ALTERED VOWS

Also by Andrew Gruse

<u>Zack Stack Series</u>

Stacked Case

Stacked Lies

Smoke Stack

The Sharpest Cut

Bad Blood

Altered Vows

ALTERED VOWS

Andrew Gruse

ISBN: 978-0-578-32961-1

To Heidi;

A guy couldn't get as lucky as I did, nor could our two sons.

Though I did have something to do with our two sons.

Sorry, but not sorry? LOL

Thank you for being you.

The best is yet to come.

XO

ALTERED VOWS

1

Andre Kitchell grabbed his handgun, dashed to his car, and sped across town towards the Dre-Zack Detective Agency with one purpose: to stop a killing.

Andre raced through a red light and accelerated past a car on the right of a one-way street. He placed a phone call via his voice feature. Mikayla answered. "Mikayla, I need you to get to the office right now!"

"Why?"

"Zack is back."

"What? Zack is back? Here?"

"He's at the office right now, and he told Lauren to leave."

"Why?"

"Zack is going to kill someone."

"Who?"

"I don't know."

"What are you talking about?"

"Damnit, quit asking questions! If we don't stop Zack, he's going right back to prison!"

Dre disconnected. Dre wanted to call Captain Ted Barnes, but he didn't. Too soon to get Zack in trouble with the police. The stoplights lined up against him, but Andre risked it. He ignored each one.

Andre stopped his car in front of the Dre-Zack Detective Agency two minutes later and ran for the main office doors. He opened the door, sprinted up the stairs.

And heard a single gunshot from a Sig Sauer P229.

* * * *

Andre rushed into the back office, gun pointed, and saw Zack Stack for the first time since December. It was now late May. There was no smile. Andre's eyes quickly surveyed the room and saw a man on his back, on the floor, with a hand on the side of his head.

Zack slowly moved the gun from his left to right hand and sat behind his desk.

"Dude! What the hell was that? You just shot me!" The man stared at the blood on the fingers of his right hand.

"I only nicked you," Zack replied. Zack opened a desk drawer, found a bag filled with assorted bandages, and tossed them to the wounded man. "I told you to shut up."

"Goddamn, Stack. Was that intentional, or did you miss?"

"Not bad with my left hand after six months in prison."

Andre kept his gun ready not for Zack but for Mark Leary, a.k.a. Kilgas, the man who worked for Senator Rosler and ordered Zack killed. Andre's suspicion was just. "What are you doing here?"

"He wants to hire me," Zack said. Zack finally looked at his business partner and best friend. "Good to see you, too, partner," Zack said sarcastically.

Andre looked at Zack, but his head swiveled back and forth between Zack and Kilgas. "Zack, I didn't know you were getting out."

"How would you? You haven't checked on me in months. No one has. Am I dead to you guys already?"

"Zack, I can explain," Andre said.

"You can explain? I spent the last six months of my life in prison, and my best friend doesn't even call once since December 17th?"

"Yeah but, wait. You remember the date?"

"Marking a calendar was the highlight of my prison life beyond avoiding gang rape in the shower."

Dre scoffed. "Come on, man. That was a country club, not some hardened prison."

"IT WAS A PRISON TO ME!"

"Zack, really. This isn't the time," Andre said, but Zack didn't calm down.

"The hell it isn't," Zack pointed the gun at Pete Kilgas, a mercenary. Kilgas remained seated on the floor as he tried to stop the blood flow on the side of his head. 'This jackass watched the prison damn near every day of the last month to see when I got out just to kill me but my own best friend?"

"I told you I don't want to kill you," Kilgas said.

"Shut up!" Zack ordered. "Dre, for Christ's sake! I played pinochle. Fricking pinochle! I'm not too fond of playing cards. Where the hell have you been? No books, no movies, no magazines, no nothing. Of all the people, you were the one I figured wouldn't ABANDON ME!"

Andre felt awful. "I'm sorry, bro. Between work and my wedding, I've been non-stop."

"Bro? Now I'm your bro again?"

"Do you two need some time? I can come back," Kilgas offered.

"Shut up!" Zack and Dre barked at the same time. Zack raised his gun at Kilgas.

"Zack, come on, man, you were fine in there."

Mikayla Dorsey rushed into the office. She saw Zack and smiled but realized it was not a smiling moment.

"It was a prison. We aren't bro's right now!" Zack snapped. "I'm pissed at you. Wait, did you say your wedding?"

"Well, yeah. Alysha and I are engaged. I proposed at Christmas."

"Well, congratulations," Zack smiled. "Come here, man." Zack hugged Dre. "That's awesome. She's a lucky lady, and you're a lucky guy. I'm so happy for you both." Zack stepped back. "But I'm still pissed." He looked at Mikayla. "And you. Where in the HELL have you been?"

2

Detective Dylan Kael stopped his unmarked police car on the side of the isolated road just north of Baltimore behind the flashing lights of county cops already there. Kael walked to the officer standing above the roadside ditch. They nodded the solemn nod cops showed at crime scenes. "What do we have?"

The officer pointed briefly into the ditch. "Body dump. A lady walking her dog found it earlier and called it in."

Kael looked down and could see the partially naked body. "What's it look like?"

"Female, late teens maybe, hasn't been here long. No telltale signs yet. The Medical Examiner is on the way."

"I'll get our crime scene unit out here." Kael grabbed his cell phone and pressed a number. He looked at his new partner. "Sometimes this job sucks. Not for the faint of heart."

Kael's new partner, Detective Fox, stared at the body and nodded.

"Another fricking murder. Jesus. What the hell is wrong with people?"

* * * *

"There's five grand in this envelope," Mikayla said.

"I tried telling Wyatt Earp over there I came with payment for his services," Kilgas said. "He didn't listen, as you can see." Kilgas kept the bandage tight to the graze wound on the side of his head.

"I listened," Zack said. "That's not why I nicked you."

"Why did you shoot him?" Mikayla asked.

"I only grazed him. Big difference."

"Why, Zack?" Mikayla pressed him.

"For one, I wanted to see if this new gun was balanced and sited accurately."

"What? You never shot it before?"

"Nope," Zack said. "For two, because I wanted to shoot something." Zack stared at Mikayla. "Glad to see you, too, Mikayla." More sarcasm.

"Zack, I didn't know," Mikayla said. "We didn't know," she quickly added with a nod to Andre.

"THAT'S why you shot me?"

"Quit your whining," Zack said to Kilgas. "I shot him since you all suddenly need to know why because I told him to stop saying we are the same."

"We are, Stack, and you know it."

Zack raised the gun, but Mikayla and Dre yelled at him to stop. Zack lowered the weapon.

"Look, Stack," Kilgas said, "I'm not here to offend, insult, kill, maim or hurt you. I legitimately need your help. Thanks to my occupation, I can't exactly go to the FBI or the cops. And I know from experience you guys get things done. This is serious. Would you please put down the gun?"

"I don't think so," Zack said.

Kilgas looked at Dre, who kept his .45 revolver ready and at the girl, Mikayla. "Ok, the five grand is just a retainer. Good faith money. There's plenty more where that came from, trust me. I don't care how much this costs; I need my problem solved."

"Why should we trust you?" Zack asked.

Kilgas understood the question. It was fair. "Like I tried to tell you because we're the same." He raised his hands at Zack quickly. "DON'T SHOOT, don't shoot, don't shoot! Let me explain, ok?"

Zack lowered the weapon again.

"Trigger happy maniac," Kilgas muttered. "We served our country. We fought the same enemy, and when we came home, each of us found a different America waiting for us. You guys went into business for yourselves as PIs. Me, and many of our brothers and sisters-in-arms, went the route I took. We did what we had to do to survive and deal with the shit. The memories, nightmares, sights, and sounds burned into our minds of our friends screaming in pain and dying right in front of us. We are the same that way."

Zack looked at his wrist minus a watch. "Now you're just being nasty."

"Stack, I was hired by someone you know to keep you alive and to keep an eye on you not long before you got railroaded by the Feds and ended up in that country club prison. The boys at National Patriot Arms had you sized for a six-foot three-inch body bag. The only reason you are alive is that I made a deal to save your life."

Zack stared at Kilgas. Zack had thought about the day the four mercs let him free a hundred times. "Erin Keyes."

Kilgas smiled. "Exactly. Remember her? Because she sure remembers you."

* * * *

Detective Kael knelt next to the body alongside the medical examiner. "What does it look like?"

Doctor Schaeffer, the new Medical Examiner, never hid his disgust. "Young female looks like raped, beaten, a bullet in the back of her head to finish the job and then dumped here. She was killed somewhere else."

"Do you have a TOD?"

"We'll have to run some tests, but it looks like a day ago at least."

Kael tried not to look at the naked corpse but had to. "See what you can find on the body."

"That's my job," Schaeffer said. "I'd hate to be the person to tell her parents."

Kael finally stood and turned away. "First, we have to find out who this is. She doesn't look much older than eighteen. I can't imagine."

"You don't have to imagine. It's right in front of you. The cruelty of humans is unrivaled on earth. Not even a virus is as evil and ruthless as humans."

Kael and Fox looked at each other, neither knowing how to respond to the doctor's strange analogy.

Schaeffer saw the look. "A virus doesn't know any better. Humans do."

3

"Your rich mistress is never far away, is she Zack?" Mikayla asked.

"I think she wants more than to be just a mistress," Kilgas said.

"Well, had she visited once in the last three months, I'd marry her since no one else bothered." Zack looked at Mikayla.

"I visited, Zack."

"Not in the last three months."

Mikayla blushed. "I'm sorry." She looked at Zack, whose stare didn't soften. "Zack, I'm sorry. It's been hard. Remember the cases you took on before you disappeared?"

"Disappeared? Seriously? That's what you're calling it?"

"Zack, we can talk about it later."

"Later? Do you think there's going to be a later? I don't. Do you know why? BECAUSE YOU ABANDONED ME, TOO!"

"Umm, excuse me," Kilgas said. "Can we focus here?"

"Zack, I didn't abandon you."

"What do you call it? I haven't seen or heard from you since February 23rd."

"You remember the date?"

"There's a lot of downtime in prison."

"Come on, to be fair, it was more like a country club," Mikayla said.

"I swear to God I am going to shoot someone."

"Seriously, people!" Kilgas barked. "Can we focus on my problem?"

"Focus? I got released from jail after six months and hitchhiked back to Baltimore. I get here to find my couch missing and refrigerator empty. Michelle is gone, which no one thought a big enough deal to TELL ME, my motorcycles and car non-existent, and the guy who tried to kill me walks into my office and wants to hire me. So what exactly do you want me to focus on?"

"I saved your life more than once, and there is five-grand sitting in that envelope," Kilgas said.

"He did save your life, Zack," Dre said.

"Dre, don't take his side."

"Let's hear him out, Zack."

"Where are my motorcycles?"

"I have them in my garage," Dre explained. "I figured I could keep an eye on them better there."

"And my car?"

"Stef is still driving that," Mikayla answered. "We all figured in this weather it wouldn't be good just sitting."

"Well, that was very thoughtful of you." The sarcasm dripped.

"Hello? I'm trying to pay you real money. Can you hear me out at least?" Kilgas, exasperated, interrupted.

"They can. I can't take this anymore."

"Zack, give him two minutes," Mikayla said. "Please."

Zack eyed Mikayla and exhaled. "Two minutes. Not a second more."

Kilgas took a deep breath. "Ok. Here it is, and I'll condense it. After our first encounter, I did some research on you, Zack. Being in my position allowed me to make some contacts that are albeit illegal but also beneficial. High places, stuff like that," Kilgas explained. "My association with Rosler and then Fairfax made me suspect your pre-military history is bullshit. Made up. Isn't it?"

"Get to the point."

"I need you to help me find a girl," Kilgas said. "A teenage girl."

Zack didn't blink. He didn't smile and barely breathed. Memories flooded Zack's senses, and he fought to remain poker-faced. Finally, after a lengthy silence, Zack inhaled deeply and exhaled slowly. "I'm sorry, Kilgas. I can't help you with that."

"Yes, you can. You're the only one I trust."

"Trust? You have some audacity to use that word to me." Zack raised the gun again.

"ZACK!" Mikayla and Dre yelled at him.

Kilgas waved his hands in surrender. "Please don't shoot me."

Zack lowered the gun.

"Stack, there is no one else. I need you and your team."

"I told you, I can't."

"Who is this girl to you?" Mikayla asked.

"Hannah." Kilgas paused. "Hannah Leary."

"The name sounds familiar," Dre said.

"It should. She's my daughter."

* * * *

Detective Kael worked at the precinct. It was a waiting game. The prints of the dead girl entered into the system, and DNA entered soon. Kael searched through missing person reports, but none matched.

It was a tough case to start with no place to start other than a dead body.

A shadow covered his desk. Kael looked up. "Hey, Captain."

Captain Ted Barnes. Back at work after a few months of rehab and healing after a near-death experience. "Kael. Anything yet?"

Kael shook his head. "It's slow. Waiting for Schaeffer. Maybe we'll have a place to start if we get her ID."

"What about a picture of her face?"

"No help," Kael said. "No one could recognize that face. Pretty brutal. They just keep getting worse."

Barnes agreed. "Don't get me started."

"I've been checking the wire, and there have been four other body dumps around the area, all similar to our victim," Kael said.

"Meaning what?"

"Well, if you prescribe to the notion that we don't believe in coincidences,"

Barnes smiled.

"Then I'd think maybe we have a serial, or something evil or something."

"None of the others in our jurisdiction?"

"No, but all within a two-hour circle of us. I'd like to look into it, Captain, with your permission."

Barnes thought for a moment. "Kael, we're already stretched thin. You can make a few phone calls but concentrate on this one."

Kael nodded, disappointed. "Are you taking off for the day, Captain?"

"Yeah. I think I'm heading over to Max's for a drink. You should stop by."

"What's the occasion?" Kael asked as he flipped over another missing person report that didn't fit.

"I got a text this afternoon that Stack is out of jail and back in town."

"He's out, huh? Wow. Six months. Who would have guessed that? Did we ever learn why?"

"Nope," Barnes said. "Didn't ask. Once I found out the FBI was involved, I knew it was best to let it be."

"So he's meeting you there?"

"No. Stack didn't send me the text. Michelle did. He usually heads to Max's, and I'm guessing he'll want a drink."

"Maybe I will. Stack is probably itching to get back to work, and he does owe me a favor."

Barnes chuckled. "Be careful what you wish for. He did a favor for Dorsey, and where is she?"

* * * *

"I was seventeen. Senior in high school at the end of four long, miserable years. I don't care what anyone says, but I say if high school were your best years, something is wrong with you," Kilgas said as he stood and walked across Zack's office.

"I hated everything about high school. I didn't fit in. Not that I wasn't athletic, because I was, or smart, because I was, and dating was easy for me. It's just that it seemed so immature and infantile to me. The clicks, drama, pressure, the dances, and formals and blah, blah, blah, blah," Kilgas carped. "I was bored with it all and tired of it all, but I was dating the homecoming queen, Sherry Bottford. Gorgeous girl. Blonde hair, blue eyes, tall, legs that started at her feet and made the most wonderful ass of themselves, and a pair of breasts, umm, umm, good." Kilgas smiled at the memories.

Zack covered his face, embarrassed; Dre rolled his eyes, and Mikayla shook her head.

"We were a couple. Sherry was the only one I could tell not caught up in all that teenage bullshit, and I swore my love to her. It was January; I remember the day well.

18

Cold as hell, and she said she needed to talk to me after school before I had basketball practice. We met at some park behind the school. She said she didn't want anyone else to be around. I remember sitting in her car; her eyes looked worried, concerned, almost scared. Now we had been a couple for almost two years. We already talked about college together and marriage and all that. You probably did the same thing, huh, Stack?"

Zack repressed the memories.

"Anyway, I asked her what was so important. She was hesitant for a while, then just blurted out: I missed my period."

Zack fought to repress more memories.

"Being seventeen, I didn't know what else to do. The girl I loved was pregnant with my child. So I asked her to marry me. I said we'll graduate, I'll find a job, and we'll start our life together sooner than we planned. She said no. We argued. She said she was going to have an abortion. I freaked out," Kilgas said and stopped as he stood near the window and stared outside.

"So you freaked out," Dre said. "What did you do? Get physical or something?"

Kilgas turned around. "No. I argued with her. Said I wouldn't allow it. If she wants an abortion, she can get one with her next pregnancy, but that won't be my child. We fought, she cried, I cried. Eventually, she told me she had to do what was best for her and left."

Those words struck Zack in his heart, and Zack felt his hands shake.

"So I got into my car and sat there with the engine running for like an hour. Then, I decided I had enough and left."

"What do you mean you left?" Dre asked.

"I left town. I made it to the Gulf Coast, Destin, to be exact. I was sitting on the beach, and a couple of military Blackhawk helicopters flew over. The next morning I walked into a recruiter's office, lied about my age; the military guy probably knew but didn't care since I was a recruit. So I joined the Army and did some time there, got out, got into some trouble, and became Pete Kilgas. You know the rest. Found work with Rosler shortly after that."

"Too many questions. You want this one, Zack, or do you want me to cross-examine him?"

Zack realized the two realities were frightening similar. He hated it. "So this girl you want us to find, Hannah Leary, is your daughter. Your girlfriend never had the abortion."

"No. I heard that Sherry felt guilty and blamed herself for me disappearing. I never told anyone, not even my parents. They all assumed I was dead, probably. She had the baby despite the problems being a single seventeen-year-old presented and used my last name either to honor me or in hopes that one day I would find her and our daughter, Hannah."

Zack thought of his child back in Michigan City. An eerie feeling crept over him.

"Why did you decide to find her now?" Dre asked.

"Recently, thanks to Stack, I came into a lot of money. I want to settle down with the woman I love. Live out my days, maybe chartering fisherman in the Gulf or something. And I want to make amends with my family."

"A real feel-good story, huh, Kilgas?" Zack's tone filled with sarcasm and bitterness.

Mikayla shot a disapproving look at Zack, but Zack didn't care.

"Yeah, I know what you're thinking, and I don't blame you, Stack. But it's the truth. Guys like me, maybe even like you, don't get many second chances. I have one. I don't want to waste it."

"But you don't know where she is?" Mikayla asked. Kilgas said no. "Have you talked to the mother? Maybe asked her if she knows anything?"

"No."

"And you think you can find her?" Dre asked.

"No. We can find her. Let's call it the singular moral thing I can do in my life. Call it easing my guilt; call it making amends. Call it whatever the hell you want. But I've known I'm a father for some time, and when I found out Hannah disappeared, it made me take stock. I know her mother worries, and if I can get Hannah out of whatever mess she is in and take her back to her mother, then maybe I'll be able to sleep at night again. Right, Zack?"

Zack remained silent.

"Zack?" Dre asked.

Kilgas spoke as Zack said nothing. "I'm getting older, Zack. We can't do what we do forever. Retirement sounds rather good sometimes. But I want to do one good thing before I ride off into the sunset."

Zack stood. "That all sounds good and dandy, but people like you, like me, we don't ride off into the sunset. We die."

"So you'll take the case?"

Zack grabbed his shoulder holster, stuck the gun in it, and walked towards the exit.

"Zack? Where are you going?" Dre asked.

"To drink."

Dre watched Zack leave and looked at Kilgas. "He'll take it. Zack just needs some time. Come back in the morning," Dre looked at the door. "Zack will be here, and he won't shoot you."

4

May 24th, early evening, but Zack didn't care. What Zack did care about was having to go back to his apartment. But there was a significant problem.

Julie Fletcher.

Zack walked past his apartment, saw the lights through the windows. He thought of Kilgas and his daughter and wondered how his baby would respond to seeing Zack.

Zack crossed the square, walked up a sidewalk, and entered Max's. The place was busy. Not unexpected. Zack saw the board with the drink specials. *Today is Thursday. The day never meant anything in Club Fed.* He recognized a couple of the waitresses. *I wonder if they miss me. Nope. Not going that route. Just go to the bar, get a drink, and decompress. This feels worse than when I got back from deployment.*

Zack wound his way through the crowd; the bartender spotted him through the crowd and called out his name. Zack smiled, and the bartender pointed to the end of the bar. Zack saw an open seat and made his way to it.

"Holy Neptune, Zack Stack," the bartender greeted. "Where the hell have you been?"

"Prison," Zack answered. The bartender shook Zack's hand.

"Well, welcome back. What can I get you?"

He thinks I made that up. Zack pointed at a tapper of a light beer. "That will do. I haven't had any alcohol in months. Gotta start slow."

The bartender laughed. "That's a good way to start. If you want alcohol, let me know, and I'll get you a real beer."

"Hey, this one's on me, Zack." The bartender placed the mug in front of Zack. "Good to see you again. Are you planning on becoming a regular again?"

"Keep the free drinks coming, and I'll move in." The bartender laughed and headed off to care for other customers.

Zack sipped the mug and forgot how the taste of beer wasn't the best tasting drink in the world. *It looks like I have to re-acquire this taste. Starting tonight. Maybe next time I get stuck in that country club prison, I'll bribe Jack the guard to smuggle in beer.*

Zack felt a pat on the back and looked. Detective Dylan Kael smiled at him.

"Welcome back, Stack. Good to see you again." Kael offered his hand, which Zack shook. "May I?" Kael pointed at the stool beside Zack, and Zack nodded at it.

"How did you hear I'm back?"

"Cap told me," Dylan said. "Said you were released yesterday and that you'd probably be here tonight. Did you talk to him?"

Zack sipped the beer again. "No, I haven't." *Who told Barnes I was out?* "So you heard I was out and just decided to come by and have a drink with me in the hopes I'd be here?"

"Yeah, why not? I thought we became friends before you got locked up," Kael said. Kael motioned to the bartender and ordered the same as Zack.

Zack didn't say anything.

"Are you back to work yet, or are you going to take a few days off to readjust and stuff?"

Zack sipped his beer as his mind raced in multiple directions. "Why are you here?"

Kael got his drink and drank from it. "I came in for a drink."

"Kael, I'm willing to bet you've been in this place exactly once since you joined the force, which tells me that you're trying to ask me something or you want information. Which is it?" Zack looked at him, irritated, and Kael recognized it.

"I'm sorry, Zack. I'm not here to upset you."

Zack finished the mug quickly. More quickly than he wanted to. The bartender filled another one and placed it in front of Zack. Zack pointed at Kael. "This one is on him. Time is precious, Kael. Talk."

"Ok, we found a dead girl this morning on the side of the road. I did some checking and found there have been similar body dumps around the area. Cap gave me a short leash; you know how it is. Hours, budgets, too many cases, so, here I am."

Zack took a deep, steadying breath. "Oh, I see. So you think your old buddy Zack owes you a favor and that I'll look into this to help you."

"Something like that. These girls need justice."

"Did you go to the police? Maybe they can help."

"Zack, come on, at least hear me out. I have a feeling it's a part of something bigger. It's the fifth body dump in the last three months in the area. One in Virginia, another Pennsylvania, New Jersey. All within two hours of Baltimore. All have been runaways missing for a while. I don't think the body they found this morning will be any different, and I'm afraid we're going to find more once we open up Pandora's Box."

"Call the FBI. They like to help." Zack swigged the beer. "I could give you the names of several."

"Zack, please. You're a good investigator with good instinct. Look, I'll get you the files. Just take a look and see if you can find anything and let me know."

Zack drank more. The beer taste already reacquired. *It sure tastes like more, only not in this crowd.* "Kael, you're a good cop. I'm sure you can handle it."

"Zack, I need help on this. Your kind of help."

Zack drank the second beer.

"Just help me by looking at the files. If you see anything, let me know, and maybe we can tie them together."

Zack finished his beer and stood. "Sorry, Kael. I don't do missing kids."

"You have a daughter, Stack. How would you feel if that happened to your girl?"

Zack stopped, his back to Kael, and he turned his head. Then, without another word, Zack exited the bar.

5

The emptiness of the square weighed on Zack's shoulders. Kael's last words felt like a vice applying pressure. Zack wanted to say it was a cheap shot. But it wasn't, and the convergence of Kael's request and Kilgas' appearance squeezed at Zack's heart. It hurt, and he stopped to look at his apartment windows again.

Zack decided he wasn't running this time. Not from her. Zack could count the words they spoke to one another since she left him in Clyde on his hands, but yet she lived in his apartment. With his baby. Zack changed directions and knocked on the door.

* * * *

Julie Fletcher enjoyed the quietness of the apartment without her parents. The renovations Julie had done made the place more baby-friendly and utilized the space more efficiently. Adding another bathroom and opening the kitchen and living room gave her the eyesight she needed to keep an eye on her baby and the privacy she needed in the master bathroom. Making that larger wasn't easy either, but now the bathroom suited her needs, and if Zack ever lived there, his needs much better.

Cate played on the carpet in front of the couch while Julie flipped channels on the television. Thursday after dinner, and this was her life. Not exactly what she had in mind. But she didn't regret having her baby.

Julie heard the knock on the door. Frightened, she didn't move. The noise continued, and Cate looked at her mother as if questioning why her mother wouldn't do something to stop this intrusion? Julie entered her bedroom, opened the closet door, grabbed her handgun from high off the shelf, hid it behind her back, and walked to the stairs. She climbed over the baby gate, walked down the stairs, and the knock stopped, but she saw a figure move in the darkness outside.

She peaked through the window, and her heart stopped.

There he was.

Zack looked taller, more muscular, more handsome. She ripped open the door and nervously stood still. Zack smiled at her, a sad smile, but it made her feel better. Julie rushed out the door and hugged him.

Zack felt the rush of warmth through him. As if the time apart didn't separate them at all. She pulled away, and Zack saw her hand. "Expecting someone else?"

Julie lowered the gun, embarrassed. "I'm sorry—just a precaution. Come upstairs. Cate can't wait to see you." She took his hand, and the two walked up the stairs. They reached the top and Zack stood still. He saw Cate sitting on the floor, her big eyes fixed on the newcomer, and a toy found her mouth, about to be covered in drool.

Zack glanced around again before he set his eyes on Julie. "Something's different."

Julie pulled him inside the apartment. "Not anymore."

Julie watched him take in everything. Even the color scheme. Soft tones of gray and white gave the place a warmer, family feel she wanted as long as she was there with her and Zack's baby.

"Can I ask who paid for the, uh, renovations?"

Julie cringed. "Well, partly me."

Zack stepped into the living room. "The only person who could access my accounts is Michelle."

"I know, I'm sorry," Julie said. "I called her, and she said I shouldn't pay for it all myself."

Zack wiped his forehead. Julie suspected he was upset. "How's Cate?"

Julie grabbed his hand and pulled him into the living room closer to Cate. "She's doing great. Healthy as can be and growing like a weed." Julie lifted Cate and held her in front of Zack. She kissed Cate's chubby cheek as Cate did little but enjoy being held and the attention. "Do you want to hold her?"

Julie watched Zack stare at his daughter and exhale slowly.

"Hold your daughter. I've been telling her all about you." Julie smiled and gently passed Cate to him. Not surprisingly, Zack held Cate like he had no idea how to hold a baby. "Cate, can you say hello to your daddy? Can you say da-da?"

There was nothing, but Julie hoped the baby would utter something. Julie watched as Zack held the baby. His eyes glossed over, and he gently rocked her. He adjusted her to make himself and Cate more comfortable. Cate fussed.

"What did I do wrong?" Zack asked.

Julie laughed. "Nothing, you're fine," she said. "Come here, you little munchkin," Julie said as she took the baby from Zack. "Does someone need a fresh diaper?" Julie asked the baby in her mommy's voice.

"No, I'm good," Zack said.

Julie laughed. "Not you, smartass. Come on. Let's teach you how to change a diaper."

Zack followed her to the bedroom, where Julie spread out a thick baby blanket with one hand while holding Cate with the other. She set down Cate and had her diaper off in seconds, wrapped tight, and chucked into a nearby garbage bin. An expert.

"Grab a diaper for me, could you please?"

Zack did.

"Now observe. When you wipe Cate, make sure you get her good and clean. Dirty is bad, got it?"

"Wait, what? You think I'm going to change her diapers?"

Julie didn't mind laughing. "Of course you are. Relax. She won't break. Next, slide the diaper under her like this, set her butt down, grab the wings, pull it tight so there aren't gaps between the diaper and her chubby little thighs," Julie said in her mommy's voice again, "then tape it like so."

"How long is she going to be in these things? Like a couple more months?"

Julie laughed again. "A little longer than that, honey." Julie lifted her daughter off the bed. "It's almost bedtime for her," Julie held Cate in front of her, "and you better sleep all night." She kissed Cate and held her close.

"Can she stay up a little later tonight?"

Julie saw Zack's eyes never left Cate. "Are you planning on disappearing for another six months?"

"I didn't plan it last time."

Julie smiled and put Cate in Zack's arms. "Then you'll see plenty of her, but she's staying on a schedule."

Cate stared at Zack and made weird noises. Julie picked up toys off the living room floor and put them inside Cate's playpen but watched Zack as held Cate. "I can't believe you're back. I'm so glad you came here."

"How does she sleep?"

"She's like her father. At least how you were with me. Once her head hits the pillow, she's out cold. Stubborn too. Don't know where she gets that from," Julie said with a smile. "But just like her father, she goes into periods where she doesn't sleep. So if she wakes tonight, she's yours."

Cate fussed a little. Julie knew the signs.

"She's tired, honey. Let me put her to bed."

Reluctantly, Zack let go of his baby daughter, told her goodnight, and Julie disappeared into the bedroom with her. Zack looked around the place. It looked entirely different than it did before. He entered the kitchen and saw all new appliances, new cabinets, and countertops, and flooring. It didn't look cheap, but he liked it. Suddenly, he felt a hand on his shoulder, and Julie appeared behind him. She stepped in front of him, wrapped her arms around his waist, and hugged him. They held each other in silence for several minutes.

Julie finally looked into Zack's blue eyes with a smile. "How about a glass of wine and we talk?"

"Aren't you breastfeeding still?"

"Stopped a month ago. Wanted to go longer, but," Julie waved her hand. Julie opened a cabinet and pulled out a merlot. "And to be honest, my boobs don't hurt anymore. Trying to get my old body back now," Julie said.

"You look great," he said.

Julie laughed. "I knew you'd say that. You haven't been with a woman in how long?"

Zack ignored the assumed rhetorical question. "You do look great, Jules. I mean that."

Julie walked to Zack with two glasses of wine and handed him one. "So do you." They stared at each other; the tension palpable. "Wow, I can't believe you're here. When did you get back?"

"Last night."

"Come on, let's sit and talk." They sat on the sofa; Julie put her wine on the table and her hand on his arm and chest. "You look stressed. What's wrong?"

Zack chuckled. "Nothing. Just readjusting."

"You're avoiding. I can tell because you won't look in my eyes."

"I am avoiding," Zack said and smiled, which led to a laugh. "I know better than to look into your eyes."

"Remember the last time we talked? We promised each other we'd always talk to one another. That hasn't changed."

"I know."

She rubbed his arm but remained silent. Each sipped the wine. "What happened?"

"It doesn't matter." More gazing at one another and silence.

Julie slowly put her hand into his. "I hope you don't mind what I've done to your place. My house is taking longer than I planned with the renovations and permitting and on and on and on. Plus, Cate only knows this place like home, and it's so close to your office," she trailed off.

"Stay as long as you want, Jules. It doesn't bother me."

"It bothers me." Julie waited until he looked at her. "You should be sleeping in your bed."

"I'm not sure that's a good idea."

"You know what I mean."

Zack looked into her eyes again and saw her smile.

Julie squeezed his hands. "Relax, Zachary Ulysses. It's me."

"I know."

"I'm sorry for not visiting you."

"Of everyone, you're the only person I'm glad I didn't see. I didn't want Cate to see me there." Zack looked at Julie tentatively. He fought with being sucked in by her eyes. "Or you."

"I still felt bad. Then I heard you and Stefani split. What happened?"

"I don't want to talk about her." Zack felt his eyes tear.

"I thought you two were on a good path."

"Well, obviously, things change. I'm sure you know more than I do about why."

Julie continued to hold his hand. "She won't talk about it. You hurt her, Zack."

Zack looked at Julie quickly. He opened his mouth but stopped. "Change the subject."

"Stefani told me the choice you had." Zack finally looked into her eyes. "You didn't have to do that."

"Yes, I did."

"Zack," Julie ran out of words. Julie pulled him close and hugged him. She kissed the side of his face. "You'll always protect me, won't you?"

Zack let out a deep breath. "It wasn't just for you." He looked at her. "I should go."

"Is it really that difficult to see me?"

"Jules," he said softly, "yes, it is."

Jules took his hands, squeezed them, and smiled before her eyes glossed over. "Your daughter is glad you're here." They stared longer into each other's eyes. "So am I." Julie leaned forward, and they kissed. "So stay."

6

Lauren Mayfield unlocked the doors of the Dre-Zack Detective Agency like she did every morning. At seven-thirty in the morning, she expected none of the investigators there.

She started the coffee pot because they all loved their coffee. Except for Lauren, she drank herbal tea in the morning before she switched to water. The boss's office door shut, which was unusual but not how she left it the night before. After the scary man that Mr. Stack attacked arrived, she hid in the office. When everyone left, Dre saw her and told her everything was fine. Lauren wasn't so sure.

Lauren readied the office and was about to sit down when a knock on the office door startled her. A delivery man smiled at Lauren and opened the door.

"Good morning, ma'am. I'm sorry if I startled you. I have a priority package for Zack Stack."

Lauren signed for the package and took it to Zack's desk. The office was dark as the shades covered the windows, and Lauren half expected to see Zack on the floor but was relieved he wasn't, nor were there signs of him.

Lauren turned on the lights to his bathroom and checked to make sure it was clean and stocked. Mikayla was the only person who used it but now, with Mr. Stack back, Lauren expected it to be worse. Mikayla was notorious for not picking up after herself. Lauren straightened a hand towel, made sure the shower was supplied, and left the bathroom.

Lauren returned to her desk, turned on her computers, and waited. She scrolled through the newsfeed, checked for any emails, new phone messages, and yesterday's mail. Lauren heard running water, ignored it, and wrote her short list of things to do today. Then, a noise from the bathroom caught Lauren's attention.

Lauren exited her office and walked towards the bathroom in Mr. Stack's office when she heard a faucet turn off and on. Lauren knew no one else was in the office and immediately thought of a haunting. She stepped forward and screamed.

* * * *

Zack stood fresh from the shower with a white towel wrapped around his waist and looked at Lauren. Lauren tried not to stare at his chest and abs.

"Where were you? I was just here, and you weren't. So how did you sneak past me?"

"Some secrets stay with me until we get to know each other better." Zack checked his facial hair. Not worth shaving. "What are you doing here this early?"

"I start early, sir. Can I get you anything, sir?"

"Lauren, quit calling me sir. My name is Zack. Zachary, Zack, Z-man, Z-force, Awesome Sauce, anything along those lines." Zack walked past her and into the giant closet where he dug for clothes. "But no sir or Mr. Stack."

"Yes, sir," she answered and watched while Zack dropped the towel and slid boxer shorts up his legs to his waist. He looked at her.

"Lauren, are you ok?"

She shook her head, embarrassed, and covered her eyes. "I'm so sorry, sir. I wasn't expecting you to do that. I am so sorry."

Zack grabbed a pair of blue jeans and put one leg in at a time. "Don't apologize. I don't care if you see me naked, but if that bothers you, we should probably work out a system where you aren't standing in my bathroom right after I get out of the shower."

Lauren blushed and lowered her head. She turned around. "Of course, sir. I'm sorry." She rushed out.

* * * *

Zack sat at his desk, saw the package, and opened it. Zack knew it came from Detective Dylan Kael. Inside was the information compiled for each of the five dead bodies, as much as Kael could get, which wasn't much.

Zack looked at the clock. Eight o'clock. *Where the hell is everyone? What kind of an operation is this? No wonder Michelle was always upset. I wonder how she's doing. I should eat something. What am I doing here? What was last night? The start of something or just the best*

32

welcome home present ever? Goddamn that Addy Jones. Prison life was more straightforward. What if Jules wants to get back together? What if I see Stefani? How did I hurt her? She left me. I don't even have any Pepsi in this place. Focus, Zack. Your buddy Kilgas may come in any second. You need an answer for him. I can't believe Erin hired that guy to watch me. She lied to me. Straight up. Just get on an Amtrak and leave town. No one will care except for Addy, who will have me executed. Maybe it's worth it. No, she'll just torture me and send me right back here.

Zack looked at the files. He read past the names and places and went straight to how each died. Similar. Raped and beaten, a gunshot in the back of the head for all five. A .22 caliber killed one victim, but no bullets found on the other four victims. Similar entry points. Dumps in different places and different states. But Kael was right; all were within a two-hour drive of Baltimore.

Zack read the files. The evidence found was minimal on each body. *Professionals or lucky? Even the rape kits turned up nothing. No DNA matches, which means whoever is doing this hasn't been caught yet if it's the same person. Or none of them have. Which means there is no place to start. I wonder when the Cubs come out east this season. I should get tickets. Zack, focus!*

There was a knock on the office door. The tentative Lauren stuck her head inside the door. "Um, Sir, I mean, Mr. Stack, um, I'm sorry to disturb you. But, um, can I get you anything?"

"Can you call Dre for me and tell him I need my baby back here now, please? He'll understand."

"Yes, sir," Lauren answered quickly and disappeared.

Zack heard her talk on the phone. It was brief. Zack listened to her chair move, and Lauren stuck her head inside the door. "Sir, Andre is on the phone waiting for you."

Zack sighed. "Lauren, I'm sorry for sneaking in here. I do that often, so get used to it. Also, when I shower, I tend to get naked. I also am briefly naked before and after I shower. I apologize for not warning you."

"Of course, sir," Lauren replied with a smile. "Andre is waiting."

"Where is everyone?"

"I'm not sure," she said. "Usually, I don't see anyone until ten, but I do know Andre is on line one waiting for you, sir."

Zack leaned back in his chair. "How did you end up here?"

"Excuse me?"

"I mean, how did you end up taking this job?" Zack pointed at the chair in front of him. "Sit down. We might as well get to know each other now that you've seen me naked."

"Sir, we don't have to discuss that."

Zack watched her be uncomfortable. "Sorry. I spent some time working on my body the last few months. If it's objectionable, I'll keep working."

"Oh no, it isn't that. You have an amazing body, I mean, but," Lauren covered her face. "Sir, can we focus on work? Andre is on line one."

"Oh, and I'm also sorry about last night. That guy is a long story."

Lauren sat with her back straight and her hands on her lap. "Sir, could you please answer the phone? I don't want Andre to think I'm not doing my job."

"I can't believe you're single."

"Thank you, sir. Now, please. The phone."

Zack grabbed the receiver. "Dre, I need my motorcycle."

"I hear," Dre answered. "Look, Zack, I want to talk with you first."

"Get my motorcycle here today, please. My baby, preferably. I'd prefer not to buy another one." Zack ended the call. "Now, where were we, Lauren?"

7

Lauren took a deep breath. "You were about to tell me who that scary man was from last night. Sir."

"Just a guy that had a lot of guys try to kill me," Zack said. "How did you end up here?"

Lauren's eyes opened wide, and her mouth dropped open. "Seriously?"

"Don't worry about him. He won't hurt you. He's seen firsthand the lengths I'll go to protect the people in my life." Zack shook his head. "Now that includes you."

"You don't know me at all."

"Well, I've been told I have a hero complex. Why disappoint?"

Lauren cracked a small smile. "Thank you, sir."

"How did you end up here?"

"Well, after I graduated from Maryland, I got a job in some firm working a business job I thought would take me somewhere. It took me about two years to realize I was just a number, and I wasn't about to lower myself to get further ahead. So I left there, worked at a couple of other places, all with the same results. Then I saw this ad for an office manager, and after I talked with Dre, Darnell, and Mikayla, I decided this is what I want."

"Why?"

Lauren seemed surprised. "Well, I'm kind of in charge here. We do important work, the hours are good, the pay is good, the vacation pay and days off are good, and the insurance is as good or bad as anywhere else. Mainly though, I'm not treated like a dumb girl. I like that."

"We offer insurance?" Zack asked, shocked. "Days off? What? Is this an alternate reality? I don't want to know. Are you good with computers?"

"Oh, yes, sir. There isn't a program out there I can't operate. I'm kind of a computer nerd."

"I don't care about an operating system. Do you have," Zack searched for the right word, unsure of how much she knew about what they did, or precisely what Michelle could do, "functional computer skills that would assist our investigations?"

Lauren thought about what he said for a moment but then grinned. "Oh. Yes sir. Count on it."

"Do you know how to check for viruses, malware, to see if anyone hacked us or anything like that?"

"Yes, sir. Why?"

"Please do that right away and daily. No one must access our systems. And you do know that at any time now, you can call me Zack or Zachary, or you know," Zack said.

"Yes, sir."

Zack leaned forward. "Do I make you feel uncomfortable?"

"Extremely, sir."

Zack nodded and thought for a moment. "Well, you've seen me naked, so perhaps that wasn't a good start. If you'd like, you can take your clothes off so I can see you naked. We'd be even then." She didn't react to Zack's joke. "Sorry. It was a joke and nowadays would get me in trouble with the pc crowd. Ok. Here it is. After they sent me to Club Fed, I thought for sure I'd be out in a week." Zack paused and watched until Lauren looked at him again. "A week passed, and it hit me. No one was saving me. A month or so in, everyone stopped visiting. No visitors around the holidays, which sucked. Then, Mikayla showed, came up a few times but then stopped in late February." Zack shook his head. "The last couple months, I was alone, and when I got out, I knew this place, that couch that you now own, was my sanctuary. I don't know why but it was the only place I could sleep without," Zack paused, "waking myself every night. The guy in the cell next to me at Club Fed hated waking every night via my," Zack stopped. "After a few days, he found me and requested I either kill myself or put several pillows over my head at night so he wouldn't hear me." Zack smiled. "We became friends." Zack saw Lauren's face relax.

"I ended up learning how to play pinochle with him and two of his friends, all inmates at Club Fed, all much older than me, they'll probably die inside. The day he confronted me about my sleeping failures before we got locked in our cells, he gave me a bible and told me to read it to help me get through the hard times. So over the next six months, as soon as they locked us in for the night, I would turn on a little lamp and open it wherever I left off. Often, I had to read passages several times. Not easy reading. I thought reading Tolkien was tough. But I read it all. Almost got through it twice." Lauren's eyes widened. "I told you, I don't sleep well. Anyway, my neighbor almost immediately was in a better mood because he slept better."

"Did it help you, sir?"

"Reading it did put me to sleep. There wasn't a spiritual revelation if that's what you're asking. I mean, I'm not knocking those who feel differently than I. Just for me, don't expect me to try to convert you. Eventually, I got to the point where I wasn't having," Zack searched for the right word as if saying nightmare would inflict him like when a golfer says the word shank or yips on the golf course sure it would strike, "episodes. I stayed awake until physical and mental exhaustion collapsed me. The gym at Club Fed helped with that."

"I noticed," she quickly said but then caught his eyes. "Sir."

Zack said nothing.

Lauren waited for more, but there was nothing. "Um, why did you tell me that, sir?"

"Because no one else will ever hear that story. What I share with you stays with you and vice versa. I'm not sure why Dre told you to be my assistant, but I need to be able to trust you. What we talk about stays between us. I'm human, Lauren, and I'm sorry if I do anything to upset you in advance. I won't even realize it most of the time, and if I do, I promise you it's not personal. And you can call me anything other than sir or Mr. Stack anytime now."

"I was leaning towards Awesome Sauce, sir," Lauren grinned.

"I like that one, but I'm not sold on it yet. So let's keep that between you and me."

Lauren grinned even wider. "Yes, sir. Sir, how did you sleep last night?"

Zack remembered what it felt like to lie in his bed with Jules beside him. "It wasn't a bad night."

"Did you make it without an episode?"

"Almost."

"Will you be returning to your apartment tonight?"

"How do you know I was there last night?"

"I didn't. You just told me." Lauren leaned forward. "Sir, it's none of my business, and forgive me if I'm out of line but be careful." She sat straight. "Sir."

"Of what?"

Lauren looked scared to say. "Sir, just be careful. I expect you're emotionally vulnerable right now."

"Duly noted. You've known me less than twenty-four hours and already given me advice on my love life."

"Well, I did see you naked."

Zack grabbed the pictures of the five deceased teenagers and spread them on the desk. "Lauren, do you see anything in these pictures that would make you think they are linked?"

She stood, walked around the desk to beside Zack, and leaned over beside him. Lauren moved her long hair behind her ear on the side of Zack and casually brushed against him. Lauren examined each picture, and Zack watched to see her reaction.

Nothing.

"What am I looking for?" Lauren said softly and turned her head to look at Zack.

"A connection. Any similarities besides the obvious," Zack said.

Lauren examined them again. "Do you see anything?"

"I may. Look closely. Every detail matters."

Lauren turned a little, brushed against Zack again; time passed. "Gunshot wounds?"

"Forensic reports suggest they may be of different makes. No ballistics so not helpful other than the victims were shot in the same manner."

"Did they find fingerprints or DNA on the bodies?"

"No fingerprints. Doubt they even checked. They did find DNA on the girls but couldn't find a match in any system, so they shelved it."

Lauren's long fingers scrutinized each picture, her hair slid off her ear and brushed against Zack's face, and Lauren quickly moved it. "All girls. Could this be a serial?"

"It could, but this looks different than a serial pedophile or rapist." They turned their heads and looked at each other. "They think differently. They kill differently.

38

It's more about power and control. They're more likely to strangle their victim to death," Zack said. "This doesn't suggest rage to me."

Lauren looked at him again. "A bullet in the back of the head doesn't suggest rage?"

"No. To me, it suggests cowardice. Not looking the victim in the eye, as if there was a trust or intimacy before."

"Is that science talking?"

"I have no idea, but I like the sound of it," Zack said. Lauren smiled and returned to the pictures.

"What are these marks?" She pointed to one of the girl's forearms. Though bloated and decayed, there appeared to be a mark of sorts. "Is that it?"

"We spotted the same thing."

"You think it's a tattoo?"

"I do," Zack said. "The girls have similar distorted markings on their bodies, but in different places."

"What does that mean?"

"Probably nothing. Everyone has a tattoo these days."

"Do you, sir?"

"No. I don't. I like the purity of the skin, especially on a female," Zack said. "Do you have one?"

"I don't. But I was thinking of getting one. Maybe like a flower or something small."

"Why?"

"I don't know. I thought it would be cool."

Zack pursed his lips in thought and nodded. "Where at?"

"None of your business, sir," Lauren smiled at him.

"When you get it, I'd like to see it to give you my professional opinion." Zack returned to the pictures.

"I'll keep that in mind, sir."

"As I said, there's probably no connection here, but despite the lack of clarity, they look similar to me. Do you concur?"

Lauren smiled. "I concur."

"Great movie line." Zack leaned back. "Lauren, I don't like doing missing kid cases. You should know that."

"Why not, sir?"

Zack leaned forward, spread the pictures slightly, and ran his fingers over them. "It becomes too emotional," Zack said softly. "I lost someone very special to me because of a missing person case."

Lauren watched Zack stare at the pictures.

"Did you find the missing person alive?"

"I did."

Lauren put a hand on his shoulder. "Sir, were you hired to find out who did this?"

"Asked to help," Zack said. "But it's more like expected to help."

"If it makes you uncomfortable, you shouldn't do it."

"The guy last night wants to hire us to find his daughter." They stared at each other. "I don't know how I can say no."

"Sir, if it makes you uncomfortable, you shouldn't do it."

"Thank you, Lauren." He put his hand atop hers on his shoulder and held it. *But Kael is right. If something happened to my daughter or son, I'd want answers.* "This is what you're going to help me with today right after I compose a letter. Are you ready?"

"Sir, yes, sir. But first, while you compose that letter, let's get you some food." She slid her hand down his back. "Should I go to the store or get something from a restaurant? A store makes more sense."

"Lauren, you're the office manager. What goes on here is your call. As long as you get me a Pepsi asap, get what you think is best. I'll show you how to access the account to pay for that later."

"Yes, sir. I'll be right back."

As Lauren rushed to the door and Zack watched her, he called out. "Lauren." She stopped and turned around. "Thank you; I mean that. And don't forget for future reference, I am sorry if I do something that upsets you."

She smiled. "For future reference, I may or may not accept your apology without making you pay." She winked. "I'll be right back, sir." She disappeared.

Zack returned to the pictures. *I hope to God none of these is Kilgas' daughter.*

8

Fifteen minutes later, as Zack put the letter in an envelope, Zack found out. He heard the door open, and the slow walk towards his office door told Zack who it was. Kilgas.

"Stack? Hey, just letting you know it's me," Kilgas said. "No need to shoot me or throw me around, ok?"

Zack had the Sig in his hand under the desk. "Come in."

Kilgas stood a little shorter than Zack and wasn't as built. He had short dark hair and a long face, not round. Hard edges and Kilgas always looked like he had a five o'clock shadow. Not bad looking, but not someone Zack would let any of the females in his life date. Kilgas entered the office with his hands shoulder height in surrender.

Blue jeans, boots, a black leather jacket, and a simple gray tee-shirt underneath, Kilgas didn't dress to impress. Zack realized he usually dressed the same. Zack didn't see a gun, but it could have been behind him. "Hey, are we good, man?"

Zack spun the pictures of the five girls around on the desk and slid them to the edge. "Recognize any of these?"

Kilgas understood what they were, and the color left Kilgas' face. He swallowed and stepped forward. Kilgas looked at each girl carefully. "It's not her. None of these."

"Are you sure? Do you even know what she looks like?"

Kilgas had no answer. "She's not one of them," he repeated.

"Do you know what she looks like?"

"She looks like her mother. She's gorgeous," Kilgas said, irritated at the questioning.

"Are you carrying?"

"No."

"Are you sure?" Zack showed the Sig in his hand and brought it above the desk.

"Come on, man. Are we going to go through this every time I see you? I told you, Erin Keyes is paying me to keep you alive. I saved your life. I think I've earned not having that thing pointed at me."

"The bullet scars in my back suggest otherwise."

"Stack, I'm not going to kill you," Kilgas said softly. "I've already lost two paychecks because of you. I'm not going to lose a third. Let's drive to Alexandria and see Erin. She's expecting you. If she doesn't convince you that I'm on the up and up, I'll disappear."

"Do you have her number?"

"Yes."

"Give it to me and go for a walk."

"Stack, what the hell am I supposed to do? Go sit on a bench and feed the pigeons?"

"They're called Rock Doves, and yes. Do exactly that. I'm starving, Lauren is coming back with food, and until I eat, I'm liable to respond to this situation poorly."

Kilgas laughed. "All right. Here," he tossed Zack his cell phone. "Press 4, but time is wasting. I'll buy breakfast on the way. I want to find my daughter before she ends up in a picture on your desk."

* * * *

"So, what's the verdict?"

Zack walked with Kilgas across the square towards Kilgas' car. "I have permission to kill you if I feel it necessary, and she won't take it personally. She said you shouldn't either."

Kilgas laughed. "Fair enough. Anything else?"

"Erin is not happy my ex is still driving the car Erin bought for me. So thank you for telling her that," Zack said.

"You know how it works, Stack. She pays me to tell her what I learn about you."

They reached the car, and Zack opened the passenger side door. "To be clear, you are my client now. Everything we talk about falls under privilege, so you will not be sharing any of this with Erin. Understand?"

"She won't be happy with me."

"Doesn't it concern you that she could have someone else on both of us prepared to pull the trigger if either of us displeases her?"

"Yes. That's why I thought it better to work for Erin. And it's why you better visit Erin and please the hell out of her. Where are we going?"

"To talk to the mother of your child."

"Um, I don't like that idea," Kilgas said.

"You said she lives in Annapolis. Let's go. We need to start somewhere, and a current picture of Hannah would be a good start."

"I haven't talked to her since that day," he said.

Zack leaned back in the car. "Trust me. I know how you feel. Let's go. You're on the clock, and my rates have dramatically risen."

* * * *

Lauren rushed back to the office with what she thought would satisfy the boss. Her arms were full of bags, and she struggled up the stairs and through the doors. Then, with a smile on her face, anxious to make up for what she perceived as slip-ups when she first met Mr. Stack, she called for him and entered his office.

"Mr. Stack?" She put the bags on Mikayla's desk. "Sir?" Lauren looked around his office. No one. The lights in the bathroom were off. "Sir?" She entered the bathroom. Empty. Lauren exited Zack's office and saw the pictures of the dead teenagers on her desk with a sticky note.

"Lauren, our mutual scary friend arrived after you left. I'm taking the case and before you comment, know that I have to. I'll be back later today. If you get a chance, can you see what you can find in these photos? Thank you. Z."

She smiled and frowned and returned to his office. Then, in the middle of emptying the items in the bags in the refrigerators about the office, Lauren heard the main door open.

"Lauren? Are you here?"

Lauren recognized the female voice. Over the past four-plus months, Julie Fletcher visited at least twice a week and sometimes even brought her adorable baby. The two, usually the only two at the office, became friends. Julie found it easier to work at this office. The place Julie stayed wasn't conducive. Lauren enjoyed the company.

"Yes, I'm in here," Lauren called back.

Julie Fletcher walked into Zack's office. "Hi, what's going on?"

"Just did some shopping," Lauren said.

Julie looked at the groceries. "You bought Pepsi," she said. "Zack hasn't changed at all."

Lauren continued to unload the groceries. "Mr. Stack mentioned he liked it, and he is the boss. Did you have a good night with him last night?"

"He told you he was with me?"

"I tricked him into admitting it. I didn't want him to sleep on the floor again."

Julie smiled. "It was a good night. I need to talk to him about it, though. Is he here?"

"Um, Jules, it's none of my business, but I can guess why you want to talk to him about last night and," she stopped. "I'm sorry. It's none of my business. Forgive me. I'm sorry."

"No, it's ok, Lauren. We're friends, and I value that. But, obviously, Zack talked about it this morning. What did he say?"

Lauren sensed she overstepped. "Mr. Stack didn't say anything about it. I tricked Mr. Stack into admitting he spent the night with you," Lauren took a deep breath. "I suspect he's vulnerable, Jules. But it's not my business. I'm sorry."

Julie understood. "And you've only known him a day." Julie smiled. "It's ok, Lauren. Zack and I are adults. We can handle it."

"I'm sorry, Jules. I shouldn't have. Please forgive me. I've overstepped."

"Not at all. Where is Zack?"

"He left. He's working a case I wish he weren't," Lauren said absentmindedly. She finished with the food in his small refrigerator and crumbled up the bags. "He's uncomfortable, and I have a bad feeling about the guy he's with."

"What guy?" Julie asked, and Lauren saw the worry on her face.

"Mark Leary," Lauren said as she continued with her tasks. "He showed up, Mr. Stack lost it and attacked the man, and then said that man was going to die."

"Mark Leary?" Julie asked as she placed the name. "Where have I heard that before?"

"Mr. Stack also called him Kilgas."

Altered Vows

"WHAT?"

* * * *

Julie Fletcher tried not to pace. She tried not to chew her nails—both mannerisms employed during times of stress. Dre sat in his office and watched Julie pace back and forth across his office in front of his desk, speaking of the inevitable doom ahead.

"Jules," Dre said, "I don't think we should worry about anything yet."

"He's with KILGAS!" Julie said. "Either Zack is going to kill him, or Zack's going to die! How can you not know where he is?"

Dre recognized the near-panic state. *That woman still loves him.* "Because I didn't ask him, and he didn't tell me," Dre said calmly.

"What about his phone? He never went anywhere without his phone," Julie said.

Dre frowned. "Lauren forgot to give it to him this morning. But it's not a big deal." Dre stood and walked to her. He put his large hands on her shoulders and stopped her. "He'll be fine."

"Fine? I called Mik, and she said how angry Zack was last night. That is all about Kilgas. You KNOW what happened to Zack, to us, the last time he dealt with Kilgas."

"Zack is angry," Dre said almost dismissively but heard his tone. "When Zack was released, no one was there for him, and we've stayed away for the last few months. I'd be angry, too."

"This is freaking me out." Julie paced even faster. "We have to do something!"

"Just chill," Dre said. "I know Zack as well or better than anyone, even you. He's fine, and Kilgas is not out to kill him."

"Dre, I'm scared to death!" Julie said. "Can you find him?"

Dre could. "He's not missing. He's working. Just pump the brakes."

"He was with you last night," Dre said. "How was he?"

Julie sighed. "Perfect. But I know Zack. I know what this case will do to him."

"He just needs time. That's all. I talked to Kilgas after Zack disappeared last night. I was ready to put a bullet in him for Zack and all of us. But I'm telling you, Zack is fine. Kilgas will keep his eye on Zack, but Zack is fine, and I'm refusing you to push the panic button."

"I see his motorcycle is outside," Julie said at length. "You told Darnell and Mikayla you figured Zack to leave the reservation as soon as he got back. Do you still feel that way?"

"Mikayla tells you everything, huh?" Dre rolled his eyes but knew there were no secrets in the group. "Right now, I'm not sure." Dre looked at Julie. "I think the equation has changed."

* * * *

The phone rang again on the edge of the desk. Another busy morning but that was ok. Moving up in the world generally resulted in more responsibility and, thus, more busy mornings. The man answered. "Ferguson."

"Ferguson, did you hear the news? Stack is out."

"What?"

"Stack was released from prison."

"On whose authority? He was supposed to be there another three months," Ferguson said.

"I don't know. I heard from the guard he got out a couple of days ago. Some lady he's never seen before showed up one day; the next morning, Stack signed papers and walked out."

Ferguson stared absently across his office. "Well, I'd say we better find out. Let me know. In the meantime, I think we better keep up the pressure. I know Stack. He'll run afoul of the law somehow. And when he does, we're going to be there."

9

The forty-minute drive to Annapolis was uneventful, and Kilgas drove straight to the house. No directions were necessary. Zack wondered how long Kilgas watched the mother of his child. The whole thing forced Zack to repress his past. Seeing the letter again sent to the agency months ago from an eighteen-year-old boy looking for his father jumpstarted his memory. *Michelle either forgot to hide it, or she left it intentionally. Maybe I shouldn't send my reply?*

Kilgas stopped the car across the street from the Italianate house. Sherry Bottford lived on the right side of the house turned into a duplex. "There it is."

Zack leaned forward to see around Kilgas. Zack kept an eye on his side-view mirror and Kilgas's hands at all times. "You ready for this?"

"No."

"Too bad. Let's go."

They got out of the car. Zack walked around to the street side and looked at Kilgas. "What does she do for a living?"

"Works for the county. Been there since college. She went to a two-year college mostly at night, got lucky with this job, and has been there ever since. That's been what? Fifteen years now?"

"How long have you been watching her?"

"Three weeks."

"Why did you start?"

"Since you were locked up and not going anywhere, I had lots of free time. So I went onto social media, poked around, and saw that Sherry had a daughter. I wanted to know if she were mine. But, unfortunately, I found out too late."

"How did you find out?"

"I can do math," Kilgas said. "To be sure, when she was at work, I broke into her house and found some paperwork where she listed the father."

"Brilliant," Zack remarked with a shake of his head. "I thought you were seeing someone else?"

"I am," Kilgas said. "I went out of my way to meet her after I learned your ex-fiancé was involved with NPA via her former boyfriend. Rather fortuitous of me if I do say so myself. She was the executive assistant for Charles Samford. Remember him?"

Zack remembered her. The woman warned Zack when Zack entered NPA.

"Poor guy had a heart attack," Kilgas said. "But not before I convinced him I was going to kill him and his secretary if he didn't pay me a bunch of money to give him you."

"You're welcome. So you conned this woman and now have a relationship with her?"

"I fell for her after the first date, so I changed my plan to include her. It turns out Samford was a real prick to work for, so Terri was more than happy to help me bilk him out of twenty-five million. She was even happier when he had a heart attack. Quit the next day."

Zack walked across the street. "And you paid me a measly five grand? I'm shooting you for sure now."

"Can you at least wait until after we find my daughter? And I did use some of that money to pay the guys who got you out of Samford's building alive."

"Gee, I guess I owe you now," Zack said stoically. "Let's see how Sherry reacts to your smiling face."

* * * *

Kilgas was right. Sherry Bottford was pretty with thick, blonde curly hair which cascaded past her shoulders. Shapely and curvy, Sherry showed signs of worry and lack of sleep on her face, but Zack saw the determination in her eyes. He had seen it before.

Sherry stared at Zack and slowly moved her gaze to Kilgas. Instant recognition. Her eyes widened, and she stepped out onto the cement porch atop the stairs at the front door. "Mark? Is that you?"

Kilgas showed a sympathetic smile. "Sherry, hi."

She slapped his face immediately.

Not the time to take pleasure in it, but Zack understood why. And took pleasure in it.

"What? How dare you show! You disappeared. You left. And our daughter did the same thing you did!" Sherry cried, and Kilgas looked at Zack, who motioned his head. Kilgas understood and held Sherry gently.

"I'm sorry," Kilgas said. "We're here to help. We're going to find her."

"Why did you leave? Why? Mark, why did you leave me?"

Zack took a deep breath. "I'm sorry to interrupt, Miss Bottford, but can I ask you two questions quickly?"

Both Kilgas and Sherry looked at Zack.

"One, how long has your daughter been missing, and two, can we have a recent picture of her?" He waited, but there was no response. "I know that sounds insensitive, but I have experience with these situations. Time is critical."

"Jesus, Stack, can you be less of a jerk?"

"Kilgas, just get me that information, and I'll leave so you two can talk."

"Kilgas? Why did he call you Kilgas, Mark?" Sherry asked.

"Stack, can you give us a minute, please?"

"I said I would. After I find out what I asked."

Sherry looked confused but seemed to gravitate toward the urgency. "Hold on." She disappeared inside the house.

"Stack," Kilgas faced Zack, "you better show a little more heart, or I may shoot you."

"I've seen you shoot. I'll be ok."

Kilgas shook his head.

"Just keep her focused on the positive," Zack said softly. "Keep her focused on helping. Inactivity breeds sorrow, tears, worry, nightmares, depression, sleepless nights. She's already suffering enough. She needs hope, Kilgas. You want to hate me, then hate me. But time is against us."

Kilgas took a deep breath.

Sherry returned. "This was the last picture I have of Hannah with her friend, Angie Simpson. They ran away together over three weeks ago." Sherry didn't hide her tears.

"She's been missing for three weeks, and you know she ran away?" Zack asked.

Sherry nodded and pulled a note out of the back pocket of her tight jeans. She handed it to Zack to read. It was simple and to the point. Hannah said high school was stupid. There was no point. She wasn't going to find herself or her purpose stuck in 'stupid little Annapolis' and said she and Angie were leaving with someone else who Hannah didn't name. Hannah finished by telling her mother not to worry and someday she'll be back.

The girl in the picture with Hannah, Angie, was just as beautiful as Hannah. Both tall, with long hair and plenty of cleavage for high school girls. At least the outfits they wore took pains to show the cleavage.

Girls rush to grow up quickly to become women who fight to stay young.

"Are you with the police? Who are you?"

"I'm a private investigator, ma'am," Zack said. He nudged Kilgas' arm. "Give me your car keys." Kilgas did. "I've been hired to find your daughter. And we will find her." Zack turned around. "I'll be right back. Don't leave here," he told Kilgas.

Kilgas and Sherry stood on the porch in silence as Zack got into Kilgas' car and drove away.

"Who is that guy?" Sherry asked.

"The guy who's going to find our daughter, Sherry." He looked at her. "Don't worry. He's good."

"Mark, what in the hell is going on? Why? What?" Sherry grabbed her head and almost screamed. "How did you find me? Start talking. I'm so confused."

10

Zack drove to the Annapolis Police Department. After talking to several officers, Zack found the detective in an office. Detective Catchings.

"Detective, here's the guy," a uniformed cop said and let Zack in the office.

"What can I do for you?"

"Detective, I'm Zack Stack. I'm a private detective in Baltimore. Captain Ted Barnes of the BPD can vouch for me."

"I know Ted. He's a good man. How's he doing?"

"Back on the job. Doubt a couple of bullets are going to slow Ted down," Zack said.

"Glad they at least got the guys."

Zack pulled out the picture of the two girls. "I'm searching for these two. They went missing about three weeks ago. I was wondering if there is anything you might share with me about the case."

Catchings grabbed a stack of files piled on the corner of his desk, sifted through them, grabbed two, and tossed them in front of Zack. "There you go. Look all you want. According to the note one left, they ran away."

Zack opened the file.

"Who hired you?"

"Mother," Zack lied. *Doubt Kilgas wants to be questioned by the police. He'd be a suspect immediately.*

"She worried we aren't doing our job?"

Zack flipped a page. "Just exhausting all of her options."

"I get it," Catchings said. "I worked her case from day one. No one likes kids disappearing. This one ran away. It doesn't make it easier for the parent but usually makes finding her easier. Kids aren't the smartest with staying off the radar."

"But these two seem to be," Zack said as he scanned the file.

"That's what struck me as odd. The note suggested the girls wanted someplace bigger than Annapolis. So, we thought New York, Baltimore, Philly, even DC and sent out an alert to every police force this side of Chicago down to Miami. Couple of good-looking girls like that I can see hitting the beach and hoping to be discovered. I figured they'd show up on an Instagram page wearing strings of yarn. Lots of girls pay their way through college that way, you know," Catchings said.

"Unfortunately. It makes me wish I didn't have a daughter," Zack said instinctively.

"You have a daughter?" Catchings laughed. "How old? I have a twelve- and fourteen-year-old."

"Seven months," Zack said and closed the file. "No hits anywhere?"

"Eh, we got leads and lookalikes, but nothing. It's like they vanished."

"You getting hits on dead bodies found in the woods, things like that? Any DNA from either to have as a test?"

"No."

"What about the Jane Does? I know of at least five dead girls found recently."

"Didn't match the two," Catchings said. "If we need it, we'll get it and run one. The rest is all in there, but I'm telling you, we got nothing. They ran away, but both girls owned a car. They didn't take the car. We think they hitched a ride or took a taxi, or got on a train or bus. Neither used a debit or credit card since the day they went missing, but each cleaned out their bank accounts, so whatever they did and however they did it, they paid in cash."

Zack put the files on the desk. "Would you mind if I had a copy? I'd appreciate it."

"You bet," Catchings said and waved to a clerk. "Make a copy of this file and make sure he gets it before he leaves." The clerk took the file and disappeared.

"How much cash?"

"The blonde, Angie Simpson, she was a little princess who took out about ten grand. Hannah only had about five grand. Guessing that was the college fund."

Zack sighed. "That much cash would make them prime targets."

"That's what I thought. We checked every ditch and forest in the county. But even with the John and Jane Does found, we got no hits. No prints, no nothing. I'm telling you, Stack, they vanished. These girls either seriously wanted to disappear,"

Zack finished the sentence. "Or someone doesn't want them found."

* * * *

Zack knocked on the door and waited. Three hours passed since he left. When the door opened, Sherry put her hand on Zack's arm. "Thank you. Please bring my baby back to me," she said. Kilgas appeared behind her. "To us," she added.

Zack nodded but said nothing. He feigned a smile.

"Stack, you ready to go?"

"Um, Miss Bottford, would you have anything of Hannah's like her toothbrush, or did she wear a retainer or something like that?"

"Why?"

"I'd like to have a DNA test run."

"Will that help?"

Zack saw Kilgas' face and suspected what he thought. "Sometimes runaways change their appearance if they don't want to be found. DNA tests are conclusive."

"Yes, would strands of hair help?"

"They would, but saliva would be better."

She disappeared, and Kilgas looked at Stack. "What are you doing? She isn't dead!"

Zack said nothing. Sherry Bottford reappeared a few minutes later with several hair strands and a toothbrush in a sandwich bag.

"I hope this helps."

Zack said yes and thanked her. "We should hit the road."

"Did you find out anything? Where did you go?" Sherry asked Zack.

"I promise you I'll do everything I can." It was a blow-off, and Zack knew it. *But what do I say? That your daughter is probably dead? I got lucky once. I wouldn't count on it again.* "Mark," Zack said, "we need to go."

Zack walked down the steps, turned, and saw Kilgas and Sherry hug and kiss. Kilgas said something to Sherry and hurried down the stairs. Kilgas walked to the car, got in, and he and Zack drove away.

"What took you so long?" Kilgas asked.

"I wanted to make sure you and Sherry had plenty of time to talk without me," Zack said. Zack sat in the passenger seat, his eyes aware of everything. "Did you two work things out?"

"Work things out? You know, I used to like your humor back in the days of trying to kill you. But now, I realize you just like being an ass."

Zack smiled. "Sometimes, I even go out of my way."

"Where are we headed?"

"Back to Baltimore after you buy me lunch. I'm starving."

"How can you eat at a time like this?"

"Kilgas, you should know this. You eat when you can. But, sometimes, you can't, and that's when you need it the most."

"That makes no sense."

"You've never been tied up in a cave before, have you?"

Kilgas steered the car into the parking lot of a burger joint. "Is a burger sufficient?"

"Not this place. They serve the wrong soft drink," Zack said.

"Are you serious?"

Zack looked at him with a straight face. "Yes. Keep driving." Kilgas did. "How was she? She coping well?"

"No. She's a mess. Confused as hell and unsure why I suddenly appeared in her life. I think she harbors some ill feelings towards me. Probably blames me," Kilgas said.

"You surprised?"

Kilgas sped onto the interstate. "A little. Time is supposed to heal wounds."

"It doesn't," Zack said. "I talked to the mother of Angie Simpson. It doesn't sound like Betty and Sherry like each other. Each blames the other," Zack said.

"Did you get a DNA sample from Angie?"

"Yes, I did."

"Did you tell her the same lie you told Sherry?"

"Didn't have to." Zack looked at Kilgas. "She believes her daughter is dead already. She just wants her found."

"Ok. I know. It's hard, that's all. What else did you find out?"

"They were best friends who did everything together. Their social media pages proved that. I got some private messages the two shared for a little insight, though most of it is benign. But Mrs. Simpson gave me Angie's diary."

"Whoa," Kilgas said. "I wonder if Hannah kept one."

"If she does, you'll need to go back and get it," Zack said. "Or have Sherry overnight it to the office. It will give us a good view of their state of mind," Zack said. "I also talked with the cops."

"You did what? Are you crazy? Stack, are you trying to lock me up?"

They looked at each other. "Should I?"

Kilgas exhaled. "Dude, that's not cool."

"Relax. I never mentioned you. I needed to know what the police have on this."

"Which is?"

"Not much. I hate to tell you this, but we're on our own."

"What do you mean? Did they give up?"

"It's cold, Kilgas. And prepare yourself for the worst. It likely won't turn out well."

11

After parting ways with Kilgas at half-past five, Zack took a walk to smell the fresh spring air. But, of course, it already smelled like early summer at the end of May in Baltimore. All the cliché things people said about spring seemed like lies and piles of cow manure to Zack. *Spring ahead? New beginning? My ass.* He looked at the office windows on the second floor. They were as dark as he hoped.

He used the front door and locked them behind him. Zack walked up the stairs, unlocked the doors to the office, and walked inside. Zack noticed the Christmas tree still in the corner to his left with several presents underneath and still lit. But he ignored that. The bathroom faucet turned on and off, and out walked Lauren.

She smiled at him.

"Lauren, why are you still here?" Zack asked curiously.

"You said you'd be back today. I wanted to be here when you did."

"You know you don't have to do that."

"It is my job," Lauren said. She walked past him and sat down behind her desk.

Zack slowly walked towards his office door. "You really don't have to do that. You should adhere to whatever Andre said the office hours are. Unless we're paying overtime now." Zack stopped. "Are we?"

Lauren smiled and lifted a piece of paper off her desk. "No, sir. I wanted to wait for you."

"Why?"

Lauren seemed perplexed. "Sir, I wanted to make sure you got your messages."

"Back one day, and I have messages? How exciting," Zack said with a touch of sarcasm.

Lauren plowed forward. "Dre wants to meet you for a drink tonight, and I'm supposed to give you this." She opened a drawer, grabbed a cell phone along with the keys to one of his motorcycles, and handed them to Zack. "I'm sorry for forgetting this morning."

Zack put the phone on the desk. "I don't want it right now," Zack said. "Maybe on Monday." The motorcycle keys went into his pocket.

Lauren stood immediately. "I think it would be best if you take the phone with you and call back Dre. Sir."

Zack saw the concern on her face and slid the phone into his pocket. "Why is the Christmas tree still up?"

Lauren smiled. "We left it up for you, sir. There are presents underneath it for you."

"Take it down, burn it, and throw out the presents. I'm not celebrating Christmas anymore." Zack turned and entered his office.

Lauren followed him into the office. "Um, sir, Mr. Stack?"

Zack sat behind his desk. "You are a stickler for formality."

"Why aren't you celebrating Christmas anymore?"

"I was alone in a prison cell on Christmas. You don't have to burn the tree, but I don't want to see it."

Lauren nodded with a sad frown on her face. "Sir, are you planning on returning to your apartment and Julie tonight?"

"Probably. Why?"

"No reason, sir," Lauren said. "I just want you to be careful."

Zack opened the fridge behind him. In the mini-fridge, he saw the seasonal Sam Adams. He grabbed a bottle and smiled. "Thanks, Lauren. Do you want one?"

She looked confused. "Is that allowed?"

"As long as the boss is, yes." He handed her his open bottle and grabbed one himself. "Though it doesn't feel like I'm the boss."

"Sir, can I ask what your history is with Julie?"

"We're getting personal after one day?"

"I did see you naked, and you said we could tell each other everything."

"That's not exactly what I said. How old are you, Lauren?"

"28."

"Really? I guessed 24 or 25."

She blushed. "Thank you. Sir, I promise you I won't betray your trust."

"Then I can assume you aren't betraying the trust of the others in the office, either." Zack drank from the beer with his eyes fixated on hers.

She lowered her gaze.

"Lauren, are they planning on a secret meeting to discuss my mental state?"

"Sir," Lauren looked at Zack, a tortured look on her face.

Zack looked from his desk to her. She was nervous and clutched the beer with both hands. "Relax, Lauren. Michelle knew how to walk the fence, or whatever the saying is. But until the end, I knew she never hid anything from me. She wanted me to think before I acted." Zack sniffed the beer but didn't drink. *I miss her.*

"I can be everything Michelle was to you, but can you at least meet me halfway?"

Zack recognized her nervousness. "Jules and I dated for over three years and were engaged. Then, because of this job and my past, she left me."

She turned red. "I'm sorry, sir. And the baby?"

"Is mine," Zack said. "I didn't know at first, or else things might be different."

"Would you go back to her if she asked?"

Zack paused. "I don't know how to answer that question."

Lauren nodded. "I heard the name Stefani mentioned. Who is she to you?"

Zack swigged from the bottle of beer. "Another girl who left me. While I sat in prison, no less."

Lauren said nothing, and Zack didn't want to talk anymore but knew she wasn't leaving.

"Two days ago, I was released from jail after six long months. My best friend wasn't there for me." Zack felt himself well up. "I know Dre didn't know I got out. I didn't know I was getting out, but I sat up there in my little room for over three months, and the only visitor I had was a woman who I don't know and scares me. I'm feeling a little disenfranchised." Zack raised his beer. "I can tell you're trying hard to tell me something without saying anything."

Lauren remained silent.

Zack swigged the beer. "Was Jules here?"

"Yes, sir."

"She knows about Kilgas."

"Yes, sir."

Zack stared at the bottle of beer and slowly spun it on his desk. "She spent a couple of days in the hospital with buckshot wounds because of Kilgas. I ended up spending a week with two bullets in my back, only inches from my heart. Better aim, and we wouldn't be having this conversation." Zack looked at Lauren. "I'm sure she freaked out. I'll talk to her tonight."

"I want you to be careful, sir."

"A sudden yet forceful suggestion. Why?"

"How you're feeling is why you should be careful."

Zack stopped with the bottle at his lips. "Lauren, you barely know me. Why the concern?"

Lauren looked lost, and as her hands trembled, she sipped the beer and wiped her lips. "I am here to do a job, and from day one, heard about you. You became this larger-than-life figure. Everyone talked about the things you did and how you survived so many things, and they made me feel like you're some kind of superhero. Perhaps a superhero with some weird idiosyncrasies, but still, all they did was talk about how great you are."

"They talked about me?"

"Of course, sir. They are your friends."

"Hmph. Why didn't they visit?"

Lauren shook her head. She continued. "I was told my job specifically is to make sure you get settled and happy and to help you in any way I can. So when you walked in yesterday, at that point, some incredible figment of my imagination, I have to admit, I was overwhelmed, and I still am, and I'm sure everything I do is wrong and that you won't like me." Lauren bit her lip, finished the bottle, put the empty on his desk, and lowered her gaze. "But, even with as little as we know each other, I can't help but care for you. And with what I know about you, I think I should worry."

"Lauren, I'm none of what they said. I'm just a normal guy. Don't worry. It causes wrinkles, and you're far too pretty to have wrinkles."

"You're anything but normal, sir."

Zack gave her another beer. "A superhero, huh?" He laughed, and Lauren smiled. "Wonder what my superhero name would be?" Zack shrugged. "Lauren, I'm just Zack. Or to you apparently, sir or Mr. Stack."

"Don't forget Awesome Sauce," she said. Lauren handed him a sticky note with an address on it. Zack knew the address. Nice apartments. "Sir, if things don't work out at your place tonight, I have plenty of space for you. Please don't sleep here. It makes people uneasy."

Zack nodded and understood. "How much are we paying you? These places aren't cheap."

"You can sleep on your couch. I promise not to walk in on you after your shower."

Zack set down his barely touched beer. "Doesn't bother me. There's no pretense with being naked."

Lauren stood. "I think you should come home with me now, but I suspect you will say you have things to do. Calling Dre would be a nice start. I'll expect you. I also expect you to take your cell phone with you from now on." She smiled. "I am the manager around here like you said, and you said what I say goes. So, I'm looking forward to having you over tonight."

"I'm taking my motorcycle for a ride. It clears my mind. Would you like to come along?"

12

The bike felt great. The engine purred, though Zack could tell the valves were a little gummed from not being exercised. Zack planned to eliminate that problem as soon as he exited town. Lauren clung to him, her skirt riding up her legs, but she pressed her legs tight against Zack. She kept her head on his shoulder and peered through the helmet as Zack, with nothing but sunglasses and a wrap-around his nose and mouth, let the air blow through his short hair.

Zack exited the town and kept an eye on his mirrors. Finally, Zack reached the road where he made his standard sixty-mile loop in the country to exercise the bike's demons and clear his mind. The bike's acceleration bogged slightly, not noticeable to most, but Zack knew it, and it upset him. *Dre should have known better.*

But the open road with no traffic helped with that problem. The bike hit one-hundred and roared. Zack felt her hand squeeze him, and he slowed with a smile. Zack returned to average speed and slowed as the turn west approached. Zack made the turn and pulled to the side of the road. He stopped and turned to look at Lauren.

She raised the visor on the helmet. "Are you having fun?"

"Feels good, doesn't it?"

"Especially in a skirt. You should have warned me."

Zack revved the engine twice. "My baby needs to be released and exercised," Zack said.

"You call your motorcycle your baby?"

"This one I do. She's been with me since I left the service. The other one was out of necessity. The other one has more horsepower and goes faster, but this one is slick and quick. She understands me," Zack said.

Lauren watched Zack's face, and his stress and worry briefly disappeared.

"I love this," Zack said softly as his eyes returned to the front of the bike, examining every inch.

Lauren put her hand on his shoulder. "Sir, can I ask you a question?"

Zack looked at her and waited.

"Why did you bring me with you?"

Zack turned around and revved the bike, both hands on the handles. "You want to know me, don't you?"

She wrapped her arms around his mid-section and tightened her legs against him. "Keep it under one-hundred, please. It's messing up my hair. Sir."

Zack smiled, revved the bike, and looked at her one last time. "Hang on tight."

They sped down the county highway barely above the speed limit when Zack noticed a black car behind him. It didn't close; it didn't fall back. But it followed him. Zack reached the intersection, stopped, turned south headed back to Baltimore. The car followed.

Zack wanted to believe it was a coincidence, but he accelerated as he approached Big Falls and a curvy stretch in the road. Zack's idea of handling a windy road was to straighten it out, and as he hit the apex of the first turn, the black Crown Victoria behind him still, Zack twisted the throttle.

Zack raced from one side to the other and straightened the road as much as he could as the bike powered through the curves. The black car fell back, not able to handle the road like Zack could. As Zack pulled out of the stretch, he broke hard at the first intersection, turned left, lowered, and accelerated. Lauren crouched with him, making herself as flat to Zack as she could.

Moments later, anything in the side view mirror disappeared. Zack slowed the bike and headed back to Baltimore in a circuitous route but made it back by nine that night. He parked the bike on the street outside Lauren's apartment building and watched for several minutes.

His mind raced more than the bike had as Lauren ran her fingers through her hair. Zack grabbed the helmet from Lauren and secured it on the back of the bike.

"Are you coming inside, sir?"

"No, I think I'll head home."

"Are you ok? You don't seem yourself right now."

Zack's mind remained on that Crown Victoria though he shook his head at her suggestion. *It was a coincidence. How could they have found me? Forget it. It's nothing.* "Get a good night's sleep. Call me tomorrow when you want your car. Or I'll pick you up early Monday."

"Monday is a holiday, sir."

"We don't work on holidays?" Zack seemed confused. "Ok, well, Tuesday, then."

"Is everything ok, sir? You drove really fast after I asked you not to. Did you see something?"

"Felt like there was a little carbon build-up in the engine. I apologize if that made you uncomfortable."

"I loved it. It was amazing. Unsafe and reckless, but it was awesome."

"Good night, Lauren. Call me if you need anything."

"Why don't you come inside and stay here tonight, sir? I think it will be best for you."

Zack paused and smiled. "I'll be fine, Lauren. Thanks for riding with me."

"Anytime, sir. I did love it."

Zack nodded at her, the sight of the black car in his mind, and he rode off.

13

Mikayla Dorsey, Stefani Oakley, and Julie Fletcher entered the Dre-Zack Detective Agency Saturday morning at ten o'clock after working out in the studio where Stefani trained. They carried gym bags, dropped them on the floor, and went to Mikayla and Zack's office, where they opened bottles of water and sat down. A regular Saturday morning routine.

Mikayla checked her computer while Stefani checked her phone, and Julie texted her parents to check on Cate. Mikayla finished. "That was a killer workout this morning," Mikayla said. "Man, those were some awesome kicks today, Jules."

Julie didn't respond.

"Those were sharp today, Jules," Stefani said. "I thought you were going to kick the bag off the chain!"

Julie sipped her water.

"Uh oh. Something is wrong," Stef said. "I can see it. What is it?"

Julie feigned a smile. "Don't be ridiculous."

"Don't lie, Jules. Mik, you can tell. Look at her. That smile is fake. What is it? Tell us."

Julie took a deep breath. "It's nothing. Just deadlines with my work and dealing with Cate. That's all."

Stefani put down her water bottle, exhaled, and decided to go in a different direction. "Did you see that creep, Jerome, today? I may ask the two of you to kick his butt. He asked me out again. I don't know why he won't take no for an answer."

Mikayla swigged from the bottle of water and smiled. "So the prettiest girl gets asked out again. We all should be so lucky."

"Ugh. Not by that guy. He's disgusting. And I'm not the prettiest girl in the room."

Mikayla laughed. "Sorry. Jules and I already decided you are."

"Stop it. You two are more beautiful than I am, and have you seen her body?" Stef pointed at Jules. "Amazing!"

Julie watched her best friend, Stefani.

Mikayla laughed at Stefani's refusal of the truth. "You're embarrassing yourself, Stef. Both of you are amazing. So what's the problem?"

Stefani let out a tired and frustrated breath. "I hate it."

"What? Are you kidding? In the last six months, because of your looks, we've gotten tables at restaurants, free drinks, doors opened for us, asked out on dates, free dinner, better movie seats, and a free cab ride. What's wrong with that?"

"You're both just as pretty as I am."

Mikayla guffawed. "Yeah, right."

Stefani rolled her eyes. "You are, so stop it. It's about confidence more than looks, and you're way more confident than I am."

Mikayla couldn't control her laughing. "Are you insane? Call the pity party police."

Stefani finished her water. "Don't take this wrong, but do you know what it's like always being the prettiest girl in the room?"

"Once. But I was the only girl in the room, so…."

"Mik, you are beautiful. But, you're too hard on yourself," Julie said.

Stefani spoke. "Ever since I was little, everyone always told me how pretty I was. At first, it made me feel good. I was popular in school; once boys became boys, they lined up to ask me to the school dance, and all the other girls were so nice to me. They all wanted to be my friend."

"Tough life."

"Shut up," Stefani said with a smile. "In high school, I realized it wasn't about me. The boys didn't want to go out with me. They wanted to say they dated me, or felt me up, or however immature high school boys brag about girls. It was all about my looks and my body. I know I was blessed, but I was into sports and exercise, and my father got me into karate at age four probably because he knew if I looked like my mother, and she's gorgeous, that guys would be attracted to me. I guess he wanted to know I could defend myself."

Mikayla and Julie listened carefully. This was unlike Stefani.

"I overheard boys at a party talk about me once. Even though I was a straight-A student, they assumed I was dumb because of my looks. They said I was using my looks to manipulate the chemistry teacher to get an A. They couldn't accept that I was smart, and chemistry came easy to me. But, of course, the teacher was always staring at my breasts."

"Did you flaunt them?"

"I dressed like every other teenage high school girl wanting to fit in. To me, I wasn't flaunting anything. Can we help it if we have boobs?" Julie and Mikayla agreed. "I wanted acceptance because of who I was, not how I looked, and all through high school, that wasn't the case."

"I hated those years. Imagine how hard it was for a late bloomer."

"Ouch, I'm sorry. I hated those years, too. I wanted to become a doctor and worked hard at school. I was on the honor roll, made the dean's list, got academic awards, a scholarship, and got into medical school. Still, at parties, all I would hear from guys was 'wow, you're a hottie,' or 'it won't be hard for you to land a good job,' or my favorite, 'with looks and a body like that, you'll land a good MRS.' Because in the eyes of the men in the class, I wasn't worthy because my mother and father just happened to be good-looking and produced me. I felt like DNA punished me."

"Many men are easily intimidated by intelligent, smart, beautiful women. We can have as many women's movements as we want. The bottom line is that this is a man's world, and many will do everything they can to prevent that from changing." Mikayla swigged her water and sighed. "What about you, Jules? How were your high school years?"

Julie smiled. "Sounds a lot like Stef's. As soon as my breasts developed, boys treated me differently, and it took me a while to understand their maturation schedule lagged behind ours. But I didn't care too much about boys. I wanted to be a journalist for as long as I could remember, and that's all I focused on." She shrugged. "I don't regret any decisions I've made if that's what this is about. Nor am I upset that God blessed me with good DNA. But I have to admit I did use it to help me get things." Julie smiled and sipped her water. "Men may be in charge, but most are easily manipulated by the bat of an eye, an extra button undone on a shirt, a cute laugh, and gentle touch of the arm." Julie laughed. "I know. It's terrible, but why not use it to our advantage?"

"I wish I had that confidence," Stefani said.

"You did with Zack," Mikayla pointed out.

Stefani said nothing.

"He was wrapped around your finger," Mikayla said. "Still is."

Stefani remained silent.

Mikayla changed topics slightly. "How did you remain single all these years, if you don't mind me asking? You get asked out every day."

"I was almost married. I fell in love with a doctor. We were engaged when I finished school and lived together until the bottom dropped out of that one."

"What happened?"

"He was done with school. I wasn't, so when I was in class, he worked at a hospital. Then, he found a younger, perkier woman that showered him with attention. I assumed it was because she was better looking, had a better body, had more to offer, anything. I wasn't good enough, and that cut me to the core. Guess I still look at men as if they're just setting me up to hurt me."

Things started to make sense to Mikayla. "What about Zack?"

Stef shook her head. "Seriously? You won't let it go, will you?" Stefani sipped her water and looked at Julie. "Has anyone seen or heard from him? Is he still in that prison?"

Mikayla and Julie looked at each other. It felt like the pause allowed all the air to get sucked from the room. Stefani read their faces.

"He's back?" Stefani traded looks between Mikayla and Julie. "Both of you knew he is back, and neither told me?"

Mikayla hunched her shoulders and looked genuinely sorry. "I didn't know if you wanted to know or not."

Stefani slowly looked at Julie.

"With what happened between you two, since you won't talk about it, I didn't know, either."

Stefani shook her head. "How is he? Surely, he went to you, Jules. Right?"

Julie shook her head. "He stopped by his apartment to get some things and to see Cate. We didn't talk much," Julie lied. Two nights in a row sharing a bed with Zack conflicted her as much as she feared. He didn't sleep well despite the lovemaking, and after a nightmare where Zack awoke with a scream that woke Cate and made her cry, Zack left the apartment ashamed. That was just after midnight. Jules didn't know where Zack went, and he didn't return any texts or calls.

"So, you're not looking to get back with Zack?" Stefani asked after a long silence.

Julie looked at her. "Stef, come on," Julie scoffed. "You know me better than that."

"Well, I'm glad he's out and hope he's adjusting. I suspect a lot is going on inside his mind right now." Stefani exhaled. "But he's got you, Jules."

"Stef, he simply stopped at his apartment for clothes. You know I'm only there because my house renovation is taking so long," Julie said. "Nothing is going on between us."

"He still went to you first," Stefani said. "He always does."

Mikayla sensed the tension. "Zack wants to know his daughter, Stef. That's what he told me when I saw him."

Stefani nodded and attempted to pretend it didn't bother her. "I know. He'll be a good father."

"Stef, stop," Jules said.

"I didn't mean anything by it. Before," Stef paused, "we talked about Cate. I knew if he and I were still together, that he would be involved with her. And if we were still together, I know I could trust you, Jules. So let's not talk about Zack anymore, Ok?"

Julie hid her guilt.

Mikayla walked to Stefani and put her hand on Stef's shoulder. "I visited him a couple of times in prison after he dumped you. Even though he wouldn't talk about you, Stef, I know he's not over you. Something is off with that whole thing," Mikayla said. "I think you should confront him."

"He knows how to find me," Stefani said. "But he found Jules first." Stefani shrugged. "Like he always does. He'd take you back in a second. I don't want to be second fiddle."

Julie rolled her eyes. "OMG. You are not the second fiddle. That's not how he operates. If you want him back, go after him and see what happens."

"Yeah, and hurry because I need to get laid, and if you don't go after Zack, I will!" Mikayla laughed.

"He knows how to find me," Stefani repeated as she sipped her water bottle.

Mikayla shook her head. "Stef, just go talk to him and figure it out so we can all either quit talking about him or start planning your wedding to him." Mikayla walked towards the bathroom. "I'm going to rinse off. Jules, can your parents babysit today? Let's go wedding dress shopping. That always cheers up Stefani. I found one that will look smoking hot on you, Stef. Zack will see your neckline and get instantly hard! Jules, call your parents. Girl's day!"

14

Zack Stack stepped into the police station with a different expectation than his last visit. The activity bustled like it always did. A few of the policemen recognized him. Some muttered something to a nearby cop and stared while others smiled at the sight of Stack and continued with their business. Finally, he saw Detective Dylan Kael.

Kael spotted Zack and walked to him. "Hey, Stack, about the other night, I'm sorry if I came on a little strong."

Zack pressed forward. "Is this by the book? Does Ted know you asked me to help?"

"He does."

Zack put two small Ziploc bags on his desk. "Can you run a DNA test on those?"

"Why and who?"

"For comparison. Two teenage girls, runaways from Annapolis," Zack said. "Been missing about four weeks now."

Kael cringed. "I got it. I'll get it done. Doc Schaeffer is in this morning. Let's go see what he's found."

"Schaeffer? What happened to Patterson?"

Kael laughed. "Oh yeah, you wouldn't know. After Barnes came out of his coma, he and the DA and IA went to work. Patterson got fired and arrested. It turns out he was in on the fix against you. He's out on bail but could be seeing some time after his trial."

"Are his examination files still here?"

"I don't know. Why?"

"I need to see a report from three years ago. Can you find one on Evan Rossum for me?"

"Who is that?"

"A dead guy, Kael. For now, that's enough information."

"Start calling me Dylan, and I will."

"Dylan. Ok. I like calling you green leafy weed, though."

Dylan laughed. "Hey, have you talked to Michelle lately? I've been meaning to see how she's doing?"

Zack smiled. Mikayla told him about the flirting in the office. "I'm going to find her later. Want me to pass along a message?"

"Just tell her hi. Listen, be nice to Schaeffer. This guy doesn't know you, so be nice. It's hard to find people who like you. Forgive me for saying this, but you look like shit. Late night or something?"

Zack remained in his wrinkled clothes from the day before and had not showered. "I, uh, had a rough night. A couple of bottles of self-pity wine, and I woke up on the roof of my office building this morning."

"You have running water in your office, Stack. I've seen it."

"Yeah, there was a reason I stayed out of my office. So, here I am. Deal with it."

The two walked to the lab and found Doc Schaeffer working on another DB. Schaeffer looked up, saw Zack, and any peace left his demeanor.

"Doc, good morning," said Kael. "You got anything on the Jane Doe?"

"Tests should be back soon. My report is on my desk. But you'll have to wait for tox to come back for anything possibly substantive."

Kael grabbed the report. "I'll make a copy and get this back to you, Doc. Let's go, Stack."

Zack followed him out. "That was easy."

"Not what you're used to, I'm sure."

"No. Julie used to get what I needed from Patterson. She used him like a dirty washcloth."

Kael laughed. "You guys are interesting. That's for sure. I'll send a copy of what I can find to your office by courier later today. Zack, I'm glad you're back."

Zack stopped and took a deep breath. "Leafy Weed, thanks. Sorry for being a jerk the other night. Just having trouble adjusting, that's all."

"I can't imagine. Give me a call next time you want me to set foot in that bar for the second time in my career."

* * * *

71

Zack entered the building Saturday with a goal. As he waited for who he asked and studied the listing of offices for a name, a bald black man turned the corner and smiled at Zack.

"Zack Stack? Holy Scooby Snacks. When did you get out?"

"Couple of days ago," Zack said. The two shook hands, and Zack observed Ty Campbell's face.

"So why are you here, of all places?"

Zack looked around, but no one paid attention. "Well, I, um, it's work-related. I hoped I'd run into you."

Ty Campbell nodded. "Oh. I get it. Come on; I'll show you around." Zack followed Ty Campbell through the floor of offices. They went to the upper floor. "Now up here is a little different. Most of the people here work on computer crimes. I thought you'd be interested to see one in particular." Campbell stopped at the door with the name Michelle Borman on the door's nameplate. "She's making a name for herself up here."

Zack stared at the nameplate. "I have no doubt. She's one of the best."

"I know. Michelle is already in charge of a group. Hell, give her enough time, and she may run this whole department. Thanks for giving her to us," Campbell said.

"Do you think I could leave a note on her desk?"

"Hell, why don't you say hi? She's inside." He opened the door, and Zack saw his former office manager, confidante, a lover from years back, closest friend and ally, seated behind a desk. Glasses on, her hair back in a ponytail, and the focused look he was used to on Michelle's face. Then, she saw Zack.

Her mouth dropped open, and her eyes widened. "Zack."

"Come find me when you're done," Ty said softly and shut the door behind Zack. Zack stepped closer to the desk, and Michelle stood. She rushed around the desk and jumped into his arms. They held each other tightly. Zack remembered what it felt like to have her in his arms. They danced at his Halloween party, the last good moment they shared. Zack knew he was the reason they weren't together.

"Why? I need to know why." That was all Zack could say before Michelle hugged him again.

"I knew you'd show, but I wish you hadn't," Michelle whispered before she squeezed him harder.

"Honey," Zack shook his head. He didn't know where to start. "I need you."

Michelle grabbed his face with both hands; tears escaped her eyes; she quickly kissed him and gazed into his eyes. "No, you don't."

"Yes, I do. I don't understand why you left. Why didn't you talk to me?"

"Zack," Michelle shook her head, frustrated. "You need to leave." She put her fingers over her lips and softly shushed him. Michelle went back to her desk, wrote something on a piece of paper, and handed it to Zack.

Zack read it and looked at her.

Michelle smiled. "You should go. It's good to see you again. Goodbye, Zack."

* * * *

Michelle watched Zack disappear down the hall through her office window. She went to her desk, picked up her cell phone, and sent a simple text. "He was just here. Keep him away."

15

Zack returned to Campbell's office.

"How did it go? Happy reunion?"

"Just saying hi," Zack said. "That's all. Can you not mention my visit to anyone?"

"Your secret is safe with me. My lips are sealed."

"There's something else. I got asked to do a couple of cases involving missing children and teenagers found dead along roads the last few months," Zack said. "Different states. I doubt they're tied together, but I thought you might be willing to sniff around for me," Zack said.

"Why me?"

"I need someone to trust. I pegged you to be a good guy back in Clyde where we met, and I'm allowing you to prove me right."

"Zack, about what happened. Look, I told you the truth."

"I hope so. That shortens the list."

"Some things might be best left alone."

"Good advice I'll try to keep in mind."

"How did you get out?"

"I signed some papers one morning and walked out the front door," Zack said. Addy Jones told Zack not to mention her involvement to anyone. Zack chose not to disobey her. "Figured someone had a change of heart. In any case, could you ask around and see if anything is going on with those DB's and potential missing girls?"

"Yeah, you bet. What's in it for me?"

"If we can tie it to anything, you get to make an arrest, help your career, and all that fun stuff," Zack said.

"So you're into making deals now?"

Zack stood. "I'm into survival."

Campbell stared at Zack. After a lengthy pause, he spoke. "Are you working on any other case?"

"I've been back two days." Zack scanned the area.

"I'll see what I can find out."

Zack nodded, left, and found the nearest bus stop. Zack wished he rode his motorcycle but decided to test his theory. At the bus stop, his phone rang. Reluctantly, he answered it. "Stack. Go."

"Where are you?"

"In Woodlawn about to get on a bus if it ever shows up."

"The FBI? Are you nuts? Jesus Christ, Stack. You must enjoy playing with fire."

"When flames surround you, what choice do you have?"

"For one, you stay the hell away from the gasoline, idiot. I'm on my way. We have work to do."

* * * *

The two men stepped out of the car. Middle of the day, outside Baltimore, in an industrial area now abandoned and forgotten, the smell and decay of the site were similar to every other city that used to have manufacturing. Now, the police rarely came to this area. But drifters, homeless, vagabonds, and sometimes runaways with nowhere else to go did.

Zack and Kilgas ambled towards a closed-down brick-walled factory. Part of it still had ceilings and walls, ideal shelter at night to stay out of the elements.

Tall 55-gallon metal barrels served the purpose of heat. Zack saw several with either flames burning or with smoke seeping out, a remnant of the night's heat supply for those here. Zack, who loved watching movies, realized that not even Hollywood could capture the area's hopelessness, despair, and filth.

"This ought to be fun," Zack whispered as they approached an area filled with women and men.

The ages of the inhabitants varied, but due to their physical condition, Zack couldn't guess. The rags they wore, likely infested with lice or fleas and dirty as could be, hung off the residents as if the clothes didn't want to be there. It didn't take long to understand what poverty and economic depression did to some people.

The rest of the world forgot or ignored the problem here, as in every city, big or small.

"Just don't get too close," Kilgas said.

"I don't plan to. I can't get past the smell." The body odor formed an invisible barrier that offended the senses. At least those not exposed to it 24/7. To those saddled with it, they didn't notice it anymore.

"Don't judge, Stack. You don't smell that great today, either. Did you even shower today, and aren't those the same clothes you wore yesterday?"

"And you just told me not to judge."

"These people have an excuse. You don't."

Zack knew otherwise.

"These people used to be someone in the real world. Who knows how they ended up here? Believe it or not, some of our brothers-in-arms may be out here. I know a couple of guys I served with came back, couldn't readjust, and ended up on the streets." They stopped. "Ok, I'll take this side; you take that side."

"And you think someone here may have seen your daughter?"

"It's worth a shot, Stack," Kilgas said. Stack looked at the picture of his daughter and her friend. "After they leave home, they have to come somewhere. This place is as good as any when you don't want the authorities to find you."

"Ok, but if I have to shoot someone, I'm blaming you."

Zack took the right side of the street-wide path between two dilapidated buildings where the occupants leaned against the wall or sat on the ground. Some even still laid under the cardboard and garbage bags they used for blankets.

Zack put the picture in his left hand. He wanted his right hand free. Zack stopped at the first man he came across. Tired looking, dirty, grey beard and mustache and unkempt hair, the man smelled, his teeth were brown, and there was no life left in his eyes.

"Have you seen either of these girls before?"

Zack held out the picture at the man. He didn't bother looking.

"Sorry to bother you, but have you seen these girls here? They could be in danger," Zack said.

The man shook his head no and returned to the emptiness of his existence.

Zack moved on, and that's the way it went for the following few people. Then, Zack spotted a man seated, his back against the wall in the middle of the block. The look in his eyes told Zack he was different from the rest of the people.

It was suspicion and anger. The man's clothes were torn and ragged but not dirty—the man's boots, Timberlands, worn but clean with new laces.

Zack stopped in front of him. "Excuse me, have you seen these two girls?"

The man looked at the picture. "Give me some money."

"Have you seen these two girls?" Zack repeated.

"What's it to you?"

"They're missing and could be in danger," Zack said. "Have you seen them?"

"Are you a cop?"

"Have you seen these girls?"

The man didn't look at the picture. "Hey man, give me some money for some food."

"Have you seen these girls?"

"Man, what do I care? Ain't my problem. Give me some money." He held out his hand.

Zack took notice. *Nicely manicured nails. Odd for down here.* "How come you're down here? Don't you have family or something to help you out? Maybe get you a bath, help you find a job?"

"Screw you, man. What do you know about it? You gonna give me some cash or not?"

"No. I wouldn't waste it giving it to you."

"Oh, you think you're better than me."

"Yup."

The man narrowed his eyes angrily. "What if I prove to you different? You act like you're looking for trouble."

Zack opened his jacket to expose the handle of the handgun under his shoulder. "Did I find it?"

The man looked away as if his time spent on Zack had expired.

Zack moved on after another long look at the man. Zack asked a few more people and decided this exercise was over. He looked for Kilgas, who talked to two men surrounding a barrel. At the end of the passageway between the buildings, a white cargo van slowly crept past. Glare off the windows prevented Zack from seeing anything inside the truck. It disappeared beyond the building.

Kilgas left the two men and headed towards Zack. Zack scanned the area and noticed the Timberland boots man walked away, unlike the way others moved. This guy moved with a purpose.

Kilgas reached Stack. "Find out anything?"

"One oddball that seems strangely out of place." Zack pointed at the man at the end of the road near the corner of the building. "That guy making like a hockey player and getting the puck out of here."

Zack and Kilgas made eye contact and headed after the man who disappeared around the corner. Zack and Kilgas ran to the end of the alley, but the man was gone. The white cargo van drove off in the distance.

Zack looked around. Nothing. "Let's get out of here. The natives don't like us here, and I need a bath."

"You sure are judgmental today. Something bothering you?"

"We don't have enough time," Zack said. "This was a bust."

The two reached the car, and Kilgas agreed with Zack's assessment. "What do you think that guy was?"

"Not sure yet."

"Tell me the truth, Stack," he said. "What's your gut feeling? Are we going to find her or not?"

"We'll find her, Kilgas." Zack didn't need to say anything else. "You find out anything?"

"Cost me twenty bucks to have the two guys at the barrel tell me they didn't recognize either. But they have seen girls come in here before. Some young, some older. And almost every younger girl disappeared within a day. Oddly, they said most people who end up there only move on in a body bag."

Zack looked one last time at the desolate area and the despondent occupants. *A body bag. Each of these people had a family but still ended up here. I suppose after a while, a body bag sounds good.*

16

The afternoon disappeared with no results, no leads, and no hope. Not what either man wanted in a missing persons' case, but not entirely unexpected to Zack. Zack entered the office with Kilgas behind him.

The two men sat on opposite sides of the desk. The alliance still didn't sit well with Zack. He knew Kilgas carried a Glock under his jacket. Kilgas looked defeated. A feeling Zack often felt in his investigative days. This case was no different.

"What do we do now, Stack? We're no further today than we were yesterday," Kilgas said.

"The BPD is running the DNA tests on the girls. That may help."

"Or it may not. That will only help us find Hannah if she's dead."

"That's usually how these cases end, Kilgas." Zack suddenly felt terrible. "I'm sorry. I didn't mean it to sound like that." *She went missing over three weeks ago, and there's no trace of her or her friend. How can two beautiful girls just disappear? Sex trade? Possible. Murdered and in a landfill. Ouch. Maybe working the streets as prostitutes. They had money. They wouldn't be doing that already. Or ever. They'd come home.*

"I know. I can't close my eyes at night without thinking the same thing. At the very least, I almost hope she is dead and not suffering somehow. I can't imagine how her mother feels."

Zack said nothing.

"Once I found out, I didn't know what to do. If I went to the police, they would have investigated me, and that's the last thing I want. As far as I know, some DC committee is still looking to ask me questions about the late Senator Rosler. If I end up in that room, I'll never see daylight again. So my only choice was to watch and wait for you to get your release as I saw it. Maybe I waited too long."

"Quit beating yourself up. Hannah didn't run away because you vanished before she was born."

Kilgas wasn't so sure. "What do we do next?"

"I don't know. If you were outside the prison waiting, you could have come inside and kept me company."

"You would have gone ballistic on me and been locked up permanently."

"Maybe. Do you know how Erin found me?"

"I heard a rumor."

Zack wanted to know how but knew if Kilgas knew, he wasn't saying. "Let's read the girls' diaries, talk to the people they talked to, and see if we get anywhere. The police did that legwork already and got nowhere, but we can try again. Sometimes people aren't very open with police, but maybe they'll talk to us."

"Ok. Let's get started."

Zack grabbed the diary from Angie Smith. "School will be out soon. So, if we plan to talk to any of their classmates, we better do it Monday."

"Monday is a holiday. No school."

Zack shook his head. Memorial Day. "Ok, we'll talk to them on Tuesday. Get them out of class," Zack said. "Pretend we're Feds. They see us waiting, wanting to ask questions, and they'll be scared shitless. We'll find out if any of Hannah or Angie's friends knew anything."

Kilgas stared at Zack. "Are you planning on torturing these kids?"

"If necessary, yes."

"You just said they wouldn't talk to the police. So why will they talk to us?"

Zack raised his eyebrows. "I'll turn on my charm. We'll need IDs that are passable. We have to be careful about walking in there. Neither of us wants our faces on camera."

"Got it. Come on, let's grab a drink and get something to eat. Then, I'll take you down to Erin's."

Zack shook his head. "No thanks, Kilgas. I'm going to pass tonight."

"What? Do you still think I'm going to kill you? Don't you trust me?"

"The jury is still out on both," Zack said. "Listen, no offense, but don't think just because you're paying me and we're working together that we're suddenly best friends."

Kilgas leaned back. "None taken, but it seems to me your other best friends haven't gone out of their way to welcome you back." Kilgas crossed his arms. "Maybe you need to begin accepting that you and I are more alike than you want to admit."

"Don't make me shoot you," Zack said. He reached back, opened his fridge, and grabbed two beers. "Here. One beer and one only. Then you leave."

"Then are you going to see Erin?"

"That's not a good idea."

"Blowing her off is a bad idea. Bad for both of us."

"Yeah, that's what worries me." Zack opened Angie's diary as Kilgas opened Hannah. "Getting inside the mind of a teenage girl ought to be interesting."

"Getting inside yours is downright scary. By comparison, this should be like going to a festival."

* * * *

Time passed. The clock hit six, and Zack's cell phone buzzed several times. Kilgas opened a second beer, but Zack didn't finish his first.

Kilgas put the diary on the table. "Man, this stuff is freaking me out. I remember being a teenager and feeling all that angst and shit, but this is next level. Read the part I highlighted."

Zack spun the diary so he could read it. Kilgas waited and watched, walked around the desk, pulled out two beers, opened them, and gave one to Zack. Zack looked at him.

"Hey, I probably bought these, and yours is almost empty."

Zack read. Hannah Leary was troubled and questioned everything. She hated her mother and blamed her for her father not being in her life. Hannah believed her mother lied about her father's existence. As Zack read, he saw the relationship deteriorate quickly as her mother asked questions, which Hannah perceived as applying pressure, about college in the fall and a decision on what she wanted to do with her life.

Hannah was an intelligent student and on the Honor Roll. She talked of becoming a doctor or lawyer or something prestigious. Something important. More than just a clerk at the county building, as she demeaned her mother. *That demeaning job Hannah's mother has kept Hannah in the front of the pack of the popular girls at school with nice clothes and a car. I spent an entire summer working for four dollars an hour to buy a three-hundred-dollar motorcycle because I couldn't afford a car and had to ride it in the winter. Spoiled is the first word that comes to mind.*

"You can see she wasn't happy with Sherry," Kilgas said. "Looks to me like poor Sherry gave Hannah everything she wanted."

"Maybe that's not what she wanted," Zack said. It made him think of his daughter. Zack remembered being told, *"you're not going to be that father, Zack!"*

Hannah dated two guys. She played them both and made each feel like the other was the 'one.' Either they both knew and didn't care, or they knew but were hopelessly 'in love' because of what Hannah provided. Zack suspected it was the latter. Both wanted to 'win' Hannah. Prove to be the best, and the sex was great. At least in the eyes of a seventeen-year-old.

"It gets better. If Sherry read any of this, she'd be devastated," Kilgas said. "The two boys, Kevin and Lee, I think we should talk to them. I see a motive."

Zack read on. Hannah doubted everything after the holidays. She questioned the value of the materialistic world and suspected many people equated happiness with material things. She asked if that was the purpose of being on earth and alive: to make money and buy objects.

Someone said something to her at school, and it bothered her., so she started a fight with a boy named Buck. He called her a plastic. Zack smiled. The reference seemed to fit, but Hannah didn't like it. A one-day home suspension put more pressure on her relationship with her mother.

"I see young boys thinking with their penis instead of their brain," Zack said. "They went to a private school. Hannah didn't feel like she belonged because of Sherry's economic status," Zack said. "I doubt the pre-pubescent preppy nerds Hannah went to school with have murder or kidnapping in their blood."

"It's a start, Stack."

"Maybe," Zack said. "She doesn't talk much of Angie in here."

"Keep reading. Remember, they were best friends. They texted or messaged, or snap chatted or click clocked, or whatever the hell teenage girls do back and forth all night most nights. No need to write about it."

Zack continued. January brought more self-doubt. Despite being beautiful, popular, and intelligent, it wasn't enough for Hannah. She kept mentioning she needed a reason, meaning, and a purpose. February brought more of the same. Only it got worse and finally a mention of Angie.

Angie and I are kindred spirits. Like two eagles soaring alone, high above the clouds, and the clouds are everyone else. So stupid and dull and content with trivial lives and an existence mapped out by their mommies and daddies. They're fake and excited about living a life with no meaning, other than another fancy car, a huge mortgage, having a mistress, or becoming a mistress. They'll spit out children they won't truly love, and then in the end, on their death beds surrounded by their families who themselves probably will grow to despise them, will wonder where it all went wrong.

Angie and I know where it went wrong. By being sheep right now. By being told by those who already made the same mistakes to do the same thing they did. How is that for irony? We aren't going to go that route. We're smarter than them. And I'm not going to be fake like that. I will have a purpose. So will Angie. We're already planning it.

Zack looked up at Kilgas. Kilgas finished his second beer. Zack saw the stress mount on Kilgas' face. Zack wanted to believe Kilgas was changed as he claimed. That would make it easier to quit worrying about Kilgas trying to kill him.

"Jesus," Zack said. "Are all teenagers like this?"

"Exactly," Kilgas said. "I hope not. Or they'll all go missing. I'll give you the Clift notes version of the rest," Kilgas said. He grabbed Zack's untouched beer and drank from it. "March is just as pathetically morose as February, only worse if you can believe it. She says she met some girl named Summer. This Summer girl seemed nice and asked a lot of questions. Then spring break happens. The two travel to Hilton Head with some friends. Rich friends. I have their names. We should talk to them, too. Anyway, Hannah mentions they talked one night about ending it all because it's all pointless. The next night she enters that they'll see what spring break brings. Summer shows up at Hilton Head and parties with them. The rest of their friends ditched Hannah and Angie, and Summer started talking about a better way. The truth, the light, all this bullshit," Kilgas said.

"Jesus."

"Yeah, basically," Kilgas said. "Hannah and Angie decide suicide is stupid, thank God, but also think this Summer chick has all the answers. Summer gets in touch with both of them and shows up in Annapolis. Summer sneaks them into a couple of bars, she tells them what the girls want to hear, and Summer says she'll be in Baltimore and asks to meet them."

"And this was about four weeks ago."

"Yep. Summer tells them they should run away with her. Summer says they'd be happy together, and she can show them a better way."

Zack put down the diary. "Guess we don't have to go talk to Kevin and Lee or Buck."

"Oh no. We do. All three were on the trip and met Summer. Summer tried to talk them all into bolting town."

"Summer. Do we have anything else on this Summer chick? Last name, picture, phone number, anything?"

"No."

Zack knew what to do. "Ok. I'll get them. This Summer was texting the girls, which means there's a record. We'll get it."

"That used to be what your girl Michelle would do. She doesn't work here anymore. So how are you going to accomplish that without going mixing gasoline with an open flame, which I'm not going to let you do?"

"Lauren. I'm paying her, so I might as well have her work."

Kilgas finished the beer. "Buy me dinner. I'm hungry and like you, being hungry makes me irritable."

"Really? I thought you were always unpleasant to be around."

Kilgas laughed. "Funny, Stack. Real funny. You should smell yourself and then ask who is unpleasant to be around."

"Go wait outside and look for a black Crown Victoria while I shower."

"And your phone? Someone is trying hard to get in touch with you."

"And you thought I didn't have any friends."

17

"You're late," Michelle Borman said.

Zack looked at his cell phone for the time since his wrist was watch-less. "It's precisely 7:02. You said seven but didn't specify which bench."

Michelle smiled. She meant the bench atop Federal Hill surrounded by large trees with dense foliage above them and around them in every direction. With the height of the hill, no one could eavesdrop on the conversation. "Well, you have me alone, and we can talk. What do you want to know?"

Zack stumbled over the words as they rushed to his mouth. "Where do you want me to start?"

"Ok, let me rephrase that since we don't have all night."

"Speaking of that, where is Ronald the Wonderboy? Sucking his way to the top or taking it in the rear to please his boss?"

Michelle grinned. "Remember when you used to like him?"

"That was before he had me thrown in prison for six months. Where is he?"

Michelle's grin disappeared. "Every Monday night, he meets with his work buddies. Usually, so he says, they watch a game, have a few drinks, and he's back home in three hours."

Zack said nothing.

"But let me explain. Ronald is insanely jealous of you, Zack. It's an obsession with him."

"He got you from me, so why does he care about me now?"

"Because you know too much and you have information, so he believes, that could damage people high in the food chain," Michelle said. "And how else to win future favors than by eliminating any potential trouble for the people that could be choosing a new FBI Director or any number of the big-time appointments Ronald wants?"

"He'd rather protect criminals for his career rather than do his freaking job? Jesus Christ," Zack griped.

"What did you think would happen, Zachary? You kicked the bee-hive."

"More like hornet's nest," Zack said. "Maybe I should kick it a few more times."

"You better be done for now," Michelle said. "Listen to me. You need to listen to me and trust me. You made sure no one saw you on the way here?"

Zack nodded. "As far as my admirers are concerned, I'm still at the office."

"How did you pull that off?"

Zack asked Kilgas for a favor he suspected Kilgas would cash in with Zack. A favor for a favor. If that prevented Kilgas from hiring someone to put a bullet in Zack, Zack was ok with that. "I'm here. That's all that matters."

"I'm sorry, Zack. But I had to leave the agency. I wanted to come to see you, to contact you, anything to let you know but I couldn't. I'm so sorry."

"We are on limited time, so just tell me why. I know we fought, and I was not who I should have been after I got involved with Lexi. I know you had Whitmore draw up the document getting me out of our business."

"How do you know that?" Michelle interrupted, surprised.

"Doesn't matter. I'm sorry. I was lost for a while. Maybe being locked up for six months made me see things a little differently. I don't want to lose you, Michelle. I can't."

Michelle smiled. "You aren't going to. You aren't the only one who can be a step ahead of everyone else. This time, honey, I was. And when you got sent to that prison, I knew why immediately."

"Ronald. Why are you still with him then?"

Michelle scoffed. "You know why. But I have a plan. I can't tell you everything, only what I need you to do. Can you trust me?"

"Since I was seventeen, I've trusted you with my life. You and Dre."

Michelle smiled, touched his arm. "There are a few other people."

"Currently?"

"Where are you spending your nights, if you don't mind me asking?"

"Well, at home, but I'm not sure what's going on."

"Oh no. You're sleeping with Jules again, aren't you?"

"Why would that be so bad? We were perfect together for the longest time, and we are parents. I don't want to let down Cate or Julie."

Michelle shook her head and held his arms. "Don't you have a song on one of your playlists titled That was then, this is now?"

"By the Monkees," Zack said. "What aren't you telling me?"

"Stefani."

"Ugh," Zack said. "Don't go there. She dumped me."

"I know you were about to ask her to marry you, and I know she was on her way up to say yes. So you need to talk to her."

"You had eyes on me." Then Zack realized what she said in its entirety. "And Stef?"

"It's more complicated than that, but of course. You're a VIP in a lot of circles, honey. Most for the wrong reason, but when I moved to the FBI with Ronald, I convinced him of my loyalty, which got me inside his head. He can never find out we're still talking. He wants to lock you up and throw away the cell."

"Then why am I out?"

"You know that, too, honey." Michelle winked. "Listen to me and listen close. Don't ask questions, and don't try to figure any of this out. You simply need to trust me. Do you think you can do that for once?"

Zack looked confused. "For once? Ok. I'll bite. What's going on?"

"It's not what's going on, honey. It's what you're going to do. Now use that memory of yours for once to help me help you."

"Did you just try to use a movie line?"

Michelle smiled. "Poorly." She put her hands in his. "Promise me, and then I'll tell you."

Zack rolled his eyes. "I promise. Talk."

18

Zack sat as a passenger as he and Kilgas headed to Annapolis to talk to the students named in the journals of Hannah and Angie. Two sentences into the drive, Kilgas suspected Zack wasn't in a talking mood. Instead, Zack stared straight ahead.

Kilgas decided to try again. "We get to Annapolis, question those kids, and move forward," Kilgas said. "Where are you planning to spend your night tonight?"

"Not sure that's any of your business," Zack said.

"Where were you Sunday and Monday?"

"I stayed in my office."

Kilgas smiled. "Bullshit. Where were you?"

"If your job is to follow me, you're doing a poor job."

"Erin wants to know why you haven't returned her calls or texts or haven't seen her?"

"I spent fourteen hours Sunday tracing phone records. Where I spent my night is no one's business."

"I thought that was Lauren's job."

"I had some free time," Zack said.

"And yesterday?"

Zack looked at the passing countryside. "We went to Annapolis, remember?"

"What about the rest of your day and night?"

Zack said nothing.

Kilgas shook his head. "You know, it wouldn't be the worst for us to be friends and allies and for you to talk to me. I saved you before. Look at your life, Stack. Nothing has changed. You may want to consider that you need Erin and me."

"I need to know why. Help me with that, and perhaps I could have a normal life."

Kilgas laughed. "Yeah, right. Have you talked to Stefani since you've been back? Maybe if you reconnect with her, you won't be such a prick to deal with."

"I believe I issued an earlier statement about business and whose it is not."

"Why did you two break up? I liked you two together."

"Am I not enunciating properly today?"

Kilgas drove on. "Jesus. Someone is in a bad mood today. Care to talk about it?"

"What is it with talk? Why is talking all of the sudden so grand?"

"Seriously, Stack. Are you asking me that? Even if it is rhetorical, you know why."

"Ok, Kilgas. I have a serious problem with you, and I need an answer. Why did you kill those girls?" Zack looked at Kilgas. "There is a large part of me that wants to put a bullet through your brain. Those girls didn't deserve that."

"I didn't kill anyone, Stack."

"You gave the orders. Same thing."

"No, Pantalini gave the orders. I supplied the men."

"You could have stopped it. You should have stopped it. You have as much blood on your hands as Pantalini," Zack said.

Kilgas looked at Zack briefly as he drove. "And I have to live with that every day."

"The families missing their daughters wouldn't accept that."

"The only person I ordered killed was you. I know I threatened to kill the rest, but that was just a threat. That's the truth. I know I should have done something, but I didn't. After you aced Rosler, I decided to try to make good. I know where I'll end up. So do you. But the rest of the days I have on this earth, I can do everything I can to make amends. That's all I can do."

"Is it?"

"You know what we do. You know the decisions we make and why. I'm not trying to justify any of it."

"Sounds like you are."

"I'm not. I'm trying not to kill myself every day because of the guilt. Until I met Terri and realized my skills could help for the right reason, I had no reason to live. Your stumbling onto the NPA case gave me a reason. Saving your life multiple times when Fairfax tried to ruin you and Stefani, yes, that was me who saved her in the motel and killed two of Lennox's men as they planned to attack you when you were at Erin's. I gave Dre the bomb to blow up Fairfax's yacht and paid the guys to drive you into the mountains and set you free. I hoped I'd earn some grace with you and Dre. It has with Dre. I understand why not with you. And for your information, the survivors of the families ruined by Rosler's sex addiction have received anonymous gifts. It won't make up for the deaths of their daughters, but at least they don't have to worry about debt. Now, saving Hannah and Angie is my cause. Having a good life with Terri is more than I deserve, and you understand that. I know what you did overseas. Not much difference."

"I never killed innocent girls."

"Never? I've heard the stories. All I ask is for you not to shoot me again and help me find my daughter. After that, like you said the other day, you don't care if you die, guess what? Neither do I."

"Good. Then we've reached an accord. You were following me. Did you tell the FBI or NPA where I was?"

"No. Not once," Kilgas said. "I took chances that you'd be better than them, and if I hurt you, Erin will have me killed. She's been quite clear about that."

"Why are you afraid of crossing her, Kilgas? Who is Erin Keyes?"

"Stack, you're asking the wrong person. All I know is that her checks are good, she has connections, and I disappear any time she wants with one phone call. Same with you. I trust her, and I think she trusts me even with the history with Rosler. You should see her. She is patient, but not that patient."

Zack looked out the window. "I need some caffeine. Stop at the next exit. I need a pop."

Kilgas laughed. "You're kidding, right? That soda stuff will kill you."

"I'm not drinking soda. I'm drinking pop. No one lives forever, so why deprive yourself during the little time we have? Plus, since we're probably going to get arrested for illegally interrogating minors while impersonating federal agents, and I know they don't serve Pepsi in prison, I better fill up."

Kilgas pulled off the Interstate and pulled into a gas station not far from the exit. "You want anything else, Stack? You want a breakfast sandwich or something worse for you like a pop-tart or those little packages of chocolate-covered donuts?"

"Et Tu, Brute?"

Kilgas laughed. "Strawberry or brown sugar?"

"Brown sugar. And make sure there's no bacon on the sandwich. Fast food bacon sucks."

Kilgas shook his head and shut the door. Zack watched and waited. Part of him expected the car to explode.

Kilgas returned with two bags. "I'm not stopping for lunch, and you have this thing about eating, so ration it out, Stack."

Zack found the Pepsi and drank from it. "This may kill me someday if you don't first."

"I'm not going to kill you."

"I hope not. I'm starting to like you buying food all the time."

Kilgas drove the car onto the Interstate and dug a breakfast sandwich out of the bag. "I'd eat up. These things suck once they're cold."

"They suck when they're hot."

Kilgas saw the signs for Annapolis ahead twenty minutes later. "You've been silent. Anything on your mind?"

"I have to give you credit, Kilgas. You believe in letting bygones be bygones."

"What good does it do to hold a grudge? Who needs that stress? Stack, you need to let some things go, man. You're wound up so tight right now you're ready to explode on someone. I can't believe you haven't."

"I'm warming up," Zack said with a stare at Kilgas.

Kilgas chuckled. "Are you going to see Stefani again?"

"Kilgas, seriously, stay out of my personal life."

"I'm getting paid well to keep Erin Keyes informed about your personal life."

"I'll tell her myself."

"Ok, boss. Whatever you say. We're almost there," Kilgas said. "In the glove box, there's a couple of official badges. You do the talking. You're better at that than I am."

"I hope they send me back to the same prison."

"You mean country club."

Zack grabbed the badges. "I swear to God, I am going to shoot the next person to say that."

19

The third boy, Kevin, was brought inside the office. Zack did this purposefully, as according to the notes and journals, Kevin was the closest to Hannah. *Make him sweat it out. He'll break if there's a reason to.* The principal and a high school counselor were present. Zack did most of the talking; the school officials believed the badges were authentic. So did Zack. Zack was shocked the school didn't call the parents, and none of the kids demanded their parents be present. A few preventive measures ensured the school's video was inoperable, and a quick check showed the maintenance department hadn't repaired the surveillance cameras yet.

The list of crimes continued.

Kevin sat across from Zack and Kilgas, with the principal and counselor flanking both of them. Kevin looked nervous. Talking to two "Federal Agents" would make any eighteen-year-old boy nervous.

After explaining why they were there to calm the kid, Zack asked a couple of innocent questions establishing Kevin's relationship with Hannah. From there, Zack moved to the spring break trip before Hannah disappeared. Kevin then spoke freely. Zack suspected this was Kevin's chance, now that he understood he wasn't in trouble, to be the big man on campus. Every teenage boy's dream. At that point, Zack asked a simple question. "Do you recall a girl named Summer?"

"Summer? Yeah, I remember her. Kind of hot but in a hippie sort of way," said Kevin.

"What do you mean?" Kilgas asked.

"I mean, she had her hair pulled back all the time. Just straight dark blonde hair in a ponytail, and she wore a headband with the Peace symbol on it. It reminded me of a hippie."

Zack hoped for more. "Is there anything else you remember about her?"

"She wore these sexy cut-off jeans. Not long but not too short, know what I mean?" Kevin smiled, obviously not afraid or embarrassed to speak freely in front of the male principal and female counselor. "She never wore a bra either. She had her bikini on under the shorts and tank top at the beach, but there was no bikini at night. She wasn't shy about making sure we all knew."

"Was she trying to seduce you?" Kilgas asked.

"I'm not sure. It was like at night, we'd all be," he looked at the principal, suddenly unsure if he'd get in trouble.

"It's ok, Kevin. Speak freely. You won't get into trouble," the principal said. "I was a teenager once, too. We all do dumb things."

Zack and Kilgas looked at each other but didn't smile.

"Well, we'd all be drinking, partying, and Summer had some weed, so we'd pass it around. She liked Hannah and Angie and spent most of her time with the girls, but sometimes she would come by Todd or me, or someone else, and things would happen."

"What things?"

"You know, things."

"Sexual things?" Kilgas asked.

"Yeah. Kissing, touching, making out, and stuff. But Summer would always stop before it got excellent. So I started thinking she was up to something, and on the last couple of nights, I pretended to be getting high like everyone else, but I wasn't. So I snuck around to see what this girl was really up to because none of us ever saw her before, and all of a sudden, she's like the best friend of Hannah and Angie and hanging with us like she was Queen shit or something." Kevin realized what he said. "I'm sorry, Principal Bakowski."

"It's ok, Kevin. I swore, too, when I was your age."

"Was she like this to everyone?"

"Oh yeah, but more to the girls. Not just Hannah and Angie but to the others. Hannah and Angie gravitated to her more, though, so that's where Summer spent most of her time."

"Other than the physical seduction and chemical enhancement she provided, did Summer talk about anything else? When you became suspicious of her, did you learn anything that made you think she was there for more than just to party with a bunch of naïve teenagers?" Zack leaned forward and noticed Kevin didn't like the naïve label. Zack didn't care.

"Yeah. The night before we headed home, those three went to the beach. They left the bonfire. I waited until they disappeared, then snuck after them and hid in the tall grass. And I heard Summer talking. It was windy, and I couldn't make out a lot, but it was weird."

"What do you mean?" Zack pressed.

"So ok, they were on a blanket and in their bikinis. Summer had her top off, so I was careful not to be caught."

"Smart move," Kilgas said.

Zack gave him a look. *Not a cop thing to say, idiot!* "Smart as in that could be helpful. What did you hear?" Zack covered as quickly as he could.

"They started kissing. They were high; I mean baked. Hannah was really high, which was odd because some others were smoking, but they weren't as baked. Even with the beer, still, no one was as ripped as Hannah. Angie wasn't as bad, but she wasn't herself either."

"How so?"

"She was giggly. She's never giggly. And I know both of those girls are straight. So what I saw next blew my mind."

Zack didn't need a description. He already knew Summer's game, but Kilgas felt otherwise.

"What did you see next?"

"Man, it was wild. It was like," Kevin caught himself. The thought aroused him, and he did his best to hide it. "They started making out. Then they were naked and going at it. It was wild."

"Ok, fast forward," Zack urged as the level of discomfort rose. "What was Summer talking about?"

"I watched for a little, and I heard Summer say something about there's a better way, and I figured she meant instead of doing it on a blanket on a beach. Then, I heard someone yell for me, so I booked out of there."

After you zipped up. "Kevin, why didn't you tell the police any of this?"

94

"I don't know."

Zack knew why. He was scared and embarrassed. Or wanted the memory unblemished a little longer. "Did they return later?"

"Yeah, about two hours later, Summer came back with Hannah. She was wrecked. Summer put Hannah in bed, and then Lee came in helping Angie. It was like they were on something, man. I've never seen anything like it."

"And the next day?"

"We went home. No one talked about it. Hannah and Angie hung out together and didn't speak to anyone. Summer wasn't anywhere around. Next thing I know, they ran away."

"Did any of you happen to have Summer's phone number or snap a picture of her or anything actually useful?" Zack asked. He didn't want to sound perturbed, but listening to a teenager's recollection of a wet dream did not help.

"Uh, I don't know. I took a bunch of pictures. Maybe I got one of Summer."

Zack looked at the principal. "Principal Bakowski, I know we already asked a lot, but I am going to reiterate this and ask for your permission and then his. First, Kevin is not under investigation, nor did anything he tell us incriminate him in any way. The same with the other students. We have no interest in them other than what they remember from the trip with Hannah and Angie and this girl named Summer. To that end, as soon as we exit this building, you'll never hear from us again because, as far as this institution is concerned, the disappearance of the two girls is a separate act not involving the school. So to be clear, there is no suspicion of negligence. Understood?"

"I do."

"Good. Now, Kevin, with your permission, can you show us those pictures and point out Summer if she is in any of them?"

"Yeah, of course. Anything to help find Hannah. And some of these pics are epic!"

Youth is clearly wasted on the young. I'm not even sure when the last time I described something as epic.

Kevin whipped out his phone and flipped through the pictures on his new iPhone expertly. He found the pics of the vacation. "Ok, here they are." He scooted over so who he thought were Federal Investigators Nolen and Larson could see. Zack made Kilgas be Larson.

The pics were as expected: seventeen and eighteen-year-old kids partying at daddy's condo on the beach in Hilton Head. Most pics were the girls in their barely-there bikinis, mainly when the girls laid in the sun or came out of the pool. Kevin, not unlike most high school-aged boys, enjoyed pics of almost naked girls and their private parts. Zack wondered if some of the girls encouraged it because Zack never even thought of taking pictures of girls like that. *Not sure I'd want to be young again but hooking up sure seems more straightforward now.*

"Ok, there's Hannah, and that's Angie," Kevin said. He scrolled through the pics. "There they are again, again, oops, shouldn't have seen that one, another one, there's, wait. That's her! That's Summer!"

Zack and Kilgas looked at the picture. Clear as day. Cute girl, pointed nose, freckles, narrow lips, blue eyes, dark blonde hair, and small breasts. Kevin made sure to get her nipples in the shot. Small breasts but effectively arousing to an eighteen-year-old, obviously as there were three more pics of Summer's breasts.

"We need a copy of those photos," Kilgas said. "Kevin, you were brilliant."

"Hand me your phone," Zack said. Zack took it and worked his way through the phone to send the pictures to his email address. Zack sent the pics, deleted his actions from the phone, and returned the device.

"You think that will help find her?" Kevin asked.

"It very well may," Kilgas said. "This is the best lead we've had so far."

"Done," Zack said and handed back the phone. "Principal Bakowski, Counselor McDermott, thank you for your cooperation." He looked at Kevin. "Thank you, Kevin, and for your sake moving forward, lay off sneaking pictures of girls' breasts and butts. They don't like that."

The two men left the office quickly. Kilgas seemed to read Zack's mind as they entered the car. "Don't even tell me you're hungry."

"It's lunchtime. We ate like four hours ago. I'm hungry."

Kilgas drove away from the school. "Do you think any of those privileged brats will tell their helicopter parents?"

"I hope so. How did you get the real badges?"

"Don't ask, Stack. If you don't know, you can plausibly deny."

Zack almost chuckled. "And I'm supposed to trust you. The Boatyard Bar & Grill is nearby. It has great seafood," Zack said.

"You are incredible. How can you eat so much?"

"Six months of prison food will do that to a person. I'm hungry."

"I have to ask Erin what she sees in you because I don't see it."

"She likes to be in control. I'm just a game to her," Zack said.

"Is that how you see it?"

"Yes," Zack said.

"Don't underestimate Erin."

"Turn here; it's up ahead," Zack directed. "I hope they have grouper."

"How do we find Summer?"

Zack stared out the window. "I'm not sure we're going to."

20

Zack looked at his wrist. Bare. He decided he had to change that. Lauren entered his office carrying a bottle of Pepsi and one of water. She walked beside Zack, set them down on his desk, and leaned over, so her mouth was close to his ear. "Here's your breakfast, Awesome Sauce." She said softly. "Are you sure you don't want something more substantive?"

"This is too early to start work. Now I know why no one else is here," Zack complained. "You shouldn't be in a good mood this early."

Lauren ran her hand across his back. "I finally know where you are. Being your babysitter isn't easy."

"If you ask for a raise, I'll give you one if you quit waking me at six in the morning."

Lauren squeezed his shoulder. "I told you where to stay. You have my address. Show up, and I'll let you sleep all day, but as long as you are going to continue on your path, well, six o'clock it is. Let's install a kitchen so I can make you a normal breakfast in the morning."

Zack rested his head on the desk as if he were sleeping. "We can order out. A lot of area restaurants rely on guys like me."

"And it's draining our funds. This is work." Lauren put a stack of notes in front of him. "Sir, you have a litany of messages. I think half the people in Baltimore are expecting a call back from you today, including Dre, Mikayla, and some woman named Addison Jones. She didn't sound happy."

"That's her normal tone. I'll get to it."

Lauren put her hand on her hip and cocked her head. "And that is exactly the response I will not accept. Call these people back. Dre was upset yesterday. And what am I supposed to tell them about the motorcycle you bought?"

After Zack left Kilgas, he traded in his oldest motorcycle for a new one. The bike he left at Erin's house before his incarceration. Erin had it a few days, it returned, and when Zack rode it, Zack felt like the black Crown Victoria followed him. Maybe it was the bike. It was a sad night.

"I only told you so you wouldn't tell them."

"Sir, they'll know I'm lying."

Zack looked at her. "Then learn how to lie better. You made me a promise."

Lauren stared at Zack, expecting more. "That motorcycle was your baby, sir," Lauren said, still looking to understand.

He took a deep breath as parting with that bike still hurt him. Zack looked into Lauren's large, blue, imploring eyes. "The engine reacted a little slow. The valves needed reboring. This one is nicer. You'll like it."

"Sir, really?" Lauren asked, exasperated. Her look turned to frustrated and angry. "Yes, sir." Lauren turned around and walked out of the office.

Zack exhaled slowly and sipped the Pepsi. Bacon and eggs did sound good. Zack looked around the office to determine if there was enough room for a kitchen.

Lauren stormed back into his office. "You aren't helping, sir, nor does it look like you care."

"I'll try, Lauren."

"Someone told me one of your sayings is try is why we fail."

"I borrowed that line from a green puppet. It means more in a Disney movie. But I'll try. Does that help?"

"I'll ignore the blatant sarcasm." Lauren set down a file in front of Zack and opened it. "Fine. Let's talk work. The pictures were too distorted to make out much, but this one," she pointed to a picture of a girl, "kind of looks like a conglomeration of symbols. I tried to isolate them to the point where I traced the individual lines and randomly connected them until I came up with this."

"How long did you work on this?"

"I barely saw you this weekend, so I had a lot of time waiting for you."

"I don't think being my assistant means literally 24/7."

"Everyone is worried about you, and it's my responsibility to," she stopped.

"To what?" Zack had an idea of what her responsibility was.

Lauren stood straight and smoothed out the wrinkle in her skirt. "It's my responsibility to help you, sir. That's my job, so I would appreciate it if you would let me help you." Lauren continued with work. "If you put what I found over the image on the body, you can almost see it. See?" Lauren slid a transparent page from the file with a tattoo image and placed it over the image on the corpse.

"What am I looking at?"

"The Alpha, the Omega, and a Phoenix rising."

"You drew this by hand?"

"Some people identify birds, others draw. What can I say?"

"You should try birding. I think you'll like it."

"I will as soon as you invite me. I think I'll like it, too."

Zack looked at the images. "I'm free tomorrow at seven AM. How about you?"

"No, you're not. Look at the drawing."

"Ok, I can see it, but what does it mean?"

"I don't know, sir; that's your job."

"This feels like a tremendous waste of time on something we aren't getting paid." Zack's cell phone rang, and he looked at Lauren. "Welcome to the Dre-Zack Detective Agency." Zack answered the cell phone. "Stack here."

"Stack, it's Dylan. Some tests came back—the dead girl from last week. We got a DNA match for a missing girl from Baltimore about six months ago, Leah Durham. She was a high school senior on the south side, and the police at the time, a different station, ruled it a runaway. The girl vanished in the wind. Sound familiar?"

"Unfortunately."

"I did some background on Leah. Good looking white girl. Cheerleader, volleyball player, decent grades, and involved in some community work. Wanna know who she worked with?"

"Queen Elizabeth?"

"Funny, but no. Hannah Leary."

Zack remained silent.

"They met at a cheerleader camp freshman year. In addition to the community work they did together, the two exchanged emails and talked from time to time. I can link the two together, but I can't locate Leah's phone. It was missing with her. It's possible whoever took her accessed it, found Hannah, and set their sights on her."

"Did anyone check the phone records?"

"I'll check with missing persons."

"What? That's the first damn thing they should have checked, and it should be in their files. Ok, can you get her phone number to me? I'd appreciate it."

"Will do. I don't know if tox will tell us much, but we have a start."

"We need a finish. I'll talk to you later." Zack disconnected, looked at Lauren, and shook his head. "This feels like it's going to be a long day." The phone rang again. Zack recognized the number. Kael. "Did you forget something?"

"Stack, how about when I call you before you hang up, you ask me if that was everything. Ok?"

"Sorry," Zack said and saw Lauren shake her head at him. "Is that everything?"

"No. You asked about Evan Rossum, remember? Well, I did some digging, a lot of digging. Patterson left no record behind other than the official death certificate. I can't find anything on his autopsy."

"That's what I was afraid of," Zack said. "Is that everything?"

"That is everything."

"Thanks, Dylan," Zack said, overemphasizing Dylan jokingly. "I'll talk to you later."

Lauren walked beside him and patted his back. "Let's get to work."

Zack concentrated on his computer. Time disappeared. Lauren occasionally walked into his office and put a water bottle or fresh fruit on his desk since she figured out Zack didn't eat healthily. They didn't speak. They didn't need to. The phone didn't ring, and it was silent. Until ten in the morning when Mikayla Dorsey entered. Zack didn't hear them talking in front. He focused on his computer, ignored his cell phone, and then Mikayla spoke to Zack.

"Hey, stranger."

Zack looked at Mikayla, and the memories of her few visits to prison and sudden exit from his life flashed across his mind.

"You haven't been around much. What's going on?" Mikayla sat on the front edge of her desk to face Zack.

"I'm working. I thought that is what we do here."

"Wow," she said softly. "Ok. So, do you want to yell at me now or later?"

"Why would I want to yell at you, Mikayla?"

"Zack, I'm sorry. I can explain. Can we talk?"

"There's nothing to talk about."

"Yes, there is. You're avoiding all of us, and we need to fix this."

"Are you seriously going to lecture me right now?"

"Do you want to know why I stopped seeing you?"

"I'm a hundred percent certain I not only don't want to hear it but don't care."

"Don't be an asshole to me."

"What should I be?"

"How about a normal person who makes a decision to have a conversation and shares things. How about that?"

"Nah, I prefer being an asshole to people who abandoned me while I was in prison."

"A prison? Ok, yes, I will accept that, but can you at least let me explain?"

"Mikayla, what part of NO don't you understand?"

"I stopped seeing you because of Stefani."

"Why do people insist on telling me things immediately after hearing I don't want to hear it?"

"You can't run and hide from everything, Stack. Maybe that's another reason I stopped seeing you. I don't like being in the dark all the time."

"You left me. Problem solved."

Mikayla stared at him. "You aren't listening at all, are you?"

"You were using me for sex, so don't even go there."

A man cleared his throat very loudly from the doorway. FBI Agent Campbell walked into the office with a smile. "Stack, I'm glad to see you're adjusting well. How's your day going?"

Zack stared at Mikayla. "Agent Campbell, good to see you." Zack sat down again, and Mikayla slipped behind him. "We were just catching up," Zack said.

Mikayla put her hand on his shoulder. "It's great to have him back."

"It looks like it," Campbell said. "Stack, I have something for you." He sat down across from Zack. Campbell plopped a thick file folder on Zack's desk. "Officially, we aren't looking into any of these, but five body dumps with similar MO's hit the radar. Over the last five years or so, there have been several young girls gone missing, possibly runaways in a territory that roughly circles two hours from here," Campbell explained. "Stories all seem similar. But, unfortunately, that's all we got on them."

Zack looked at the file. "Any leads?"

"No. You asked me to sniff around, and this is what I came up with."

"You guys have people who study this daily and write the playbooks on how to catch a serial killer or whatever this is. What do they think?"

"They think something is off about these. So if the deaths are connected, which it appears, whoever is doing it is careful."

Zack nodded. "They always slip up, Ty, you know that."

Campbell smiled. "They do. I'm not officially talking to you about any of this."

"Of course not. What aren't you telling me, Campbell?"

"Stack, if I were you, I'd keep your head low. Keep a low profile. Rumor is that people in high places don't like snoops peering through the windows."

"Agent Campbell, you know I prefer to keep low and stay off the radar."

Campbell stood and smiled. "I do know that about you. Let's have a beer sometime. I mean that. Somewhere a little quieter." Ty Campbell nodded and left.

Mikayla moved from behind Zack and sat on the desk beside him. "What was that whole bunch of nothing about?"

"A warning," Zack replied quickly. He looked at Mikayla. "Don't worry about it. It's only me they want to persecute. So, is there anything else we should discuss?"

"Zack, I'm sorry."

"I should have stayed in prison."

"You don't mean that. I know you."

He stood from his chair. Zack walked to his closet and grabbed his leather jacket. "Where are you going?"

"For a ride."

"Zack, maybe you should hang out here. Let's talk. I can apologize a couple hundred more times," Mikayla said with a smile. "I am sorry, Zack. I'll come with you. We could use some time together."

"Maybe another time. Listen, I know why you stopped visiting. I did enjoy the visits, and I can assure you when we are together, I'm not thinking of anyone else. But you made the right decision. You're off the hook." Zack walked to her. "It is all about confidence, Mikayla, and you do have plenty of that." Zack winked, leaned forward, and surprised her with a kiss on her lips. "And you are beautiful," he said softly. "Tell Lauren not to wait for me today." He hugged her. "Thank you." Zack went to the bathroom and left. A couple of hours on the motorcycle, his new BMW S 1000 RR in a silver metallic finish, to clear his head.

Mikayla thought about what he said and shook her head. "That sneaky little prick."

21

The phone call snapped Agent Ferguson from the focus on the computer screen. It looked like his department was about to bust open another computer-scamming ring, and Michelle Borman's group looked good. A good hire, to be sure. Ferguson didn't rush to answer the phone. It was important for the caller to believe Ferguson was busy and, thus, more important. A power move.

"Ferguson here," he answered.

"Our office received a call this morning from an upset parent. Two men claiming to be Agent Carter Nolen and Agent Derek Larson went into a high school in Annapolis yesterday and interrogated several students there. Two of the kids were only seventeen. There was no parental consent."

"Uh-oh."

"Fergie, the problem is that Agent's Nolen and Larson weren't in Annapolis yesterday."

Ferguson exhaled. "Stack."

"That was my first thought."

"Can we prove it was Stack?"

"The school's video surveillance was not operating yesterday. Stack was with a white guy, so it wasn't one of his employees."

Ferguson shook his head. "Concerning. What was he investigating?"

"The disappearance of two runaways. One is named Hannah Leary, the other Angie Smith."

"Quietly sniff around. Link Stack to something. I'll talk to Nolen and Larson." Ferguson ended the call and waited. A message finally returned. Michelle Borman agreed to have lunch with him.

* * * *

Mikayla exited Zack's office and saw Lauren busy at her computer. "It's ok, Lauren. You don't have to pretend you didn't hear." Mikayla sat in the chair in front of Lauren's desk.

Lauren made a scared look on her face and whispered. "I hear a lot of things I probably shouldn't."

"Don't worry about that. I don't know if there are any secrets here. And now you know the nature of my visits to him in prison."

"I heard, but it's none of my business."

Mikayla chuckled. "That's what I thought when I first started here, but I found out the people here are different. They're closer than family, and it is their business."

"Mikayla, you don't have to explain anything to me."

Mikayla ignored Lauren. "He's tough to deal with sometimes."

Lauren looked at Mikayla finally.

"I wish I could explain. Things haunt Zack, and he doesn't know how to deal with it."

"I think he wants me to be Michelle," Lauren confessed. "How can I compete with her memory?"

"You can't. Michelle and Zack are close, and she left without saying goodbye to him, so I'm sure that stung." Mikayla watched Lauren and thought about what Zack said and did before he left. "Zack and I have a different relationship. At times we're like oil and water, other times like peas and carrots." Mikayla smiled. "The bickering keeps us fresh."

"If he wasn't seeing Stefani, why did you stop visiting him?"

"Because I wasn't Stefani, and I couldn't hurt Stef. I wanted to believe it could be more, but like my normal love life, I picked the wrong man at the wrong time."

"What's the deal with him and Stefani? Why aren't they together? I can't find a thing about her to dislike."

Mikayla smiled. "None of us can. She cast a spell over Zack that he can't or won't break, but he also won't talk to her, nor will she talk to him, which isn't like them at all. Why he dumped her via a letter is beyond me."

Lauren thought about it. "I haven't heard him mention her name once. And if he's so in love with Stef, why is he spending his nights with Jules?"

"Every night?"

Lauren worried she said too much. "I'm not sure. What I do know is that Mr. Stack is confused, in my opinion."

Mikayla thought about what Lauren said. "Does he talk to you?"

Lauren again worried she said too much. "Not really," she quickly corrected. "It's more about what I've learned from all of you about Mr. Stack and listening. He doesn't talk much." Lauren chuckled. "You know that."

"I do."

"And about Stefani? Will he talk to her?"

"He won't. He's stubborn, and so is Stef. Something is off, though." Mikayla sat next to Lauren. "Enough about him. We have work to do. Could you show me what you're doing? Maybe I can help, and we can get Zack off this case quicker."

22

Zack turned the corner, saw the cars lined along the street, maneuvered onto the sidewalk, rode up to the house, and parked the motorcycle on the sidewalk of the front door. He got off the bike, and the door opened.

Zack looked at the tall, sleek, dark-haired, green-eyed woman and couldn't help but smile. She wore her customary black mid-thigh length satin robe over whatever color bra and underwear she felt like today. Erin Keyes crossed her arms.

"What brings you here?"

"I figure since you drove all the way up to New York to see me in prison exactly once, in six months, I could return the favor and visit you once."

Erin slightly grinned. "Is that a new bike?"

"Yes. I traded in the old one." Zack stepped closer. "Disappointed?"

"Only that you're still riding that thing. I bought you a car."

Zack shrugged. "Are you going to let me inside?"

"Why should I? You're still not the Zack I'm waiting for."

"I'm not sure that Zack exists anymore."

"He does. You just need to find him." Erin Keyes stepped back from the door, and Zack stepped inside. She shut the door and put her arms around Zack. "Maybe I can help you."

Zack smiled but refrained from the response she desired. "I need to talk to you. Do you think you can give me answers this time? Or are you going to obfuscate more?"

"Obfuscate? Someone has been reading a dictionary in prison." She kissed him, and though his lips moved, it wasn't what she hoped. "You're here on business," she frowned. "Now I am disappointed."

"Is it our time, Erin? Is that what you're telling me?"

Erin turned around and walked into the living room. She spun and sat on the couch. "What do you want?"

"How did you find out where I was?"

Erin smiled and shook her head. "Are you staying long? If you are, I think we should have a drink."

"It's not safe to ride and drink."

Erin got off the couch, her robe opened, showing a red bra and panties, and she walked across the room. "Then let's have a drink. You want something from me; I want something from you. Let's see who flinches first." She poured two glasses of red wine and brought one back to Zack. "I still have connections in the government. It was torturous, but I found you. My turn." Erin handed one to Zack, but he set his down. "Where have you been spending your nights?"

"I'm sure Kilgas already told you."

"I want to hear it from you."

"I've been staying at my place for part of the night," Zack said. "Who is Addison Jones?"

Erin sipped her wine. "I don't know that name, but if she has you worried, I want to meet her. What about the other part of the night?"

"My office," Zack answered quickly. "I'm being followed by someone other than Kilgas. Is it the FBI guys who shafted me?"

"I don't know."

"But you can find out."

"Zack, darling, you should be careful. You sound like you're about to offer me something if I help you."

"I am. You know who Fairfax hired to investigate me. You know everything about me. So how do I know you won't use it or sell it?"

Erin put her arms around his neck, still holding her wine glass. "Because of us, darling."

"Can you tell me who it was?"

"I can, but I don't think it will do you any good. You have far too many things on your plate right now. I think we should concentrate on one crisis at a time. Which one do you want to concentrate on first?"

"Where do you want me to start?"

"How about starting with giving me what I want?"

"We didn't when you visited me in Club Fed. Why now instead?"

"You weren't over your precious Stefani, and I'm not a rebound girl. I'm hoping you're over her now. Or are you serious with Julie again?" Erin rolled her eyes. "Though even asking hurts me."

Zack ignored her. "I got rid of my bike because I was afraid you had a GPS tracking device placed on it. Somebody followed me the other day."

"You think I had your motorcycle tampered with?"

"I don't know. That's why I'm asking."

The smile left her face, and her green eyes narrowed. Zack recognized ire. "Get out, you ungrateful bastard. If that's what you think of me, get the hell out of here and don't ever come back."

"I'll take that as a no; you didn't."

"I protected you! I spent money on helping you get Stefani back, I bent over backward to keep you safe, and you STILL don't believe in me? You're a bigger asshole than everyone says!"

"Define everyone."

"You can leave anytime now."

"I will. But we need to talk. So talk. Do you know Addison Jones?"

"I am certain my last instructions to you were for you to get the hell out of my house."

Zack sipped the wine and set down the glass. "I don't think you're seeing things through my eyes."

"I said get out. After everything I've done, for you to accuse me of that? HOW DARE YOU?"

"I don't know who to trust, Erin, so give me a break. I'm sorry," Zack said. "Now please, can we talk? Do you know Addison Jones?"

Erin put down her glass and put her hands on her hips. "Yes."

"That's how you found me and why you warned me to keep quiet in prison."

"No one, not even me or Kilgas, could protect you in there. We wouldn't be having this conversation if you made a stink about your being there and even mentioned why you were there and what you uncovered with NPA. I shouldn't have stepped foot inside that prison, but I did to save your life. So please leave and consider our association finished."

"Why do you care about me?"

"Why do you think? Are you really that dumb?"

"Apparently."

"Why is everything with you so difficult?"

"Pot and kettle, dear."

They eyed each other angrily, no words spoken. Finally, Zack lifted his glass and gulped the wine in one swallow. "Do you ever wear any clothes?"

"I asked you to leave."

"I don't think you meant it. I'm sorry, Erin. I don't know what to think. Let's start over. Now, do you ever wear any clothes?"

Erin tried to hide her smile. "Am I wearing too much or too little for your liking?"

Zack rubbed his forehead. "Why do you make things so difficult?"

"Now you understand what it's like to deal with you."

23

The picture of Hannah and her friend Angie never left Zack's vision. When Zack shut his eyes, he saw the girls vividly. It reminded him of Derek back in the town of Clyde and the missing children there. His stomach knotted, and Zack felt like throwing up at the thought, but he sat up, and the acid returned to his stomach.

He left Erin Keyes' house and returned to Baltimore only to receive a text from Julie asking him not to stop because Cate was fussy, and Julie worried Zack's presence would worsen her mood. Zack asked if he could stop by after Cate went down for the night. Julie declined.

It gave Zack time to think alone.

Which, Zack learned in prison, was not a good thing.

Zack slept on his office floor that night but decided as the sun rays found his face on the office floor, he didn't want to listen to Lauren chastise him for his sleeping choices. Nor did he want any advice about Jules. Zack didn't even know what he wanted out of that.

After a quick shower, Zack exited the office from the alley-level garage and drove off on his motorcycle. He rode around town for a while, stopped at a few distinct places but ended up on the waterfront and watched the few birds fly past. Then, his phone decided the day began.

Zack returned to the office. He climbed the stairs and saw Lauren alone at her desk, head down, working furiously at the computer. Zack opened the doors and pointed at Dre's office. She said no.

Zack walked towards her desk. "Gee, if I weren't the owner, I'd think you're the only employee of this place."

"I feel like that a lot, sir."

Zack sat down across from her. "I'm sorry for disappearing."

Lauren nodded and returned to work.

"I'm trying, Lauren."

She finally looked at him. "I know, sir. Quit failing." She winked.

"Is the check on Zack meeting tomorrow?"

"Probably."

"Do you tell them everything?"

"Not everything, sir."

"Do you tell me everything?"

"It's complicated, sir." They stared at each other. "Sir, can I ask you a question? Why don't you just meet with them and work out the problem? They care about you."

Zack thought about that. "Maybe. And doing what you suggest would be beneficial." Zack looked around.

Lauren took a deep breath. "Do you regret that I'm here?"

"What? No. Not at all."

"Did you talk to Michelle more than you talk to me?"

"That's an unfair question. I've known Michelle since I was seventeen, and she's the reason I'm here today. I've only known you for a week. Our relationship is different." Zack watched Lauren analyze what he told her.

"Sir, of course, it will be different. I want our relationship to be unique. Ours. Ok?"

Zack examined his bare wrist again. "I know."

"Would it help if you call me Michelle?" Lauren stared at him. "Sir."

"Listen, can I buy you dinner tonight and try to explain to you some things? Especially about Michelle."

"Don't you have plans with Jules tonight?"

Zack did not have plans with Julie or anyone. "Why would you think I have plans with Jules?"

"Because I'm not stupid." Lauren grabbed her water bottle and stood from her desk. "I did warn you."

Zack said nothing. "Ouch. What aren't you telling me?"

Lauren walked across the office and filled her water bottle without responding.

Zack decided that conversation died and changed his focus to work. Zack scanned the office. "High school girls live on their phones. What we need to know is on their phones."

"I think you'll want to see what I found. It may be what you're looking for." Lauren returned to her computer. "The Church of a New World Order for Christ. It's a mega-church but look at this symbol."

"Looks like Greek letters to me. Not conclusive, but," Zack trailed off.

Lauren touched the screen. "It looks similar to one of the tattoos we saw." She watched his face and expected more surprise, but there was none. "The cell phone number of that Summer girl belongs to a corporation that has a headquarters in the 540-area code. They're headquartered in Ireland, but when I dug deeper into that corporation, one of its holdings was this mega-church in the middle of nowhere in Northern Virginia."

"A corporation owns the church which doesn't pay taxes, and the corporation is based in Ireland to get out of paying US taxes. What else does the corporation do?"

"I'm trying to find out, sir."

"Didn't we agree that try is why we fail?"

Lauren bit her lip. "Is that supposed to be funny, sir?"

"It is. All right. You win. I'll work here with you for a while. I have some things to do today; then, I'll take you to dinner. Deal?"

"Suspiciously sounds like I'm a backup for you tonight."

Zack walked into his office. "If you get a better offer for dinner, let me know."

24

Mikayla filled her mug, smelled the coffee, added a little creamer, and sat on the couch. The rest of the group did the same Thursday afternoon, one week since Zack returned. Lauren sat anxiously on her desk front and watched the group mill about and talk. She finally had everyone in the office, save Zack.

"This coffee isn't too bad," Darnell said.

Dre put his mug down on Lauren's desk and sat on the corner. "I can't tell the difference between this and the Hawaiian coffee, but it bothered Zack, and Michelle loved it when she ticked him off, so I went with it." He laughed at the thought.

"You can't tell the difference? I can," Mikayla said. "Getting under Zack's skin is fun at times."

"All in good fun," Dre said. "So, how was he today, Lauren?"

Lauren leaned forward. "I think he was himself. At least as far as I can tell."

Darnell sat on the couch and rested on the arm. "Where did he go?"

"Mr. Stack said he had some things to do. I presumed he met with that creep Kilgas." Lauren noticed they waited for more. "I don't like Mr. Stack around him. That Kilgas guy worries me."

Mikayla spoke. "He's not worried about Kilgas."

"I think he should be," Lauren said softly.

"Lauren, did he say what his plans are tonight?"

"Well, he said he was going to take me to dinner." Everyone looked surprised at her, and Lauren understood why. She blushed. "It's not what you think. It's his way of apologizing and trying to let me get to know him without him allowing me to get to know him. I was warned, if you recall."

Dre smiled. "I do recall. Good luck. Try to find out what's going on inside his head. He's not sharing much with the Kilgas case, and that worries me."

"Or any other case," Mikayla pointed out.

"Dre, why don't I order a new couch for him and have it here?" Lauren suggested. "Mr. Stack told me this was his sanctuary. Maybe if I restore it, he'll open up."

"That's a good idea, Lauren," Darnell said. "Dre, when are you going to talk to him? I mean, we can sit around here all day and night and talk about what's going on with our boy, but you're his bro. Me and him are tight, but not like you and Zack. That dude would take a bullet for any of us, but he'd be dead and still find a way to take a bullet for you, Dre."

"He's avoiding me."

Lauren spoke. "I shouldn't say this, but he does feel alone. Mr. Stack doesn't know who to trust. He wouldn't tell me why or what, but something is bothering him. I'm not sure if it's because he's confused about Jules or working with that Kilgas guy, or maybe it's something else."

"Why wouldn't he trust us?" Dre asked. "Why would he be confused about Jules?"

Lauren's surprise was evident. "Didn't you know? I thought everyone knew everything about all of us."

"What about Jules?" Dre asked again.

"He's been sleeping there since he came back. Last night he slept on the floor in his office, and that was the first night since he got back that Mr. Stack hasn't been with Jules."

Mikayla heard Lauren say that before. "Wait. Is he sleeping there, or is he sleeping with Jules?"

"I'm not sure Mr. Stack would approve of me telling everyone about his love life." Mikayla shook her head.

Dre ran his hand over his head. "Did he mention birding?"

"Several times. He's upset because he missed migration."

Dre spoke. "I think he needs that hobby to keep sane or steady. Down to earth. Know what I mean?"

"He asked me to go birding, but I told him we had work to do. Should I have said yes and left with him?"

"Probably," Darnell said. "Dre, you need to talk to him."

Dre nodded and stood. "You're the only person he's talking to, Lauren," Dre said. "Until he talks to me, find out what's going on with him. And don't tell him you told us about Jules."

25

The familiar car of Kilgas parked, luckily, in front of the Dre-Zack Detective Agency. Late in the day, conveniently before dinner time, Zack spent another afternoon asking questions, searching for clues and leads, and getting nowhere with Kilgas. Hannah Leary was not to be found.

Zack got out of the car, and Kilgas exited the driver's side. The two men stood on the sidewalk. Zack scanned the area, but it looked normal to him with all the people on foot and cars moving about.

Kilgas scrolled through his cell phone. "Nothing. Damnit, Stack, we're getting nowhere."

Zack nodded. "I know."

"And you're ok with that?"

"I won't take offense at your incredulity," Zack replied. "We know she hasn't been found yet, and, in this case, that's a good thing. We'll scour through more phone records and tackle what we can tomorrow."

"So what about tonight?" Kilgas asked, the impatience in his voice growing with each passing day.

"We keep our emotions in check, Kilgas," Zack said sternly. Zack spun and looked at the doors of the agency and then at the second-story windows. "And we start mending fences." Zack turned back to Kilgas. "Go home and have a good night with Terri. Remember the life you want to have after we find your daughter."

Kilgas stared at Zack but relented. "Ok, fine. You're right." He exhaled. "This wears thin in a hurry. I'm supposed to call Hannah's mother tonight with an update. What the hell do I say?"

Zack scanned the area again in search of anything out of place. "Tell her this is difficult, but we're giving it our all. And despite what you hear on the television shows, every day she's not found means she's still alive. That's what you have to get her to believe."

"And get her hopes up so I can crush her when some local schmuck finds Hannah's body in a ditch while walking their stupid dog?"

Unusual for Zack, he put his hand on Kilgas's shoulder. "Yes. Remember, hope is a good thing."

"That's poetic. You should put that in writing," Kilgas remarked full of sarcasm.

"Can't take credit. That's a line from a movie. Name the movie, and I'll buy lunch tomorrow."

"Asshole. I'll be here at eight in the morning."

Zack smiled. "Don't worry about bringing breakfast. There's a kickass breakfast diner nearby."

Kilgas shook his head, got into his car, and disappeared. Zack waited a moment before he went inside.

* * * *

Zack sat in his office and dialed his cell phone. She answered on the third ring. "Hi, Jules, it's me."

Jules chuckled. "I know who it is, silly. What's up?"

Zack paused. "Well, I didn't see you yesterday, and I thought maybe the three of us could have dinner or hang out together tonight."

"I'd love that," Jules said, "but I can't tonight."

"You have better plans?"

"I'm sorry, honey. I do."

Zack waited, but the silence became too uncomfortable. "And you don't care to share them with me?"

"It's nothing. I have something for work to do, and I might be late. My parents are taking care of Cate."

Zack waited again, and again the silence became uncomfortable. "You're working?"

Jules laughed. "Zack, honey, it's nothing, so don't concern yourself. I know how you get. But, listen, maybe tomorrow night or Saturday we can get together, Ok?"

"I can watch Cate. I'd love to," Zack said.

"Babe, I know. I wasn't sure where you'd be, and my parents are already here." Jules chuckled. "Unless you want to hang out with my mother tonight?"

"You could have asked me. No worries," Zack quickly said. "So, maybe tomorrow?"

"Yes." Julie paused. "I'll call you."

Zack rubbed his forehead. "Ok. Hey, so you know, I enjoyed the time we've spent together." Zack shook his head at the statement. As it replayed in his head, Zack wished he could rewind and start again.

"So have I. I should get going. I don't want to be late and don't worry about me, ok?"

"That's a dumb thing to say to me."

"I know. I'll call you tomorrow. Have a good night, babe."

Zack nodded silently. "You, too." They disconnected, and Zack fought his urges. He left his office and saw Lauren at her desk. Lauren looked at Zack.

"I don't have other plans, but I despise being your backup plan." Lauren stood and grabbed her purse. "I think you need to reprioritize your priorities."

Zack looked at his bare wrist. "Keep up the unsolicited 'I-told-you-so' advice, and you'll be eating alone."

Lauren smiled. "I doubt that. You're still trying to figure me out, and you won't walk away until you do."

"You think you know me, huh?"

"Let's have Italian tonight. I want to see how good you are at picking out Italian wines."

Zack finally smiled. "Prepare to be impressed. Let's get out of here. That wine is the best thing I've heard all day."

* * * *

The men sat inside the van, the windows down to let in the fresh air, and they watched. They weren't sure what or even why. Their job was to obey orders. Simple, and it paid well. The driver had the easiest job. He just drove. The other four had to do the work if there was any.

One man, who sat in the front passenger seat, was known as the Scout. He typically worked his days in places vagrants and runaways stayed. Being out this late in the day during the week irked him. A wild goose chase is what the official term designated this assignment as. And the Scout decided to let the rest know.

"Again, why are we here? Is there anything substantial about this?"

A man in the third-row seating, with a computer in his lap, rolled his eyes again. "I told you. We got a hit on the website, but it terminated our reverse search before we landed a solid location."

"So what? So whoever hit the site decided it was all bullshit and left."

"That's not how it works," the man known as the hacker replied. "You don't understand how our system works, so just let us who know handle it."

The Scout now rolled his own eyes. "Why are we here?"

"Because we were able to trace the IP address to this area."

"Great," the scout droned. "That narrows it down to what, like five thousand computers near here?"

"Something like that," the hacker agreed as he continued his search. "But this one was different. They knew how to terminate the connection and stop our search. They were a little late, but they still knew what they were doing, which means someone may be investigating us, making the boss worried. That's why we're here, so instead of complaining, keep your eyes open."

"For what? This is like searching for a needle in a haystack."

"By comparison, that would be easier," the hacker said. "Needles would be drawn to a magnet. The hay would not."

The scout inhaled slowly and sat quietly for another five minutes until the magnet finally attracted the needle. "WAIT! That guy, that's him!"

"Which guy?" Two men in the back seat said simultaneously.

"That guy, the tall one with the hot chick getting on the motorcycle. That's him!"

"Who?"

"I saw him at the boneyard," the scout said. "He and some other dude were looking for those two girls, remember?"

"That's him?"

"That's the guy who talked to me, showed his gun, and thinks he's a badass. That's him, all right," the scout said.

"And he exited the Dre-Zack Detective Agency," the hacker said with a smile. "Interesting."

"Gentlemen, I think we found our location," the driver said. "What's next?"

"We keep low and keep an eye on him," said one of the men in the second row of seats. "I'll phone it in and get directions. Hacker, see what you can find out."

26

The motorcycle stopped in front of Lauren's apartment building. Zack set the kickstand, felt Lauren's arms unwrap around his mid-section, and he waited as she got off the bike as delicately as she could in a skirt, her chosen work apparel.

"Are you coming inside?" Lauren asked. She stepped close to him. "I have a nice Bordeaux inside. Perhaps you could open it for me?"

Zack took the helmet from her hands. "In the grand scheme of things, how high does that rate on the bad idea scale?"

Lauren grinned. "Why would it? Do you think I'd let you work your charm on me to get into my bed?"

"I wouldn't dream of it. But you should know that the past few nights I've,"

Lauren cut him off. "Mr. Stack, it's not my business, so stop right there. I'm simply asking if you want to come inside for a glass of wine. After that, if you decide to stay, which I think you should, you have your old couch to keep you company." They walked to the door of the building.

"I should just go back to the office. How do I know you won't try to work your charm on me?"

"There's only one way to find out."

"Or not find out." Zack leaned forward and kissed her cheek lightly. "I like you even if there is something about you throwing me off. And I don't know what is going on with my personal life. So the last thing I want is to drag you and us into the middle of something that could ruin, well, ruin us."

"Ok. I understand. I still think you should stay here tonight. No wine. I'll lock myself in my bedroom, so you'll be safe."

"It's not me I'm worried about." Zack winked. "Goodnight, Lauren. Thank you for an enjoyable evening."

"Thank you, sir. Can I ask you to stay one more time?"

"You can, but the answer will be the same. You were right about one thing. I'm emotionally vulnerable right now."

Lauren touched the side of his face. "I know, sir. At least promise me you'll go straight back to the office and stay there alone tonight. Please."

"I promise."

"Call me when you get there. I want a video chat to prove it."

Zack smiled. "Yes, mother." He kissed her cheek again. "Now go inside before I change my mind."

Lauren slowly removed her hand from his face, turned, and walked inside. Zack watched her, and his mind raced though he couldn't pinpoint anything particular. Every woman in his life briefly appeared and vanished. And then the faces of the two missing girls appeared, and the boy's words from Clyde while in the hospital popped into his head and shot an arrow of guilt through Zack's heart. *"I want to be like you, Mr. Stack."*

Zack shook it from his head. Currently, Zack didn't even want to be like Mr. Stack.

His cell phone rang, and Zack saw it was Kilgas. It stopped and rang again. "What, Kilgas?"

"Stack, you're being…" the line cracked and broke up.

"What? You broke up."

Zack heard static then nothing; Kilgas's voice returned briefly. "Three," but it broke up again.

"Dude, I can't hear a word you're saying. Call me back." Zack put the phone in his pocket, turned for the motorcycle, and suddenly understood what Kilgas tried to tell him.

Three men grabbed him; one punched Zack in the stomach while the other two grabbed his arms. The men said nothing. They straightened Zack, hit his stomach again; the puncher pulled an object out of his pocket and came at Zack.

Zack couldn't identify it but didn't want to be the recipient. Zack's legs were free, the mistake amateurs always made. Zack's right leg quickly kicked the man's arm with the device and a second kick smashed the man's genitals. A third kick hit the man's jaw, the man bit through his tongue, blood spurted out of his mouth, and the man hit the ground.

The other two men moved to stop Zack's legs. Another mistake. Zack ripped one arm free and shot his elbow back into the man's nose. In an instant, the free fist spun and hit the third man in the face.

Now free, Zack turned to the first man who struggled to his feet, but a spin-kick ended with Zack's heel separating the man's jawbone from his skull. The other two men attacked. One grabbed Zack, but he was smaller and weaker. Zack lifted him off the ground, whipped him around, and tossed the man into the other standing.

Both hit the ground. The two scrambled; Zack saw headlights brighten. The vehicle accelerated, and Zack saw one of the three men brandish a handgun. Zack ran as the auto headed for him. Zack jumped in front of the vehicle but timed it perfectly, and when Zack hit the ground in a somersault, he withdrew his Sig and spun. The sound of one gunshot echoed. The sound of the second and flash from the barrel of the Sig eliminated the threat.

Zack stood; his gun aimed at the assailants, but they remained motionless. Zack crossed the street, lights in apartments in the building now blackened, and darkness prevailed. Zack heard the sound of an engine accelerating, looked, and saw a van speed at him, its lights now off. A Chevy white cargo van; Zack saw it before.

Zack dodged away from the van, somersaulted again, spun, aimed, and fired once. The rear window shattered. The vehicle zig-zagged from right to left, smashed into the motorcycle, corrected its path; Zack fired again and knew the bullet passed into the van. The brake lights briefly brightened, but the vehicle sped away. Zack saw his new motorcycle on its side, mangled and destroyed.

"Goddamnit," Zack muttered, and his hand clenched the gun. "Brand spanking new and now trashed."

Zack returned to the three men, two unconscious; one clutched his leg and moaned as if death was imminent. Zack made sure it wasn't.

But Zack reconsidered.

Zack kicked away a .25 caliber pistol and stuck his gun into the man's eye socket. "Looks like things went to hell in a hurry, huh? You have three seconds to tell me why you're here. Ready, set, go."

"Whoever sheds the blood of man, by man shall his blood be shed."

"Seems fair. I'm good with that. Two seconds."

"You will rot in hell, heathen," the man said.

"Oh, I'm already living it. You'll have to do better than that."

The man smiled. "He who strikes a man so he dies shall surely be put to death."

"Wow. I'm feeling all Old Testament giddiness. It sounds like it's an eye for an eye time. Or, in this case, just your eye for my bike. I liked that bike. I hope you liked your eye as much."

"You will die. You are not worthy."

Zack nodded. "Everybody dies, worthy or not." Zack thumped the man's head with the handle of the gun. Out cold. The man wasn't worth a bullet.

Zack heard footsteps, spun, and pointed the Sig at the movement. A man appeared from the dark. Kilgas's arms went high in the air.

"Don't shoot, don't shoot! It's me."

Zack lowered the pistol.

"I tried to warn you. Sorry. Damn cell service. We should find that 'hear me now' guy and beat his ass. Are you ok?"

Zack holstered the weapon; his adrenaline surged. "Yeah. But they killed my motorcycle."

Kilgas saw the twisted carnage on the side of the road. "Sorry, man. Damn, that's cold."

"Not as cold as I want to be. They killed my freaking motorcycle!"

"Relax. You have another one. What do we do now? Load them up, take them to the country and torture them until they talk?"

Zack shook his head. "We can't. We're on camera. I better call Barnes."

"Cops? You're calling the cops?"

"Either that or they'll be knocking on my door and taking me to jail tomorrow. I'll call here. Keep an eye out." Kilgas stood above the men while Zack dialed a number on his cell phone. He waited. "Captain Barnes, I'm sorry to call you this late. It's Zack. Three guys just attacked me. Currently, they are all alive, but I'm having second thoughts. Is there any chance you or Kael can get over here immediately?"

"Stack, don't do anything stupid! What else should I know?"

"One got away in a white Chevy cargo van. I shot out a rear window."

"Damnit, Stack. Stay put. This is not how I wanted to see you again."

"Me, neither. I'll be standing outside Lauren's apartment. You know where."

Zack disconnected, and his phone buzzed. It was Lauren saying she heard gunshots, and she was scared. She wanted to know where he was. "Kilgas, can you hang here for a moment?"

"Stack, are you nuts? I am not dealing with the cops."

"Then come up with me and don't scare Lauren. I'll deal with the cops."

* * * *

Zack knocked on Lauren's apartment door. "It's ok, Lauren. It's me." The door unlocked and opened immediately. Zack stood there. "I got your message."

"What was that? Did I hear gunshots?"

"You did." Zack took a deep breath. "Um, I need a favor."

"What?" Lauren crossed her arms.

"Can you allow Kilgas to stay here while I deal with the police outside?"

The smile left her face. "What's going on?"

"I told him not to scare you, and if he does, tell me. I'll remove his elbows." Zack pulled Kilgas from the hallway. "Play nice."

Lauren's face turned white.

"I'm not a threat, Lauren. I don't want to deal with the police."

"It will be ok, Lauren. I'll be back shortly." She nodded, and Zack disappeared down the hallway as the sound of police sirens filled the air outside.

Kilgas stepped inside and shut the door. "I'm sorry if I upset you."

Lauren, her arms crossed, walked to the kitchen. Kilgas saw an open bottle of Bordeaux and two glasses.

"While I wait, do you mind if I have a glass of wine?"

"Not that one. That's for Mr. Stack. I have a red blend I'll open for you."

"I see how I rank," Kilgas muttered.

"You know exactly where you rank. What happened outside?"

Kilgas waited until she opened the red blend bottle of wine. He poured himself a glass. "It could be just a group of jerkoffs trying to make a quick score."

"Mr. Stack was attacked?" Lauren asked, alarmed. "Here? Was he involved with the gunfire?"

Kilgas sipped the wine and watched Lauren worry. "You must not know him well enough to expect gunfire regularly if he's involved." He had more wine. "What I'm hoping, Lauren, is that we've stuck our noses where we shouldn't have, which, by the way, is another trait of your boss. That's how we met."

"I know. If you hurt Mr. Stack, I'll kill you."

Kilgas smiled. "Duly noted."

"Don't patronize me. I will kill you."

27

Captain Ted Barnes found Zack outside twenty minutes later. Barnes spotted Detectives Dylan Kael and Aaron Fox. Barnes wasn't surprised to see Kael and Fox. Nor was he surprised to see other cops and two paramedics. Barnes scanned the area, and other than three bloodied bad guys, he saw little.

Barnes had his memories from this apartment complex. Months earlier, while responding to a B&E call, Barnes received multiple gunshot wounds and nearly lost his life. Yet, Barnes shook that out of his head and walked forward.

Dylan Kael saw Barnes and walked over. "Captain, glad you came down."

"How could I miss this? Our favorite customer is here. What happened?"

"Stack dropped off Lauren; three men attacked him as he tried to leave. After that, Zack did his thing," Kael said nonchalantly. "The one on the stretcher has a hole in his leg received after he brandished the .25 caliber over there." Kael pointed at the gun.

"Never a good idea with Stack around," Barnes said softly. "Surprised he's still breathing."

"So am I. Did you see what those guys did to Stack's motorcycle?" Kael shook his head. "One of the men tried to jam this syringe into Stack," Kael said as he held a bag containing the syringe.

Barnes noticed Zack. The two exchanged acknowledgment but nothing else. No smile. No nod.

"Any IDs on the men?"

"None, and judging by their condition, I doubt they'll be talking anytime soon," Kael said. "A witness from a nearby apartment corroborated everything Stack said, but we'll do due diligence and collect video."

Barnes looked around. "Can anything be normal with this guy?"

"I'm beginning to think this is normal with Stack, Captain."

Barnes begrudgingly agreed. "Good job, Kael. Do us all a favor and make sure Zack gets absolutely no press on this one, ok? I mean none. Bury the video. If they ask, say the girl is a cage fighter or something, but no mention of Stack."

"Count on it."

Kael left, and Barnes walked closer to Stack. Stack looked at him again. "Zack, are you ok?"

Zack nodded.

"Can we have a word in private?"

Zack nodded again; the two walked away from the commotion and around the corner of the building. Barnes faced him and smiled.

"Thank you," Barnes said softly and pulled Zack in for a hug. "And you still owe me that hundred bucks."

"Not yet, I don't."

Barnes laughed. "We'll see," he said softly. "Please tell me what you told Kael is the truth."

"100%, Captain. Swear on my life." Zack understood the look Barnes gave him. "I swear on my baby's life."

"Ok. Good enough. Did any of the three men, before you prevented them from being able to speak, say anything?"

"One mumbled a couple of verses from the bible. Genesis chapter 9 verse 6 and another from Exodus or Leviticus. I don't remember for sure."

"Bible? You memorized Bible verses?"

"Hank gave me a Bible to read in prison after several nights of waking him with my nightmares." Zack shrugged. "I didn't sleep much at night, so I read the Bible."

"Who is Hank?"

"The guy in prison who gave me the Bible."

Barnes rolled his eyes. "Did it help?"

"I wasn't looking for help. I was looking to fall asleep."

"Maybe you could use a little salvation."

"I find my salvation in being a wine snob, a good shot, and occasionally a good lover."

Barnes stifled a laugh and looked around. "Not sure if I'm glad you're back or not."

"How are you doing, Ted? Becki and the kids doing ok?"

"Doing great. Thanks for asking. Is the video from the surveillance cameras going to show anything different?"

"No. But it will show a guy I'm working a case with showed up right afterward. He's now upstairs in Lauren's apartment."

"Why are you here this late?"

"I took her to dinner," Zack said. "The office has an Alert Watch on me right now, and to prevent Lauren from having to lie about my whereabouts after other plans fell through, I bought dinner."

"Alert Watch, huh?"

Zack nodded.

"Who's the guy?"

"Don't ask, Ted. It's not important."

Barnes groaned. "You better be operating on the right side of the law, Zack. We all sleep better when you do that."

Zack shook his head. "All work and no play makes Zack a dull boy."

Barnes laughed. "Shut up, Stack. I'll stop by in the morning."

"Why?"

"So you can tell me what you're not telling me right now. Why don't you tell me everything in the beginning? I'm going to find out anyway."

"Ted, now is not the time to be skeptical. Just a cheating spouse case."

Barnes nodded and grinned. "Your bullshit is such bullshit. This game you play with me is tiresome."

"But it keeps us fresh, Ted."

* * * *

Barnes found Zack at the Dre-Zack Detective Agency the following early morning outside the building. Barnes slept, but Zack did not, and it showed.

"How was your night?"

"After I told Lauren what happened, not fun. We had to leave her place within the hour of you leaving."

"Did you go back to your place?"

Zack scoffed. "No. That would have been a major mistake."

"Jules." Ted nodded. "She has a right to be worried, you know."

"Yeah, thanks for reminding me," Zack remarked.

Ted changed the subject. "What do you think? Related to anything?"

Zack shook his head as his eyes scanned the entire area. "Lately, what isn't?"

Barnes spoke. "The compound in the syringe was a form of LSD. It might not have killed you, but you would have been out of your mind. You didn't take up drugs in that country club you stayed at, did you?"

"Damn you, Ted. I swore to shoot the next person who said that. But, no, you know I don't do drugs. And, after Lexi, do you think I'd even try any? I don't know what that was about."

"Why haven't you seen me since I woke up?"

"For one, I stopped and talked to you, and for two, I was locked up, remember?"

"I know. Becki had a recorder in there to replay for me after I woke." Barnes smiled. "You so owe me, just like you said."

"Forget everything I said. I just made that stuff up to try to get you to wake up."

Barnes laughed. "I will enjoy being your boss."

"You should think twice."

"Becki and I want you over for dinner tomorrow night. Seafood pasta night. We know you love it. Bring whoever you're currently dating."

"I'm not dating anyone."

"Yeah, right. Bring Stefani."

"What about Julie?"

"Ships and ports, Stack. Bring Stefani. She's your future."

"She dumped me. I haven't talked to her since December. So why would I bring her?"

"Is that how it happened?" Barnes shook his head. "See you about six. Bring plenty of wine. I like drinking your wine and since we're responsible adults, plan on spending the night."

"Ooh, a sleepover. It's like we're in sixth grade again."

"Or I can have a squad parked outside and bust you for DUI. Smartass. Stay out of trouble, and please, this time, Zack, if shit gets crazy, talk to me before you do anything stupid. Got it?"

Zack watched Barnes walk away. *Sounds like a relative term in this situation.*

* * * *

His office phone rang. It was less of an intrusion than Agent Ferguson thought. Phone calls meant he was needed and wanted. Eventually, that meant a promotion, and it seemed every four to eight years, a new head Director of the FBI was required. Ferguson viewed himself as that man. Eventually. Today, he answered the phone.

"Ferguson here."

"Hey, it's Nolen. Can you talk?"

Ferguson hit a button on his phone. He had a device installed, so his phone calls scrambled with the press of that button. No one listening would understand a word. "Go ahead."

"Susan B. Anthony. That's the name of the lady who visited Stack the day before he got out. According to our source, she spent at least two hours with Stack inside a protected room."

"Susan B. Anthony, are you kidding me? It's a fake. Do we have her picture?"

"No. You know how that place is. We got a shot of her walking towards the protected room, but not her face, just build. We got nothing."

"Protected room? What the hell is that? It's a prison."

"Well, apparently the entrepreneurial spirit is alive and well there, and since it's unregulated due to the private nature of it, there isn't much we can do. I guess it's for conjugal visits. The guards profit well off it."

Ferguson ran the possibilities through his head. "So Stack has a woman in his life. Are we sure it wasn't that Oakley woman?"

"She hasn't visited since before Christmas, and the description doesn't match with any other female in his life."

"Keep looking. Whoever got Stack out is someone to watch. What else?"

"Interesting development. Three men tried to jump him last night outside the apartment of one of his employees. They're in police custody right now."

"Find out who they are and why they jumped Stack."

"We're on it—one other thing of interest. We spotted Stack with a man we couldn't find but got a picture of him. We ran his face through our facial recognition app, and it came up as Mark Leary, former US Army Ranger. Guy disappeared from the planet not long after his discharge from the military. He must be working for cash or running around under an alias. Can't find anything about him."

"Keep looking. I think Stack and that Leary guy used you and Larson's names to illegally interrogate some high school kids. Catch Stack with a fake FBI badge and bust him on that."

"How do I do that? I just can't get a search warrant so we can find a reason to throw him back into our prison."

Ferguson understood even they had rules, even when doing something illegal. "Keep watching him. If Stack as much as Jaywalks, I want him back in that country club. I want to know everything he does, and I mean everything and find out who that woman is." Ferguson hung up and sighed. He stared absently at his computer monitor and decided it was time to take a walk. There was one person in the building with inside knowledge of Zack Stack. She likely wouldn't talk about the past with him, but it was worth a shot. Agent Ferguson left his office in search of Michelle Borman.

28

Kilgas watched Zack work on his computer. Kilgas questioned what Zack absorbed. Zack's eyes scanned everything on the screen, but he changed the screens quickly. Kilgas wondered if Zack simply worked like this to keep from talking. Zack wrote an occasional note on a legal pad but worked in silence.

"So Erin left yesterday. She wanted me to give you a message."

"She left?"

"Had to go to Europe. Erin said she's sorry she had to leave and wants to see you when she gets back. Erin wants to call you and apologize."

"What? Why didn't she mention it?"

Kilgas smiled. "Maybe you kept her so preoccupied she never had a chance."

Zack slowly opened his desk drawer and grabbed his Sig. He held it and looked at Kilgas.

Kilgas put up his hands. "I know, shut up, or you'll shoot me. Jesus. She never mentioned having to leave to you?"

Zack leaned back in his chair. "Not once."

"Last minute thing, I guess."

It felt odd and disappointed Zack. "Can you do me a favor and scan the area for anyone suspicious outside? I think last night wasn't random, and if they found me there...."

Kilgas understood and left the office.

"And don't frighten Lauren," Zack called as Kilgas walked through the door.

"I know, or you'll shoot me." Kilgas shut the door.

Zack picked up his phone and dialed a number. Zack waited until the other end answered. "You wanted a callback."

"I expect you to call me back a lot quicker."

"I'll work on that. I need to see you."

"Zack, that's not how this works."

"It is now. Where and when I'll let you decide, but it is happening," Zack said.

The silence on the other end didn't last long. "You're taking charge. It's about time. I'll be in touch." The line disconnected.

Zack put down the phone. *We'll see why Addy Jones suddenly appeared in my life.*

He dialed another number. Julie.

"Hi. I'm glad you called," Julie answered.

"Hey, are you free tomorrow night?"

"I am, actually. Why?"

"Well, I'd like to spend some time with you. Maybe we could talk." Zack listened, but no response. "I remember how that was one of your biggest complaints about me. I don't want it to be anymore."

"I think I like the new you." Jules laughed. "Can you stop by today after work?"

"You bet. Also, Ted invited me to dinner at his house tomorrow. I'd like you to come. He told me to bring a date."

"You should take Stefani."

Zack audibly sighed. "Do you want to come with or not?"

"Zack, of course, I will, but you should ask Stefani."

Not exactly what I hoped you'd say. "Great. I'll stop by later today, Ok?"

"Perfect. Cate and I will be here."

Zack disconnected and heard the door to the front office open. There was no talk which meant Kilgas returned. Zack left his chair, walked to the window, and tried to sort a hundred things in his mind. Too many distractions, so he left his office. Zack entered the main office, walked behind Lauren's desk, and grabbed a Pepsi. He opened it and tried to take a drink, but Lauren stood and took it from him. No words needed to be said. Zack was being rationed.

"Anything?" Zack asked Kilgas.

Kilgas stared straight at Zack. Zack understood.

"Solid or loose?"

"Loose. Routine, probably."

Zack opened the fridge behind Lauren and grabbed the bottle of Pepsi again. He heard Lauren sharply inhale and saw the ire in her eyes. Zack winked, but she still clutched the Pepsi.

"You agreed to the rules, sir. And you already had your limit today." Lauren took it from him again and handed him a bottle of water.

"Today has sucked."

"I don't care. It's been that way for all of us since you returned."

Zack sipped the water and sat on the edge of Lauren's desk. Kilgas grinned at him. "Why is the Christmas tree still up? It's June."

"Because there are gifts under it for who I am beginning to realize is the most ungrateful and possibly selfish person on the face of the planet," Lauren replied. "Sir." Lauren stood and entered the bathroom. The door shut.

"I like seeing you get told off," Kilgas said.

"I bet. What's outside?"

"A cable company van oddly out of place, and a black Crown Victoria parked a block away with a clear shot of the front door. Both have two men inside."

Zack looked at the Christmas tree and saw the presents underneath. "Feds?"

"Probably, but I didn't ask."

"Did you know about Erin's sudden departure to Europe?"

"Nope. Caught me by surprise, too."

Zack picked up a box Andre left under the tree for Zack. He shook it and guessed what it was—a bird book. Zack smiled. "Kilgas, we need extra eyes. Can you access any we can trust?"

"Stack, you don't want to wade into that pool."

Zack looked at Kilgas after he put the box back under the tree. "I don't have a choice. If people are after me, if they're watching me, they know about my daughter."

Kilgas understood.

"We need to know who is watching us and why and if you are of interest. I don't think you want that. I can't put Jules in danger. Or Lauren or anyone. I went through that before, and it almost killed me."

"I said I was sorry about that."

"And I can't end up in that Club Fed again. So do what you have to do, please. Just be clear about the objective and make sure it matches mine."

Kilgas nodded at Zack. "Trust me on this. It does."

Zack returned to his office, Kilgas followed, and they sat down. Zack typed on his keyboard, and Kilgas heard the printer in the front office print. Zack hit more commands and leaned back. Zack leaned forward again and scratched his unshaven chin. Rarely did he go unshaven.

Kilgas leaned forward on the chair in front of Zack's desk. "Stack, those men cost money. Mercs don't work for free. But thank you for saying please."

Zack smiled. "I was told I need to try harder."

"A new you?" Kilgas chuckled. "What is going on?"

"Don't get used to it. You made millions off me, and Erin can buy the state of Vermont if she wants. I'm sure between the two of you, a solution to our problem exists that won't cost me anything more than a favor as long as we remain on good terms. And like you said, there might be a DC committee looking to question you. So if someone is about to grab you or me, we need to know beforehand."

Kilgas smiled. "You are desperate, aren't you? Promising me a favor. Wow."

"I need certain people in my life safe, Kilgas." Zack eyed him. "If they aren't playing by the rules, neither should we."

"Ok, I'll make some calls, but you better think long and hard about that decision. Not every merc is as reputable as I am."

"I expect you to use your considerable influence and explain the downside of crossing me. Don't forget about Lennox."

"None of them do. Lennox was a friend to some of them."

"Good. Then they understand hierarchy."

29

Lauren appeared with the printed papers. She put them on his desk and left.

"What are those?" Kilgas asked.

"Phone records from Hannah and Angie and Leah Durham."

"Who is that?"

"The girl found in the ditch the other day," Zack said. Zack scanned the numbers.

"Since when do you do research? I thought that was Lauren's job."

"It is. Do me a favor, go to the front office, and grab a bottle of Pepsi. Lauren keeps them out of my fridge. Say it's for you. I didn't sleep last night and need a caffeine kick."

"Ok." Kilgas walked out to Lauren and tried. Zack heard Lauren tell Kilgas no, he's not doing Mr. Stack's dirty work. Kilgas returned. "I tried, Stack. You're on your own there. Hey, I'm going to make a call and take a ride to see if I can lure the jackasses outside away from here."

"Have fun."

Kilgas left, and Lauren entered Zack's office. She shut the door and crossed her arms. Her weight on one leg and the other slightly bent; Zack saw that look from women before.

"You're upset with me."

"Sir, how can you pretend like nothing happened last night? Those men were after you, and they found you at my place!"

"They weren't after you, Lauren."

"But they were after you, and anyone can figure out who I am. Sir, I'm sorry. But I don't want to live there anymore."

"Do you still want to work here?"

"Of course. I just can't go back there."

"Ok. I'll ask around. I think there might be a couple of places open close to here if you want to live around here."

"How can you be so calm about this? Sir! I'm a nervous wreck!"

"I can see," Zack said calmly. "And I'm the one who didn't sleep last night."

Lauren looked away. Once inside the hotel room down the street, she curled next to Zack on the bed and slept soundly.

"Lauren, nothing is going to happen to you. I promise. Take a deep breath and chill. I'll find you an apartment quickly. I'm sure there's at least two open within walking distance."

"Closer to work than where I live now?"

"Yes. Like a few doors down close." Zack returned to the pages but realized Lauren stood in front of him. He walked to her and hugged her. "It's ok, Lauren. Nothing is going to happen to you."

Lauren clung to him, and he felt her tremble and her tears through his shirt.

"It's ok, Lauren. I promise you."

"I'm sorry for snapping at you in front of Mr. Kilgas."

"It made his day. Are you ok? Do you want to take the rest of the day off?"

"No, sir." Lauren slid her hands down his arms. "What's going on with Jules?"

"I'm not sure. Everyone keeps reminding me of Stefani, and I haven't talked to her in months." Zack shook his head. "Jules left me for the right reasons, and I don't know what's changed."

"I warned you," Lauren said softly.

"I know. I feel like I should be with Jules, and I love being with her and Cate."

"But?"

"But we are here to work. Not dissect my private life."

"They appear to go hand in hand. But, you know, Mr. Stack, you aren't always the tough guy you pretend to be. Showing your soft side is appealing." She rubbed his arms. "Even you need to talk about things sometimes, and I'm a good listener."

"Jules' most significant problem with me, besides the guys trying to kill us, was my lack of communication. But when I'm with her, I have a hard time saying what I want. Part of that is because I'm not sure what I want anymore, but more importantly,

I'm unsure what she wants. And after we get together and put Cate down for the night, we have a glass of wine and go straight to sex."

"Clearly, she wants sex from you."

"Why wouldn't she? We're great at that together," Zack said. He looked at Lauren. "Do you think she's using me for sex like Mikayla was?"

"Ask her. And if she is, after you stop seeing her and aren't in love with Stefani, I may see for myself." She winked.

Zack shook his head. "Ok, enough of that. How did you get me to talk? Were you a psychology major, or do you watch lots of movies on Lifetime?"

Lauren laughed. "Sir, if you haven't noticed, I'm the only person you're talking to, and you need to talk. So don't beat yourself up. She loves you; you know that. But, sir, you know there's always a but."

"I know. What happened last night is exactly why she and I can't be together. It's why she left me in the first place. I didn't want to admit it. Shit." Zack stepped back and rubbed his forehead. "I asked her to dinner. She accepted."

"Well, that's a horrible idea, Mr. Stack. Are you a glutton for punishment?"

"What?"

"What? You'll go to dinner; you'll have a great time, you'll have a drink or two, you'll feel things, and you'll sleep with her only to get your heart broken again. What is wrong with you?"

"What if things are different this time?"

"You idiot. You're vulnerable. I told you to be careful."

"Ugh. Whatever you do to get me to talk, stop. I don't like it." He went back to his desk.

"You feel better, don't you? I told you the other night I'm good for you. How about if I allow you one more Pepsi for today? Then no more. It's not good for you."

"Yes, mother."

Lauren shook her head, turned, and left but returned with the soda. "Don't be a smartass to me. I can make your life hell."

Zack smiled. "Should I not take her to dinner?"

"Only if you want to be heartbroken again."

"We can make it work. We love each other."

"Do you truly believe that, sir? Is that what you want, to be with her?"

"I was ready to ask Stefani to marry me. I had a ring and everything," Zack announced to her like it was cathartic. Lauren set the plastic bottle in front of him and listened. "I bribed the guard at Club Fed to extend me a favor he shouldn't have."

"What happened?" Lauren asked as she sat on the desk beside him.

"Christmas." Zack stared ahead emptily, nothing in his focus other than his thoughts. "I got a Dear John letter. We haven't spoken since."

"Maybe you should. I think settling things with Stefani would be wise before you try to commit to Jules. You have a past, Mr. Stack, with Jules and with Stef."

"That's not the half of it," Zack said. "Do you know something I don't?"

"I'm saying you need to be careful. And sometimes, Mr. Stack, you just have to let go of the past." Lauren leaned over to touch his face. "If you're not in the present, you may miss the future."

Zack heard what she said and took a deep breath.

"Maybe tonight we should talk? I'm free and won't be upset at being your fallback plan."

Zack picked up the Pepsi, almost opened it but gave it back to her. He smiled and winked. "We'll see. I want to see Cate."

"I know, and you should. But remember everything you just told me. Ok?"

"I can't acknowledge you are right this early in our relationship."

"There's hope for you yet. By the way, sir, Dre had me rent you a vehicle for the week. After I told him you complained about the carbon buildup, he said I should rent this for you while he has your other and last motorcycle tuned to your liking. He said it might rain, and you don't like to ride in the rain."

"That was thoughtful of him." Zack returned to the papers. Lauren walked around and saw them.

"What are those? How did you get them?"

"Phone records," Zack said. "Sorry. I have sources."

"Sir, that's my job. I'm supposed to do that. So you don't think I can do the job as Michelle could." Lauren shook her head, leaned over, and moved her hair to behind her ear so it didn't impede the vision between them and pointed to the papers. "The phone numbers from the two girls. I've been studying them. Look at this one.

I was able to find who the similar numbers were. All were their friends from school, except for one." She pointed, her hair fell from behind her ear and brushed against Zack's face. She guided it behind her ear. "540-area code, and it belongs to a church in Virginia called The Hope of Christ." Lauren moved her fingers down the list and noted several calls and texts to and from that number. "Sir, call me crazy, but that has got to be more than a coincidence."

Zack saw the dates. "They stopped on the date the girls went missing, and you're crazy, but it is more than a coincidence."

"Sir, I don't know why the cops didn't follow up on that, but the girls were so active on their phones I can see why. Each must have talked to thirty different people that day," Lauren said. "From there, I took that number and dug into it deeper. Do you want to know about the Hope of Christ?"

"I read all about it in prison."

"Funny, sir." Lauren rolled her eyes. "It's a small church in rural Virginia. There isn't much about it other than who owns the property, the Colson Brothers. The church pays monthly fees to them. I am still looking for anything on the Colson Brothers."

"Who's the priest?"

"Priest?" Lauren looked confused.

"Sorry, that's my Catholic education. How about minister or pastor or preacher or whatever. It has to have a leader, right?"

"It does. Minister Bradley Pollard. It turns out he has a police record and a bit of a fetish. The church has no affiliation with a national church or denomination. It's odd. It doesn't even have a website or is listed as a church in the yellow pages."

"The yellow pages?"

Lauren smiled. "Sometimes, Mr. Stack, the best information is found via the old ways. I kept looking at the phone numbers, and because no one else had anything for me to do, I remembered a list of phone numbers you found before you went to prison."

"Lauren, thank you for not saying I left."

"I know that bothers you, sir. The others are afraid of how to speak to you, so you know. They think you're on edge, ready to explode."

"What do you think?"

"I know I'm safe. Now, for these numbers. I need to do some checking, but there's at least two that caught my eye."

"Show me, and what list are you talking about?"

"Andrea Whitehead, the madame, remember her?"

"Not personally. Hey, do you like being tied up for sexual pleasure? Or any of that bondage, sadism, masochism, or dominatrix stuff?"

Lauren turned her head, and the two stared at each other. "Is that a proposal?"

"I've been tied up before. Not happening again. Not sure I want to be whipped, either. How about you?"

"I might have fun with a few things, especially if you keep calling me mother, but no one is tying me up. This number here and this number here. Do you recognize them?"

"Should I?"

"I'm not sure. One is from the church, the Hope of Christ." Lauren turned to look at Zack again. "Bradley Pollard."

"The other?"

"Well, I developed a program that cross-referenced all the phone numbers I found in lists around the office, including the list from the dominatrix, the missing girls' contacts, and ours, and it is a long list, but one appeared several times, but I can't trace it. It called the yoga studio once, and your BDSM lady regularly."

"What day of the week?"

"Usually on a Monday but sir," Lauren turned her head and looked at him, their faces only inches apart, "the same number called you the day the Feds hauled you to prison."

"Lauren, I swear to you, I have never seen that woman or any of her associates."

"I hope not, sir. Do you remember taking any calls that day?"

Zack shook his head.

"I'll keep digging. I thought you'd want to know about Bradley Pollard."

Zack stared at the number. "I don't remember my phone ringing once that day. I texted Dre. That was it. Then the Feds grabbed me."

Lauren continued her long stare at him. "I'll look into it. It is illegal for me to do this; you understand that, right?"

"What fun would it be if it weren't? Just don't get caught. If you do, I'll see if they'll put us in the same prison."

"Sorry, sir. But I don't find that funny."

"I was serious." Zack stared at the numbers. "You'd make my stay there a lot happier."

"Don't count on that," Lauren said. "Sir, Mikayla helped me with this. She saw the Andrea Whitehead name and got excited. Then, she said something about Dan Banks. I haven't seen anything about that name. Should I have?"

Zack rubbed his forehead. "No. Neither should she. Lauren, I'm going to see Bradley Pollard. Could you do me a favor and call Detective Dylan Kael. Tell him everything you just told me and ask if he can dig on the Colson brothers. Tell him Michelle specifically asked me about him. If Mikayla shows, can you tell her I need to speak to her about the Rossum case and have her wait here for me? That should pique her interest. Maybe she'll listen to me. I'll see you soon. Good job."

30

"**A**re you kidding me?"

"What?"

"That? I'm supposed to drive that? What am I, a suburban housewife with four kids?"

Lauren looked at the minivan and suddenly felt like she had failed again. "Sir, I'm sorry, but for the week, based on availability, it was the cheapest vehicle they had."

"A minivan. You got me a minivan. Do you know what my other car is?"

"I'm sorry, sir. It seemed more practical."

"Dre told you to get that, didn't he?"

"Yes, sir."

Zack looked at Lauren. "Subtle. Very subtle. I'm not giving up my motorcycle, Lauren. Make sure everyone knows that when they ask you." Zack shook his head and looked around the square. No cable van or Crown Victoria. "Stay here today and lock the doors at least until Dre or D get here. I'll be back later this afternoon to get you settled for tonight."

"Where?"

"I don't know yet. Maybe I should get a bed for my office, and we can stay there."

Lauren smiled. "That would make things awkward here, sir."

* * * *

The church wasn't majestic. Its walls weren't filled with giant stain-glass pictures from Bible scenes or of Jesus welcoming His people. It didn't have wings like a crucifix or was built with stone and brick, ornately mimicking a European creation celebrating the extravagance of the church.

This building looked like it was built in the early 1900s of wood. The wood now weathered to an uneven gray. Few windows on the church lined the walls, and tall, wide wood doors stood beneath the church bell's steeple and atop that, a rusted, aged cross.

Green grounds surrounded the church. Mature trees dotted the landscape, but mostly it was green grass and a sidewalk around the building. Next door, a white picket fence surrounded a simple Cape Cod-style house, newer than the church, that Zack guessed housed the minister. The yard around the house contained a swing set, a flower garden, a vegetable garden, two young red maple trees, and a children's play area complete with the playset with ropes and swings and a fort.

Zack stopped the minivan in the empty parking lot on the opposite side of the church and house. The lot was big enough for a hundred cars. But, as isolated as the church was in the middle of the rural setting, Zack wondered how it survived minus affiliation with a national church.

A gentle early summer breeze blew across the land to warm it and encourage late spring growth. Zack walked towards the church but discovered it was empty. Three in the afternoon on a Friday, most churches were vacant.

Zack walked to the house and knocked on the front door. After three separate knocks, the door opened. A man opened it, balding with hair only on the sides of his head, glasses, dressed casually in khakis, and a short-sleeved dress shirt. He looked at Zack. "Can I help you?"

"Are you Bradley Pollard?"

The man didn't move. "Who's asking?"

"Right now, just me," Zack said. "Can I come inside?"

"No, you may not," Pollard said. A woman appeared behind him.

"Honey, who is it?"

Pollard turned around. "Just a friend from school. We'll step outside to talk to not bother the children," Pollard said. He stepped outside and shut the door behind him. "Who are you?"

"Doesn't matter," Zack said. "What matters is why you are running a youth ministry but have a police record. You're a sex offender with a charge of statutory rape against you. Care to explain?"

Pollard rammed his hands into his pockets. "I demand to know who you are."

"I'm sure you do." Zack pulled out the badge supplied by Kilgas on Tuesday at the school. "Carter Nolen, FBI," Zack said. *If impersonating an FBI Agent with a stolen badge doesn't get me locked up, nothing will.* "I'm investigating a series of missing teenage girls."

They reached the church, and Pollard used a skeleton key to open the large wooden doors. "So why come here?"

"Some contacted a phone number listed under your name," Zack said.

Pollard opened the door. "A lot of teenagers contact me."

"Which is peculiar considering your police record. Start there."

"My high school girlfriend was a sophomore. I was a senior. Her parents didn't like us dating. They caught us; her mother called the cops. Because of my age, even though it was consensual, I was charged with statutory rape by law. They pressed charges, I was convicted, but they recanted their desire to punish me before sentencing. The judge, being conservative, still sentenced me to five years and another two on probation. That girl, Melissa, waited for me, and six months after I was released, we were married. That was her inside the house. We have three children and have been married for ten years now. The law isn't as forgiving or understanding as the Lord." Pollard walked up the center aisle of the small church.

The inside was as un-decorative as the outside. One wooden crucifix with a likeness of Jesus on it stood tall behind the altar, which contained one bible. Basic and Zack reasoned all that was necessary, if a building was necessary, to worship. Only fifteen rows of pews filled the area.

Pollard knelt, did the sign of the cross at the altar, and headed towards the sacristy. Zack remembered spending a lot of time as a young altar boy goofing off in the church and the sacristy. God must have had a sense of humor, or lightning would have struck him down at an incredibly young age.

Pollard opened the door and entered the room. "I'm not running from that, and many of my congregation know about my police record. And they all adore Melissa and her pies. So, if you want to cause trouble with the police and my youth ministry, go ahead. You'll find no one will listen to you."

Thank you for confirming everything Lauren already told me. "Your youth ministry, tell me about that."

Pollard sat in a chair with a closed cabinet behind him. He swiveled on the chair and explained in detail all that his youth ministry did for the youth. It was for children ages ten to eighteen who wanted to share their experiences and lives without being judged, graded, or pressured by adult expectations. Some wanted more religious education; some just wanted guidance and to talk about how teenagers grew anxious.

"To me, it sounds like most of the kids you deal with are normal kids, is that right?"

"Yes, of course, that is our adult version of normal. But unfortunately, they don't understand what normal is. So my goal and those of my fellow parishioners that assist is to accept who they are as normal, not the normal society projects."

"That's great. Do you ever get runaways?"

"We may. Typically we don't ask when they come to us. It makes them uneasy."

"Just them?" Zack scoffed as he pulled out the pictures of Hannah and Angie. "How about these two? You ever see them?"

Pollard studied the pictures. "I'm sorry. They don't look familiar."

"They both called or texted a phone number registered to you and this church several times and notably on the day they went missing. Care to explain?"

"I don't know what you're talking about," Pollard said.

"Take another look at those girls. You're going to tell me that you've never seen them even though I traced their phone records to a number listed under this church and specifically your name. Is that what you're going to do?" The skepticism in Zack's voice told Pollard this wasn't a joke.

"There are several phone numbers listed to this church that the church, under my name, provides to the assistants of our ministry. It's a service we have to encourage involvement."

"Someone filled these girls' heads with tails of a better world with no trappings of capitalism or personal vendetta. Real bullshit if you ask me. It sounds like they wanted to escape the normal expectations that society projects. Does that sound about right?"

"Certainly, Mr. Nolen, you remember the pressures of being a teenager. Fast forward twenty years till today, and everything has been exacerbated a hundredfold for youth. The troubled youth that comes to us is lost and needs guidance, perhaps

149

through scriptures, perhaps through exposure to a simpler way of life with fewer expectations and demands with a routine they can handle until they reach physical, emotional, and psychological maturity. Life on the street can't and won't do that. I dare say schools can barely provide that if they even try. With our youth ministry service, the youth of all ages can learn, explore, and mature at a pace that suits them, and we can gradually intertwine the real world with their lives rather than out there where it is cast upon them without regard for their welfare."

"Yeah, that's great; I'm deeply touched," Zack said without hiding his sarcasm. "Look at this picture really hard, Pollard."

"I don't know them. I've never seen those two girls before and have no idea where they could be."

"Ok. Where is this Utopian youth ministry? I notice you have no lost youth looking for themselves in your yard."

"I'm sorry," Pollard replied, clearly displeased with Zack's dismissive attitude.

"Not yet, you aren't. Where are all these lost kids who don't go home at the end of the day?"

"I can't tell you that."

"You can't tell me that, or you won't tell me that?" Zack's patience stalled.

"Both. Someone like you wouldn't understand, but that is part of the promise we give to these lost children of the Lord."

"And part of the promise I give to the parents is to torture the people responsible for abducting or hiding their children. The God I believe in is good with that." Zack stared at Pollard. "These lost children have parents that love them. Is your calling more important than that?"

"Love is a fickle thing, wouldn't you agree? One person's love is another person's smothering, often abusive, penetrating act of control and violence. Which one are you?"

Zack smiled. "Right now, I'm leaning towards the violence part." Zack opened his jacket to show the handgun under his arm. "So you don't know these two girls, you don't know where they are, but you are the person listed as the head of the ministry?"

"Don't believe me, but I don't personally help every troubled child that comes in touch with our ministry. To gain their trust, we have to assure these souls that they are completely safe, and sometimes that means even I am not aware of all we take in. As an FBI agent, though you don't dress or look like one, you should know that loose lips sink ships."

"No, torpedo's do," Zack said. "So, you want me to believe you do not know these two girls, or where other runaways took in by your," Zack paused, "ministry are?" Pollard nodded. "Mr. Pollard, in my business, we have another name for that."

"You don't strike me as a churchgoer or believer in the Word, so I'm sure you do."

"Believer in the Word?" Zack chuckled. "Do you even care about how these kids' parents feel? But, of course, you don't. So somehow, you must profit from this."

"Excuse me!" Pollard objected and stood.

"Sit down," Zack said dismissively. "Pollard, I also discovered that you make bi-weekly calls to a place in Baltimore. Same time each week, which suggests a meeting. Do you care to talk to me about that?"

"I have no idea of what you're talking about."

"I bet the Dominatrix you see for whatever fetish you pay for would disagree."

Pollard stared angrily at Zack.

"Does the money you collect at your church service pay for that visit? Is that the Lord working in mysterious ways? Is that believing in the Word?"

"I think you should leave."

"I'm sure you do. You better talk because I'm running out of patience."

Pollard took a deep breath. "I love my wife, and we enjoy our," he paused, "love. But there are some things she doesn't like, nor would I ask her to do for pleasure."

"Finally, an answer I can believe," Zack said. "Who do you contact with the lost youth who won't go home?"

"I'm sorry. I won't betray that trust."

"That trust is possibly resulting in hiding a murderer."

"Do with me what you will, I won't say."

"I'm about to." Zack withdrew his gun. "Are you going to continue to obstruct me here?"

Pollard sat firm, but Zack saw the color of his face change, his breathing quicken, and beads of sweat form on the sides of his face. "I didn't know the FBI allowed such brutish behavior."

Zack smiled. "Carter Nolen; remember the name, Pollard. You don't want to see me again." Zack holstered the weapon. "Pollard, I'm going to give you a shot at redemption and salvation, something you'll understand. You're going to call your network and find out exactly who talked to these two girls and where they are and when I come back in five days, you're going to tell me."

"And if I don't?"

"I saw a movie where some psycho strapped a priest to the ceiling and lit a fire underneath him that engulfed the church and fried the guy. Gruesome. I can't imagine the horror and pain one would feel from that." Zack leaned forward. "But I'm curious and would like to watch." The glare from Zack told Pollard what he needed to know. "I bet this tinder box will burn very fast."

"Sometimes runaways don't want to be found, typically for extremely personal and credible reasons. The Lord agrees."

"Yeah, well, this is my jurisdiction, not your Lord's. So tell me, how do you afford multiple cell phone plans for your youth ministry?"

Pollard raised his chin as he swallowed. "The Lord provides if one believes."

Zack smiled. "Jesus Christ. You know how to peddle that shit. It sounds like fleecing, but what do I know? I'm just an FBI Agent. Have a nice day."

Zack left and walked through the church. Zack crossed the altar but did not kneel, genuflect, or give the sign of the cross. Something about this place told him it wasn't a place of worship. The girls weren't there, and Pollard didn't help much. But Zack had the phone number and guessed Pollard would make a phone call quickly. That would give Zack a direction. And set things in motion.

* * * *

Bradley Pollard watched the man leave. He picked up the phone and dialed a number. After several rings, the other end answered.

"Yeah, hi, listen, a guy named FBI Agent Carter Nolen was just here looking for the two Annapolis girls. He knew an awful lot about me and traced the girls to our ministry. I'm only in this because of you. I need protection" He listened. "Yes, I'm worried, I'm telling you, he knows a lot, and he's coming back in five days to find out who dealt with the two girls, and he was very intent on finding them." He listened. "I don't care, but I can't have him disrupting what I'm doing over here, and I think it would be in your best interest to think the same way."

Pollard hung up the phone, looked out the window, and saw his wife and three children playing in the backyard. He smiled. Pollard left the rear of the church to play along with them. This life was his. This is what he wanted. No one was going to interfere.

31

Zack returned to the office at five o'clock. He hadn't heard from Kilgas, but Zack trusted Erin wouldn't let Kilgas kill Zack. Uneasy alliance at best, but it was the best Zack currently had. He entered the office to find a colossal sofa/sleeper in his office. Lauren decided to save the business money and would stay there until Zack found her a new apartment. The downside was that she was too afraid to go to her apartment, so Zack had to head over to get things for her.

Zack made sure to grab her pillows and the fluffy comforter she liked. Zack got back to the office with a suitcase of things for Lauren. She sat on the new couch and flipped channels of the television on the wall.

"This place isn't too bad, Mr. Stack. We really should consider adding a small kitchen."

Zack ignored the comment. "I had to rummage through your underwear drawer to find the pair you wanted," Zack said seriously. "But I'm pretty sure I got everything you requested."

"I said just grab whatever was on top," Lauren grinned.

"Yeah, those were boring. What I picked are much more interesting." He lifted an exotic pair out of the suitcase. "Very interesting."

Lauren ripped the leopard print thong from his hand. "Did you see anything else you like?"

"I did," Zack said. "Fascinating drawer."

"Jerk," Lauren blushed. "Thank you, sir."

"How are you feeling?"

"I'm not worried about me, sir. I'm worried about you."

"I'm fine," Zack said. "I made some calls. If you like the area around the square, a couple places are available."

"I do. Can you show me tomorrow?"

"I'll see what I can do."

"Thank you. Did you cancel your dinner plans?"

"No, but I did get a text from Jules saying she was busy tonight, so I can't go see Cate. Have you heard from Mikayla? She's not returning my call." Zack watched Lauren put her pillows and the comforter on the pulled-out sofa bed already.

"I haven't. Have you called Dre?"

"No. It's unlike Mikayla to not return my call."

"I haven't heard from her all day. Why? Are you worried?"

"Frequently. Has Kilgas or anyone else called for me today?"

"No, sir. My guess is they are tired of waiting for you to call back and gave up on you."

"Shit. I'm going to find Mikayla. I'll be right back," Zack said. "If Mikayla calls, let me know."

"Are you coming back here tonight or sleeping elsewhere?"

Zack heard the tone and saw Lauren cross her arms. "Don't wait up."

32

Mikayla Dorsey sat in her car. She parked far enough down the street to remain unseen, but the lens on her camera made up for it. She could see the front door and side of the two-story house and anyone who visited. So far, no one had entered other than the female owner, sans her husband, the elusive Dan Banks. It looked to be another long, lonesome night, but Mikayla understood after she chose to forego her career with the police department to work as a private detective at Dre-Zack, there would be many nights like this one.

Mikayla saw the sun in the rearview. Sunset approached slowly, but Mikayla kept her eyes on the house. Cars occasionally passed by, unaware or unconcerned about her vehicle. She sat low, so it was difficult to see her. But enough light to take pictures or look through the telephoto lens. A car turned the corner, crept slowly towards the house, parked on the opposite side of the street. A man exited the car and headed to the front door. Two knocks later, the door opened, and the female occupant ushered him in the door.

Mikayla snapped as many pictures as the digital camera would allow. Perhaps she could get a shot of the car's license plate and find out who is visiting the home of Susan Rossum. Maybe that would help her find what Emma Rossum wanted. Perhaps it wouldn't.

Mikayla studied the house again. One dark window upstairs but the rest covered with drapes or curtains so no movement could be seen. She looked at her phone, sheltered by one hand so the light wouldn't give her away. She saw yet another missed call from Zack and another message. Mikayla ignored it and slumped lower in the seat.

Suddenly, the passenger door opened, a man slid inside, and the door shut in a flash. Mikayla jumped in fright then recognized Zack Stack as he turned off the dome light inside the car and stared at her. She realized the angry look on him. She didn't know what to say, but Zack spoke first.

"What did I tell you about keeping your doors locked? Damnit, Mikayla."

* * * *

Mikayla knew she had made a mistake. "I poured out my cold coffee and forgot. I'm sorry."

"Sorry is going to get you killed. Why are you here?" Zack demanded, and Mikayla understood this was more than a reprimand.

"Because Emma Rossum deserves an answer better than we couldn't find anything," she defended herself.

Zack lifted the camera and focused on the house. "Top window. Why is it black while the others aren't?"

"I don't know. It was like that all night."

"I told you to stay off this case. Was there something in my tone or words that suggested to you that I phrased my position incorrectly?"

"No, but Emma Rossum is sure her brother Evan didn't die of a natural heart attack, and since you aren't talking to me, I decided to take matters into my own hands."

Zack nodded. "Get us out of here."

"What?"

"I said get us out of here. I parked nearby. Drop me there and then go home."

"No. Someone entered the house twenty minutes ago, and it wasn't Dan Banks."

"Because there is no Dan Banks. It was a made-up name. You should know that, and maybe you would have if you wouldn't have abandoned me."

"Oh, is that what this is about? What do I have to do, Zack, to not be in your doghouse?" Mikayla stared at Zack, but he looked out the window. "Do you want to have sex? Would that help?"

Zack looked at her. "Right here in the car? Not very comfortable."

Mikayla gasped. "Ok, should we go back to my place, and I'll screw your brains out. Would that help us? Let's go right now."

Zack considered it with a playful look on his face. "I bet I can count on one hand all the times I've turned down an offer like that and with our past I have no doubts my brain would not be operating properly after you finished. However, at this particular juncture in time, I think that would be an extraordinarily bad idea for both of us. Tempting, but no."

"You can be such a jerk."

"Is it jerk or asshole? Because I had a teacher once that said the second rule of personnel management was that it's better to be an asshole than a jerk."

Mikayla let out a scream. "Ok. You're an asshole. Zack, why won't you talk to me?"

"I am talking to you. Get us out of here."

"Zack, we need to figure this out. We can't work together like this, and I like working here with you. So please, talk to me. Yell at me, do whatever you have to do but help us get past this moment right now where we hate each other."

"I don't hate you, and I'm not mad at you. But you could have told me you were using me for sex." Zack looked at Mikayla. "I heard you tell Stef and Jules."

Mikayla dropped her head. "That's not entirely true."

Zack looked out the windshield towards the house of Susan Rossum several places down the street. "Her maiden name is Susan Banks. She was married to Evan Rossum, who did die of a heart attack. But it wasn't in his sleep, nor was it caused by over-exertion at his weekly basketball rec-league earlier that night."

"Are we not talking about us now?"

Zack looked at Mikayla. "She had Evan cremated after Doc Patterson did his examination, which isn't suspect nowadays, but what is suspect is the several communications she had with Patterson before and after the examination."

Doctor Steve Patterson was the former Medical Examiner for Baltimore County. Patterson's history was impeccable, and his reputation was renowned across the Eastern Seaboard. He regularly shared suspicious deaths with Julie Fletcher when Julie worked the crime beat as an investigative journalist, and Zack knew Patterson had a crush on Julie. Patterson later was implicated in doctoring/creating evidence to incriminate Zack in the death of his at-the-time girlfriend, Alexis Parker.

"How did you find this out? You said you had no way of communicating with anyone when you were in prison."

"Jack, the guard, isn't above cash payments for the use of a secure computer," Zack said. "I haven't found a smoking gun, just a bunch of circumstantial stuff. The policies paid out full without much fuss. Susan Banks remarried only a few months after the death of Evan."

"Yeah, to Dan Banks. Who is he?"

"Edward Rossum. Evan and Emma's brother. The middle child of the four."

"What? He can't be the middle child if he has three siblings."

"Edward was a twin, was being the operative word. His twin brother, Eldon, died as a teenager. History shows a pattern of mysterious deaths surrounding Edward, starting with their childhood pets, five dogs over the years, and then Eldon. It only gets worse from there culminating most recently, as far as I can tell, with his other brother Evan."

"Are you serious? Why would Susan stay with him?"

"She's just as sociopathic as he is. Evan was her second marriage. Guess how the first one ended." Zack didn't let her guess. "Guy died when he fell into a silo at his parents farm. Oddly, Susan was the only person with him. That only gained her a half million in life insurance. That doesn't go far these days. So Edward and Susan found each other somehow, probably at a convention for murderous sociopaths, and unfortunately, Evan was in the way. Add a little poison to his sports drink, cash in on some life insurance policies, and Edward and Susan can live happily ever after. Maybe if we let them alone, they'll kill each other."

"Why is he going by Dan Banks?"

"Because a private investigator hired by Emma Rossum turned up mysteriously dead after she hired him to investigate Evan's death." Zack looked at Mikayla. "Edward Rossum's name was mentioned. I don't want you near this place. I'll tell you about the rest over dinner."

Mikayla started the car. "I'm a big girl. You don't need to save me, Zack. How do you know all of this?"

"I talked to Emma the other day, and I investigate."

"Then let's finish it and get those psychos behind bars!"

"We will, but not right now. There's too much going on, and we're spread too thin. I have to get this Kilgas case taken care of, and I, as you saw, have to be super careful. I doubt the next prison they send me to will allow you to visit."

Mikayla turned right at the intersection before the house. "Why didn't you tell me?"

"I told you to stop snooping around. That should have been enough. I'm still the boss, aren't I?"

"Zack, that's not how we operate, and you know it."

"When it comes to the people in my life who I love, yes, it is. Turn left up ahead."

"Why aren't you and Stefani together? I know you still love her, and she still loves you. It doesn't make sense."

"They say that all good things must stand someday, and autumn leaves must fall."

"Really? That's your answer. You dumped Stef with a letter, Zack. Why did you do it?"

Zack's head snapped to attention. "What?"

"Come on, Zack. You broke Stefani's heart and won't talk to her, but she still drives your Jag. What's going on?"

"It is a nice car."

"Why did you dump her?"

Zack said nothing.

"Fine. I'll change the subject. What's the deal with Jules? Are you trying with her again?"

"Who said anything about Jules?"

"Stack, WTF! Talk to me. I want to know about Stef and Jules. They are my friends, and I don't want to see them hurt again."

"What about me?" Zack looked forward. "Come on. Let's go to dinner. How about the Charleston?"

Mikayla snapped a look at Zack.

Zack rolled his eyes. "I'll buy, you cheapskate."

"And you'll talk?"

"We'll see. Maybe. Probably. I don't know, but if it will get you to get off my back about not talking, ok. You're a good investigator, Mikayla. I don't want to lose you."

Mikayla laughed. "The first thing you've said to me in a long time to which I agree. We should change the name of the business to The Mik-Dre-Zack Agency."

"That has a nice ring to it. I'll consider it."

* * * *

Back at the Susan Banks house, after Mikayla started the car and drove away, a shadow moved from the dark second-story window. The man upstairs closed the curtain and lowered his binoculars. It was time to act. People would not respond kindly if this operation became known. And he knew who owned that car.

33

Night fell on the vast estate. The lands went dark except for the main house, the house of the minister. A woman near forty years old entered the estate grounds accompanied by two guards. Opulence necessitated protection. She had been here before but under different circumstances and now felt anxious. Her main focus was to tend to her flock of people on the west end of the property. She dressed plainly, as all the community did. The trapping of material worship was a plague this group fought.

The guards led her down a well-lit brick walkway lined with extensively manicured flowers, blooming shrubs, and fruit trees. A water feature trickled along one side of the path and ended in a Koi Pond, all red and orange. The top of the pond contained an overflowing stream that circled back through the magnificent gardens and provided areas for birds to bathe and drink. All beautifully lit with strategically placed back-lighting.

The woman always hid her shock in the wealth surrounding her while she and her flock, who followed and worshipped the man and his beliefs she would soon see, lived so plainly. But, she knew, belief in God provided all they needed. A devout woman of faith, her single purpose in life was to spread the word and help people in need of guidance.

They turned the corner, and she saw the minister, the leader of the church, sitting at a table near a large in-ground pool, a canopy over him, a portable decorative heater not far away, as he worked on his laptop.

"Sir, a disciple is here to see you," one of the guards announced.

The leader, dressed in casual clothes, saw her and smiled. He rose from his chair. "Ah, Sister Anne, how good it is to see you? What brings you here this evening?"

"Minister, thank you for seeing me. Something alarming happened again in our flock." The woman called Sister but not because of the ordination of any church. It was a title achieved in this ministry via the length of service and devotion. The woman was still allowed to wed and have children.

"What?"

"One of our flock, Talia, has gone missing. She is not on the grounds, and we cannot find her," Sister Anne said.

"What? How is that possible?"

"She must have gone missing after we did nightly rounds and went to bed. Talia wasn't there this morning, and we checked and double-checked everywhere. At first, we thought maybe you summoned her, but she hasn't returned. Sir, I'm sorry if this reflects upon me, but what are we going to do?"

"Did she run away? Perhaps unhappy with her ministry or the direction of her teachings?"

"I don't know if she ran away. As for her happiness, she seemed down last week, perhaps unsettled, but she wouldn't talk about it. Sir, this is the sixth member of our church to vanish in the last few months. I'm worried."

The minister stood, worried, hand over the lower half of his face, and he paced on the patio in front of Sister Anne. "This can't be happening again."

"Minister, I wish to call the police. At the very least, we should notify their families. Perhaps the child returned home?"

The minister nodded in thought. He put his hand on Sister Anne's arm and rubbed it. "Anne, let me handle this. I will take it under advisement with the council as to how to best proceed. I don't want to alarm you or allow the rest of our family to be frightened, but we have suspected there may be predators in the hills to the south and west of our property. Perhaps they are responsible. I'll talk to the local police. They are our friends." He stepped beside her and put his arm around her. "Anne, why don't you stay up here with me tonight? Let me pour you a refreshment to settle your nerves."

"No, minister, I must return to our flock. With the unease amongst them, me being away will make them worry more."

The minister smiled and put his hands on her arms, and gently rubbed her. He smiled his disarming smile. "I'll make arrangements to increase the watch tonight. I'll have part of the ministry head down and have a special feast tonight. That should settle the flock. They'll be safe, I assure you. But you look worried, Anne. Stay with me tonight and relax. Then, in the morning, you'll be refreshed and have a new sense of divine spirit to enrich the flock with positivity. You'll see. I insist." He stared into her eyes. "You'll stay with me tonight."

Sister Anne lowered her head and smiled. She knew, too, no one said no to the minister. "Of course. His Will Shall Be Done."

"Now, come inside. Let's have a drink to help you calm down."

They entered the mansion with the minister's arm around her. He held her hand and took her into a large, glorious room filled with paintings, ornate furniture pieces, floor-to-ceiling drapes, and luxury everywhere. He led her to a chair and had her sit while he poured two drinks out of a bottle of something she didn't see. Then, he came back and handed her one.

"Anne, here's your drink. I'll be right back. I want to call about Talia and ensure the safety of the family. Just sit tight." The minister handed her the drink, leaned over, and kissed her cheek. He left the room, closed the door behind him, and entered another den where he picked up a phone and dialed a number.

"Hey, it's me. Another girl went missing. What the hell is that all about?"

"The usual."

"Increase the guards around the compound, so they see it's safe. And let the outside guards know that Anne is staying with me tonight and send a couple of the ministry down. Then, order out pizza or something and have a feast for them to calm their nerves. Call it a celebration of life."

The voice on the other end laughed. "Will do."

The phone call ended, and he returned to the study with Anne. He put on his smile and walked to her. The minister took her hand in one and his drink in the other. "Everything's fine. Now, for the rest of tonight, it can be just about us."

34

Zack took the phone call at 6 AM. By 7 AM, he stood in the center of the Baltimore Cemetery and overlooked the vast number of graves. A lone vehicle, a black Cadillac Escalade SUV, entered the main entrance and slowly made its way through the roads until it stopped across a large partition from Zack, the area of a city block away.

A tall blonde exited the rear door, and the Escalade pulled away. The woman in a long navy-blue knee-length coat kept her hands in the front pockets as she trekked between the gravesites towards Zack. She stopped in the middle of the block and waited until Zack stopped in front of her.

"You wanted a meeting. Here I am. I hope meeting early on a Saturday morning didn't upset your date."

Zack looked around the grey and sullen area. "What date? Addison Jones of the Federal Government. Would I be wasting my time if I asked you for any more information about who you are, who you work for, and how you found out about my situation, as you called it?"

"You would be," Addy said. "I hope this isn't why you demanded this meeting."

"Don't insult me. I like you," Zack said.

Addy looked at him and smiled. "Let's walk." The two slowly walked between the graves. "Has your homecoming improved?"

"It's up and down. What did the people who put me there have to say about my release?"

"Like you, they're trying to find out who I am." She stopped and faced him. "Do you have a plan? Because they certainly have one for you." The two stared at each other before they walked more.

"It's a process. I need time. I can't access any bank accounts. Hence, I may have to rid us of them via a non-traditional way."

"Mr. Stack, I hope you're not thinking along the lines of how you rid us of Michael Rosler."

"This isn't admission, but why? Would you frown upon that?"

She looked at him with clear disapproval on her face.

"Ok, plan B. If you have friends at the DOJ, keep them on speed dial."

Addison Jones grinned and put an arm around Zack's arm. "Ooh, I like it when you talk like that."

"Addy, do you know Erin Keyes?"

"Never heard of her."

"Does she work for you?"

Addy Jones chuckled. "I don't think you're hearing properly this morning."

"You sent her away, didn't you? So she and I are not part of the master plan, right?"

"You have an outlandish sense of drama, Mr. Stack."

"I've been told several times I'm a different breed. I've never heard that until I met you."

Addy Jones didn't hesitate to chuckle again. "And a vivid imagination. If you ever retire from being a troublemaker, you should write novels."

"I'll consider romance novels and start with a descriptive chapter about your visit to me in Club Fed."

"That's one way to end up in an early grave. I'd stray far from romance novels if I were you, Mr. Stack."

"Pity. I think that was the first time I've heard you laugh. You should do it more often. It's charming." She said nothing. "Addy, I've been found on multiple occasions where I shouldn't have. I need to know how."

"And that would tell you what?"

"Who I can trust. Erin Keyes. Start with her."

"I already said I've never heard of her."

"You're lying."

Addy looked at him.

"You know Erin. What are you hiding? Why are you protecting her? Is she an ally or not?"

They reached a fork in the road and turned north. The Escalade appeared and trailed behind at a fifty-foot distance. Addy put her hands in the pockets of the long overcoat. She sniffed. "Smells like rain today, Mr. Stack. I love June rains, don't you?"

"Almost as much as I love torturing people."

Addy stopped and turned. A gust of wind blew strands of hair across her face. She didn't flinch. "If you're threatening me, you should know if you touch me, you'll be shot."

"Can you make the sharpshooter shoot something specific other than me, so I know she's a good shot?"

"Why do you think it's a she?"

"I smelled her perfume earlier. She is northeast of us. She would have been better off setting up a hundred yards south beside the monolith. Even cloudy, there's enough glare in that direction that detecting her would have been nearly impossible with my naked eye." Zack turned and walked. "Plus, men don't have figures like hers, and she should have worn desert camo, not black. The black is too conspicuous in a cemetery."

"I know of your military exploits. I've seen the unredacted files. I daresay I believe you do enjoy June rains." She walked again. "I won't have her prove she's a good shot. Unless you provoke me."

Zack laughed. "Why do you think I'm a threat? You're the one with all the cards. Tell me about Erin Keyes. Throw me a bone. Convince me I can trust you."

Addy walked alongside Zack. Grey clouds formed a barrier between the sun and readied for battle. "You know all about her, Mr. Stack. Focus elsewhere."

Zack shook his head. "Just tell me whether she was the one who contacted you to get me out of that Club Fed or you contacted her to warn me to keep my mouth shut."

"Mr. Stack, do you like this cemetery?"

"Not enough to become a permanent resident. Why is answering me so difficult?"

Addy wrapped an arm around his and walked close to him. "Erin is an ally. She did come to me, but that's all I can tell you."

"Was that so hard?"

"In my position, yes."

"I think you know you can trust me. Plus, I don't want to get killed by your sniper. Having to admit that I knew where she was and still allowed myself to get taken by her would be embarrassing in the afterlife."

They turned at an intersection and continued the slow walk around the empty cemetery.

"Mr. Stack, tell me about that gap in your history before your military service."

"There is no gap."

Addy Jones laughed again. "Zack, I got you out of that prison. Don't lie to me. I can do much worse than have you shot and left for dead this morning. So treat me with respect."

Zack took a deep breath. "My guess is if you know Erin, you already know about my gap."

Addy tightened her grip around Zack's arm. "You're in deep. You understand that, right, Zack?"

"More than you know."

"Don't underestimate how much I know." Addy stopped and faced him.

"Then why ask about my past?"

"I need you to tell me."

"If the truth comes out, I'm going to prison, as is someone close to me. Possibly more than just one person, and I can't allow that. I can accept the repercussions, but I can't accept those repercussions spreading to anyone beyond me. This is getting out of control, Addy, and whether it's by your doing, my doing, Erin's doing, whoever's doing, I have to regain that control."

"Control is an illusion."

"Says the woman with a sniper rifle pointed at me."

Addy took a deep breath. "Trust Erin. I don't know how they found you, I'll look into it, but our mutual friends are watching you. They are afraid of you, and you know why. What you're into now is serious, Zack, and I wish I could have prevented you from getting involved. I'm not sure involving your FBI friends was a good idea."

"That could end up working in our favor, Addy. Even the FBI has limits."

Addy looked at Zack through the corner of her eye and almost smiled. "You're playing a dangerous game."

"I'm playing to win, Addy. So are you, and right now, you need me."

"And you need me."

"What a wonderful relationship we have."

"You would be wise to trust your instinct instead of ignoring it out of fear of what it means. Don't forget that, Mr. Stack. In time, perhaps we'll reach a point where I can tell you more, but I think we're still proving one another to each other. Does that sound about right?"

"Can I take your sniper out to breakfast? Not only am I hungry, but I'm curious as to what she looks like."

Addy didn't smile. "Watch it, Mr. Stack."

"Are you telling me I'm off the market?"

Addy motioned to the Escalade. "You're off the market as far as my assets are concerned."

"And I do enjoy your assets."

Another smile by Addy caught Zack off guard. "As I do yours but remember that was only to get what I wanted, which I did." She winked. "I'm surprised you let yourself be used so easily. Was losing Stefani that difficult on you?"

Zack lost his smile. "Yes, it was. And that was a cheap shot."

The Escalade stopped beside them. "Was it?" Addison Jones touched his nose. "Sometimes, when things are right in front of us, we can't see them." Addy glared at him. "You are one of my assets now. It would behoove you to get your affairs in order. Too many cooks ruin the broth, Mr. Stack, and if your head isn't right, if you slip with your tongue, I will be forced to utilize the power you don't accept I have."

"I think you should have your sniper kill me now. I don't like you anymore."

Addy smiled, leaned forward, and kissed him. "Now I understand why Erin says you're adorable. Be careful with your search for that missing girl. The next time we talk, I expect to hear your history. And keep those lips soft. Formaldehyde ruins that."

35

Detective Dylan Kael stopped his unmarked police car at the edge of the scene, and his partner Detective Fox took a deep breath. The two got out of the car and walked towards the gathering along the closed-off road as lights from squad cars flashed.

The detective on site saw the two and nodded. "Hey, thanks for coming. I thought you'd want to see this."

Kael and Fox looked around the area. "What is it?"

"Another body dump," a uniformed county sheriff said. "Sometime during the night. Take a look for yourself."

Kael and Fox walked to the ditch along the county highway just outside the city.

"My chief got a dispatch saying you guys had a similar case last week and are looking for a couple of missing girls," the county sheriff said. "We don't give a crap about that jurisdiction nonsense. The word serial popped up more than once this morning, and if that's the case, the more of us working together, the better, right?"

Kael nodded. "Thanks, Tom; we appreciate the call though we'd prefer to see you at our bowling league instead."

Sheriff Tom Masterson smiled. "You city boys better not bring in another ringer this season. We're tired of losing to you. Anyway, she looks like a teenager, sixteen to eighteen, naked, with a bullet hole in the back of her head. A guy found the body while walking his dog this morning. We got tire tracks and footprints. CSU is on the way, and I told them to bust ass since it's going to rain soon."

Kael and Fox crept closer. "Schaeffer on the way?"

"Yep."

"Fox, what do you think?"

Fox knelt and examined the dead body. "I see some defensive wounds on her, so this one fought back." Neither touched the body. "I don't see a lot of blood, so she wasn't shot here, but no exit wound. Small caliber shell, probably. What the hell, man? She's a young girl."

Kael looked closely at the body. Scratches marked her arms and upper torso. Traces of blood spattered on her in addition to the gunshot wound. "Tom, will you make sure I get everything on this? We need to ID this one. It's the second in just over a week."

"Count on it." They heard distant thunder. "Come on, hurry up, people," Tom muttered. Moments later, the vehicles he wanted to see arrived. Sheriff Masterson yelled. "Let's get a cover over her before it rains. Pronto!" He rushed towards the crime scene unit personnel. "We aren't losing evidence. Hurry!"

Fox backed out of the ditch as cameras flashed all over the place. They saw Doctor Schaeffer arrive and waited. A few minutes later, Schaeffer called them over.

"Detectives, you might want to look at this." He pointed to the front of her body. "You said that Stack guy noticed tattoos on other victims. Does this one look similar?"

Kael looked closer and saw what looked like a tattoo. It was difficult to discern with the blood and dirt and scrapes. "It may. Once she's at the lab and cleaned, get me a picture of that. Anything else?"

"Other than I'm already tired of seeing this, no. Looks like the girl we found last week," Schaeffer said. "It's as if someone gets tired of them and just disposes of these girls like they're garbage."

Kael looked at Fox. "And it will continue if we don't stop it. So let's get to work, Fox."

* * * *

Fire engulfed the van, and the flames shot high due to liberally applied accelerants. The community watched as an organized congregation.

The service doubled in purpose. For one, as a funeral for one of the family. A longtime disciple and true believer. The second purpose was the beginning of the Church's Holy Week. Early morning service to kick off the week and preach the importance of their beliefs and why only theirs were the true beliefs.

The leader dressed in his cascading gold-lined white robe and held his head low. The loss of a family member created a somber atmosphere. Other Enlightened Ones sat on the stage. Off the stage, in order of importance, sat rows of the congregation. All searched for the truth and embraced the teachings of the Leader, the Chief Minister, the Prophet.

The flames lessened, and the black smoke rose into the darkened sky as thunder rumbled in the distance. Finally, the leader stood straight and walked to the pulpit, a stage in the middle of the community. Wooden and majestic, a giant golden crucifix stood tall behind him and a symbol they all recognized on the front of the pulpit. The Alpha, the Omega, Infinity, the Phoenix rising from the ashes all morphed into one character.

It meant the Leader was all-knowing; his wisdom and knowledge and the power of this community would rise from the ashes the world will soon become and last forever. Like God's Eternal Love because that is what the community received from believing.

The Enlightened Ones.

They were all a part of it.

The redemption and hope; the meaning and purpose; the direction and teaching; the answers. Belonging. Acceptance. Equality, fairness, individuality inspired by God, good for the community, not just the lucky few or those born with a silver spoon. For Everyone Who Believed.

The Leader raised his arms and the congregation silenced.

"Enlightened Ones, Disciples, community members, true believers, I speak to all of you. To all of Us. Each of you has been chosen. Not by me, but by a higher power. A higher power that few understand as I do and as the Enlightened Ones understand. And we impart that knowledge and wisdom on you so that you, too, achieve Enlightened status."

"But today, we meet as a family to mourn the loss of one of our own, a dark moment to start our Holy Week, the greatest week of our faith. Avishai was one of my first disciples. He believed as all of you do. He saw a better way and came to me to seek it out. Avishai found what he needed. He fulfilled his search by accepting the Word as spoken by our God, and as an Enlightened One, he spread his seed amongst many of you. And as I know Avishai, he would say to us to not mourn, but to celebrate his life and cherish our memories of him and strive to keep his faith, his purpose, his life within us alive."

"Tragedy occurred." The Leader lowered his head and paused. The emotion of the moment too much for him without a pause. Many in the congregation wept. They knew Avishai.

To them, as the name indicated, he was a gift from God.

"We cannot let that pass! The sinners out there," the Leader said forcefully and pointed towards the direction of civilization, "the heathens and evil-doers, the non-believers, the lost souls and Godless people of a corrupt society obsessed with the pleasures of money and flesh, they stole the life of our beloved Avishai!"

The congregation gasped.

"They took our Avishai. He innocently went into the city and was not welcomed. He was not met with love and open arms. Avishai merely wanted to purchase items for a grand feast to celebrate all of you. To show how meaningful and grateful he was for all of you," the Leader paused. "But he was not met with the love and acceptance you show and have been shown. NO! The evil spirit possesses those outside these walls, and they cast their wicked spell on our Avishai! They killed him in cold blood, without provocation, with no remorse but with the malice only those who embrace the teaching of Satan can wield! Outside these walls is how we would be treated. As selfless as we expect from a soul as pure as Avishai's, only thinking of others, always putting someone else's needs in front of his own, he was gunned down. Cowardice, evil, murder!"

"And to those we pray. Yes, I say we pray! For we must pray for those who embrace sin and who are blind to living a life designed by God like all of you are now. And we must forgive them for they know not what they do, for they are agents of the devil. They are the fingers of Satan! They are bred with hostility, with nothing but desires for wealth and status and care more about their image than they do for their fellow brothers and sisters in the Lord's eyes."

The Leader scanned the crowd. He saw the tears, the weeping, the sobs, and the open crying—his gift. The people followed. He took a deep breath and wiped his eyes as if clearing his tears from them. Thunder and lightning followed as if perfectly timed by God.

"Family, I ask of you now to pray with me for our brother Avishai. We ask that when he is received with open arms at the Gates of Heaven, he is sent back to us so that his love and spirit can continue to guide us all through our journey towards Enlightenment."

He raised his arms, and the congregation joined hands. In the front row stood several females, all clasped hands together and stared at the Leader. One, a girl now named Suday, bowed her head and prayed with the rest of the congregation. She missed her friend.

Sometimes.

Most of the time, she felt nothing.

The Leader made sure of that.

* * * *

The Leader finished the service early. He told the deflated crowd the inevitable rain forced the remaining service and activities inside the communal hall, which the congregation knew meant He would not be there. But he left the crowd feeling upbeat with a brief speech of the significance of their Holy Week and the Confirmations at the week's end. Despite the negative message necessary to indoctrinate the herd, as he called them, leaving them with a feeling of hope was better than of despair.

He left the area in a Jeep and traveled back to the house with his top three Enlightened Ones, one of which his brother. The four men drove through their property to the estate to get out of the falling rain. The men retreated to a large kitchen, and each grabbed a beer. The rest of the day, thanks to the rain, meant little responsibility for the men. Instead, they would enjoy luxury in the wealthy estate on the edge of a larger tract of land in the farm country and hills of western Maryland and eastern Virginia. It was home to all of these men—the product of their expansive endeavor.

The brothers added another two thousand acres to the land inherited from their parents. The land included farmland, forest, hills, rivers, streams, and difficult access to most. They took over the family farm but realized that milking cows and growing corn was not creating the profit margin they desired. And the smaller plot of land didn't give them the privacy they required.

Altered Vows

Once the parents finally died and the brothers gained control, they turned their back on their strict-religious upbringing. Providing and serving did not afford them the life they wanted. The cars, the money, the glamor and fashion, the women, the yachts, mansions, vacations, and worldwide travel weren't something people from the church of their parents saw except on TV shows.

These two dreamt of more, and their religious upbringing showed the brothers how to get it. It was all right in front of them, for the taking. The revelation occurred to both before the death of the patriarch of the family. Being born only a year apart, they grew up together and thought alike.

And one day, when mother and father took them to a new church outside of a small town in Virginia almost an hour away from their farm called the Hope of Christ, the boys realized how to get what they wanted.

And who they would get it.

Ten years later, the farm had expanded. These four men lived in the main house. A seven-thousand square foot mansion with ten bedrooms, ten bathrooms, two full-size kitchens, a theatre room, offices for each man, a gaming room, and another room simply for the men to gather and play cards, pool, throw darts, watch games, drink beer, and isolate themselves from the rest of the world.

One room filled with racks of rifles, both semi-automatic and for hunting. Shotguns, pistols, revolvers, grenades, knives, and body armor. An arsenal fit for Kings. Or police forces.

Or simply people who feared being discovered and vowed to fight to keep their operation safe.

The leader, the oldest brother, rarely left the grounds. Someone brought him everything he needed. That was the beauty of being the strongest, the smartest, the most charismatic, and the best fighter. Everything he needed. Food, drink, clothing, women, money.

Whatever he wanted, he got.

After all, only one could rule in any Kingdom. Or else it would lead to chaos.

And this place dispelled chaos.

One of the men left the kitchen, climbed stairs to the second floor, entered the control room, and sat at a desk with several high-tech computer stations. Large, fast, and modified to be quicker and more intelligent than the average computer, the computers did their work once he designated a target. The hacker built the system to protect their sites, access information they needed from potential prospects, and block anyone from snooping. It was a full-time job.

Their sites received multiple hits per day, but most were accidental landings on their sites. Some clicked to the next page, and as soon as they did, a notification chimed on the home computer and let the hacker know they had a bite.

That's when he went to work.

And the person perusing the site had no idea they were now a target.

Technology. It's wonderful until it isn't.

But there was nothing worthwhile, so he returned to the rest of the gang and enjoyed his beer.

The oldest brother, the leader, went outside and sat poolside under a large awning to protect from the rain. His brother shortly joined him. The leader worried about things the others didn't, which included plenty.

He worried about the missing persons from his flock and how it could negatively impact the operation if word got out. If there was any possibility of the girls being linked to the ministry, it could be devastating. At the very least, it would create a public relations nightmare and distrust. In addition, it would ruin the weekly services, and the collections would suffer.

And it could eliminate the protection they received from being spiritual advisors to people high on the food chain.

Everything could change.

The Leader had other thoughts. Risk, reward, benefits all went into his contemplation.

The Leader chugged his beer and dialed his phone. "Sister Anne, good morning. Could you have someone send up Suday at lunchtime? I'd like to talk to her about her teachings. With our confirmation coming up, I want to make sure she's taking her studies seriously. Confirmation is a big deal." The Leader smiled. "Thank you, Sister Anne. His Will Shall Be Done." He hung up and smiled at his brother. "Make sure the others are scarce when Suday arrives."

"You bet. What about Suday's friend?"

"The indoctrination is not taking place. Perhaps she needs a visit in the pit."

"I'll see to it. What about the three that were caught the other night in Baltimore?"

"Take them to Arizona in search of a new ministry and kill them. They're failures, and we don't accept failures. Take whoever you need with to complete the mission." He drank from his beer. "This week should be a good one. I don't know, brother; what do you think about starting new?"

"I think it would be a good idea. Have you heard about that FBI agent yet?"

"I made a phone call. That's only one-half of the fire, though. So I'll kindly ask you to extinguish the other half upon your return."

"His Will Shall Be Done."

The Leader laughed. "Yes, it will."

36

Zack took one deep breath before he entered his apartment. It was early in the morning, and he didn't know what to expect, but something drew him there. He climbed the stairs to the quiet apartment, stepped over the baby gate, and looked around. Clean with the unmistakable signs of a baby living there. "Jules? Are you here?"

He heard no noise and stepped forward. "Jules?"

The bedroom door opened quickly, and Alex Fletcher, Julie's father, came out in his pajamas with a smile. He quietly closed the bedroom door behind him and walked to Zack with his hand extended. "Zack, how great to see you! I'm so glad you're finally back."

Zack knew the greeting was genuine. "Me, too. Where's Jules?"

"Ju-ju went to work this morning. She left about thirty minutes ago with your friends Andre and Mikayla."

"What? Why are they with her?"

"Oh, I don't know," Alex brushed off. "She's excited about her new project. I just stay out of her way and hope she makes the right decision. You know she likes to butt heads with her parents." Alex laughed as he walked towards the kitchen. "So, what brings you here?"

"Well, Mr. Fletcher, I hoped to see Jules and Cate." Zack saw the look on Alex's face. "We've both been busy."

Alex nodded but smiled. "I'm sure you two will work it out. Cate is sleeping, so is mother," he said about his wife. "Ju-ju had us come over last night. I'm sorry for sleeping in your bed. Ju-ju thought it better because she didn't want to wake Cate when she left this morning after last night." Alex shook his head. "It was a long night with Cate."

"Why? What happened? Is she ok?"

Alex stood straight and saw the concern on Zack's face. "Oh no, it's ok, son." He put his hand briefly on Zack's arm to settle Zack. "The girls told me it was just Cate being Cate. They both mentioned your name when describing Cate's attitude last night. It's best you didn't hear. Eventually, she calmed down and went to sleep." Alex began a pot of coffee, and Zack bit his tongue.

Zack still despised the smell of coffee and didn't like it in his apartment. Alex pulled a quart of orange juice out of the refrigerator. Zack noticed no Pepsi existed.

"Zack, can I ask you what happened? Why did you get sent to that prison?"

Zack opened a cupboard, grabbed two glasses, took the orange juice from Mr. Fletcher, and poured two glasses. Zack handed one to the man he once hoped to call Father-in-law and took a deep breath. "Well, sir, I was given a choice, and the way I saw it, the best choice was to do time."

Alex Fletcher nodded his head and eyed Zack. "Thank you, son," he said softly.

"For what, sir?"

Alex flashed a hint of a smile. "For protecting my baby girl." He sipped the orange juice. "I still don't understand what happened between you two. And her mother is bewildered why Ju-ju insists on staying here, but I think I know why." He sipped the orange juice again. "Can you stay for breakfast?"

Zack smiled. "I'd love to, sir, but with all due respect, I think that would be awfully uncomfortable."

"I see your point. I'm working on it."

"Thank you, sir. I did hope to see Cate. Is that possible?"

"Oh! Of course, I'll go get her." Alex laughed. "You better stay here. I don't want you to see Margaret in her bloomers."

"That would be even more uncomfortable." *And would turn me off women indefinitely.*

Alex disappeared into Zack's bedroom but returned quickly with a bundle of blankets and a seven-month-old sleeping girl in his arms. Alex smiled at the baby, walked to Zack, and handed Cate to Zack. This time, it felt comfortable. Zack cradled his beautiful daughter in his arms and smiled at her. He knew his eyes glossed over.

"What do you think, son?" Alex asked softly.

"Sir, I think she is the most beautiful thing I've ever seen."

Alex beamed. "She is. I hope you don't mind if her grandparents spoil her."

Zack smiled. "I wouldn't have it any other way." Zack watched Cate sleep. His mind raced, and the thoughts lapped each other again and again in a blur. But Alex Fletcher wouldn't have known because Zack slowly rocked his daughter in his arms and watched her sleep. Zack sniffed and exhaled slowly. "You better put her back to bed, sir. I don't want to be the cause of her being cranky today. I suspect I'll hear about it from Jules in a not-pleasant tone." Zack smiled, and Alex stifled a laugh.

"I'm sure you would. I'll take her."

Zack lightly kissed Cate on her forehead and handed his daughter back to Alex. As Alex took Cate back to bed, Zack went to his back-bedroom closet and grabbed a bag. He filled it with folded clothes on the top shelf. Zack came back out and drank his orange juice. Alex returned.

"Are you coming with us to help work on our new winter home? Jules and Cate are coming to New Mexico with us for a few days."

"When are you leaving?"

"Tomorrow morning. Didn't Jules say anything to you?"

"She never mentioned it," Zack said. "I wish I could come along, but I have things here I have to tie up." Zack lifted the bag. "And I should be going."

"Leaving already?"

Zack slung the bag over his shoulder. "Mr. Fletcher, sir, I wish I could stay. I really do. But duty calls."

Alex nodded, a frown on his face.

"Please let Jules know I was here. I'll call her later."

"I'll let her know. Take care of yourself."

Zack left and locked the door on his way out. He slid raingear over his clothing as the rain fell, got on his motorcycle, and headed for his next stop—the feeling of holding his daughter in his arms fresh in his mind.

* * * *

The industrial area once thrived. But like almost every other part of the country, recession after recession hit, globalization attacked, and soon, American industrial might, though still powerful, became a rusty, dilapidated shell of itself. And quickly, many of the industrial centers were abandoned.

Altered Vows

This particular one had been largely left alone. The city didn't have the funds to raze it, nor did the private investors think the area was worth anything. And the companies that once owned parcels and factories and yards either merged, defaulted, shuttered their doors, or vanished. To many, it became the death of the American Dream without even realizing it.

This particular area in Baltimore became a haven for drug use and homelessness. Gangs didn't bother with this area because there was nothing there. Just rusting metal factories, ancient relics of a better time when the middle class had good-paying jobs and a fighting chance. Now, the buildings rotted and slowly fell in on themselves, weathered and beaten by time and nature and the normal process of no one giving a damn.

But it was a hotspot for some. The police didn't bother the area too much. What could they do? There was no place for the people to go and the prevailing attitude was as long as the downtrodden and desperate remained isolated in this rundown area, the rest of the city was free from their presence.

Hardly a recipe for revival, but to one operation, it sometimes proved fruitful. And Sundays were as good as any day to find potential recruits. The scout was familiar with the area and sent frequently. Pickings had been slim lately, but with warmer weather, history showed chances would improve.

The scout found his position against the wall, an excellent location to see the area's inhabitants. So he sat and waited, purposefully dressed as downtrodden as the rest. Sure, it was miserable, particularly in the rain, but the pay was good, the benefits were better, and the bonus was even better if the right candidate showed.

* * * *

By noon, the scout decided the day was over. New potential recruits typically arrived early morning after not knowing where to go after leaving home the night before. Everyone knew of the area, so it was only a matter of time before new runaways out of money and hope and nowhere to go but too proud to go back home ended up here, if only for a while. The other scout had a much better way of finding recruits. And she had a considerable advantage; she already knew the target was troubled and therefore easy prey.

Andrew Gruse

The scout saw the white van slowly drive past the end of the street-wide passageway between two empty, decaying buildings and knew it was time to go, which was fine by him. He slowly stood and mimicked the actions of the rest of the 'residents' of the area: slow-moving, uncaring, weak, tired, hungry. He walked down the center, but no one paid attention to him. The van crept slowly, and the man motioned with his arm to notify the van he was aware.

He turned the corner and saw an empty doorway. The urge to empty his bladder struck, and the scout stepped into the door. The scout unzipped and let it flow. The rain washed away his urine, and he zipped up. The scout turned around, saw no one still watched or cared about his presence, stepped away from the door, felt a hand cup his face around his mouth, and yank him off the ground.

Lifted off the ground, he ripped through the air and hit the floor inside on his back hard. The scout caught his breath and saw the man standing above him dressed in jungle camo gear of black and white. The scout rolled to his feet and charged the man. A kick dislocated his knee, and as the scout fell again to the ground, a fist smashed his face. His world turned silent.

37

A large amount of water splashed into his face and woke him. The scout blinked, cleared his vision, and tried to move; only he couldn't. He jerked his arms and legs but was immobile in an old chair. He tried to yell, but a piece of tape constricted his mouth. The scout looked and saw the man in front of him, smiling. The scout recognized him, and his eyes changed moods. The man fought with the bindings but realized it was useless.

Zack Stack stared at him and held up a thick roll of black tape. "Gorilla Tape. This shit is the bomb," Zack said. "Regular duct tape works generally, but since some ten-year-old girl showed how to get out of regular duct tape bindings on some video, guys like me have changed our ways." Zack put the tape in his backpack and picked up an iron rod found on the floor. "First, I want to apologize for the primitive tools I'm about to use here, but improvisation is necessary sometimes."

The scout mumbled something.

"Let me guess; you just issued me some threat about how I don't know what I'm dealing with or how you're going to kill me or something like that, right?" Zack chuckled. "I think I've heard them all already."

The scout mumbled something again. Zack feigned interest. The scout repeated his mumbling, but Zack sighed.

"Believe me; I understand your frustration with not being able to talk and part of the whole gig here is for me to let you speak. And you will speak. But first, I have to know you're not going to try to scream and yell." The scout remained silent. "It will get worse for you, in the interest of sharing. Unless, of course, you cooperate." Zack ripped the tape off his face. The scout took a deep breath and spat at Zack. "Cock flavored spit. Interesting."

"They're looking for me, and when they find me, they'll find you."

"And I'll do to them what I'm going to do to you. Are you ready to get started?"

The man glared at Zack.

"The picture I showed you before. You know where those two girls are, don't you?"

"I don't know what you're talking about."

Zack gripped the two-foot-long one-inch-thick iron rod in his gloved hand. "Ok. Let's try again. And before you lie to me, I know you work for someone because you're wearing newer Timberlands and have clean fingernails. Plus, you don't smell like you've been in a sewer for the last week. Of course, you were smart enough not to have ID on you or a phone, but this," Zack pulled out a 9-mm Luger pistol, "this isn't something the ordinary homeless person carries around. So, here's your chance. Who are you, and who do you work for?"

"Screw you. I'm not telling you anything." The man grinned. "And I know who you are. You can't do anything to me because the second I get out of here, I'll go to the cops."

Zack nodded. "Yeah, I already considered that. I suspect I'll have some explaining to do in the afterlife, but I'm guessing Old Testament God will show up at my hearing, and after He hears about what you lowlifes are doing to these young girls, I'll get a stern warning at worst." Zack stuck a rag in the man's mouth right before the iron rod smashed into the man's left hand. Blood spurted from the crushed fingers, and the man screamed in pain, muffled through the rag. Zack watched until the man stopped his fight to get loose, and the pain subsided in his hand. "Again, I apologize. This isn't how I like to do this. It just seems less professional." Zack squatted in front of him, his eyes never leaving the glare from the man. "Do you want to try again?" He yanked out the rag.

"I'm not telling you anything."

"You should reconsider. You're about to lose your ability to masturbate and as ugly as you are, I'm guessing the women aren't lining up to date you. But, of course, if you don't talk, you'll end up castrated, so what difference will that make? That is what we call a predicament for you. Where are those two girls?"

The man remained strong. "You're going to have to kill me."

Zack smirked. "Only when you beg me to."

* * * *

Andre drove. He enjoyed this gig: operating a camera and recorder while also playing bodyguard to Julie as she did her work. Julie employed Andre and Mikayla often, as well as Stefani and Darnell. Whoever was available, but Julie always took two people with her when she did her interviews.

Mikayla was abnormally silent in the backseat, but she didn't intend to remain that way. She leaned forward and put her hand on Julie's shoulder. "Jules, I have to ask you something, but I don't want you to get upset with me."

"Why would I get upset with you?"

"It's about Zack."

Andre remained silent.

Julie turned in her seat to see Mikayla easier. "What about him?"

"What's your intention with him?"

"What?"

Mikayla swallowed and knew this was difficult terrain. "I'm sorry. I know it's none of my business, but Zack is one of us. He's a friend, even Stefani's."

Julie pretended confusion. "What are you talking about?"

"You two are sleeping together. Are you a couple again?"

The bluntness made Dre cough.

Julie dropped the blank look and frowned. "Did he tell you?"

"He didn't have to," Mikayla said.

Julie sat normally. "He's been by a few times just to see Cate. That's all."

Dre looked at Jules.

"What about Stefani? She'll be devastated if she finds out."

Julie sighed.

"Jules," Mikayla paused, "I'm sorry. Zack hasn't been himself, and we're worried about him, that's all."

"I know," Jules said softly. "I don't want to hurt him if that's a concern."

"We know you don't want that. None of us do," Dre finally spoke.

Julie looked at Dre. "He invited me to dinner tonight with Ted and his wife."

"And you're going?" Mikayla asked.

"It will be ok," Julie said. "We need to talk anyway. We'll figure it out."

"When you talk to him, convince him to talk to me," Dre said. "He's been back over a week and hasn't talked to me beyond getting his motorcycles."

Julie sighed. "I'll try."

38

Lauren looked at the time. Three o'clock. Her boss, Zack Stack, was a no-show after promising to show her apartments he heard were open today. She sat on the couch in his office and watched television, unhappy with the situation. Worse, she had no idea where Zack was as he wouldn't answer his phone or return a text.

So, Lauren sat in the office, flipped channels, and waited.

Then, the bathroom door opened, and Zack stepped out. Lauren screamed.

"How did you? Where were? OH MY GOD! You scared the hell out of me!"

Zack walked to his desk, opened a drawer, and removed his phone. "Sorry. I had something I had to tie up today."

"How did you come out of your bathroom?"

"By foot," Zack said. He listened to his phone update.

"You are frequently late and out of reach, aren't you?" Lauren asked as she shook her head.

"I am. I've been told it may be one of my most annoying traits."

"The way you avoid answering questions and change the subject is the one that annoys me most. But your refusal to listen is a close second. Third would be how you disappear." Lauren walked close to him. "You should know it's not conducive for making women happy."

"I know. I'm beginning to think that since I screwed up all of my relationships with women that karma is telling me to remain single."

"I've only known you a week, and I agree." Lauren followed Zack into his closet, where he took off his clothes, threw them in a hamper, and took them to a washing machine in the main bathroom. Lauren followed him the entire time. "Why won't you talk to anyone?"

"I'm talking to you," Zack said as the dirty clothes went into the machine, and Zack pressed the necessary buttons to make a heavy wash occur. He turned to her. "Sorry, I'm late."

Lauren watched his every movement. Zack walked towards the shower, turned on the water, and glanced at her. Lauren smiled. Zack shook his head and removed his remaining clothing before he stepped into the steaming hot water and let it cascade over his body. He felt a revival inside of him. Zack turned his head and saw Lauren stand against the sink, watching him. "Why are you staring?"

Lauren uncrossed her arms. "I'm curious about the scars on your body."

Zack washed the soap from his eyes and looked at Lauren. "How much time do you have?"

"I'm not going anywhere."

"Do you still want to see those apartments?"

"You're going to have to show me those apartments, or you can put in a kitchen, and I'll live here. You'll have to get used to sharing a shower with me."

"I should marry you right now."

Lauren laughed. "Solve the mysterious case of Stefani first."

"What's so mysterious about it?"

"Sir, everyone here tells me you love her, and she loves you, yet you two won't speak. So, either you don't love each other, you're secretly seeing her, or something keeps you from her, and don't even get me started with Jules. Sir, forgive me for saying so, but your personal life is a disaster."

Zack wiped the water from his face. "Well, that's a lovely assessment. Don't expect any more marriage proposals from me."

"I'm not marrying someone in love with another person," Lauren said with a grin. "You're trying to change the subject, which tells me I'm onto something. What is it?"

Zack washed suds from his face again and rinsed off. "I've noticed that you aren't calling me sir or Mr. Stack."

"You're very astute today. Talk to me. I'm going to get asked Monday morning when you aren't here, so give me something, so I have something to say."

Zack shut off the water and grabbed a towel. "I'm doing my job. Tell them that. Tell them to do theirs. Do you want to see the apartments or not?"

Altered Vows

* * * *

Lauren fell in love with the first apartment only two doors away from Zack's. It had twice as much square footage as her current apartment and brand-new appliances. The kitchen island with seating for six on one side, new solid wood floors, a security system, a walk-in shower along with a giant soaker tub in the master bath, Lauren told Zack to tell the landlord she'd take it if she could afford it. After Zack told her the price was half of what she currently paid, she wanted to faint. Instead, she jumped onto Zack, hugged him, and kissed him out of excitement. They went back to the office, and Zack left.

Lauren didn't like being alone, nor where Zack headed. So Lauren sat behind Zack's desk and ran her fingers along the wood grain on the edge of the desk. It was a comfortable chair and desk. Lauren understood why Julie preferred to work here.

Zack's laptop sat silently on the desk, which made Lauren think about what Zack was thinking. Hacking into Zack's computer seemed mischievous and secretive, but Lauren thought about Zack's lack of communication skills.

"I'm sorry, Mr. Stack."

She knew his password and clicked on history; what Lauren found amazed her. She saw a file named Hannah Leary. Lauren opened that and was even more amazed. "That secretive little shit! He's been holding out on me. He already knew everything I showed him."

Lauren saw saved pages of a website. It was obscure, hidden behind links and pages and sites that sold worthless trinkets, but Lauren could tell it was professionally done and protected. And there, hidden deep on the website, was the symbol she showed Zack.

Lauren scrolled to another saved page which talked of a place where people come to find themselves. And the purpose behind it all. Lauren noticed the vagueness of the prose. *Behind what all? What purpose?*

The page talked of inner peace, tranquility, humility, and lastly, of escaping the monotony and mutiny faced in everyday life. *The brutal day-to-day triviality, struggling to exist, to matter, to be noticed, to be more than a number, an excuse, an alibi, an acquisition, or a conquest. Why subject yourself to the corporate reality of raping the many to profit the few and exist in obscurity?*

189

Lauren read on, and the message was clear. There's a better way.

It talked of a materialistic world where people gauged themselves by how much they had, not by how much they grew. It talked about how people compared themselves based on their house, their automobile, and their yard.

And said there is a better way. There is only one way.

Lauren scrolled more. The text continued to sell her on how bad her life was and how she missed the point of life and living. But it promised to help the reader out of the rut, the gloom, the insufferable existence, and money-based superficialities of a meaningless life. And if the reader is willing to take the next step, click here.

Lauren saw that Zack had clicked here and saw he added several commands which blocked his identity, location, IP address, everything. He was invisible. Lauren opened her mouth but grinned. "That sneaky little shit."

The page asked for information, which Zack provided, albeit fake. The website said if the reader were desperate for immediate answers and help, the reader could give a cell number, and an *Enlightened One* would make direct and quick contact.

They asked for an address, *for mailing vital information to help you escape the abyss of the modern yet so primitive world.* Lauren facetiously liked that line. So pessimistic, yet it almost made her believe she needed help. Precisely what they wanted, she suspected. And Lauren suspected Zack did a spit-take during hysterical laughter.

Then, the site requested specific questions the reader needed answers to, what problems bothered the reader, and Lauren's favorite: what purpose in life does the reader feel they have or not understood and needs direction?

And lastly, another simple plea for the reader to save themselves from becoming a statistic where so many people are searching for answers they never find and make the ultimate sacrifice: suicide.

But, the text continued, if the reader were ready for enlightenment, improvement, the answers, and a significant purpose both rewarding and fulfilling, please hit the submit button and begin a dialogue with one of the few Enlightened Ones.

Lauren understood the message. *You need to be heard, and we will make sure one of our best will listen.* She couldn't have taught copywriting better herself. *They don't want to be sold; they want to buy. Same principle here. They need this; only they don't know they need it. Yet.*

Lauren saw what Zack drove at, and soon the site turned to a page filled with social media emblems and asked her which ones Zack belonged. The text asked if someone bullied the visitor on any site, ever felt inadequate, ashamed because of looks or body or physical attributes, or felt as if the world didn't understand them and social media exacerbated the problems?

Lauren suspected she understood what the site wanted, but Zack was way ahead of her. The site asked if they could see just one private account to investigate the harmful and debilitating incidents and scathing commentary so *quickly spat out by the self-aggrandized cowards hiding behind a keyboard and a false sense of self-worth while you search for true meaning.*

Lauren smiled. "Sound predatory," she said. Zack commented here that a questionnaire appeared seeking highly personal questions. Male or female. Age. Involved with a significant other. Live alone or together. Zack commented that this was a mining operation. Lauren thought about it and understood.

And she finally saw the symbol repeated. Zack got the screenshot of the character and ended contact there. "Why didn't he tell me? Why have me duplicate his work? How did he find this?"

Zack documented everything clearly, which completely contradicted what most believed about him. And she saw what Zack felt about working with Kilgas. Conflict with a simple note saying check pad for more. Nothing else on his computer; Lauren opened his desk drawers until she found a legal pad with his notes. She read them in awe. "How does he find all of this out? I am so going to let him have it!"

Then the office door opened though she had it locked. And Lauren realized who it was.

Michelle Borman.

Lauren didn't know what to say as Michelle stopped in front of Zack's desk, where Lauren sat. Michelle took a deep breath and smiled.

"Michelle. I've heard a lot about you," Lauren said.

"And I've heard a lot about you, too, Lauren."

"Zack's not here. No one is," Lauren said.

"I know. I came to see you."

"Why?"

"Those men the other night who attacked Zack. Remember them?"

Lauren nodded.

"They found you because of you, Lauren. Not Zack. It was your search that brought them here."

Lauren turned white. Michelle recognized it.

"If you're going to work here for Zack, you need to know a few more things. You're good, but not good enough. Let me show you, and don't tell Zack or anyone I was here." Michelle walked to Lauren's desk, and Lauren followed. Michelle sat down. Lauren stood beside her. "Now, when you're searching as you did, you did almost everything right. But you need to understand fully, nothing, and no one can ever find out what goes on here. And no one can ever look into Zack. I'd like it if you kept me and Dre and Big D in that focus, as well. So, when diving deep into a website like you were, you need to do this first. Pay attention."

39

The minivan door shut quietly; Zack walked around to the driver's side door and got inside. The van started with the push of a button, and Zack secured the seatbelt. Julie Fletcher watched Zack put the vehicle in drive and slowly drove away from the home of Ted Barnes after a nice dinner.

Zack looked at his bare wrist then checked the dash for the time. Half-past ten.

"What's wrong, Zack?"

"What?"

"What?" Julie laughed. "You had two glasses of wine all night, you didn't talk much, and you barely looked at me. Your mind is elsewhere. What's wrong?" She reached across the consul and grabbed his arm.

"Why didn't you tell me you're leaving town?"

"I planned to tell you tonight after we get home. It's only for a few days. Is that Ok?"

"Of course. I'm not your boss," Zack said. "Just as well. I have work anyway."

"For Kilgas." Julie took her hand off of Zack. "How could you work with him after what he did?"

Zack took a deep breath. "It's complicated."

"Because of his missing daughter. You feel you have to save the day again."

"That is my job, Jules, and he did pay me well."

"You shouldn't be working that case. I know how you are, Zack."

Zack turned down another street headed back home. "That sounds like something a girlfriend would say." He looked at her. "Are we there now?"

"That is the mother of your child voicing her desire to have Cate's father in her life a long, long time."

"I will be in her life for a long, long time." Zack looked at Jules. "As long as you let me."

"Of course, I'll let you. It doesn't always have to be you, honey. That's all I'm saying."

Zack made another turn, and the two rode in silence for two minutes. "It's complicated, Jules. This time, it has to be me. What if this were Cate in sixteen years?"

"Don't do that, Zack. That isn't fair. Kilgas almost had you killed, and I spent time in a hospital. Remember? Leopards don't change their spots."

Zack remained silent.

"I know you, and I know you won't back off. But some other people need you, too."

Zack continued to drive. "Are you one of those people?"

Julie sighed. "Zack, is that why you're not yourself tonight? Do you want to talk about us?"

"Is there an us? You and everyone else keeps reminding me of Stefani, and I recently learned I dumped her."

"You did. I saw the letter you sent," Julie countered.

"Yeah, that's what I keep hearing. But yet here we are. What is going on, Jules?"

Julie looked forward but remained silent.

"Jules," Zack said as he parked the minivan in front of his apartment, "what are we doing? Where is this going?"

Julie undid her seatbelt. "Let's go inside so you can see Cate, Ok? Dre and Alysha are babysitting. Dre mentioned you two hadn't spoken much since you've been back."

"I think maybe I'll just head back to my office and sleep there tonight."

"Your pride is more important than your daughter?"

"That's unfair."

"But yet you choose work over Cate." Julie shook her head.

"That's not it, Jules, and you know it."

"No, I don't. Come inside and see your daughter. Prove to me you want to be her father. Then, when I come back, I promise you; we will figure us out."

40

Zack dressed in his closet at the office Sunday morning and looked in the mirror at his tie.

Lauren stood behind him with her arms crossed. "Where are you going dressed for a funeral?"

"Church."

"Which church?"

"The new world order for Nazis and Conmen, or whatever that cult is called."

"You're a treasure chest of bad ideas, sir."

Zack smiled. "You are consistent. It's the start of their Holy Week. Best week of the year to scam their customers."

"Customers?" Lauren rolled her eyes. "Why are you going?"

"I need intel. I got a few morsels yesterday but not enough. Everything about it smells like horseshit, which is an insult to horses, but for lack of a better analogy on short notice, I'll stick with that." Zack fiddled with his tie until Lauren shook her head, moved his hands away, and fixed the knot.

"Sir, I saw what you saw, and they know about you. This is a horrible idea. They'll recognize you immediately."

"I know," Zack said again. "I'm kind of hoping for that."

"Sir, it's time to turn it over to the police before you get injured. If that was who attacked you, what chance do you have if you walk right into their church?"

"Someone said something to me yesterday morning that makes me think we're onto something, Lauren."

"Who? That woman you won't tell me about?"

"Yes." Zack watched Lauren's eyes as she fixed the knot on his tie.

"Who is she, and what did she say?"

Andrew Gruse

"Just a couple of cryptic things. I have to do this, Lauren. If those girls are down there, I have to know. Another girl was found just outside of town. It's just a matter of time before one of them is Hannah or Angie."

"You can't go alone into that church."

"I'll be fine. Besides, rumor on the street is that I have a hero complex."

"Sir, you aren't listening to me! You aren't going alone. Call Dre."

"Sweetheart, religion, in general, isn't as open-minded as you are. So I don't think Dre and I would be accepted there."

"Then I'm going with you."

Zack checked the duffle bag on the floor and zipped it. "Lauren, it's just church. I'm sure it will be some singing, chanting, calisthenics, more chanting, emptying of the wallets, and then a festive song as we leave. Nothing will happen."

Lauren hated his response. She tried a different tactic and put her arms around his neck. "Sir, let's go birding today instead. Birding helps clear your head, and you need to do that. Take me right now. Let's go to a quiet place on the coast and just lay on the beach. We can spend the night somewhere and just chill. Let's go right now."

"Why do you think birding clears my head?"

Lauren turned red. "Mr. Stack, for me, please? I'm asking for this, and I promise you we'll have a great day together. You didn't sleep at all last night after you showed up in your office at three in the morning. You aren't thinking clearly. I told you not to take Jules to dinner. Please, sir, I need you to do this for me."

"Lauren, I saw Cate. I understand how Kilgas feels."

"No, you don't. He's not like you, sir," Lauren almost whispered to him. "No one is." Lauren stared into his eyes. "I'm begging you to listen to me. Please."

Zack hugged her; she clutched tight to him; her fingers dug into the back of his shoulder blades. "Stay here until I get back."

"If you go, I won't be here when you get back if you get back," Lauren said defiantly. "I'm not joking, sir. I will quit right now. So you either take me with you, or I'm quitting."

Zack looked at her. "Lauren, you're not quitting."

"Then I'll quickly get dressed."

"Lauren, you freaked out when three guys attacked me outside your apartment."

"I'm coming with you, or I'm leaving. It's that simple. I'm not allowing you to prescribe your way or the highway here. I know what's going on in your head. I know how this is affecting you, and you need someone with you."

"How would you know how this is affecting me? Are you inside my head? Do you know what I went through in Clyde? Do you know how that ruined my relationship with Jules?"

Lauren sighed and put her hands on the sides of his face. "Yes, I do," she said softly. She let go, walked to his desk, and pulled out the legal pad in his lower left-hand drawer. "I read it all. I'm sorry, Mr. Stack." She walked back to him and stopped inches away. "I'll be ready in ten minutes."

41

"Is that it?"

"Yup."

"The place is huge." Lauren looked through binoculars at the giant building and shook her head. "That place can probably hold five thousand people."

"Eight," Zack said. "Two services per week normally. But this is their Holy Week, so one every day. The parking lot is filling. Never ceases to amaze me." Zack put the minivan in drive and drove towards the property owned by the Church for a New World Order for Christ.

"Sir, religion is essential to some people."

"I know." Zack slowed the car in the line of cars waiting for a parking spot. Well-dressed men directed the cars to line up in an orderly fashion in the mowed field beside the church. "If I have to pay for parking, I'm shooting this guy and driving off."

"You don't like this, do you?"

"I should have taken you birding." Zack looked at the expanding crowd. "Jesus Christ. Remember, we're searching for a new church because the pastor's message at the one we attend doesn't resonate with us. Got it?"

"Don't worry about me, sir. I got this. The worry is you. Besides being recognized, your love of religion ought to make this day exciting. So try to fake it at least, ok?"

"Jesus Christ," Zack muttered again.

"And stop saying that."

The two were directed to follow the next car and pointed where to park. Zack parked, walked to Lauren's side, and opened the door for her. She exited in a black dress, form-fitting, stopped at the knees, with two-inch open-toed heels. The necklace and earrings matched the diamond ring on her ring finger supplied by Zack to complete the ploy. Zack likewise wore a wedding band.

"I have to say, Mr. Stack, you do dress up nice." Lauren smiled at him as they held hands and walked through the parking lot towards the church. "You look good, sir."

"Thank you. You look amazing. I'm not sure that dress is suitable for church."

"You grabbed it. And you picked the heels I would have grabbed. You have good taste."

Zack observed all the activity, including that of the church personnel. "If any of the bullshit we're about to witness appeals to you, you're walking home."

Lauren laughed but spoke quietly. "You better keep your comments quiet. These people don't look like they'd appreciate your views on religion."

"My views are just that, mine, just as theirs should be. I like sex, but I don't go shoving my genitals in their face to prove my way is better, do I? And what we are about to witness is not religion or the practice of it. It is the rape of the vulnerability of people we are about to see, not to mention the obscene profiting of a few via spreading their compromised word of Christ. I promise you this is not what Jesus preached." Zack kept Lauren's hand in his. "If anything does happen, do as I say. Ok?"

"Yes, sir," Lauren grinned with a military-style response.

Zack looked at her and smiled. "You like this, don't you?

Lauren smiled. "So far, being pretend married to you is fun."

"Then wait until the pretend honeymoon."

They walked across the field, past the long line of vehicles to the paved lot, filled with cars and dotted with picturesque plots of landscaping and blooming flowers and small flowering trees. Finally, they approached the massive mega-church. An octagonal shape, the enormous structure was more expansive than a football field.

New and shiny, the building and landscaping around it were nicer than any office building Zack and Lauren had seen on the trip. Thousands of people filed inside. Zack and Lauren approached the main doors and were let inside but had to produce a pass to enter the great hall. A younger pretty woman smiled at them and asked if they were new visitors.

Lauren introduced her and Zack and explained why they were there. The lady pointed them to the far end of the entrance hallway and told them they'd have to register.

"We want to get to know all of our congregation. It's important for us to spread the word of God to our family," she said. "You picked an extraordinary week. It is our Holy Week. What made you choose us?"

"After we heard of this and read the message on your website, we had to come," Lauren said.

Lauren held Zack's hand as most married couples did in the great hall before passing through the high-arched doorways into the congregation hall. The church itself. Zack pretended the part but watched everything. The posters were propaganda but nothing of note.

They came to a table with a professional sign above it for 'New Family Registration.' A pretty woman, early-twenties, stood behind the table. She had dark blonde hair with added light highlights. Full-bodied and dressed well in a tight dress, she smiled widely at Zack and Lauren.

"You must be new," she said. "I know all the families here. My name is Autumn, and I'll be your sponsor for today." She held out her hand to Lauren first and then to Zack. "We would like to be able to follow up with you after your visit here today, so we ask if you would please give us some information."

"Of course," Zack said.

Autumn had a clipboard ready to go. "You're a lovely couple. What are your names?"

"Um, Patricia," Zack said. "But she goes by Pat, and I'm Philip. Phil, for short," he answered. "One L in Philip."

"Of course. And your last name?"

"That would be McCracken. Two C's. The first one small."

Autumn wrote it down and smiled. "Ok, so Pat and Phil McCracken."

Lauren stared at Zack, who didn't even smile.

"Ok, here are your visitor badges for today's service. You can find a seat in the left sections labeled visitors of the church and enjoy. Afterward, I'll be outside in the garden area. Please find me so we can talk further." Autumn smiled again. "You are such a lovely couple."

* * * *

Zack and Lauren walked hand-in-hand to a seat in the back of the visitor's section. Many well-dressed men in nice suits, younger men, like ushers, or security, walked the aisles and stayed spaced evenly about the church. A vast stage with tall red drapes with gold piping stretched from the floor to the thirty-foot tall ceilings filled the front of the great hall. Ornate yet with a hint of the deity inside a church.

Floodlights pointed all over the stage with microphones spaced twenty feet apart. Zack had seen pictures on television of the megachurches and the televangelists preaching from the giant sets. This place did not take a backseat to any. But Zack focused on something different.

Video cameras covered every square inch of the place.

"Smile, honey, we're on candid camera."

Lauren smiled at Zack and casually glanced around the area.

"Pat and Phil McCracken?" Lauren chuckled. "You are such a child."

Zack tried to hide his pride in that creation. "Yeah, I like that one. I don't think Autumn got it."

"I hope not. The quote-unquote ushers looked like they are packing heat," Lauren said.

"Oh, sweetheart, there's a load of cynical comments there." Zack quickly noticed she was right.

Lauren slightly elbowed him. "Remember where we are. God is listening to you. Is it cold in here, or is it me?"

"It's cold in here. Here, take my jacket." Zack slipped off his coat and put it over her shoulders.

"I don't need everyone to see my nipples."

Zack looked, but she covered her chest with his coat. "I've had a difficult time not staring at you in that dress. I should have picked you something less provocative."

"I like what you picked, and I've noticed where your eyes have been, but you were also with Julie last night, so calm down. I'm not interested."

"She wants me to quit what I'm doing. Jules doesn't want my current life to be anywhere near her or Cate," Zack confessed.

Lauren's mouth opened, surprised. "What did you say?"

"I didn't know what to say."

"So that's why you came back late and couldn't sleep."

"Mainly." Zack looked at Lauren. "We didn't talk much."

"What do you want?"

Zack took a long, slow breath. "Honestly, Lauren, where I'm at now," he shook his head, "what I want doesn't matter." Zack looked at Lauren. "I'm not the one in control."

The lights lowered as the drapes rose. A ten-piece band appeared behind the drapes and played. Zack and Lauren followed suit as the rest of the congregation stood, not wanting to be the outcasts.

The songs continued. And went on and on. Zack watched as the congregation swayed and clapped and sang along. All had the same message: Jesus Saves, so put your faith in Him.

After several songs, the pastor or minister walked out on stage with applause.

"He's attractive," Lauren said. "I can see why he's popular."

"He's a conman," Zack scoffed. "You like facial hair?"

"Not on you," said Lauren. "But on him, it works."

"I can grow facial hair if I want."

"You know my stance."

The man spoke, and to Zack, it sounded like a thinly veiled telemarketing call. An overly long and pious infomercial. Like a well-written piece by an advanced copywriter convincing the masses to buy something they didn't need and couldn't afford, and the masses would buy it without hesitation, for they knew the answer they sought was contained in that purchase.

Zack looked around with hopes of seeing members of the youth ministry. They had to be somewhere. But he saw no one even remotely similar to Hannah Leary or her friend, Angie.

More singing. More talking. More stories of people who believed and were saved and how their problems vanished. Not by magic beans bought at a farmer's market that grew into the clouds and provided riches, or even science, but because of their faith in God. The message they received specifically from this church and this church alone. All they had to do was put their belief in this God and this Church because the preacher, the man on stage selling his version, said he talked to God. He has been chosen, touched by the Hand of God, so, therefore, everyone needed to listen to him and only him.

Zack leaned into Lauren. "This guy you find attractive is a jackass."

"You sound like you're jealous."

"If things were different, yes. He talked to God. Are you freaking serious? This guy may have been touched, but it wasn't by anything divine."

"Stop it. You should feel guilty for even thinking that here."

"It's a freaking money laundering scheme, not a Catholic Church. And believe me, the Catholics cornered the market on guilt. I don't see a confessional here. So I'm ok."

Lauren shook her head and softly elbowed him in the side. "I am sure you spent plenty of time in the confessional when you were in school."

"Forgive me, Father, for I have sinned. It has been a month since my last confession, and since that time, well, where do you want me to begin, Father? It's been a good month," Zack joked as if he were in the confessional booth. Lauren covered her mouth to stifle her laughter.

"Stop it. We're here on business."

"If I only had a nickel for all the Our Father's and Hail Mary's I recited from my knees after confession."

"Should I make an inappropriate altar boy joke now?" Lauren covered her smile with her free hand.

Zack almost laughed aloud. He pretended to suppress a cough when other worshippers looked at them. "Thankfully, that never happened where I was an altar boy. Still, with all the Rosary's I had to recite, I'd be a rich man."

"Blessed are you who are poor, for yours is the kingdom of God."

Zack looked at Lauren. "I'm impressed. Suddenly I have an image of you in a Catholic schoolgirl uniform, and it's turning me on."

Lauren leaned close to him. "I still have that uniform. It's a little tighter now but would do the trick." She winked at him. "Too bad you're still in love with Stefani. And Jules. And who knows who else. You're a mess, so that is not going to happen. Now quiet. We're in a church. Stop talking like that."

"By the way, being poor sucks."

"Shut up. They're looking at us."

More singing followed the preacher's rants, and then after nearly two hours, the preacher blessed the congregation. He reminded them the magnificent hall was because of the generosity of God and how God has shown how giving is more important than receiving and how the meek shall inherit the earth.

"The rich are destroying the earth," Zack whispered to Lauren. "They'll be nothing left to inherit, and if there is, the meek won't want it."

"Why would a church like this need so many cameras? Are they broadcasting or searching?"

"Good question." Zack suspected the latter.

The preacher kept going as the ushers appeared with collection baskets and processors for credit and debit cards. They passed them up and down each aisle.

"Give me 20 bucks," Lauren said to Zack.

"Why? Are you buying lunch on the way home?"

"Haha, funny. No, to put in the basket."

"What? I'm not giving this thieving liar any money. He believes less in God than I do, and I've been called Godless. He's not getting any of my money."

"We'll be the only ones not to give."

"And that gives me a sense of satisfaction and pride."

Lauren shook her head at him and dug in her purse. She put her last four dollars in the basket as it went by. "Isn't pride a Cardinal Sin?"

"No, rooting for St. Louis is a Cardinal sin." Zack looked at Lauren expectantly. "Get it?"

"Ugh. Is that a baseball joke? I happen to like the Cardinals. Take me to Busch Stadium any day."

"I will and leave you there. By the way, they should give you a receipt for that since they don't pay taxes."

"Can you at least try to be a little less cynical?"

"I could try, but then I wouldn't be true to myself. Is that schoolgirl uniform plaid? That would be a hot look on you."

Lauren elbowed him in the ribs. "Yes. Focus on why we're here," she whispered forcefully.

"Can you believe this windbag?" Zack whispered. "Lauren," Zack nudged her arm, "I'll bet you twenty bucks the Cubs finish ahead of the Cards in the standings this year."

"Make it forty. The Cubs suck. Now hush."

"This guy is a fraud. He's bilking these poor people out of their life savings." Zack shook his head. "This isn't the place. She's not here. Let's just leave. I feel like my soul is getting sucked out of my body and incinerated."

Lauren turned her head and gave him an evil look as others turned towards Lauren and Zack. She put her index finger over her lips.

Finally, the service ended. The people stood and filed out as orderly as they left. Many knew the people beside them, and they talked as they walked out. Zack and Lauren waited until the place thinned before they headed for the same doorway they entered.

Not surprisingly, Autumn waited for them.

42

Zack saw the vast majority of the seven thousand worshippers headed for their cars unimpeded as they stepped outside into the beautiful sunlit day. Zack put on sunglasses, as did Lauren after she gave him back his jacket. The wide-smiled sponsor, Autumn, met the two quickly.

"Mr. and Mrs. McCracken, it's so good to see you again," Autumn said, her arm extended. She grabbed Lauren's hand first and shook it. Zack saw her shirtsleeve rise on her forearm and show the lower half of a tattoo.

"So, Patricia and Philip, how did you enjoy the service?"

"It was," Zack paused as if searching for the right word, "enlightening."

"Yes, it was enlightening," Lauren said as she eyed Zack.

Autumn caught Zack's eye but focused on Lauren, and her wide smile returned. "Excellent. We hope we connect with new visitors. Come with me into the garden over here."

They walked down a decorative stone paver walkway into a garden with blooming orchids and daffodils and ornamental dogwoods and fruit trees. Tall golden grasses swayed in the light breeze, and Zack heard song sparrows and goldfinches singing in the distance.

They stopped again by Autumn under a tent with a welcoming table. Three other sponsors talked with new visitors. Zack eyed each one, but none fit the description of Summer.

Behind his black sunglasses, Zack scanned everywhere. Particularly the area behind the megachurch conveniently blocked by solid rows of arborvitaes, spruce, and cedar trees.

And several well-dressed men walked in tandem along the front edge. Zack counted four pairs of men, and two of the pair lounged within eyesight and watched Zack and Lauren with the girl named Autumn.

"We always like to spend a little quality time with new visitors to discuss why they visited and see if our prophet's message touched you," Autumn said. "We preach acceptance, not exclusion. God's love was not intended for those based on skin color, societal status, or whether you can afford to attend their school. We don't judge based on tithing or history. We are all the same in God's eyes," Autumn said.

"Not in America," Zack said. Lauren glanced at Zack. Disapproval.

Autumn pretended not to see or hear Zack's cynicism. "In today's society, too many people are left out for far too many unfortunate and unnecessary reasons," Autumn said. "It's easy to get lost amidst the struggles and chaos of today's world with the political divide, the overt corruption, the privilege based on race and wealth, and the fake prophets out there. Ours has truly spoken to God. His word resonates through our messengers. You can see that with the quickly growing congregation."

"That's fascinating," Lauren said, still holding tight to Zack's hand.

"I'm so glad you agree. I have a questionnaire we ask all of our congregation to complete." Autumn smiled and touched Lauren's arm. "Of course, there is no obligation. We merely wish to know what it is you're seeking. Why don't we step inside?" She pointed to a side door of the building. "We have refreshments inside for new guests. It is a gorgeous day, but it is warm under the sun, so why don't we go in and at least have a cup of water to cool off?"

Zack noticed the crowd of suits staring at him and Lauren. It didn't look good. "Oh gosh darn it all," Zack said. "Patricia, darling, we can't." He put his arm around Lauren and gently squeezed her, a signal. Alarm. "We have to be going. I lost track of time." Zack smiled and laughed at his mistake as he kept a close eye on the group slowly gathering around them.

"What?" Lauren said.

"Honey, you know we're expected at your mother's for supper. The last time we were late, all she did was complain the entire time we were there. I couldn't even enjoy her pecan pie, and you know how I love her pecan pie. She lives north of Richmond, so we really must be going."

Lauren showed a faux over-acknowledgment. "Oh, that's right. I can't believe we almost forgot. It was the sermon that spoke to us."

Autumn watched the two and reached below the table.

Zack tightened his grip. "Sweetheart, I promise you we'll come back soon." Zack smiled at Autumn. "I don't want to seem rude, but we really do need to be at her mother's. The first Sunday of the month, she has the family over, and now that my darling Patricia is pregnant," Zack rubbed Lauren's belly, "Mama Cass insists she sees her baby girl as often as possible."

"Oh, you're pregnant? That's so exciting," Autumn said. "I understand. Can you leave an email or phone number so I can follow up with you soon? You're such a lovely couple," she said again.

Zack took the pen. "I'll do it, honey." He wrote down the email address Michelle Borman had specifically for unwanted senders. Michelle was the only person who could access it, and once her response arrived in the inbox, the sender was in a world of trouble. Zack handed back the pen and quickly looked at the men behind them. They stared at Zack but didn't move. "Autumn, thank you so much for your welcoming hospitality. The church is lucky to have someone as lovely as you to do their bidding."

Zack quickly turned and pulled Lauren along with him.

"Oh wait, here," Autumn said as she ran after them carrying a teddy bear. She handed it to Lauren. "It represents our feelings to you. Welcome with open arms, ready for an embrace."

"Thank you," Zack said. "I promise you we'll be back. Thank you again." Zack finally extracted him and Lauren from the premises. They got inside the minivan.

"We attracted a crowd."

"It was either your dress or my charm." Zack started the vehicle. "How about a ride in the country?"

"West?" Lauren smiled. "I'd love to, Phil McCracken."

"I love it when you talk dirty to me. Especially after church."

43

Zack drove the Kia minivan out of the lot and saw the hills of Virginia ahead. He didn't drive leisurely. Three miles down the road, his eyes on the rearview mirror, Zack finally spoke. "Lauren, I need you to slide under me and take over driving."

"Ok."

Zack expected questions and objections, but instead, Lauren kicked off her heels and slid her body under Zack's. Her hands took the wheel, her leg slid under Zack's, and hit the pedal. Zack popped into the passenger seat and then the rear seat. Lauren drove.

"Impressive. Take a right on the next road," Zack said as he took off his sport coat and tie. "That was a great knot, by the way. You'll have to show me how you did that."

"I'll be happy to, sir. What are you doing?"

"Changing. I don't want to ruin this suit." His dress shirt came off. Zack took off his shoes and socks as Lauren took the turn. "Keep an eye on the rearview."

"I am. I told you this was a bad idea. They recognized you the second we walked inside. Did you see anything that could help us?"

Zack folded his dress pants and put them on the seat next to him. "Well, we know they have video surveillance on one-hundred percent of the property we saw, and they are well-staffed with armed guards." Zack unzipped the duffle bag and pulled out his military camouflage clothes. "And we know the missing girls were not inside that church. Follow this road about a half-mile; then you'll come to a left. It won't look like much but take it. That will wind us to where we want to go."

"This is creepy, sir."

Zack dressed as she drove but concentrated on his boots after he got his pants over his knees. Lauren turned at the place Zack noted and realized it was more of a trail than a road. Tall grasses brushed against the vehicle.

"Sir, this isn't a road."

"Just stay on it. It will wind us into the hills and lead us to a logging road. Take a right on that, go down about three hundred yards, and pull off. It's the only opening. That's where we're parking."

"Are your clothes on yet? Sitting back there almost naked telling me we're parking makes me suspicious of your intentions."

Zack chuckled as he finished tying his boots. "You're the one who begged to come along."

"Someone has to keep an eye on you. That's me, sir."

"I've noticed." Zack put on a long sleeve shirt and buttoned it. "You're much better company than Kilgas, that's for sure, though he does buy food, unlike you. Here it comes, pull over up there."

She did and drove as far into the brush as she could. Then, she turned off the vehicle and turned to watch Zack finish dressing. He looked at her and pulled a set out of the duffle bag. "You're next unless you want to stay here or hike in that dress."

"This is a Vera Wang. I'm not ruining it today." She exited the minivan, opened the side sliding door; Zack got out, and Lauren spun. "Unzip me." Zack did. Lauren turned again, and the dress dropped. She stepped out of it, naked, picked it up, and smiled at Zack. "I forgot to tell you I'm not wearing undergarments."

"I already knew. Get dressed."

Lauren grabbed the camouflaged patterned military fatigues. "Will these fit?"

"They'll be close enough." Zack added his sidearm and binoculars to his gear. His Ka-bar slid into a sheath around his leg. "You look good in camouflage. Probably hotter in that school uniform, though."

"You look pretty hot yourself, Mr. Stack. Do I get a weapon?"

"We shouldn't need weapons. You ready?" Zack grabbed water bottles out of the cooler, locked the vehicle, and stuck the keys deep in a pocket. Lauren tied her boots, stood, and nodded. "Let's go. Stay close and keep your eyes open. The last time I went hiking in a forest, well, let's just say it didn't go well for me." The two trekked into the woods back towards the west end of the property containing the church.

* * * *

Zack and Lauren hiked towards the destination. The two stayed close and talked little until they reached a tall crest and could see the grounds to the east, north, and west of the megachurch.

Zack took Lauren's hand, and the two sat. Zack rested his elbows on his knees for support and fixed the binoculars on the land ahead. Still a half-mile out, Zack couldn't see people, but he saw buildings. Several of them, all one story, made of wood, nothing fancy, and what looked like gardens about the area. Smoke rose from a chimney attached to the most prominent building.

"What is it?"

Zack took the binoculars from his neck and handed them to Lauren. "Looks like an encampment, doesn't it?"

"Yeah, like one of those old-time settlements," Lauren said. "Looks fairly primitive. What are you thinking?"

"I'm thinking we may have just found the troubled youth that Pollard and his freaks decide are too troubled to go home," Zack said. Lauren handed him the binoculars. He studied the area again. "Talk about changing the environment for those kids."

"You said they take them to a place where they can gradually intertwine these kids with the real world."

"Like reprogramming."

"Let me see again." Lauren looked through the binoculars and swept the area slowly. "There are four tiny buildings, like outhouses, a few hundred yards east of the encampment. What do you think they are?"

Zack had a thought, and it froze him.

"Sir, are you ok?"

Zack looked at the ground to regain his composure. "Yeah, just thinking."

"If I didn't know better, I'd say we're looking at a cult. I mean, look at it. It's isolated from the world, hidden from society, and looks like the people are living fairly simply. Can we get closer? We need to get closer." Lauren looked to see if it were possible.

Zack stood, grabbed her hand, and yanked her off the ground. "You don't sound like an office manager right now."

"When in Rome, right?"

＊＊＊＊

The last half-mile disappeared slowly. Zack heard every sound beyond each cautious step. To his relief, there were many. That told Zack he and Lauren were alone, save the wildlife, which alerted other animals of Zack and Lauren's presence. They slowly descended the last hill and crouched before a ditch alongside a dirt road. The tree-lined road showed signs of regular use, evidenced by potholes filled with recent rain and tire tracks.

On the other side of the road, amid the thick vegetation allowed to form an almost impenetrable barrier, stood a ten-foot-high chain-link fence topped with a foot of razor wire. To Zack, the obstacle served one purpose.

To prevent leaving.

"Look, down there is a gate," Lauren pointed. "Let's see what's on the other side." Lauren moved, but Zack quickly grabbed her arm and held her back.

"Our day is done. We need to head back."

"Why? Sir, they could be on the other side of that fence. We can put an end to this today."

Zack pointed across the road, elevated to above the fence, thirty feet high. "If we press this position, we get ended today. We're on camera. We need to move out now."

44

Four men exited a white Jeep, two exited a black Jeep, and four left a Dodge Durango. They all stared at the Kia minivan. They held long rifles, AR-15's, and dressed in body armor, a knife strapped to their leg and ammo clips and a sidearm in a service belt.

"They'll be heading back this way. Twenty minutes ago, they left the fence. Break off into teams of two. Stay low, stay quiet."

"And when we find them?"

"You heard the boss. If we can take the man, we take him to find out what he knows. If we can't, we kill him and leave him out here. The woman we take back. The boss wants her."

"I'd like to get a crack at her," said one of the men.

Another chuckled. "Fine piece of ass. Did you see that dress?"

"To hell with the dress. Did you see that body? Damn."

The leader disapproved of the banter. "Be alert. We don't know anything about this guy. Spread out." The leader pointed the teams in the direction and heard the thump-thump-thump of an approaching helicopter. He spoke into his radio. "Eyes in the sky, what do you see?"

"Nothing but canopy. We'll keep flying low and drive them to you. Over."

"Roger that. Over and out." He hooked the radio to his belt. "Let's get to work, gentlemen."

* * * *

Zack watched through his binoculars as they spread out. He sized up the men quickly. Militia wannabes. They dressed the part and acted the part, but Zack smelled it on these men. Acting the role was the polar opposite of being there and doing it.

Zack had been there. It was easy to spot the pretenders.

"Oh goodie," Zack said softly to the crouched Lauren beside him. "We attracted a search party." He handed Lauren the binoculars.

"They have bigger guns than you do. This is not good. What do we do, sir?" Lauren watched the men fan out as they scampered down the hill through the trees and grasses in search of their prey.

"We do nothing," Zack said, emphasizing we. "I will get us out of this, but you are going to hide where I tell you."

"What?"

Zack took Lauren's hand and led her north as the men fanned out east by southeast and northeast. They descended a hill, reached a stream, hopped over it, dashed through a small clearing, and settled on the edge under a thick canopy, hidden by waist-high brush and grasses. "You're going to stay here. I'll clear us a path so we can get back to the vehicle and get out of here."

"No, I'm coming with you. It's ten to one without me. That's too many for you."

"I don't recall seeing twelve years of combat training on your resume."

Lauren gave him an angry look but silenced.

Zack put his hand on her face. "Don't worry. Nothing is going to happen to you."

"Sir, make sure nothing happens to you."

* * * *

The wind gently swayed the grasses and tree branches. A soft whooshing noise and a few bird and animal noises prevented complete silence. A low-flying helicopter stayed south of the area Zack and Lauren hid. Zack handed the binoculars to Lauren as he eyed the closest pair of men on the far north end of the line they established to flush Zack and Lauren. "Don't lose those. That's my favorite birding pair. I've seen over two thousand species with those."

"Of birds? Are you kidding me?"

"And I plan to see at least that many more," Zack said. He kept his focus on the two men nearest them, a hundred yards away.

"Get us home safely, and I'll travel with you to see each one."

Zack quickly winked at Lauren. "Stay here and don't make a sound."

Two men approached, but one continued east as the closest man veered north, straight at Zack and Lauren's position. The birds stopped squawking, and only the wind and distant helicopter created any noise. The closest man stopped, listened, heard the stream, and trekked towards it. The man remained alert as he reached the stream. He knelt, took a canteen out of his beltline, unscrewed the top, and held the canteen under the water.

The man looked around, thought he heard noises, returned to focus on his canteen, lifted it out of the stream, and took a drink. He screwed the top on the canteen when a hand grabbed the back of his head and slammed him into the stream. The man struggled, but his head remained entirely underwater. He kicked and fought and splashed, he reached for his sidearm, but his assailant slammed an elbow into his head, hit his shoulder blade with something hard and metal. The man coughed for air, felt himself get lifted, and got bashed.

The struggle stopped.

* * * *

Zack yanked the man out of the stream, drug him to the hedgerow, and dropped him. Zack knelt next to Lauren.

"Well, that was subtle, Mr. Stack," Lauren said. "I assumed you wanted to be quiet." Lauren stared at him in disbelief.

"Have you ever fired a gun?" Zack pulled the AR-15 from the man and his sidearm.

"This is America. Who *hasn't* fired a gun? Give me the handgun. I don't like assault rifles."

Zack handed Lauren the 1911 Ronin pistol. "This is ready to fire, but do me a favor and don't shoot me." Lauren motioned for the gun, but Zack kept it from her a second longer so she'd look at him. "I'm not negotiable on that. Don't shoot me."

Lauren showed a smile. "You must have a history with past girlfriends to say that." She took the gun and readied the chamber. "I'm not your girlfriend. Don't worry."

Zack slowly pulled Lauren lower in the grasses. "Here comes his partner. Stay here."

* * * *

The man's partner soon realized his pairing wasn't there. He looked to his right but couldn't see the other pair as they descended the next hill. He turned north to find his partner and reached the stream. His partner's canteen lay on the opposite bank. "Doug?" The man wrapped the strap on the gun around his forearm and crouched, ready for battle. "Doug, where are you?"

He hopped over the stream, picked up the canteen, and saw the drag marks. He followed them, saw his buddy's boots splayed, and knew Doug was either dead or unconscious. The man grabbed his radio from his belt, put it to his mouth when a log smashed over his head.

Zack tossed the large branch aside, grabbed the radio, and heard the approaching sound of a helicopter as he removed the handgun from the unconscious man, unloaded it, and tossed the gun into the stream. He snapped the AR into two pieces and tossed them aside while he returned to Lauren. "Move fast. We have to get to those trees." They ran south to get behind the other eight men.

They reached a solid stand of Butternut Hickory trees as the helicopter flew over, circled, and flew back towards the compound. Zack waited until it disappeared, and the whomp-whomp of the whirring blades didn't distort his hearing.

"Where are they?"

"Two are directly east of us," Zack said. "One of them is wearing too much cologne. Can you smell it?"

Lauren sniffed several times and grinned. "I can."

"Which means if the wind changes, they'll smell your perfume."

"We could make a straight line to the vehicle from here."

Zack scanned the area as much as he could, but the foliage made it difficult. The helicopter circled again. "No, we can't. Not yet. There's still too many of them, including the leader who likely stayed close to our vehicle." Zack watched Lauren, but her eyes didn't give away her mood. There was no fear or trepidation. Instead, she acted calm and measured. Zack ducked. He heard twigs snap in the distance, southwest of their position. "Stay here." Zack disappeared.

Lauren didn't stay there.

45

Zack readied for the two men, split by twenty yards, as they unknowingly approached. Zack waited for them to separate. The wind rushed past; a woodpecker shrieked an alarm and flew off. Then silence. The closest man to Zack stepped over a fallen log, approached a thick bramble patch, and circled it, unwittingly putting himself in the line of fire.

The man looked to his left and right, stepped around the tree, a hand clasped over his mouth, and slammed him against the tree. Stunned, he lifted off the ground, went sideways, and his body collided violently with the earth. Before he could react, the AR-15 ripped from him, and the butt of the gun smashed into his face. Out cold.

Zack knelt, looked around but didn't see an armed man at the crest of the hill to the west, directly in sight of Zack. The man crouched and aimed his AR-15. The target and his back sat square in the scope: one shot, one kill.

* * * *

A hand grabbed the barrel of the long rifle, ripped it straight up and out of the gunman's hands, ripped the strap off him, spun the gun around, and the butt smashed into the man's face. The man hit the ground, was kicked ferociously, and lost consciousness. Lauren quickly knelt beside the man, her eyes barely on Zack, who heard the commotion and looked. Zack didn't see her, nor did she want him to. Zack was good, but only one. And she, Lauren knew they believed, was just a helpless woman.

Pity them.

* * * *

Zack saw his victim's partner move through the rough underbelly of the forest. The prey looked uneasy and nervous. The man climbed over an embankment, knelt, and readied to fire though he didn't know at what. He viewed the thick forest through his scope but saw nothing, so he hurried down the embankment and climbed a low ridge. He wanted to yell out but knew he couldn't.

He felt alone. And scared.

He picked up his pace. They had been out there too long not to have found the couple. The man took a deep breath. "Will?" He called out. He moved forward, stepped on a thick branch. The branch rolled; he rolled with it and hit the forest floor. Ten feet later, he stopped at the base of the ridge on his belly. He raised his head and saw two feet in front of him. He looked. Zack smiled.

"Hi. How are ya?"

The rifle smashed his head.

Zack retraced his steps and returned to where he left Lauren, but she wasn't there. Instead, Zack heard footsteps, crouched, and readied his weapon. Then, Lauren appeared with a smile on her face.

"Sorry," she said. "I thought I heard something and hid. What now?"

The helicopter returned and flew overhead. Zack heard chatter on the radio. Zack realized the leader discovered some of his men weren't replying.

"We retreat to the car before they do and get out of here. Are you ok?"

Lauren nodded, a concerned look on her face. "Get us home, sir. Your new couch is waiting."

* * * *

The leader leaned his back against an oak tree to steal a sip of water. Atop the crest at the edge of the clearing where they found the Kia minivan, the leader waited if the couple outsmarted his crew and returned. They weren't getting past him. They had been out there an hour. No sounds or sight of the couple, but they couldn't get far. He sipped the water, replaced his canteen, and grabbed the radio. He stepped away from the thick oak, heard the helicopter circle, and head east, pressed the button and the barrel of a Sig Sauer P229 pressed against his forehead.

In front of him was the man they searched for, Zack Stack, with a big grin on his face, and he shook his head no. Stack took the radio from the man and tossed it away. Stack pulled out his large knife and sliced through the strap of the AR-15 easily. The gun dropped to the ground. The leader watched Stack's eyes. They never wavered, blinked, anything—pure focus.

Next was the leader's sidearm. Again, removed from the holster and tossed into the forest.

"Where's the girl?"

"Interesting question," Zack said. "You're one wrong move from losing your frontal, parietal, and occipital lobes, and you're asking about the girl."

"I'm just making it easier for my men to kill you both," the leader said. "There's a sniper on that ridge with you in his sites right now."

Zack shook his head. "No, he's not. You don't have to die. Neither do your men. I'll let you walk. Tell me what goes on inside that fence."

"The work of God. Something you know little about."

"Ugh. You're one of those. You people are so tiring."

"We'll kill you and when we find the girl," the man smiled.

"Now, *that* is most definitely not the work of God. I want to read whatever version of the Bible you psychos read. It must be fascinating to be able to self-righteously pick and choose which of Jesus' preaching's you follow, and disregard based on your *beliefs*."

"Says the man with a gun at my head. You won't shoot. A man of God, such as yourself, won't shoot me. Not after that nice speech attempting to point out my hypocrisy."

"Trust me. I am most definitely NOT a man of God."

The leader yelled. "HE'S RIGHT HERE! STACK IS RIGHT…"

The sudden gunshot stopped the man's voice. Zack expected yelling, gunshots, anything. Instead, the only movement or sound was Lauren exiting the brush alone. "Start the vehicle." As Lauren started the minivan, Zack shot out the tires of the other vehicles. He reloaded his Sig and walked back to the minivan. "Where's the stupid bear?"

Lauren handed him the teddy bear. Zack ripped open the head.

"Check the heart."

Zack did and found the transmitter. A GPS location device. He chucked it and the shredded bear out the window. "Let's see how this thing handles."

"Before you destroy it, Mr. Stack, remember I didn't pay for the insurance."

"Good to know. Would you mind monitoring the radio? Sooner or later, they'll find out their leader just got a botched lobotomy. That might cause them to follow us."

"Something tells me I doubt that," Lauren said as she grabbed the confiscated hand-held receiver/radio and turned up the volume.

After several minutes of spirited riding on the poor mountain roads, there was chatter. The helicopter requested an update from the wolfpack leader. Nothing. Again, the aircraft called for an update but received no reply.

"There were ten. Why aren't any of the others responding?" Zack said.

"I don't know. Maybe the others realized they were playing pretend soldier like you said, panicked when they saw you shot their boss in the face, and ran away like cowards, again as you said they would."

"Well, forehead technically, and I did warn him. That doesn't make sense," Zack said.

More chatter from the helicopter, and finally, the aircraft called the base. Zack and Lauren listened.

"Base, this is Eagle One, over. I've tried repeatedly to contact Wolfpack One. There's been no reply. Please advise."

After a moment of static, the reply came. "Eagle One, this is base. Were all radios working properly before incursion? Over."

"Affirmative, base. Five teams, five radios. There's no response. The canopy blocks the view, but we've seen no movement below. I recommend sending out another team. There could be trouble down there. Over."

More static. "Roger that, Eagle One. This won't make the boss happy. Hold position until further notice. Over."

Zack grabbed the radio, rolled down the window, and chucked it. The radio shattered into several pieces as it hit the paved road. Zack pressed the accelerator, and the minivan raced west, far away from the area with no helicopter in sight.

Lauren looked at him. "Your hand is bleeding."

Zack noticed the wound on the back of his hand. Superficial. He saw her left hand: the ring was gone. He noticed something else. "So is yours."

Lauren looked. "I snagged it on a bramble. Hurt like hell. Are you ok? You aren't yourself, sir."

Zack knew he wasn't the Zack Lauren knew. This was combat.

"Adrenaline, that's all."

Lauren took a deep breath. "How long does it take for you to calm down?"

"Several hours. Why?"

"However you do it, count me in. I'm pretty pumped right now, too."

46

Lewis Colson entered the estate after a long day on an airplane and dealing with airports. He dropped his bags as a servant ran out to greet him. He recognized the servant. With them for almost a year, she followed orders, no matter what.

Lewis dealt with the servant and asked where the Minister was. The servant told him, and Lewis dismissed her. He would summon her if needed again. Lewis walked through the estate hallways and rooms and found his brother seated behind a big oak desk in the study. A magnificent study with walls lined with bookshelves and portraits, ornate draperies, chandeliers, and of course, a well-stocked wet bar.

Lewis went straight to the bar. He poured himself a gin and tonic and swigged it. Garrett looked up from the ledger he studied.

"Nice to see you, too, brother. How was the trip?"

Lewis finished the gin and tonic and poured another. "Successful. All should be good now."

"No, it's not. We have serious problems. The PI was here today. He stepped foot inside our church, and we saw him snooping at the western edge of the property," Garrett barked. "I sent ten men after him. Four were killed. The rest were incapacitated. All is not good now."

"Did they escape?"

"What do you think, Lewis? Yes, the PI escaped, and he's getting too close."

"Then we have to stop him."

"I'm afraid we're getting too much attention."

"Then you should make some phone calls, Garrett. You're the boss around here. Not me."

Garrett Colson shook his head. "I think that Stack sonofabitch was the guy who caught and tortured our scout. If he's working with the police,"

"So what? Baltimore police can't do anything to us. If they turn it over to the locals or the Feds, we'll be fine."

"You're missing the point, Lewis! This has gone too far."

Lewis finished his drink and sat down. "Relax, Garrett. No one is going to knock on our door. We have friends in high places. We paid for those friends and that protection. If we don't get that protection, we threaten to sing. That will keep us safe."

"Are you not listening to me?" Garrett wiped his face. "I think it's time to relocate. With the girls you keep dumping, it's getting too hot here."

Lewis laughed. "Are you kidding? They'll never tie those girls to us."

"Can we afford to take that chance?"

"Ok. Let's suppose you're not panicking. What do we do next?"

Garrett paced slowly. "First, I'll call our clout. That sonofabitch better have a backbone. Second, Pollard is weak. The FBI already talked to him once. I can stop that investigation, but if they put pressure on him, he'll crack. It could spread. If they come in and dig up the bodies on the grounds, we'll be finished." Garrett sat and adjusted his position in the fluffy black leather chair. "I think we have a huge sermon next weekend and clear out of here."

"What about Summer? Is she still in the field? We either have to cut ties with her or bring her with us."

"I sent her on a mission. Then we eliminate her. But I need to know what they know and who else knows. Somehow, they got onto us, and I want to know how." Garrett watched his younger brother.

"I'll make arrangements for our departure. I'll put the jet on stand-by."

"I think that would be prudent. We'll see what our spiritual guidance is worth. Giving large donations and suggesting to our congregation who to vote for doesn't come without strings."

"And the flock?"

Garrett didn't hesitate. "Pick our four most ardent believers, have them load the flock on the motorcoach, and send them to Arizona. Make sure they understand how important the delivery is. Then, once they get to the desert in Arizona or wherever the hell they end up, they can all experience a rapture. It's what they all expect since we convinced them this world isn't worth living. Make sure Summer has plenty of eyes on her."

Lewis never underestimated the brutality and heartlessness of his brother. Garrett, after all, was the one who first started to kill the young girls who didn't commit to the Enlightenment. Garrett, however, shot the girls in the face as they cried and begged for their lives. Lewis felt his style of execution was more humane. In the end, though, Lewis knew Garrett wouldn't hesitate to kill him if he failed his older brother. "I'll get on it right after I blow off some steam. I think the servant will do tonight."

47

The office of the Dre-Zack Detective Agency filled early that morning with one notable exception and one odd addition. Zack was missing. Kilgas, however, sat in the front office with Dre, Darnell, Lauren, and Mikayla. Dre waited for the group to assemble and checked his timepiece regularly. Once everyone grabbed their coffee and settled, Dre began the frequent "Zack's Status Meeting."

"Ok, does anyone know where Zack is?"

No one knew.

"Lauren, you don't know?" Dre asked directly.

She held her arms across her chest and shook her head no.

They all looked at Kilgas.

"Don't look at me. I never saw Stack. I looked for him, but he disappeared before I got back from my other engagements yesterday morning."

Dre looked at Kilgas. "Other engagements?"

"Relax. I'm currently getting paid well to provide protection, including for everyone here and our missing leader."

"If you don't know where he is, how can you protect Zack?" Mikayla asked.

Kilgas smiled. "I can't. Perhaps Lauren, with all due respect, is holding out on us."

Lauren's face changed to shock as she looked at Kilgas.

Mikayla exhaled through her nose. "What are you saying?"

Kilgas shrugged. "I know he has been spending his nights with Julie, but she left town, and Zack wasn't at his place. So I just figured Lauren would know his whereabouts."

"I don't know where he is, and if you are insinuating something beyond a working relationship between Mr. Stack and me, you are dreadfully wrong," Lauren scoffed.

Kilgas smiled. "I meant no disrespect."

Darnell shook his head. He didn't like Kilgas at all. "We hired her to care about him. That's her job."

Kilgas said nothing.

"Is he working your case?"

Kilgas nodded. "He is. Not exclusively, though. You guys seem to have a lot of work and not enough human resources."

"Currently, we are in a state of flux," Dre said. "Does he take calls from anyone?"

"Sometimes he answers my calls," Kilgas said.

"He'd probably answer a call from Jules or Stefani," Darnell said.

"I wouldn't bet on that," Lauren said. "He seriously dislikes his phone currently. I don't know why."

Kilgas spoke. "I know I'm not one of you guys, but what happened there? That guy was so head over heels with Stefani; why aren't they together?"

"We don't know. Stef said he dumped her."

Kilgas nodded. "How?"

"Via a letter."

Kilgas rubbed his forehead. "Stack wrote her a letter and dumped her?" He laughed. "That ain't Stack."

"Well, that's what happened," Mikayla said. "I've talked to Jules a lot lately. She's worried about you, Kilgas."

"I have told you all repeatedly; I'm an ally. And I need you guys to find my daughter. Besides, I'm getting paid well to keep him alive, and consequently, all of you."

Darnell spoke. "And what happens when someone pays you to kill Zack?"

Kilgas looked at Darnell and knew Darnell didn't trust or like him. Kilgas understood he deserved that. "I promised Stack I'd talk to him first so we can make a deal. But, I'm telling you, that's not me. I like you guys."

"Dre, you need to talk to him," Mikayla said. "He's good with me again, mostly, but he's guarded. It has to be you. We need to know what's going on so whatever he is doing doesn't blow back on us."

"It's not like I'm not asking him to meet. I'll keep trying. Lauren, he talks to you. What's going on?"

"He doesn't say much to me. As far as I know, he's spending all his time finding Hannah Leary and her friend."

"I'll track him down and talk to him. I think once we get this case closed, he'll return to being the Zack you guys know," Kilgas said. "Maybe then we can figure out what happened with Stefani."

Dre stared at Kilgas. "Do you know something we don't?"

Kilgas shook his head. "Nope. I wish I did."

"You've been following him for a long time, Kilgas," Darnell said. "What aren't you telling us?"

Kilgas felt all eyes on him. "I don't know anything. I'm just speculating based on my observations, and I'm telling you Zack would never send a letter to Stefani to dump her. That man was and still is in love with her. He wouldn't send a letter. Stefani's a bull in a China shop. If he were to send her a letter, she would have dropped everything, driven up there, and beat his ass. Something doesn't feel right about that." Kilgas watched everyone ponder his analysis. Kilgas's phone buzzed, and he looked at it. Kilgas stood. "Speak of the devil. Our boy wants to meet. Says we have business to tend to." He looked at everyone. "Don't worry. I won't let anything happen to him. I'll meet with him, find out where we are on my daughter, if I'm fortunate, he'll be in a rare talking mood."

The group chuckled at the possibility or likelihood of it not happening.

"And if he doesn't talk to any of you, I'll be back tomorrow to give you an update." His phone buzzed again, and Kilgas typed a text reply. "He's in a mood, ladies and gentlemen." Kilgas smiled. "I better get going."

Dre, Darnell, and Mikayla stood silently for a moment after Kilgas left until Darnell shook his head. "How in the world did it become that guy is the one we're relying on for information about Zack?"

"Where did Julie go?" Lauren asked.

"Her parents have a winter home out west somewhere," Dre said. "She's there."

"Only for a couple of days," Mikayla said. "Does Zack know?" They all looked at Lauren.

Lauren answered. "Yes." She knew they expected more, but she remained silent.

Mikayla walked to the door. "You know what? I think I'm going to find Stefani today and talk to her. Rumor has it a couple of shots, and a glass of wine gets her to talk. So I'll try it."

Dre and Darnell shook their heads. "Man, if we did that, we'd end up in jail."

Mikayla laughed. "It's all about confidence, so I've been told." She winked and left.

Dre looked at his watch. "I'm late for an appointment. I'll be back later."

Darnell stood and nodded at Dre, then to Lauren. "I have business myself. See you later."

Lauren watched everyone leave. "Now I know what Michelle must have felt like all the time."

48

Zack walked onto the porch and scanned the area as Kilgas knocked on the door of the house. The farm country of Northern Virginia didn't sing as loud or shine as bright as usual. Clouds scattered across the sky but kept the sun behind a blockade. Another June rain seemed imminent.

"Nothing," Kilgas said. "I don't see a car, and there's no noise inside. How was the church?"

"Unlocked but empty," Zack said. "And the sacristy was sacked."

"Sacked? Like a quarterback or?"

"As in like the fall of Rome. Some say ransacked. I was trying to use fewer syllables today so thank you for ruining that plan."

Kilgas smiled. "Robbery?"

"No, something else," Zack guessed. "The computer was smashed. If it were a robbery, they would have stolen it. Other than the five-dollar per liter of wine, there was nothing of value in there."

"Five dollars per liter of wine is value?"

Zack noticed that no Eastern Meadowlarks or Song Sparrows sang, which they should have been in that habitat. "If you can't afford good wine, yes. Do you think it's quiet, or is that just me?"

Kilgas listened. "We're in the middle of nowhere with no people within twenty miles. How loud should it be?"

"Look in a window or something, and let's get out of here."

Kilgas walked to the nearest window and looked inside. Then, on the third window, as Zack walked off the porch to see further in each direction, Kilgas spoke. "Uh, Stack, we have a problem."

Zack spun around. "What?"

Kilgas wiped off the window. "Come look at this and don't touch anything."

* * * *

The front door opened, not locked, and the two men stepped inside carefully. They both wore latex gloves. They weren't about to leave fingerprints. The reason lay on the floor in a pool of blood.

Bradley Pollard.

"He's dead. Shot in the back of the head," Zack said. "Just like the girls." Zack looked at the blood. "Relatively fresh. This is not good."

"Where's his family?"

The two men looked at each other, then frantically searched the rest of the house. Finally, Kilgas returned to the body when Zack returned from the kitchen with a note in his gloved hand. "Safe, thank God," Zack said. He showed Kilgas the message.

"Fortuitous, lucky, or planted?" Kilgas asked. Pollard's wife left a note saying she took the kids to her parents at their summer home in Virginia Beach for the weekend.

"We're not going to stick around long enough to find out," Zack said.

"I agree, Stack. But this is an opportunity. Badge or gun?"

"What?"

"Don't ask questions. Badge or gun? You know what I mean."

Zack thought for a moment and remembered Michelle. "Ok. Badge."

Kilgas handed Zack a badge.

"How did you get his gun?" Zack asked as he tossed the badge into the living room, kicked over a table, knocked over chairs, and put the couch on its back. A couple more distressing actions and Zack stepped back.

"The same way I got his badge. You have your friends. I have mine."

"Does he know it's you or, more importantly, me?"

"You're smarter than that, Stack. This FBI agent won't be singing or coming looking for either of us. Step back. This isn't going to be pretty." Kilgas aimed the gun and fired it into the dead man four times.

"There are laws about that, and any decent investigator will know these shots were postmortem," Zack said.

"So what? Make it look like the gunman had to escape quickly and dropped the gun."

"You got it." Zack picked up a chair and threw it through the front window. Zack checked the area one last time before they stepped onto the porch. "Do you hear that?"

"Yup. Sirens coming from the east."

"I'll drive."

The two ran back to the minivan and sped down the road to the north. They both watched, but no one followed. The cornfield stopped at a country road, Zack turned west onto it and stopped on the shoulder. The land to the west was a tree-covered hill. "Let's take a look," he said. With the house barely visible on the horizon, Zack and Kilgas found a vantage point and viewed the house via Zack's spotting scope.

"First responders," Kilgas said. "An ambulance, volunteer firemen, and a cop from town. They had to be called."

"But why? He couldn't have been shot more than twenty minutes ago. So why call it in?"

"You're the detective. You tell me."

"There was no one around. They couldn't have seen us," Zack surmised.

"Look at us right now."

"We're on the right track. They're closing shop, Kilgas."

"Which means my daughter is in harm's way. Do you know where she is?"

"Not exactly." Zack carried the scope to the minivan.

"So, what do we do?"

"Get the hell away from here. A helicopter is coming. Hear that?" They got into the minivan.

"Yeah, so?"

"We don't want to get spotted. Trust me. Let's get back and go fishing. Since I'm helping you, you're going to help me."

49

Ronald, the FBI Guy, always took a different route to his Monday night appointment, and he always kept a watchful eye. Ronald spotted an unwanted sightseer before; he didn't want any other onlookers spotting him again.

Always suspicious, Ronald kept track of all the vehicles. He knew how to spot a tail.

Ronald reached the neighborhood he desired, confident in his privacy. He had a seven o'clock appointment only two blocks up the street. Ronald carefully watched each car or motorcycle he passed, inspected each person walking on the sidewalk, and parked in the regular spot across from the house after declaring it safe.

The house of Andrea Whitehead.

Ronald sat in the car three minutes since he was early. Promptness was appreciated and rewarded in this line of work. Here, he experienced an erotic pleasure his girlfriend Michelle Borman would never accept, encourage, or participate. The archaic Puritanical views of much of America, brought over from England and Europe during the migration to the New World, still prevailed in the minds of many.

But to others, both men and women, some itches needed to be scratched. And Andrea was good at it. And her clientele and the clientele of the others associated with Andrea required secrecy. Because of the protection he and a few of his colleagues could provide, Ronald benefitted twofold. First, tonight was the primal benefit he enjoyed. Second, because of this, it allowed him to maintain a normal, albeit stale, sexual relationship with Michelle. Perhaps someday, he'd flirt with the idea of sharing some of it with Michelle to see if she'd be open to experimenting in submissiveness, dominance, objectification, or queening. Ronald experimented and enjoyed everything but ensured no bodily marks were left that wouldn't disappear before he got home.

Ronald made a phone call. "Where is he?" Ronald asked when the other line answered.

"Looks like he's still in his office. He returned earlier with that Leary guy, entered the front door, and no one has left since."

"Do you have eyes on the back?"

"He can't get into that alley without us seeing. So he's still there."

Ronald kept an eye on the neighborhood. "Good. I have an appointment. I'll check in after."

Confident in the area's security, Ronald got out of the car, walked across the street, knocked on the door, and waited. Finally, the door opened, and the beautiful Andrea Whitehead smiled, opened her home to him, and the two kissed on the cheek as he entered.

Directly across the street, inside the house in a second-floor bedroom, sat Kilgas. He watched Ronald enter the house as his video camera captured everything. Kilgas smiled and said to no one, "Stack, you owe me again." The night was complete. He packed his gear, walked downstairs, handed the owners another stack of fifty hundred-dollar bills, thanked them for their cooperation, and reminded them their silence was essential in the investigation.

Kilgas left through the backdoor and realized he enjoyed impersonating a federal officer.

If only the job paid better.

50

Lauren needed clothes. Her refusal to return confused Zack after witnessing her fortitude yesterday in the hills of Virginia while being hunted. Not what he expected. Her lack of shock or surprise after watching him operate confused Zack as well. Zack knew he had eyes on him but still rode his motorcycle away from the office.

Another cat-and-mouse exercise.

Losing his followers was a fun habit for Zack. He got to know the streets of Baltimore so well; Zack felt he could ditch anyone following him. He was right again this night.

Alone now, Zack made his way to Lauren's former apartment. He parked his only motorcycle on the side of the street across from her building and scanned the area. Though after dark, people did walk along the waterfront. Some with dogs, others just to walk with their significant other. Nothing looked out of place. Zack secured the motorcycle and headed inside.

The hallways and stairs were empty. Zack reached Lauren's door and used the key to enter her apartment. It didn't look different than when he visited before. Zack locked the door behind him, flicked on the lights, and entered the kitchen. He opened the refrigerator, saw a six-pack of Sam Adams Boston Lager and one lone plastic bottle of Pepsi. Zack smiled. He went to the bedroom and packed clothes. His phone rang. Lauren.

"Hi," he said.

"Are you at my old place?"

"Packing clothes as we speak."

"Good. Will you be long?"

"Nope. Have your stuff packed almost."

"Ok, Awesome Sauce. Did you learn anything today?"

"Enough. But no police knocked on our doors, so I think we're good. Anything else?"

"No, sir," Lauren said. "Just checking on you and making sure you're not causing trouble."

"Not tonight." Zack exhaled slowly. "Not tonight. I'll see you soon."

"Ok, bye."

Zack put down the phone and stared at it. He realized he had too many things to sort, starting with Julie. Then, the mysterious case of Stefani. He thought of Stefani. Seeing her with another guy hurt more than he thought it would. *Why did she convince everyone I dumped her? And why would she fake a letter to prove it? I need to talk to her.*

Zack showered and slipped into the clean clothes. Keeping an extra set at her place was Lauren's idea. He looked at his cell phone. Mikayla texted, 'call me.' Dre and Darnell both messaged about a drink special and said to meet them. Zack texted them all, saying he got busy and they'd talk tomorrow. Fortunately, he received no replies. Then, Zack heard Michelle's voice again. *It's time to put water under the bridge, Zack. Quit being stubborn and just talk to them.*

Zack wondered why it was water under the bridge. *Was it ever over the bridge? Why is there always a bridge? Cross that bridge when we get to it, bridge over troubled water, water under the bridge. What is it with bridges?*

Zack walked to the kitchen and heard a knock on the door. Zack opened the door and saw the blonde in front of him. He knew his face gave it away and saw her face recognize his recognition.

She stood there, looked both ways, and stepped closer. "I heard you're looking for me."

"Summer."

"The one and only."

The girl stood in cut-off blue-jean shorts and a yellow tank top with no bra. A sun emblem on the front with a rainbow of colors cascaded from the sun, but the chilly hallway made the no bra evident, and Summer wasn't ashamed.

"How did you find me?"

"You're an easy man to spot. You shouldn't have entered the church yesterday."

"What can I say? I felt the Lord's calling. What are you doing here?"

"I'm interested in a parley," she said. "I've played their game too long. I need out, and you're the only person I think can help."

Zack listened and waited. He quickly stuck his head out the door.

Summer chuckled. "I'm alone. It wasn't easy."

"Yeah, if you found me this easy, I'm sure they can." Zack grabbed her, yanked her inside, and pushed her against the locked door. "What are you doing here?"

"I just told you," she said uncomfortably. "You're hurting me."

"Not yet, I'm not. Why are you here?"

"I told you! Oww, stop," Summer cried. "Mr. Stack, I swear to you. I want out. They'll kill me if they catch me here. I need protection. I need your help. That's the truth."

Zack stared into her blue eyes. She was young; Zack guessed early twenties. He let go and stepped back. "And how do I know you're here alone?"

"You don't, but if I weren't, the guys they sent with would have already tried to take you. I escaped, and I'd say we have another hour." Summer stepped forward. "You want to interrogate me now? Let's get started. But not here," Summer added.

"Why not?"

"They'll find us here. We should go to your office."

Zack checked the closed window-shades. "That's oddly specific. Why there?"

"You have information on the people kidnapping those kids. I want to see it. I think I can fill in the gaps for you." She smiled. "You impress me as a guy who likes to fill gaps, right?"

Subtle. "Not yours." Zack grabbed her arm, spun her around, and pressed her against the door. He raised her arms against the door. "Hold them there." He kicked out her feet, ran his hands over her clothing, breasts, shorts, and checked her pockets—all empty.

"Is this your idea of foreplay?"

"I promise you, if this is some game or a trick of yours, you'll be the first one dead."

Summer turned around and put her arms around his neck. "I don't care if I die. But if I do, we could at least make tonight special."

Zack removed her arms. "Not a chance. Stay there. Don't move, and I mean it." Zack texted Kilgas. A simple text. "Is the office clear?"

The reply came quickly. "Yes. Everyone left. So did I. Do you need me for anything?"

Zack hesitated as he stared at Summer, who did her best to look seductive and available. Zack had no interest. He texted back. "Should be good. See you in the morning. Tomorrow promises to be a productive day."

Zack grabbed his keys and gun, put on his jacket, and grabbed Summer by the arm. "Ok, let's see what game you're up to."

Zack opened the door, looked both ways to see clear halls. Zack pushed Summer towards the stairwell, where he expected an ambush. Nothing again. They exited the building, made it to his motorcycle, and Zack put the helmet on Summer.

* * * *

Zack sped towards the office but didn't take a straight route. Finally convinced there was no one following, Zack steered into the alley behind the office. Zack slowed the bike as he neared his garage and was about to hit the remote door opener when a vehicle turned into the passage ahead of him. Zack stopped. The alley was narrow, almost too little for the motorcycle and vehicle to pass.

It wasn't unusual, but it was rare. Rarer still was the vehicle that drove into the alley behind him. Both with their bright lights on, and both accelerated. Zack got off the bike, pulled Summer off; she yanked off the helmet, and the two dodged behind a garbage bin. Then, the first vehicle plowed into Zack's motorcycle, destroying it. The bike scraped along the blacktop alley, sparks flew, and pieces busted away. The van stopped and reversed quickly, dragging part of the bike with it as the other cargo van steered towards Zack and Summer.

Summer screamed; Zack lifted Summer, threw her into the bin, and leaped off the ground as the van crashed into him and the container. Zack flew over the dumpster and into the wall, the dumpster slammed into the wall beneath him. Zack hit the pavement hard. He heard doors slam as he fought to clear his blurred vision.

Two hands lifted Zack off the ground and a fist buried in his stomach. "We got you now," Zack heard. Three more fists landed in the center of his stomach. He hunched over. They dropped Zack to the ground, and a foot landed in his side. Zack tried to curl as the blows continued.

He heard sounds, gunshots possibly, a yell, a scream, and saw the feet in front of him disappear. Zack shut his eyes as the pain from the collision with the van, wall, and pavement overwhelmed him. Moments later, he felt two hands on his shoulders.

"Stack, wake up. Damnit, I said wake up!"

51

"**I**'m getting tired of saving your ass, Stack."

Zack rubbed one of the many places of pain on his body. "I'll try to make it up to you."

Kilgas dragged Zack's motorcycle into the open garage.

"Did they all get away?"

"They did, and they won't be coming back. And they sure as heck won't call the police. But I made sure she stayed put." Kilgas pointed to the blonde-haired girl tied to a chair in the middle of Zack's garage.

Zack saw Summer strapped to the chair; a gag tied around her mouth. "Sonofabitch. My bike is destroyed."

"Everyone keeps telling you to quit riding these things," Kilgas said. "I hope you had it insured."

Zack looked at the motorcycle. Brand new and now ruined. "Sonofabitch. That's both now. They killed my bikes!" Zack sat a moment and stared at his demolished motorcycle. Two in a week destroyed.

"You're lucky to be alive. Again."

Zack looked at Kilgas. "Why are you here?"

Kilgas knelt next to Zack. "It is my job to keep you safe. I know of a good nurse who should probably take a look at you."

"I think she's looking at someone else's body as we speak," Zack said.

"So that's where you disappeared earlier. Interesting." Kilgas laughed. "You love her."

Zack looked at Kilgas.

Kilgas smiled. "I've followed you for a long time. I'm not stupid." Kilgas pointed back at the girl tied to the chair. "Now, what should we do with her? She made it clear she wasn't talking, and I didn't want to kill her without discussing it with you first."

Kilgas helped Zack to his feet, and Zack walked to the prisoner. Zack tapped her face, though she stared at him. "Hey, are you still interested in a parley?"

She mumbled. Zack moved the gag. "Screw you." Zack moved it back. He exhaled, disappointed.

"That's what I thought you said. So tell me, when you woke this morning and planned your day, did you imagine that by nightfall, you'd be strapped to a chair in a soundproof garage wondering if we're going to peel your skin like a potato?"

She mumbled.

"What's that?" Zack moved the gag.

"Screw you."

Zack returned the gag over her mouth and added additional ties. "One of your friends told me that the other day. It didn't work out well for him. Have a good night."

* * * *

Zack and Kilgas walked around the building to the front and entered the office. Zack immediately slumped onto his couch and took a deep breath. "I need some ibuprofen. It feels like a truck hit me."

"It did. Then so did the wall and pavement and three thugs."

"Why did they run?"

"I shot out their windshield and had six guys behind me. They broke the first and only unbreakable rule of a gunfight. They showed up without one."

Zack adjusted his painful position on his chair. "They know she's here," Zack said. "They waited for her to bring me back here. It was a trap all along."

"No shit, Sherlock. What's your next brilliant deduction?"

Zack rolled his eyes. "We need backup in case they storm the castle."

"Way ahead of you. I warned you, but you're in my world now, Stack. They like working with you, by the way. Tonight was the best coordinated non-lethal activity any of them have done since joining the merc world."

Zack felt the pain continue to reverberate through his body. "This is still my world, Kilgas. Make sure they understand that."

Kilgas said nothing as he watched his ailing friend. "You should have had me meet you there." Kilgas found a bottle of bourbon in Zack's desk and two glasses. He poured bourbon in each and handed Zack one. "We hold all the cards now, Stack. We get her to tell us exactly where Hannah is and get her back."

Zack sipped the Henry McKenna single barrel bourbon. "She won't talk. She's a tough one. And now that we have Summer, there's a chance they are panicking, cleaning house, and we'll find your daughter in a ditch like the others. We should turn it over to the police right now."

"No. No way, Stack. That's NOT what I paid you for. WE find Hannah. The police will screw everything up, and she'll end up dead. We bleed that bitch dry until she tells us where Hannah is, then we go get her."

Zack stared at Kilgas. "We'll get her back. I promised." Zack moved a little, and pain overwhelmed him. After that, he didn't move again. "Calm down. We need to think this out."

Kilgas raised his hands. "Stack, I'm sorry. This is emotional. I'm tired of hearing Sherri cry every night because Hannah isn't home. We need to get Hannah."

"And we will. I want to know who Summer is. She needs to stew down there and realize they tried to kill her, too. I'll break her and get what we need. Until then," Zack looked at Kilgas, "I need you to be patient."

"The girl your cops found the other day. Her name is Talia Bodzinski. She knew Hannah and disappeared a month before Hannah and Angie."

"How did you know that?"

"Your cop friend sent over the info to your office manager, Lauren. I saw it on your desk. Stack, you know we don't have much time."

"Where is Lauren?"

"Tired of waiting for you and went to your apartment. I'm guessing Lauren likes being around you."

Zack struggled to readjust himself, and pain surged through his body. "Go home to Terri and remember the life you want after this is over. You want a second chance, remember?"

Kilgas hesitated. "Do you think you can save her, Stack? Is that what this is about?"

241

Zack knew the accusation was supposed to sting. "She's going to help us, Kilgas. I can see it in her eyes. She wants out, and we're her best chance. Summer's parents want her home, too. She'll end up in jail the rest of her life deservedly so, but she's not dying. You're a father. You know how it feels." They stared at each other. "My focus is bringing your daughter home alive, Kilgas. Don't forget that. Come back in the morning."

"You got it, boss. Stack, you slipped tonight. You got lucky." Kilgas glared at him. "The Stack I know is better than that. Get your head straight, or we'll all die."

Kilgas left. Zack slumped back onto the couch and realized Kilgas was right. *Everyone says I'm getting too easy to follow. How can that be?*

Zack struggled into the front office. He looked at the Christmas tree, still decorated with presents beneath them. Zack walked to the tree and knelt. A long, slim box stuck out, and he saw the note attached. "To Zack, Love SR." He grabbed the box, smiled, and opened it.

A watch. A Seiko Prospex Street series watch. Zack put it on his wrist and stared at it. *Get your head straight, or we'll all die.* Zack grabbed the office phone, about to dial a number he memorized, but Lauren entered the office carrying a pizza box and a bag. She saw Zack, and the smile left her face. Zack put down the phone. The call to the person everyone told him to talk to would wait.

"What happened? I can see blood all over your clothes from here."

* * * *

The lights flicked on when Zack opened the secret hatch to the garage ceiling. He lowered himself to the floor as Summer watched. Zack smiled at her and set the bag, a kit kept in Dre's office, on the top of a bucket. He walked to Summer and eyed her up and down.

"Is your real name Summer?"

Summer looked away from him.

"For transparency's sake, I am skilled in getting answers. Some call it torture. I call it proficient. But I don't want to do that to you." Zack hid the pain throughout his body well. Inside, his body screamed, and he wanted nothing more than bourbon, ibuprofen, and sleep. But to Summer, he looked like nothing had happened. "If you recall, I lifted you off the ground and tossed you atop the garbage dumpster right before the van slammed into it. The goal of that van was to kill us both. I avoided both of my legs getting crushed by inches. If you think they sent you out here to find me so they could ask me questions, and you all would go to your hideout in the hills of northern Virginia laughing about it, you're wrong. This would be more than an opportune time for you to get serious about that parley."

She mumbled. Zack ignored it.

"Is your real name Summer?" Zack removed the gag.

"I'm not telling you anything."

Zack put the gag back on her. "I suspect you think you won't. Admirable."

She mumbled. Zack pulled down the gag. "Go to hell. They know I'm here, and when they come back, you're dead. I'm not telling you anything."

"If they come back, they better bring body bags. I need your fingerprints; hence, I need you unconscious."

"So what are you going to do, big man? Hit a girl?"

Zack smiled. "No. I used to date a super-smart nurse. She should be a doctor. She would not like what you pulled tonight. You know something, I miss her." Zack thought about the admission. Truth. "We talked a lot, and she told me a few things." Zack reached into the bag and pulled out a syringe and a vial of clear liquid. "I just hope I remember how she said to do this. I'd hate to kill you accidentally."

52

When Zack walked out of prison a free man, he hoped to spend a week at a beach to soak up the sun and watch birds fly past on the wind. But, before that fateful letter, he imagined Stefani in his arms on the beach, the wind blowing her hair wild, a smile on her face, and the two of them figuring out what to do next. Together. Walking into a crime lab alone to deliver blood and fingerprint samples to a guy in love with Stefani was nowhere on his bucket list of things to do. But there he was. And there was Caleb, the lab tech.

Caleb stood there in his white lab apparel, working away on the latest in the long line of samples to process. Zack looked around, but not surprisingly, no one paid attention to him. Then, finally, Caleb lifted his head and recognized Zack. There was no smile.

Another response Zack got used to. *It definitely is me.* "Caleb, right?"

Caleb nodded.

"You know who I am, so I'll just get to it. I need a favor."

"Why should I help you? Aren't you dating Stefani?"

"No. Stef dumped me," Zack said. "Are you dating her?"

"No. She dumped me," Caleb said. "She dumped you. Seriously? Why would she do that? She loved you."

"So I hear. No matter." Zack set a brown paper bag on the counter.

"What's that?"

"I need some help identifying a person of interest. I have her prints and a blood sample for DNA in case her prints aren't on file. My guess is she went missing in the last five or six years," Zack said. "If so, I found her."

"I don't work for you. I could lose my job for this."

"You wouldn't be the first."

"That's my point. I don't want to be the next Dorsey."

"Nor do I," Zack said. "Tell me, does anyone else in the lab know about the paternity test Stefani had you run on me?"

"That was on you?"

"Confirmed to Stefani that I have a daughter. Had I known, I would have told her myself. Nonetheless, does Schaeffer know now that Patterson is gone? You weren't working with Patterson when he framed me, were you?"

Caleb looked around the room. Still, no one paid attention. "What do I get out of this?"

"Satisfaction of a job well done and knowing you may have saved lives," Zack said. "How soon can you get me results?"

Caleb frowned. "I'll rush it. The prints will go a lot faster. I'll turn them over first. Give me a day or so."

"I may not have a day or so," Zack said.

"I can't rush science. Give me your cell number. I'll text you. But, if I lose my job,"

"You won't. Tell Barnes or Kael it's for me. Either way, I'll owe you a favor. Good enough?"

"Are you not dating Stefani?"

"No, I'm not. But if you want, I can relay a message."

"Nope. I want nothing to do with her. Tired of being used."

Zack nodded. "I'm sorry, Caleb. You deserve better. Thanks." Zack exited the lab without seeing anyone else and sat in the minivan. Caleb did deserve better. So did a lot of people. Zack decided so did he. But he fought his instinct and returned to his office.

* * * *

Zack woke on the new couch as sunlight shone through the window of his office. He didn't sleep much, but Lauren ensured he wasn't interrupted after his early morning visit to Caleb. Zack heard the click of heels on the wood floor from Lauren but no voices. That meant his silent respite was about to terminate.

His office door opened, and Lauren entered. "Time to get up, sir," she said. "How are you feeling?"

"If I felt any better, they'd make a law to prevent it."

"Liar." Lauren sat on the edge of the couch and lightly touched his bare chest. "Worrying about you was in the job description. I thought it was just a joke, but now I know differently."

Zack looked at his new watch.

"I see you finally opened your Christmas present from Stefani."

"How did you know this was from her?"

"I'm a woman. Have you talked to her?"

"No." Zack tried to sit, but his aching mid-section stopped him. Lauren pulled him up. "I should talk to our guest."

"You should turn her over to the police."

"I know." Zack pushed the blanket off his legs and stood. Lauren stood beside him.

"Sir, please do that for me. Please."

"Let me find out some information first."

Lauren frowned. "Sir," she shook her head. "Get dressed. I'll get you something to eat."

Zack watched her walk out, found his shirt on the floor, and put it on. Five minutes later, he slipped through the shower wall into the inner walls of the building and made his way to the garage.

When the panel in the garage ceiling opened, the light automatically lit. A precaution Zack employed to not stumble over his motorcycle. He lowered to the floor. The girl tied to the chair in the center of the room opened her eyes, squinted, and watched Zack. Zack made sure the panel closed and sealed before he walked to the girl.

"Are you hungry?"

"I'm starving," the girl said. "And I have to pee."

"Then pee."

She looked astounded. "I'm not going to pee myself. Please, just untie me and let me go. I'm not going to talk. Guys will be here soon to get me out of here."

"No, they won't," Zack said calmly. "I want you and I to help each other before this goes any further."

"Let me go, and I'll do what I can to stop them from killing you."

246

"Who's going to stop them from killing you?"

They stared at each other. The girl finally frowned. "I really have to pee. Can you untie me?"

Zack shook his head no.

"I mean it. I am going to pee myself. I can pee in the drain over there."

Zack relented. "Don't make me regret this." He moved behind her, untied her, and watched as she tried to stand. The blood slowly returned to her legs.

"Even prisoners are given food and water."

"I know."

Summer stood and walked to the drain. "Turn around. I don't like people watching."

Zack did and waited. He heard the unmistakable sound of the girl peeing and waited. It was quiet, and then Zack heard the girl grunt. He turned, and the chair swung through the air at him.

Zack raised his arm to block the chair; it crashed into his arm. Summer charged and tried to pin Zack against the wall with the chair legs. She fought and screamed and tried to hurt Zack, which convinced Zack to break one rule.

Never hit a woman.

Much like the rules of the English language, an exception to every rule was the norm. This one, however, Zack felt terrible about and knew he had to be careful.

One swipe knocked the chair away, and Summer looked at him as if she knew she had made a wrong choice. But unlike a wise person, she pressed the position and came at Zack again. And Zack broke his rule.

One hit, and she hit the floor.

He lifted her off the floor and put her slumped body back in the chair. Zack strapped her to the chair again. Zack waited a moment and then tapped her face. She woke.

"I did warn you." Zack grabbed her chin and made her look at him. "What did you think you were going to accomplish?"

She said nothing as defeat swept over her. Zack recognized the look on her face. Zack let go and wiped his hand on his pants. "Are you going to talk?"

"No. I know how guys like you work. You think a little threat and scare tactic will make me give up anything you want. So go ahead and smack me around. Be a big man. Does that excite you?"

"Not at all. That's not how I do things," Zack said. "It's unprofessional. I am sorry for hitting you. However, you were acting irrationally and needed a subtle reminder that you are not in charge here. I am."

"No, you're not, big man. How many other women have you hit? A bet a lot."

"You were the first, and I almost feel bad about it. You and I are not seeing eye to eye. You think you won't talk, and I know you won't talk using primitive methods. You survived working for whoever you do because you learned to play their game to stay alive." Zack watched her eyes. "You played me last night, so I know you're smart. My guess is you were kidnapped or tricked into running away like Hannah and Angie were, and you realized survival was more important than your integrity, pride, and self-respect. Maybe your home life sucked. Maybe you were confused with life or scared of leaving home like Hannah was, and someone like you promised you a better way. An easier way. A path to some teddy bear-filled land of Oz or like Willie Wonka's Chocolate Factory. I don't care how you ended up here. What I do care about is why you believe that by stonewalling me, your life is any safer than it would be with the guys who nabbed you probably when you were sixteen?"

"You don't know a thing about me," Summer said defiantly.

"But you do know Hannah and Angie, and you will tell me where they are."

"I'm not telling you anything. I was prepared to die every day for years. Today is no different."

"Today is a lot different. In a few hours, I'll know who you are. And when I find out who you are, it will be easy to tie you to at least six dead bodies found in the last three months. You see, Summer, that tattoo on your ass, kind of tacky, and it ruined a nice ass if you ask me, is similar to tattoos I identified on three of the bodies. Some tissue work will connect the bodies to one killer. Which, my dear, will lead the police, both local and federal, since the bodies were found in different states right back to you. That makes you complicit. Sure, it may be circumstantial, but this is America. We lock up people for twenty years for having an ounce of marijuana. Imagine that. Your pretty blue eyes and teary-eyed performance isn't going to work, sweetheart."

"You don't know nothing."

"Double negative," Zack chuckled. "I love those."

"You think you're so smart. There's nothing you can do to make me tell you anything. You messed with the wrong people. I've seen what they can do and know they have connections. And you're on their list. You're as good as dead."

"Yeah, the thing is, there is nothing as good as dead. Dead is dead. You like to act like you're tough and not afraid to die, but you are. I see it in your eyes."

She stared at him. "What else do you see in my eyes? How about you untie me, and we go back to my place, clean up, and we make magic? Neither of us needs this life. You and me, we can disappear. What do you say?"

"And leave all this behind?" Zack smiled. "Nah, I'll pass on your offer. So let's do this. I'm going to eat and maybe catch a movie. One of the cable channels has a John Wayne movie marathon today, and I'm hoping The Searchers is one of them. I haven't seen that in a while. And then, maybe I'll stop back, and we can talk some more."

"Wait! Are you going to leave me here? That's inhumane! I'm starving, I need a bath, I need a bathroom, and you can't leave me here."

"Time is precious, sweetheart. I'm not wasting anymore with you." Zack opened the door and heard her curse at him. She pleaded. She said she'd talk. Zack shut the door, and as it closed, her voice silenced. Zack looked both ways in the alley, saw no one, went to the fire escape, and climbed to the roof.

53

Zack returned to his office. The cell rang. Captain Barnes. "Stack here."

"Stack, I see you've hijacked my lab. I should have you arrested."

"I'm guessing that's not the first time you thought that."

"Caleb, the lab tech called me directly. I'm seriously considering sending units over."

"Is he at least processing what I took to him?"

"Yes, I gave him permission. That's how this works, Zack. You ask me, I decide, and then I have my department do it. You don't go in and order it."

"I asked nicely. Well, maybe coerced. But it was an agreement."

"Don't dodge this, Stack. What's going on?"

"Ted, I need a name. It's for a case, and I have a lead to help find two missing girls."

Barnes paused. "Oh, I get it. That does explain things. The person you're looking for, well, I should rephrase that. The person you overtook my lab for and probably have tied up somewhere is named Sophie Flowers. Now, can I ask you how you got her blood and fingerprints?"

"You can, but I'd prefer not to answer. What else do you have?"

"She went missing about six years ago—age fifteen. Parents weren't sure if she ran away or was abducted. Never found, obviously. DNA and prints were on file."

"She's only 21?"

"Not yet. Still 20."

"Where is she from?"

"Charlottesville, Virginia. Cute girl. Now how did you get her blood?"

"Ted, can I beg for some leniency today?"

"You are pushing it. What do you need?"

"A few hours and whatever you have on her."

"Zack, this does not sound good at all. You just got out of prison, for Pete's sake. So this better not be what I think it is."

"What do you think it is?"

"Later. How is Stefani?"

"Why are you asking?" Zack took a breath.

"Becki and I want you and Stefani over Friday night for dinner."

"Why in the hell would you want her and me at your house right now?"

"Well, you blew it with Julie. That was obvious Saturday night, and I want my hundred bucks. But I thought you might have a chance with Stefani."

"Thanks for the vote of confidence, Ted. Fax the info over immediately."

"Zack, can you do me a favor and please include me this time?"

"Ted, I don't think that's a good idea."

"Let me decide. How about you call me over to the office later for an off-the-record meeting?"

"I'm trying not to ruin your career, Ted."

"That ship has sailed. Let me know what time." Ted ended the call. Zack sat behind his desk and noticed his office door was closed. The fax machine rang. Ted was quick.

Zack reached behind his desk and grabbed the allowed Pepsi. He called Kilgas, but it went to voice mail. "Kilgas, where are you?" He disconnected, and Lauren entered his office carrying the papers.

"You're drinking that soda before you eat?" Disgusted, she set down the papers, walked to him, and took the soda away. "Sir, the answer is no. A late lunch will be here soon. Then, maybe."

"Lauren," Zack said, suddenly speechless. He dropped his head to his desk. "It's pop and just one, please."

"No.

"I'll raise your rent."

Lauren smiled and walked around the desk to his side. She leaned over and put her arm around him. "No, you won't," she whispered and kissed the side of his face. "All that sugar isn't good for that body."

"Lauren, before you judge me, please try to understand me."

She looked long into his eyes and nodded. "I do. But you better understand me. I'm not training a new boss. And you dead or in prison does not bode well for me." She kissed him. "Understand?"

"I do. Why did you kiss me?"

"Because that's the only way to get you to pay attention." She winked, turned, and left.

* * * *

Zack opened the garage door carrying two pails of water. The garage door shut behind him. "Hey, wake up," Zack said and splashed Summer with water.

Summer, now known as Sophie, squinted her eyes to adjust to the light and stared angrily at Zack. Zack was careful only to wet her midsection and below. Zack flipped over the empty pail and sat on it five feet in front of her. He had a backpack slung over his shoulder but said nothing.

"You're back. How nice. Did you bring me some food? I'm starving. Prisoners have rights."

"You're not a prisoner, Sophie," Zack said. "You're free to go whenever you want."

She wanted to say something but heard what he said. "My name isn't Sophie, and how can I leave? I'm tied to a chair."

"Untie yourself, and you can walk out that door," Zack said. "Sophie."

"Why do you keep calling me that?"

"Because that's your name, Sophie. And your parents want you home."

"I don't know any Sophie."

Zack stood, lifted the other pail, and carefully poured it over her mid-section and legs. Then, he set it upside down and placed the backpack on it. He opened it, and the first thing Zack withdrew was his Ka-bar. The second was a stack of photos and the information Barnes sent over. Then, Zack pulled out a hypodermic needle, a pair of pliers, and a roll of Scotch tape.

"Interesting contents, huh?" Zack held the knife and studied it. "Sophie, you have an interesting past. You're 20, and of course, your name is Sophie. You're from Charlottesville, Virginia. You have a little brother and sister named Tucker and Ophelia, your parents are Southerners and still believe the South will rise again, and their names are Forrest and Scarlet. You had a good childhood. By all accounts, you were a spoiled rotten brat who got whatever she wanted. Not sure why you'd run away," Zack said.

"I don't know what you're talking about. I don't know any of those people."

"These pictures say otherwise." Zack showed her a family portrait taken on Sophie's birthday only a month before she disappeared. "Cute girl. A real Southern Belle."

"I don't know those people! You're a liar!" She yelled.

"But because boys made fun of you because of your small breasts and because you stuttered and the other girls made fun of you, you grew up unhappy with your situation. You questioned why you had to go to church every Sunday when your friends were at the swimming hole and why even though mommy and daddy gave you everything, you didn't get the pony you wanted or the car. I get it. The teenage years can suck, and they're confusing. Maturing isn't easy. Some never do. Hell, I was in the military with guys who swore their best years were behind them. These were 19-year-old kids who thought their best years were in high school. Imagine that?"

"You don't know anything. Quit wasting my time and let me go. I'm going to make sure you rot in jail if I don't kill you myself!"

"Scarlet said you had a problem with authority. You always resorted to yelling and threats—kind of like now. You hate being told what to do. It still makes no sense to me why you ran away, but you did. You likely met someone who was like you are for who you work for now. That person was understanding, cool, older, wiser, experienced, and promised you a better way. A better life. A new life without all the bullshit you despised as a spoiled little teenage girl. Sound about right?"

"You never talked to anyone. You don't know anything."

Zack quickly jabbed the knife into the chair between her legs, only an inch from her. "Hold that for me, would you?" He stuck another picture in her face. "Look at it." She looked away. Zack grabbed her face and made her look at it. "I said LOOK AT IT!"

She wouldn't open her eyes.

"I have a solution for that. Allow me to introduce to you this thing called Scotch Tape." Zack unrolled a piece and stuck it to her top eyelid and eyebrow. "Believe me;

this is going to hurt you a lot worse than it hurts me." He did the other eye. Sophie's defiance was almost something to be proud of if not for so sad.

Zack taped several pictures on the wall. Twelve in total in four rows of three. Then he grabbed her chair, dragged it to the wall, and made her sit as close to the wall as he could. Zack grabbed his knife and slowly ran the tip along the side of her face while he breathed close to her ear. "Sophie, why don't you take some time to remember your family. When I come back, I'll introduce you to the pliers, the needle, and the rubbing alcohol. It's a fun game I call 'let's see how many fingernails I can remove before you pass out.' The record is eight. The thumbs are the worst." He looked at the picture. "Damn, you are an adorable girl." Zack tapped the knife on her quivering lips. "Don't go anywhere. I'll be back."

54

Zack returned to the office. Lauren talked on the phone, so Zack waited until she disconnected the call. "How are you?"

"Better now." Lauren smiled. "Sir, Julie called. She'd like you to call her."

Zack nodded. "Has anyone been in the office lately? Like Dre, Mikayla, or Darnell? You know, the other employees?"

"No, sir. Darnell is working out of town today on an insurance fraud case. I haven't heard from Mikayla, and Dre said he'll be in later this afternoon. He asked if anything was going on with you. I didn't know what to tell him."

"Yeah, let's keep what is happening between us, Ok?"

"You got it, Awesome Sauce." Lauren put her hand on Zack's thigh. "Sir, had I known no one visited you, I would have visited you every week."

Zack squeezed her hand. "I know you would have. It would have cost me a fortune, too." He winked. "I'm going to take a shower after I call Julie. Don't let anyone in my office, please."

"Even me?"

"We're working now. Maybe later." Zack went to his desk and dialed the number. She answered right away. "Julie? Hey," Zack said. "How are you? Everything ok?"

"Hi. I'm good. You?"

"Eh," Zack said. "You wanted me to call?"

"I did. I'm glad you called. I'm at my parents' place in New Mexico with Cate." They were silent. "How are things there?"

"Boring," Zack lied. "When are you coming back?"

"There's so much to do out here. Probably through the weekend. I swear mom and dad haven't cleaned a thing out since they bought the place. It's nice, though. I think you'd like it. I saw some weird birds already I've never seen before."

Zack smiled. "How's Cate?"

"She's fine. When I get back, you could stop over and have a play date with her."

"I'd love that. Will you be along?"

"Honey, count on it. I think maybe I've been unfair. Have you talked to Stefani like I asked?"

"She was busy with another guy when I stopped by her place," Zack said. "I don't think we need to worry about her."

"I worry about you, Zack. And she is my best friend. Oh shoot, mom and dad are here. I have to go. Zack," Julie paused. "I'll talk to you soon, ok?"

"You bet. I'm looking forward to it."

They disconnected. Zack thought of the prisoner downstairs. He called Kilgas and waited, but there was no answer. Zack left another voice mail. "Kilgas, it's Stack. You're conspicuously AWOL, and that makes me worry. I'll be away from my phone for the next fifteen minutes. Call me after that." He disconnected, stared at his bathroom, thought of everything, and knew the water called his name. Twenty minutes later, after the shower, Zack decided it was time to deal with that bridge.

He called his best friend, Andre.

* * * *

Zack wasn't fond of driving the minivan. It was conspicuous, too big for tight city parking, definitely not his vibe, and didn't handle the greatest when taking corners quickly to thwart the tracking of any following cars. He vowed to himself, now that he was minus both of his motorcycles, to either track down Stefani and get his Jaguar back or track down Stefani and confront her about what Zack believed was the lie she told everyone about who dumped who.

In that case, the car could wait.

Though Zack wasn't keen on dropping a few grand on a new bike, testing the boundaries of his insurance company was risky. Neither motorcycle destruction was his fault, but two in a week certainly would raise eyebrows. And rates.

If they didn't drop him.

Pay all that money year after year, never make a claim, then boom! Try actually to use insurance, and the insurance company has a fit.

Zack shook the thought out of his head. Dealing with the wealthy trying to justify legally stealing from the people wasn't one of his favorite topics. The last time he did, Zack spent six months in prison. Cozy or not, it didn't matter. It was a prison.

Zack parked the minivan on the street and didn't hesitate to walk to the door and ring the doorbell. The wait wasn't long. Dre answered the door. He smiled, but the words wouldn't form.

Zack nodded a self-deprecating-fully-aware nod. Zack knew he would all along.

"Zack, good morning. What brings you here?"

Zack smiled. "Lauren has been busting my chops about our employees not starting work before noon. So she made me go house to house to find you guys."

Dre laughed. "Come on inside. You'll see I was working."

Zack followed Dre into his house and, indeed, saw Dre working a case on his computer. Unlike the television shows suggested, most of the investigative work was research. In the era of information, misinformation, or disinformation, sifting through piles of information of whatever kind to get the correct answer took time.

Dre chose to spend that time at home.

"Oh, hi, Zack! Oh my God! Dre told me you were back, and I've been waiting to see you again," said the new fiancé of Dre, Alysha. She walked to Zack, and the two hugged.

Zack's genuine smile didn't lessen. "It's good to see you, too, Ally. You look great. Congratulations. I could not be happier for you two."

She hugged him again with a beaming smile. "Thank you. Now, if I can get him to pick a date." Ally rolled her eyes at Dre. "What brings you here? Can I get you something to drink? Pepsi, perhaps?"

"You always knew how to win me over," Zack laughed to Ally. "But no. Unless Dre will join me, and we can take that in a to-go format."

"Why? Are you going somewhere?"

Zack looked at Dre. "I want to talk to my best friend. I hoped we could take a walk."

Dre nodded at Ally. "That sounds good. Two to-go, baby."

Ally disappeared but returned with two bottles of soda pop. Dre and Ally kissed; Ally gave Zack another hug, and the two men exited the home and walked down the street with no destination. Zack took the initiative.

"Look, Dre, let me start and don't interrupt, please. I know the last few months before my incarceration, and since I've been back, I've been a lot of things. But, for the sake of brevity, I'd prefer if we don't name them. I feel awful enough already."

Dre chuckled. "Can't I even list a couple?"

"I guess that I already know, and none equate to a pat on the back." Zack looked at Dre, who smiled and slapped Zack on his back. The two men laughed.

"So, are you back, or just back?"

Zack stopped, unscrewed the cap off the plastic bottle, swigged it, and stared at the cap. "You know, every time I have one of these, I'm contributing to the world's destructive and decimating reliance on plastic. Maybe I should switch to cans."

Dre laughed. The two walked. "What's going on with Kilgas? I've talked to him a few times, so you know," Dre said, which earned a surprised look from Zack. "He's either one hell of a poker player, or he's a liar. I don't trust him."

"Why not?"

"Because Lauren doesn't," Dre said.

"Does she know about our past with Kilgas?"

"A little."

"Then we'll be going off my instinct. I think he's trustable, at least this time. Besides, if it's not kosher with Kilgas, he's only going to kill me." Zack stopped and turned to Dre. "I've been a piece of shit, but I'm making the flush. Dre, I've asked more than any person could ask of a friend, but I need to ask,"

Dre cut him off. "Shut up, man. You think you're going alone?" He shook his head. "Not a chance. I need you, too, man. I cut you a lot of slack for good reasons. From here on, you need to tell me everything. As far as I can tell, you aren't talking to anyone else."

The two walked again. "Lauren sure is trying hard. Like a teenager on prom night. We're about four blocks from the water. Let's walk. I'll talk. There's a lot you need to know."

Dre swigged his beverage. "Where do I start?"

"Well, first, let me tell you about the girl tied up in the garage under our office."

"I was hoping you'd tell me before I had to let you know I'm aware."

Zack shook his head. "Barnes?"

"Of course. We got a full alert watch on you. I had faith you'd come to me like you are now. Mikayla, not so much."

"And Big D?"

"He wouldn't sell you out for all the tea in China. But he was stressed about it. So what's going on?"

The two crossed the street. Zack could see the water ahead and felt the soothing of his soul, which was odd because he didn't like being on boats very much. "Kilgas and I, I'm afraid all we did was awaken a giant."

Dre rolled his eyes. "A movie reference. Yup. You're definitely back."

55

The clock chimed on the wall of the office. Four hours passed before Zack returned with Dre beside him. Zack looked both ways in the alley, no one in sight, and opened the garage door. The girl sat in the chair exactly where Zack left her.

The two men stepped inside and shut the door. Sophie didn't turn her head, so Zack walked to her and spun the chair.

"This is her." Zack took the gag off her mouth.

Sophie breathed as if she hadn't had a gasp of air in hours. She stared with her manipulated eyes at Zack, spit at him, and turned away.

"I don't think she wants to talk yet," Zack said. He wrapped the gag around her mouth instead of stuffing it inside. "But she will. Sophie simply hasn't agreed to my stipulations yet."

She mumbled. Dre smiled. "You haven't changed at all, Zack." Dre stepped forward and looked at the pictures on the wall. "Cute girl with a nice-looking family, albeit a bit Confederate looking for my liking. Why doesn't she want to go back?"

"I'm not sure," Zack said. "But that's not the biggest concern."

"What is?"

"It's a toss-up between who she works for, their connections, or the fact that I had Kilgas enlist mercs to watch our back."

Dre's shoulders slumped. "Out of the frying pan into the fryer. Nice."

The two men stared at Sophie. She stared back with her eyelids Scotch-taped to her eyebrows.

"Dude, maybe you should take the tape off. Her eyes are freaking me out."

"Ok. I get it. Show a little compassion."

"I don't give a damn about compassion. We do what we have to until she talks. But her eyes are freaking me out. I never liked it when you did this before, and we didn't give a crap about the enemy then, but this broad ain't the enemy."

Zack scoffed. "Dude, look at my mangled motorcycle. It's because of her. She's the enemy."

Dre saw it and thought for a moment. "I see your point. At least put sunglasses on her."

Zack rubbed his forehead. "Let's go get some lunch and think about it. I'm starving."

"Let's hit that burger joint you love. It has the best double cheese in the area."

"I'll buy. Let's go."

They turned for the garage door and heard Sophie attempt to yell beneath her gag.

"What?" Zack asked. She mumbled until he took off the gag.

"I'm starving, and I need a bathroom. Please untie me."

Zack laughed. "I fell for that one before. We'll be back." Zack moved her, so she had to look at the wall of pictures of her family.

* * * *

The two walked quickly around the building, both sets of eyes careful of the surroundings.

"We can't keep her there."

"I know. Can we get a room at the Inn and sneak her there?"

"Only if you want to include Big D and Mik. We should get Barnes and leafy weed involved."

"Ruin two careers at once?"

"You ruined Mik's. Why stop there?"

Zack stopped outside the front door. "Ouch. You went there, didn't you?"

"Cheap shot. I know. And it was unfair. I take it back. If they are connected that deep, what chance do us and a few of Kilgas' mercs have?"

"I'm still analyzing that."

"First, you need to get her to talk."

Zack opened the door and smiled. "That, my friend, is what I do best."

56

Zack dropped to the garage floor and saw tears running down Sophie's face. She had her head turned away from the pictures. She saw Zack.

"Get this tape off my eyes. Get me away from those pictures. Please, I'm begging you," Sophie cried.

"Nope, I don't think so."

"Please, Zack, please. I'll do anything," she said, and the crying overtook her. "Please."

Zack walked over to her. "Hold still. This will hurt." He yanked the tape off as quickly as he could on both eyes.

"OWW!" Sophie shook her head and cried more. "Please untie me. Please."

Zack leaned against the wall and crossed his arms. "You haven't given me what I want," he said. "That's the deal."

"Untie me," Sophie cried. "Please!"

Zack didn't move. "Six young girls were murdered and dumped on the side of the road in the last few months. They are the ones you recruited but didn't work out, aren't they?"

"Please untie me. Please. I can't feel my legs or arms. Please."

"Ok. We'll play it your way. I don't want to do this. I'm untrained, but I did take good notes." Zack picked another syringe out of the bag along with a vial with clear liquid. He inserted the needle, withdrew a fair amount, and pressed the plunger to expel any air.

"What are you doing? What is that?" Sophie yelled. "Don't! Please! What is that?"

Zack grabbed Sophie's bicep and jabbed in the needle. He pushed in the liquid and yanked the syringe out. "Talk and talk fast," Zack said, the menace in his voice reaching a tone that scared Sophie. Zack tossed the needle away, pulled another vial out of the bag, and unwrapped it. "You have maybe ten minutes. If I don't inject you with this, you'll lose feeling in your arms and legs. Then, you won't feel anything as paralysis overwhelms you. You won't be able to speak and if I let it go, breathe. It's a nasty venom that kills hundreds of people each year. I saw this in Africa. It was horrible to watch a grown man die that way. And they never see the snake that bites them. Well, I'm the snake this time, Sophie. I told you, you will talk."

The fear in Sophie's face made her tremble and cry. "Please! No, I'll talk. I'll tell you everything. Please. I don't want to die."

Zack stepped forward and knelt in front of her. "Sophie, that is your name, isn't it?"

She nodded.

"You know Hannah, don't you?"

"Please, give me the antidote! Please. I'll talk. I'll tell you everything. Please."

Zack returned to the wall. "I don't want to hear what you think I want to hear. I need the truth, Sophie. I'll give you the antidote, but it won't help, and it's getting late. I already delayed my dinner plans." Zack pulled the Sig out of the back of his beltline. "If the venom doesn't kill you, I am going to use this on you. You won't die from the wounds. You'll only wish you died. So talk and talk fast. Nine minutes."

"They'll kill me. They'll find me and kill me. That's what they do! If I talk, they'll kill me. You can't protect me."

"Sophie," Zack said, "I won't let them kill you. I have friends in the right places, and I promise we can protect you. But you have to tell us everything, and you have to do it," he looked at his watch, "in eight minutes. Your hands are already white. Maybe six minutes."

Sophie breathed heavily, a panic attack. "Oh my God," she said repeatedly. "Please, please don't let me die. Please."

"Talk, Sophie. Where is Hannah?"

"She's at the compound in the hills in Virginia. It's hidden. She's there, and so is her friend, but they're going to kill her friend. I'll tell you everything. Please don't let me die."

Zack looked at his watch again. "How many others have they killed?"

"I don't know."

"Quit wasting my time," Zack barked. "You're saving your ass because you think you can flash your pretty eyes and manipulate me. That's what you do. You use people and lie to stay alive."

"NO! PLEASE!" Sophie cried. "I really don't know. They've killed at least a dozen since I've been there. It's probably more." Sophie pleaded and watched her captor do nothing. "They get tired of the girls. They get too old, or they don't indoctrinate and fight back. They kill them."

"Where is there? Who are they? Five minutes. You're losing the color in your face," Zack said. "Your heart is racing towards bursting. You better make up your mind to tell me the truth and do it quickly."

"The Church of a New World Order for Christ. It's them-the minister and his brother. They're sex fiends using the church to get rich. Please. Help me!"

"By bilking gullible, poor, old people?"

Sophie panted frantically as if her lungs were shutting down. "No, there's more. Please give me the antidote. I'm dying!"

"What more? Tell me."

"They steal from the families-anything they can do for money. They're evil. Please! Don't let me die."

"The Church of a New World Order for Christ," Zack said. "That rolls off the tongue like peanut butter stuck to the roof of your mouth." Zack held up the gun as if examining the aim. "You know, not too long ago, I told some rich, privileged, self-entitled scumbag that money may be the cause for all evil, closely followed by religion. I'm beginning to think the two go hand-in-hand."

"Oh My God! I'm dying. I can feel it. Please help me!" Sophie yelled frantically.

Zack knelt in front of her and stared her in the eyes. "I need to know where the two girls are, the layout of the place, how many men are there, how many people are there against their will, everything. Are you going to tell me the truth?"

Sophie breathed frantically.

"Your eyes are turning color. You don't have much time."

Sophie realized she was going to die and dropped her head. She cried. The tears flowed and dropped to her pants, and Zack watched. "I'm so sorry," she said. "I don't want to die," she said softly. "Please tell my parents I'm sorry."

Zack walked around and untied her. She didn't move. He knelt in front of her again. "Are you going to tell me everything?"

"I will. I swear on my life. I promise I will never lie again. Please give me the antidote."

Zack lifted her from the chair. "I injected you with water. You're fine. But if you clam up, I have something in that other vial you will not want in your system, so keep your facts straight. Follow me and don't touch anything. And understand I won't hesitate to kill you." Zack squeezed her arms and made her look at him. Sophie lost, and she knew it. She nodded her head and did precisely what Zack said.

57

"I was sucked in easily," Sophie said. "Everything you said about me, Zack, was true. I was spoiled, but I didn't feel loved. I felt different. My breasts were smaller, I did stutter, and the boys did make fun of me. I felt like my family actively betrayed me every day because I was different. The girls were ruthless. Don't ever kid yourself. Girls are worse than boys when it comes to bullying. The boys just stopped showing interest in me, and if one did, that boy would get ridiculed until he stopped talking to me. So yes, I wanted out. I wanted to run away, and then I met a girl named Sunshine. Her name wasn't Sunshine like mine isn't Summer. That's the names we get after Garrett and Lewis Colson brainwash us."

Sophie sat in Zack's office surrounded by Zack, Kilgas, Lauren, Dre, Ted Barnes, and Detective Kael. Once out of the garage, she talked freely.

"Later, I found out her real name was Wendy. Once she aged, Garrett decided she was of no use and had her disposed of," Sophie's bitterness was apparent. "I liked her. She was the reason I am who I am now and how I survived. Like me, she understood what was going on there. They promise a better life, a better way, becoming one with God and understanding the true meaning and all that garbage, but they only want us for sex and money. Everything else is just a dog and pony show."

"Wow," Ted said. "She sounds like you, Zack."

"Don't get him started," Dre said.

"Go on, Sophie," Ted said.

"As Zack guessed, I did what I did to survive. I saw girls come in and then disappear, and even though some bought into the brainwashing, I never did. I didn't want to go back to my life, but I realized I had made a huge mistake. My only way out is dead. So I played the game. I manipulated and lied and did what I had to do. No one was better at," she raised her hands and made air quotes, "believing than me.

So they elevated me to an Enlightened One. My job was to recruit. Thankfully, I got too old for them and didn't get summoned to see The Prophet, so gross," Sophie said, disgusted. "So I got to leave the compound and follow leads generated by our computer searches."

"Computer searches? What do you mean?" Ted asked.

"They don't find the lost souls by chance," Sophie said. She ate another piece of pizza and drank one of Zack's soft drinks while she talked. "It's hard work. They have a team of experts, and four of them do nothing but search websites like Facebook and Instagram and everywhere else young girls hang out. They make up multiple fake identities as young girls and do nothing but identify and relate to their targets. Some take the bait, and then I'm sent in. That's how we got who you're looking for." She looked at Kilgas. "I'm so sorry, Mr. Kilgas. Please understand I did it only to stay alive."

Kilgas said nothing, but Zack saw the ire in his eyes.

"I can show you their mining operation later, Ted. Move on, Sophie," Zack said quickly. "Why didn't you try to run away?"

"Once you're there, there is no escape, except for ending up dead in a ditch. I'm sent out but never alone. There are always at least six guys nearby in teams of two in different locations, making sure I can't escape, and they often had me wired. To get around that, I stopped wearing a bra because that's where they hid the wire. They promised they would kill me if I did anything dumb."

"Where are they keeping my daughter?" Kilgas asked.

"They aren't keeping her anymore," Sophie said. "She's been indoctrinated. She's there by choice. Some buy into it. It's not a bad life at first," Sophie explained. "There's plenty of food, whatever you want, anything you want. It just appears. There are several buildings on the property. And the security is impressive."

"Is anything illegal taking place there?" Ted asked.

"You mean besides kidnapping, rape, theft, murder, and brainwashing?" Zack asked.

"They have an armory. I've seen inside it once. I've never seen so many guns. At least a hundred men are guarding the place. They're enticed by the money and by having the opportunity to have their way with the girls. Some stay on and accept their existence. But, as I said, some don't."

"That many men can't stay there," Zack said. "Can they?"

"I don't know. I haven't seen the entire compound. The property is huge. We aren't allowed on most of it. Only a few of us are even allowed in the church. The rest have a small sermon every weekend given by the Prophet himself. It's sickening."

"I need the layout, Sophie. As much detail as you can give about the place," Zack said.

"Mr. Stack, you should call Agent Campbell," Lauren said. "They should know about this."

"Zack, you already know what I'm going to say. First, you're kidnapping and torturing people, and now you're talking about an illegal incursion onto private property. Lauren is right," Ted said. "Listen to her."

"In my defense, Sophie was sent here to have me killed."

"Which means they know she's here, Zack," Ted replied. "They probably have men parked outside waiting for the right moment."

"There won't be one," Kilgas said. "If they try, they'll be massacred."

Ted Barnes looked at Zack. "Zack, why didn't you tell me everything before?"

"Sophie, keep talking," Zack said.

"There's a lab where they make their LSD. The recruits don't realize it is part of the indoctrination," Sophie said. "And they use their computer skills to steal the identities of the parents of the kids they kidnap. They access bank accounts, credit card numbers, retirement accounts, you name it. If it's worth being stolen, they steal it. They have to pay for everything somehow, and the weekly parishioner's donations are huge, but not that huge."

"Can you give us proof that they killed any of the six we are investigating right now?" Ted asked.

Sophie shook her head. "I know they killed them, and I know they killed more. They started by burying the bodies on the property and had a lavish ceremonial funeral for each victim, as they called it. But after a while, the flock, as they call us, started questioning all of the sudden, unexplained deaths. Teenage girls don't suddenly die. So, Lewis Colson decided to invent the predator watching the compound story. Naturally, everyone believed someone was snatching the girls in the middle of the night, but in reality, they were girls who realized it was all a sham, and they wanted to go home. Lewis and Garrett can't have anyone talking about what's going on there, so they killed them and dumped them all over, hoping to throw off the police who found the bodies." She looked at Zack. "Zack, this is bigger than you think."

Zack looked at Lauren.

"You need to call the FBI." Lauren's tone said it wasn't a suggestion.

"The minute the FBI gets involved, they'll kill my daughter," Kilgas said. "That's not happening."

"Mr. Stack, you need to call the FBI," Lauren said again.

"You don't have that much time," Sophie said.

Zack paced while he rubbed his forehead. "Maybe we do." He stopped and faced the group. "It's their Holy Week. The Prophet convinced his congregation that Jesus' Resurrection happened on June 9th specifically. He says that because the Christians allow their Easter celebration to be based on the moon's cycle, they are false prophets and not true believers. It's a bunch of crap, all of it, but the followers buy it, and donations are huge on that week of the year. They'll take in almost a million dollars this week. It is a huge week."

"How do you know that?" Sophie asked.

Zack pointed at Lauren. "Their website, some digging, and hacking their accountant. Lauren is worth every penny we pay her."

"Easter in June. That seems odd to me," Kael said.

"*That's* what seems odd to you?" Ted Barnes asked.

"Garrett is smart. Better weather equals better attendance and he learned that spring and early summer donations are higher. I don't know why or how he figured that out, but Garrett did. Maybe that's when people get their tax returns back. I don't know. But Easter is a huge day for them." Sophie looked at Zack.

"Nothing equates sacrificing the Son of God for the good of mankind like guilting people into emptying their wallets to help conmen live on easy street."

Dre chuckled. "You are consistent, Zack."

"They know you and are looking for you, Zack. They need to know how much you and the police know." Sophie kept her eyes mainly on Zack when she spoke. "They were concerned about an FBI agent sniffing around one of their satellite churches asking about Hannah and Angie. He's probably dead by now."

"What satellite?" Barnes asked.

"Bradley Pollard. He's a freak, but he hides it better. He talks a pious game, but he's just as evil as the rest. He's a front. He runs a youth ministry and if one of the brothers spotted one they liked, guess who disappeared next?"

"Kael, contact the VSP, find out if Pollard is on their radar for human trafficking."

"Pollard is dead," Zack announced. "Kilgas and I found him dead the other day. We have time, but not a lot. They are closing shop."

Dutifully, Kael left the room, went into Zack's office, shut the door, and made a phone call.

"You *found* him dead?" Barnes asked skeptically.

Zack stopped his pace and stared at Barnes. "Ted, you know me better than that. If I killed him, he'd just be missing."

"Same here," added Kilgas. "Besides, I don't kill the small fish."

Barnes tried to not show his incredulity.

Dre kept them focused. "Where are they holding Hannah Leary?"

"Her name is Suday now," Sophie said. "It means gift of God. They do that to convince the newcomers they are special. She might be in the house. Garrett likes her."

"That's the fish I'm going to kill," Kilgas mumbled. "Stack, we can get in and get her out. We have eyes now."

"No, Zack," Ted said. "There is no way I or anyone can protect you from that."

Zack thought of Addison Jones.

Lauren looked at Zack and crossed her arms.

"Zack, over a hundred men are guarding the place. It's suicide," Sophie said. "Zack. I'm telling you this is bigger than you think."

58

Zack sat on the edge of Lauren's desk. "We can worry about the big picture later. I need to know what's going on right now. This is about time, Sophie. What's the frame? What are they thinking?"

Sophie took a deep breath. "Garrett mentioned moving. I think he's looking to get out. He sent Lewis to Arizona earlier this week with the guys you beat up outside her apartment." Sophie pointed at Lauren. "It looked like a funeral to everyone in the compound, but Lewis took them to Arizona and killed them. Other than finding you, Zack, Garrett hasn't sent me on any recruiting missions since I got Hannah and her friend. It makes me think he's tired of the area or feeling the heat. I'm afraid he's going to pull a Jonestown and bolt town."

"You said satellites. How many other places do the Colson's have?" Barnes asked.

"Helping them with their harvest?" Sophie asked. "That's what they call it. I'm not sure. I only dealt with Pollard."

"He claimed to have more than one person helping him with the lost children, as he called them," Zack said. "Is that true?"

"I only dealt with Pollard," Sophie said. "But I'd guess yes. It's tough to deal in human flesh having a life where no one expects it unless you have help." She looked at Zack. "I'm sorry. But they all need to suffer."

"Stack, the rest will fall like dominoes once we cut the head off the snake. The snake is Colson. We go in, get my daughter, and let the chips fall where they may," Kilgas said.

"Easy for you to say. You're not on the radar of the FBI," Zack said.

"Mr. Stack, you have a friend there, and you need to call him right now," Lauren said again.

"Friend? They locked him up for six months without a trial. They aren't friends," Kilgas said.

"Mr. Kilgas," Captain Barnes said. "I remember you from your Senator Rosler days, and Zack, since you're associating with him, my intuition tells me both of you are breaking the law. Zack, we specifically talked about this. You are on probation. You do realize that, right? Your ninety days weren't over when you got sent to prison. They were extended. If you go to wherever this place is and start shooting people, I cannot protect you; do you understand that?"

"I get that," Zack said. Everyone looked at him. "Look, this isn't about me being a hero."

"It's not?" Lauren asked.

Zack looked at her. "No, it's not. I didn't spend a dozen years in the military to let someone else do the dirty work. They didn't send us in first so we could hide and wait for reinforcements with the excuse of if we get injured, what good are we? That's not how we're wired."

Dre and Kilgas nodded appreciably.

"But we have to think this out," Zack added. "They know we have Sophie which means they'll suspect she talked."

"Meaning she's dead if she goes back," Dre said.

"We're not letting her die. Her parents deserve to see her again, too."

"So do Hannah and Angie's," Kilgas said.

Zack looked at Captain Barnes. "Ted, can you protect Sophie?"

"Zack, if you ask me to get involved, I have to do it by the book."

Zack nodded and understood.

"Zack, listen to me. We call the FBI, she tells them everything, and they can breach the area and get the girls out safely," Ted said. "It's the right call."

Zack looked at Lauren and saw the tear trickle out of the corner of her eye.

Ted eyed Zack. "Damn you, Stack." Ted shook his head. "Zack, getting killed is not in the plan, do you understand? This is too much for us."

Zack remained silent but steadfast in his look.

Ted took a deep breath. "You are one hard-headed individual."

Kilgas looked at Sophie. "Sophie, can you spot the guys looking for you?"

"I don't know," Sophie said. "I never knew how many there were." Sophie looked around the room and saw all eyes on her. She quickly reverted to Zack. "Zack, I'm sorry I did what I did, and I know I deserve to be punished. They'll kill me."

"Bro, I'm not sure we want to get into a fight with a hundred gun-toting brainwashed idiots," Dre said.

"How many men do we need?" Kilgas said.

"No," Ted barked. "Absolutely not. We're not going to war with mercenaries."

"No offense, Captain," Kilgas said, "but it's not your daughter, and it's not your war. I respect you and everyone here, but only if your objective is the same as mine."

"Are you out to save your daughter or exact revenge?"

"Save my daughter. I only do revenge when I get paid. No one is paying me. I'm paying him." Kilgas pointed at Zack.

Zack rubbed his forehead. "Let me think about it. Criminals won't pass on free cash. And they have one every day this week. So let me think about this, at least overnight." Zack said.

"And what about tonight?"

"Dre, can we sneak Sophie to the Inn, lock her inside and make sure she contacts no one," Zack asked. "We can't keep her here."

"I'm not safe anywhere," Sophie said.

"As Stack said, you aren't dying, princess," Kilgas said. "My daughter is coming home alive."

Lauren kept her eyes on Zack.

Dre nodded. "I think so. Ted, can you arrange some diversion to keep eyes away from this side of the square?"

"I can. But I don't think it's a good idea," Ted answered.

"Mr. Stack, I don't think you should," said Lauren.

"Lauren is right again," Barnes said. "Zack, you look like shit. When was the last time you slept? February?"

Zack said nothing.

"I can stay with her," Lauren volunteered.

"No," Zack said quickly. He pointed at Kilgas. "No."

"I'll take the first watch," Dre said. "Mik and Big D can take the second watch. That will get us to daylight."

"I'll make a call. They'll be enough activity on the other side of the square, you'll be able to drive a herd of cattle through this side, and no one will notice," Barnes said reluctantly.

Detective Dylan Kael exited Zack's office. "I just got off the phone with a Virginia State Police Captain. Bradley Pollard is dead. Murdered at his home yesterday."

Barnes looked immediately at Zack.

"One bullet, a nine-millimeter from a Glock 17 to the back of the head. Four more center-massed on his heart from the back," Kael said.

"Well, that's interesting," Barnes said, his glare still fixed on Zack.

"What's more interesting is that they found an FBI badge on the premises. It looked like there was a struggle in the front of the house. The primary suspect is Agent Carter Nolen. It was his badge, and Pollard allegedly reported a visit by Nolen and how Nolen threatened him."

"Stack, Kilgas, anything to add?" Barnes said.

Zack shook his head. "I shoot a Sig. It wasn't me."

"I shoot a 1911, .45 cal."

"VSP and the Feds are fighting over the investigation right now," Kael said.

Tears leaked from Sophie's eyes. "I'm sorry, Zack. I really am."

Barnes stood. "We'll meet tomorrow morning at six and go from there. Agreed?" Barnes looked specifically at Kilgas.

"Don't worry about him. If we fail, I'm the only one he'll shoot," Zack said.

59

Agent Carter Nolen drove to the office Tuesday morning. He had a nine o'clock meeting with a task force, then an eleven o'clock off-site meeting with Agent Ferguson to update on other "important" issues. Nolen arrived an hour before his first meeting to settle into the day. Customary procedure.

He locked the car and approached the front door with his lanyard, ready to swipe the secured door. Out of the corner of his eye, he saw men in suits and uniforms approach slowly from the left and right. They all watched him. Nolen smiled at the leader as he stopped next to the door. "Good morning, gentlemen," Nolen greeted them.

"Agent Carter Nolen?" The man asked.

"Who's asking?"

The man showed his badge to the Department of Justice. "Tyler Zimmerman, DOJ. Mr. Nolen, you're under arrest for the murder of Bradley Pollard. Cuff him," Zimmerman ordered, and two agents quickly locked Nolen's wrists behind his back.

"What? I don't know a Bradley Pollard."

"We found your badge and gun on the premises of the victim."

"Wait, my gun was stolen."

"Did you report it missing?"

"No."

"And your badge? Did that go missing, too? Badge, gun, your cell phone off, no known whereabouts of you at the time of the murder," the agent said. "Do you want to talk or not?"

Carter Nolen sensed a sell-out. "I want my attorney."

"Read him his rights and take him away."

Across the parking lot, on the street, sat a black Cadillac Escalade SUV, with a rear passenger window slightly lowered. A tall, blonde woman sat in the back seat and watched. She saw the FBI Agent carted away in handcuffs and knew that man's existence suddenly took a turn for the worse. Much worse. A man sat next to her.

"Make sure he doesn't talk to his attorney until after you talk to him. Give him a chance to roll over on his cohorts."

"Yes, ma'am. I'm on it." The man quickly exited the vehicle and rushed off.

She smiled, rolled up the window, and tapped on the seat in front of her. The driver casually drove away from the area. Addison Jones held her cell phone and sent a simple text to her new friend. "Good start. Well done." She didn't expect a return as Zack Stack rarely acknowledged her. This time he did. It simply said, 'stand by.'

* * * *

Zack sat in his office late Tuesday afternoon and waited. The phone was silent, and that was the last thing Zack expected. He made calls and sent texts. Zack felt he put in the effort this day. Save for one person.

Zack wasn't ready for her. Yet.

The phone finally rang. Zack answered and listened to Dre talk.

"It's done. No one saw us move her, and the watch has started."

"Good. I'll take the late shift. I can't sleep anyway."

Dre didn't hesitate. "No. You're not part of the watch. You need sleep, per Lauren's orders."

"Better me than Kilgas. I have to see a couple of people now but let's meet for dinner at six. Can you make that?"

"Your treat. See you, six o'clock, Max's."

"When is it not my treat?"

"Don't be late. Ally will be with me."

* * * *

Zack entered the rear door of his apartment rarely. This time he figured it to be the fourth time ever. Maybe the fifth, but he wasn't about to stop and count when he walked through the kitchen.

"What are you doing here? I just left you at the office."

Lauren smiled. "You hid in your office for so long; how would you have known if I left?" She looked at Zack. "In fact, how would anyone else know, either, since no one is ever there."

"You're there, Lauren. That's what we pay you for. Why are you here?"

"Checking on you, sir."

Zack looked at his watch. "I'm supposed to meet Dre and Ally for dinner at six. Want to come along?"

"Sir, I'm not getting involved with you. We've covered this before."

"I'm not asking you to get involved. I'm asking you if you want to come along for dinner with Dre and Ally. Believe me, the last thing I want right now is to be involved."

"Really?" Lauren's doubt resonated.

Zack sat down. "Yes, really. I have to see about a couple of things before dinner. The offer still stands. Max's six o'clock."

Lauren watched Zack and frowned. "Sir, there's something I need to tell you. Promise me you won't get mad."

Zack watched as her eyes glossed over, and a tear leaked out. "That has never been said to me where the following conversation ended in me not being mad."

"Please let this be the first time, sir. I'm sorry. I'm so, so sorry."

"What, Lauren?"

"When I was researching the symbol, I came across the church. Unfortunately, I wasn't careful and," she trailed off. "Sir, when they found you at my apartment and attacked you, it was because of me." Lauren held her breath, but the tears flowed. "They found you because of me, sir. Michelle stopped at the office the other day and told me. She has been watching what we do and discovered how they traced me." Lauren finally looked at Zack. "I'm sorry, sir. They recognized you because of the guy at the abandoned factory site. That's how they found you."

"Michelle knows this?"

Lauren nodded and sniffed as she wiped tears off her face. "I'm sorry. I was sloppy, but it will never happen again. Michelle showed me."

Zack sighed. "What if I hadn't shown?"

"Then they would have taken me instead," Lauren said softly. "You saved me and didn't even realize it."

"That's not how it felt."

"I feel like I've made a mess of things with us. I'm sorry, Mr. Stack."

Zack walked to Lauren and hugged her. "We poked the bear. It was bound to happen. You can meet me or come with me now. You choose."

"Just dinner. Nothing else. I mean it."

60

Zack exited the shower Wednesday morning and slowly dried himself with the thick, oversize towel. The ceiling fan hummed and sucked away the steam effectively. He stared at his face in the mirror, and thoughts started. The directions scattered, and soon, there was too much swirling inside for him to focus. He tossed the towel aside and continued to stare into the mirror though he didn't even see himself.

Briefly, he wondered where it all went wrong because it felt wrong. Everything felt wrong.

Mikayla burst into the bathroom.

"Stack! OH MY GOD! Put some clothes on!"

"I just got out of the shower, and this is my bathroom," Zack replied.

"Get dressed now! We have a problem."

"What?"

"Sophie. She's not there."

"WHAT?"

* * * *

Zack stood inside the room. It was empty. He turned slowly, noticeably upset, and faced Mikayla, Dre, and Darnell. "How in the name of a sore MONKEY'S ASS did this happen?"

The three looked at each other.

"Anyone? Anyone? Bueller, Bueller?"

"We got tricked," Dre said. "I'm sorry. I went home and slept after we had dinner. I got a text from Mikayla saying she took over for Big D."

"But unfortunately," Mikayla said, "at the same time, I got a text from Dre telling me he took over for Big D."

"Where were you, Darnell?"

"I, uh, left."

"You left Sophie here alone?"

"I got a text from you telling me you were in the lobby. You said to leave via the back door to eliminate suspicion because you thought people followed you."

"I didn't send you a text."

"I know that now."

"I never," Zack started but stopped, frustrated. "Ok, water under the bridge, right? Doesn't matter now. We were all outsmarted."

Darnell dropped his head. "I'm sorry. This is all my fault."

Zack disagreed. "Kilgas. Sonofabitch."

"So what do we do, Zack? We call the FBI, right?" Mikayla said. "That's the right call. We know what he did. He grabbed Sophie and went to their place."

"And he's going to get himself and her killed," Zack said.

"Darnell, go back to the office and stay there. Mik, you go with him. Dre, let's go for a ride."

61

"They're somewhere on that property," Zack sat on the crest of a ridge and looked through his binoculars at the land owned by the Colson's.

"So are a bunch of brain-washed gun-toting idiots," Dre said. "If we go near that place, we'll get gunned down in a heartbeat. Look at all the heavy artillery patrolling the grounds." Dre scoped the area with his binoculars. "What are those outhouse-type buildings further up the slope from the compound?"

"Well," Zack said. "I have an idea, and I don't like it."

Dre understood. "Dude, this is not good."

Zack lowered his binoculars. "Let's go. If he isn't dead yet, he soon will be. Same with Sophie and, most likely, the two girls. I'm guessing behind one of those doors of one of those outhouses; we'll find who we're looking for."

"What are you planning, Zack?"

"Let's get back to the office. If we do anything, we do it at night. We'll have the advantage." The two crouched low and headed back through the hills and forest and got to the minivan. Two hours later, they sat inside the office with a larger audience.

* * * *

"You two shouldn't be here, and you won't talk me out of this."

"I know better than to try," Ted Barnes said. "Thank you for finally including me, though, before it gets out of hand. And now, this is when I do what I do and tell you to call the police or FBI."

"I already did," Zack said as he looked at Lauren. "Sometimes, I do listen and act on good advice." Zack winked at Lauren, and she smiled briefly. Then, Zack walked to her desk, sat on the front edge, and looked at his watch. "Here he comes now."

Agent Ty Campbell of the FBI entered the office, acknowledged the crowd, and sat in an empty chair as if the head of the class. "Stack, introduce me to everyone."

Zack pointed at Campbell. "Everyone, this is the one guy in the FBI I believe we can trust. Ty Campbell. He helped Jules and me in Clyde last year. Ty that is Darnell," Zack pointed at each person in the room. "That's Dre. You've met Mikayla and Lauren. Together, we are the employees of our little agency. The two men on the couch are Captain Ted Barnes and Detective Dylan Kael of the Baltimore Police Department. Ty, these two men I definitely can trust."

The group gave genuine but tempered pleasantries. Ty stood and walked to a position to see the entire group. "So you're all aware, Stack explained the situation to me."

Captain Barnes nodded. "And the position of the FBI is what?"

"We have no position," Campbell said. "We aren't investigating the Colson brothers or their ministry."

"Despite the criminal activity," Barnes said. "We know of murders, kidnappings, illegal drugs, rape. Do I need to go on?"

"I need proof to take this anywhere. Stack kidnapped and possibly tortured a girl who may be saying all of that to slander them."

Barnes looked at Zack. "This is a new you, Zack. So you told him everything?"

"Just about," Zack said. "He knows enough."

"So the two missing girls, what about them?"

Campbell didn't like the news he gave. "We have a bigger problem, and by we, I mean you and your lot, Stack." Campbell walked around the room, grabbed a mug, and filled it with coffee. The group waited. "To update, Stack has some enemies at the Bureau, and the Colson brothers have some friends in higher places than that. So waging war against the Colson brothers is a bad idea."

"They're criminals, Agent Campbell," Barnes said.

"That may be so, but there's always an election around the corner. Power begets power. You guys should know this as well as anyone. And people in power hate two things. One, losing that power, and two, losing that power. They'll do anything to keep it, and this time, Stack, if you pursue any action against the Colson brothers, you'll end up in the crosshairs of that power."

"Gee, there's a surprise," Barnes muttered.

"If they come after me because of the Colson brothers, simply to protect their reputation and the reputation of their spiritual advisors, they're inviting trouble. That's not on me."

"The IRS audit will be," Campbell said. "And they'll undoubtedly find something. Or, until they do, they'll cease your assets and close your doors. They'll take everything from you with one clear message: keep quiet or else."

The group remained silent. Barnes decided it was time to add to his coffee intake for the day and filled a mug. He sipped it slowly, thoughtfully.

"Is that official?"

"No. It's not even unofficial. But it's more than speculation."

"So you can't help," Dre declared.

"I tried telling you all," Zack said.

"Now is not the time for an I-told-you-so, sir," Lauren reprimanded Zack.

"Stack, if I convince my superior to investigate, to descend upon the Colson compound in search of those girls, he'll go to his superiors, and so on. Ultimately, what will happen is," Campbell sighed, "well, you know the saying about what rolls downhill. Stack, you're at the bottom."

"You aren't the first person to tell me that. But Kilgas threw gasoline onto a simmering fire. So, my hunch is they'll close shop there to bury what they're hiding forever, move to a new spot and continue with a new congregation."

"You're probably right," Campbell said. "But I can't even put it under surveillance. You have no evidence of wrongdoing other than the word of that girl, and you can't produce her. My superiors would want to talk to you. You already know how that would go, Stack. Not even your girl, Michelle, couldn't protect you."

62

Barnes walked to his former seat and settled himself. "Zack, I see that look in your eye. You need to forget about it. Even a soldier like you knows sometimes it's better to walk away to live and fight another day."

Zack ignored the comment. "Sophie said their made-up Easter date will be their biggest scam of the year. Even with Kilgas' shenanigan, I doubt they'll forego the heist. But after they cash in, they'll bolt town."

"What did his merc friends say?" Dre asked.

Zack crossed his arms. "No one left the premises. He may be dead, but he's still there."

"Merc friends?" Campbell asked. "You're dealing with mercenaries?"

"That's what Kilgas is, Campbell," Stack said. "And he's saved my life more than once."

"That doesn't mean you owe him yours, sir," Lauren injected.

Zack sighed. "If the feds or police go in, Kilgas will be fried."

"If he's still alive," Dre said.

"I have to assume he is," Zack said.

"And you're willing to risk your life on him after all he's put us through?" Barnes asked.

"He's one of us," Zack said and pointed at Dre. "At least he was. I owe him that much."

"Do you?" Lauren shot at Zack.

Zack remained silent.

Dre walked across the office and grabbed a coffee for himself. "You owe him nothing, Zack."

"It isn't just Kilgas. I promised Sophie she'd see her parents again," Zack said.

"Sir, she is not your responsibility," Lauren said firmly.

"Then whose responsibility?" Zack asked sharply.

"Stack, are you thinking of an incursion to rescue that girl and the other two? Because that's not a good idea," Campbell said. "And if you're caught going in there, they will kill you. It won't be your word against theirs. You know that."

Zack walked to the fridge behind Lauren's desk, grabbed a bottle of water, and swigged it. "There's only one way this ends, and it ends tonight. I'll go alone. Ty, I need your word that you know nothing of this and will say nothing, regardless of the outcome."

"Stack, you have my word. But I'm urging you to reconsider. Even if you're successful, you won't be successful. In this case, the heat will only flow one way."

"Any other way and they all die. You can't and won't do anything, but I can."

"And what chance will you have?" Campbell said. "This is also unofficial, but I can tell you they have over one-hundred-armed men, and they are ready for a fight."

"There doesn't have to be one. I go in before dawn," Zack said. "It's best if all of you go home and forget about this."

"Stack, you'll end up in prison or dead."

"I know," Zack replied to Campbell. "But no one else will. This is where it ends."

Lauren turned around and left the room. She entered Zack's office and shut the door.

"Think about what you're doing, Zack," Mikayla said softly. "People care about you here. Dying doesn't help anything. We need you alive. You're a father now, Zack. Think about that."

"I am. I'm thinking about the other fathers that can't do what I can."

Mikayla raised her hands in defeat. "This is another reason I stopped seeing you." Mikayla exited and shut the door after she entered Dre's office.

Dre stood. "You go, we go."

"No, you're not. Go home and forget this meeting ever happened." Zack left and entered his office.

Lauren sat on his desk, her back to him. Zack saw her shoulders heaving as Lauren cried. Zack walked to her and put his hand on her shoulder. Lauren jumped off the desk and swiped his hand away.

"Lauren," Zack tried, but Lauren knocked his hands away again.

She cried and knocked his hands away again before finally, she let Zack take her in his arms, and she clung to him tightly. Lauren cried into his shoulder.

Zack felt her emotion, wanted to reconsider his stance but knew he couldn't. He felt his eyes gloss over but fought it off. Zack let her cry for several minutes and waited until Lauren stopped before he pulled back, wiped the tears off her cheeks, and stared into her eyes. "Lauren, I'm sorry. I wish I could explain why."

Lauren took a deep breath. She kept her arms around Zack's neck. "I already know why. That doesn't mean I have to like it or agree with you." Lauren wiped her cheeks and exhaled. They looked at each other before Lauren quickly put her mouth on his and kissed him deeply. When she pulled away, she breathed heavily. "Goodbye, Mr. Stack."

63

Midnight struck as Zack stopped the minivan behind the office for a couple of final provisions. Then, as the garage door opened, the light flicked on, and Zack saw three men, dressed in military fatigues, arms crossed.

Andre Kitchell, Ted Barnes, and Dylan Kael.

"What are you doing here?"

"We drew straws," Dre said. "We lost, so we're coming with you." Dre shrugged his broad shoulders. "Sorry, bro, but I can't let you go off and get yourself killed. I made promises, too. Besides, you know how we roll."

Zack showed a brief smile. "And you think I'm dumb."

"I know you are. But I'm just as dumb."

"And you two?" Zack looked at Barnes and Kael.

"Mikayla and Lauren made us. Something about returning your dead body so they can spit on it," Ted said. "I'm sure there are a few others in your life who would like that honor, too."

"Zack, I know what you're thinking," Dre said. He lifted two rifles from the floor. "But they can shoot. More importantly, they can shoot from a distance."

Zack stared at the three. "Big D and Campbell?"

"Campbell promised he knows nothing. I'll take his word," Dre said. "Big D was upset, but after we die, I told him the business is all his. It didn't mean much until I showed him all your bank accounts. He's still pretty upset, though."

"Ok then. Let's finish this. And remember, you three come back alive no matter what."

"So do you, Zack," Dre said. "So do you."

* * * *

Two AM. More than four hours before sunrise. Zack stopped the minivan in a forest five miles west of the target. Five miles of hills, trees, vegetation, and no people in between. He drove it off the road as far as he could.

Four men exited the vehicle. Barnes and Kael watched the two men ready themselves. Neither knew what to expect. Zack checked the Bushmaster ACR 3 rifle and the additional clips in his belt, the Ka-bar secure in its sheath, and his side-arm with extra ammo. Dre did the same, almost in unison. Both checked their sidearms and secured them in the hip holster. Zack looked at Dre, and the sight reminded him of the two preparing for a mission back in the military. Dre handed him a grenade.

"Where did you get this?"

"You have your contacts; I have mine," Dre said. "Here's some smoke grenades and flashbangs. Use them wisely." Dre watched Zack blacken his face with eye black. "White privilege biting you in the ass now, isn't it?"

Zack smiled, put on his helmet, and adjusted the night-vision eyepiece. "This isn't privilege."

Zack and Dre grabbed two M24 Sniper rifles, handed one to each Barnes and Kael. Zack gave each a magazine for the rifles. "You're getting a crash course tonight," Zack said. "Number one rule there is no discussion on is simple. Don't shoot Dre or me, accidentally or otherwise. End of lesson." Zack handed each one last item. "Night vision. You'll need this. Don't look into any bright lights with it. You'll be temporarily blinded, and in combat, that is a bad thing. Flip this switch, and we can talk but keep it to a minimum. Any questions?"

"You think we're going into combat?" Dylan Kael asked.

Zack looked at Dylan but said nothing. "Follow us, step for step. Stay on course and keep up. This is our domain now, gentlemen."

Barnes tapped Kael's arm. "Just do as they say, and we'll be fine." The two followed only feet behind Zack and Dre.

The telltale call of a familiar nightjar, a bird, typically heard and rarely seen as it came out at night and ate flying insects, echoed inside the forest.

"What is that?" Dre asked.

"Chuck Will's Widow, it's a bird," Zack said. "You should come birding with me and learn this stuff."

"I was going to before you got locked up. I didn't have anyone to teach me after that. How about after we get out of here, you take the girls and me to see some birds?"

"Don't mention Stefani's name. I mean it."

Dre almost laughed. "Tell me why you dumped her, then."

"I didn't." Zack looked at Dre.

"What? That's not what she said."

"I didn't, Dre. I was going to ask her to marry me."

Dre stopped and stared at Zack. "What?"

"Something happened, but I don't know what. I'll find out but keep that between us, ok?"

"Why? Maybe you should tell her. You should tell her."

"Just keep it between us, ok? There's a lot of other stuff going on I need to finish first."

"What about Jules? What's going on with her?"

"It's complicated, Dre. Can we move on?"

"I want to know."

"Um, excuse us, gentlemen," Barnes interrupted. "This isn't a soap opera. Can we get on with this?"

They trekked towards the destination silently for a few more minutes.

"This brings back some memories."

"Not ones I like to recall."

"At least this time, we know why we're doing what we're doing."

"We always knew why we were doing what we were doing," Zack said. "Because we were told."

"Ours is not to reason why," Dre began.

"Ours is just to do or die," Zack finished.

"Zack, is your head clear?"

"Crystal."

"Remember when I told you not to try to bullshit me?"

"I do."

"This is real, Zack. I need rampage Zack to be present and accounted for."

"Don't worry."

"Do I know everything about this situation?" Dre asked.

"Campbell was right. The Colson boys made a phone call to exercise their considerable financial influence to prevent any investigation of the Colson's operations," Zack said.

"You know this how?"

"I made a phone call. Tomorrow will be interesting." *I hope I get to listen to the lecture I'm sure to get from Addy tomorrow.*

"You could have mentioned this earlier," Barnes said.

"Just don't shoot anyone who looks like Secret Service," Zack quipped.

"So we're about to go to war with the US Government?"

"It's becoming a habit for me. But not the whole government. Just one side."

"Which side?"

"The one in power."

"Jesus Christ," Barnes muttered.

"What about Jules? Does she know you're about to get us all killed or locked up for life?"

"Do me a favor and look after her and my daughter, ok?"

"We're both making it home today, Zack."

"Just make sure you look after Jules and my daughter if I don't, Ok? And keep an eye on Stef."

They walked further. A compass guided the group in the right direction. The darkness of the night made seeing beyond an outstretched hand impossible, but night vision eliminated the treachery. To Zack and Dre, the words of one their commanders in the military gave them confidence: "We own the night."

64

The early dawn hours. Still ninety minutes before sunrise. The coldest part of the night. This day was no different. Atop a hillcrest, two hundred yards back, Zack and Dre placed Barnes and Kael. Both had clear views of much of the grounds, but not all. Neither liked their position but remained as Zack and Dre disappeared in the black of the night.

Zack and Dre reached the ditch beside the overgrown dirt road. Across from it lay the property inside the fence. Video monitors spaced thirty feet apart slowly scanned the area. Dre and Zack watched.

"They'll see us," Dre said.

"Maybe," Zack answered.

"Is the fence electrified?"

"Probably."

Headlights and the low rumble of a diesel engine coming from the property on the road ended the conversation. The headlights lit the forest, and the two men ducked behind a tree.

"It's a bus," Zack said. "A charter bus."

The bus reached a gate, two men exited the bus, unlocked, and opened the gate; the bus pulled forward, the two men closed and locked the gate and boarded the bus. The bus lurched forward before the engines roared, and the bus moved forward on the narrow, vegetation-covered dirt road towards a county highway a mile away.

Zack and Dre reached the edge of the forest, hopped over the narrow ditch beside the road, and watched the red taillights of the bus disappear.

"They're clearing out," Zack said.

"What if the girls are on that bus?"

"We better hope they aren't. Let's go find out," Zack said as they hustled to the gate. "Cut the chain."

"Why are you always giving the orders in the field?"

"I was promoted faster than you. And this is payback for you not visiting me for my last five months in prison."

The small pair of wire cutters clipped at the chain. "How long are you going to remind me of that?"

"I'll bring it up during the toast I give at your wedding to show what a great best man I am. Then, after that, I'll drop it for good." They looked at each other. "Probably."

Dre grunted as the cutters popped the link and the chain dropped to the ground. "Well, I'll give you that one. I can deal with that for the next month."

"You set a date. Really? Why didn't you tell me? When is it?"

"The weekend of July 8th, and we picked it right after you stopped the other day. I'm sorry, by the way, for the hundredth time."

"Forget it. Wait, what? A wedding in the middle of the summer in Baltimore, and we'll be wearing tuxedos?" Zack shook his head. "We'll be swimming in ball soup! Are you out of your mind?" They pushed open the gate and crept inside.

"It was the only day we could get both the church and the reception hall. She didn't want to wait until fall. Something about the symbolism of fall and shit like flowers losing their blooms and all that crap," Dre said. "Just toss extra baby powder down there that day."

"Please tell me it's at least inside in air conditioning."

They looked at each other.

"Jesus Christ! Are you insane? Outside, Baltimore, middle of July? It's either going to be 95 degrees with two thousand percent humidity or raining! You know what that will do to the bride's and bridesmaid's hair?"

"Zack, what was I supposed to say? No? I love this woman and want to give her what she wants."

"I'll bet you a vacation for the four of us to St. Lucia that she'll want air conditioning before she says I do."

"Deal. What is it with you and St. Lucia? You have a bet with everyone we know to go there."

"It's in the Caribbean, it's gorgeous, sure it's hot, but the ocean is right there, and half the island is a wildlife refuge. Can you imagine the birds there?"

"There you are," Dre tried not to laugh out loud. "So by four of us, you mean Stef and you, right?"

"Dre, you sound like a broken record. How did you set up a wedding in a month?"

"I'm not sure. I think Ally had it planned all along. But you are bringing Stef, right?"

"What is wrong with you and everyone else?"

"Hey, can you two get on with this and quit the chit-chat?" Barnes spoke into the headsets they all wore.

"This is SOP, boss," Zack said. He looked at Dre. "You ready?"

"Ready as ever. Age before beauty, right?"

"I'm five days older. Five days."

"Which makes you older. You lead." They headed south on a trail inside the fence. Dre remembered their military days. So far, this was the Zack Dre knew in combat. "Is this the escape route?"

"Not sure yet," Zack said.

"That's encouraging," Dre deadpanned. "R.O.E.?"

"We do what we do but let's try not to kill anyone," Zack said. "We find those girls; we get out."

"And Kilgas?"

"Secondary. I think Kilgas would agree with me on this. Stay sharp. We're flying first class to the island; you're buying the first round of drinks on the beach, and yours has to have pineapple in it."

Dre smiled. "Bro, whatever happens, we go home alive. Don't forget that."

"You're taking us, too," Barnes said. "Now get to work."

Zack looked at Dre. "It's rampage mode time, partner. Let's get this done."

65

The two moved to opposite sides of the dirt road as they entered the property owned by the Colson brothers, which included the megachurch, the Colson's large estate, the compound ahead of them, and thousands of acres of open and treed country. They walked a quarter mile before reaching the end of the trees, shrubs, and vegetation surrounding the entire property.

They stopped at the edge and scanned in every direction—no signs of life. No movement.

The compound included several buildings, all single story, with plenty of green space. A half-dozen gardens located about the property provided fruits and vegetables for the inhabitants. One penned-in area contained chickens for eggs and likely chicken meat. One building was larger for all of the inhabitants to gather.

Zack and Dre scanned the area, made a complete circle, and looked at each other.

"What do you think?" Zack asked.

"I think the owners of this place don't want anyone to see what's going on here," Dre said.

"My thoughts exactly. Which begs the question, how did we get to the center of this compound so easily?"

"Because they let us," Dre answered. "We need cover."

The two rushed to the edge and crouched low.

"I don't like it," Dre said.

"It's a trap," Zack said. "But they're avoiding a firefight. Why?"

"This would be the perfect place to attack," Dre said.

Zack scanned again. "We have to search those buildings. Boss?"

"No bogeys," Barnes reported.

"I got the point," Zack said. Zack moved ahead, and Dre followed at an appropriate spacing with their night vision still employed. Zack crept low but fast until he reached the first building. Zack opened the unlocked door and peeked in quickly. "Clear."

No one inside with six empty beds. The subsequent three units revealed the same.

"They moved out," Dre said as they stepped outside the large hall. "That was them on the bus. They cleared out, and this is one giant trap."

A thick line of trees and brush lined the end of the compound. Beyond that, nothing but open country mostly uphill with shallow valleys heading east towards the estate and megachurch to the east-southeast.

They approached the tree line and crept through twenty yards of the forest before they reached a path. They looked both ways. Nothing but both knew what it was.

After another twenty yards of trees and brush, they reached the large clearing that led to the estate without impediment. Zack saw the four small buildings in the distance. A standard-sized door and a tiny rectangular building looked about four feet wide and five feet deep.

"Those aren't shitters, are they?"

"They're not shitters," Zack said with a hint of dread in his voice.

"Uh, gentlemen, you are nearing the extent of our range. We need to move forward," Barnes chimed over the mic.

"Negative. Stay there," Zack said. There was no reply.

Zack dashed from the edge of the brush into the grass-covered clearing. He reached the first outhouse and knelt low. Unnoticed. Zack looked at the door handle.

"Be advised, bogey twelve o'clock, just appeared on the side of outhouse number 4," Dre said. "Fully armed."

Zack remained motionless and saw the man lean against the shed. The men withdrew a cigarette and lighter and lit the stick, one of the many rules not to break when watching night. Zack saw it all.

Zack crept to the backside of the first shed and quietly maneuvered to the second and then the third. Zack heard the man talk. Another rule broken.

"What is he doing down there? How long does it take?"

Zack crept to the rear of the fourth shed. He heard the guard laugh.

"Maybe he'll let us take a shot at her. We do all the work, but they get all the fun."

Zack thought of his options. His knife would have worked easiest, but he remembered his pledge. Zack set down his rifle and peered around the corner. Nothing. He stepped on the side, and the man talked again.

"God, he's going to just shoot the bitch, so why is it taking so long? It's late, and we don't get paid enough to listen to him screwing these girls."

Zack heard and understood the plan. He also suspected that the Colson brothers didn't expect the incursion so soon after the Kilgas fiasco. The man laughed and paced in front of the shack. The man turned around; Zack put one hand around the man's throat; the other arm crashed across his head, and the man slammed to the ground. Zack pounced atop the man, his knees pinned the man's arms and his hand over the man's mouth. The man struggled to get free. The guard's boot kicked the door, and Zack decided it was time to end it. His elbow slammed into the man's face and stunned the man. Briefly silenced, Zack knocked the man out with a vicious right cross. Zack quickly grabbed the man and pulled him aside. The other guard emerged after the noise alarmed him.

The door opened. "Hey, where are you?" The guard inside stepped out. "Dude, quit playing. Where are you?"

"Here," Zack said as the butt of his rifle clobbered the man's face. He hit the ground unconscious. Zack dragged him aside and looked at the door. "Dre, I have to go in. It must be to a tunnel underground."

"Uh-oh. No, partner. Don't do it. I'll do it. Come back now."

Zack shook off the memories and fought the freeze his body attempted. He opened the door to see stairs leading underground, as he feared. Zack's mind played tricks on him. Images of Pigface and the other cretins in Clyde raced across his mind; the sounds and smells of Zack tied underground filled his senses. Pigface's laughter filled his ears, and the feeling of Zack's weapon pressed against his head.

"Zack, come in. I'm on my way." Dre feared Zack let the trauma affect his actions. This was a trigger. Dre exited his safe vantage point and ran towards the four sheds.

Zack shook it off.

Zack opened the door and descended the stairs. A narrow strip of light escaped under a wooden door, so Zack removed the eyepiece, reached the door, and heard a girl plead and cry. And a man laugh.

Altered Vows

*

Ted Barnes crouched low as he reached the road with Dylan Kael at his side. They raced across and through the gate. They couldn't see ahead of them or behind them, but they knew where they previously were was not optimum for helping. So they trudged through the shrubbery and trees headed east, where their partners searched.

Sticks and leaves crumbled under their feet as they crept forward. Once they reached the edge, Barnes stopped them, silence surrounded them, and they continued.

The two dodged to the first of the buildings, but the first wasn't the objective. Instead, Barnes wanted the best vantage point he could get, so they continued to the edge of the encampment. Barnes needed to see Zack and Dre, but at the last building, Barnes realized this was as far as he and Kael safely could continue.

66

The wooden door splintered off its hinges, and Zack stepped inside. A large man jumped in fright, stared at the door, and Zack recognized him immediately. Lewis Colson. He tried to pull up his pants, and Zack identified the victim strapped to the exam chair, her legs open wide and naked from the waist down, tears streamed down her face, and she looked at Zack expectant of relief. Zack suspected a bullet to the head was the relief she begged for, as anything would have been a relief from what she suffered. But Zack had a different plan.

The embers exploded. Zack morphed into rampage mode.

Zack rushed Colson and kicked him into the wall. Zack grabbed the back of Colson's head, spun him around, and slammed his face into the wood-planked wall three times before Zack turned Colson again and buried a fist in his stomach. Colson hunched over, and a knee met his nose. Zack grabbed Colson's head again and smashed it into the metal chair. Colson hit the floor, dazed, bloodied, and in pain.

Which was just the beginning.

Zack kicked his face, stomped on Colson's genitals, and pressed and twisted his foot as if squashing a bug. Colson howled in pain but didn't pass out. Zack lifted him again by his neck, dragged Colson across the room, and smashed his face on the metal chair again. Colson was out. Another kick to the head ended Zack's assault.

Zack looked at the girl on the chair and saw the horror on her face. Angie Simpson. "I'm getting you out of here, Angie," Zack said. "Can you walk?"

She stared at Colson but breathed rapidly, as if in shock.

Zack looked around for her clothes and saw ripped underwear and pants that looked like pajama pants. He grabbed the pants and, after he undid her legs, slid the pants up her legs.

She stared at Zack in fright.

"Angie, we have to go. Do you know where Hannah is?"

The girl shook, the events not computing in her head.

"Where's Hannah?" Zack said as he undid the binds on her hands. The girl's movements were sluggish, but she said nothing. Zack recognized it.

"Can you walk?" Zack watched. Zack helped her out of the chair, but with weakened legs, she fell. Zack caught her before she hit the floor. Zack's mind flashed back again, and he froze. He remembered Derek Willows. Zack shook it off. "Come here." Zack grabbed the girl, swung her to his back, and shifted her higher. She held on with her arms and legs. "Hang on. We're taking you home."

The girl couldn't take her eyes off the man on the floor. Lewis Colson. Neither could Zack. He grabbed his Sig, aimed, and fired. Lewis Colson's kneecap disappeared.

* * * *

"Hold your position and keep watch," Zack replied. "Can you see our location?"

"Clear as day."

"Then you disobeyed an order. We have a passenger and need immediate extraction. Can you comply?"

"Roger that. I'll send leafy weed."

"Ten-four." Zack flipped off his mic. "Dre take her to Barnes. I'm going to check the other three holes."

"There are no guards. They're probably empty."

"I hope so."

Dre scooped Angie in his arms and ran west into the dark while Zack went to the third shed and ripped the padlock off the door. He didn't care about noise and didn't move slowly down the stairs. Zack kicked the door off the frame, the room lit, and saw a man in the middle of the room. His feet and hands tied to a normal chair, but nothing wrapped around his mouth. He squinted as his eyes adjusted to the light. Zack stepped forward and yanked out his Ka-bar.

Zack undid the wraps on his feet and walked around to untie his hands. The man in the chair leaned forward and rubbed the mark on his arm.

"It's about damn time, Stack. Another twenty minutes, and they were going to light me up with some kickass LSD then kill me."

"My timing has always been bad. I told you to be patient."

"I'm sorry, but we have bigger problems. Look." Kilgas pointed to a corner of the ceiling.

"Well, that doesn't look good at all," Zack replied nonchalantly. Zack recognized the setup. Explosive prima cord wrapped around the room's ceiling along with a block of C4 plastique on opposite sides of the ceiling corner. "I should leave you here to get buried."

"Stack, I'm sorry. I had to find Hannah."

"Yeah, how did that work for you? Now they have Sophie, too." Zack walked to the explosive.

"She ratted me out the first chance she got, Stack. She knows where Hannah is."

"To save your ass and hers and buy time for me," Zack snapped. "I earned her trust, Kilgas. Whatever she did, she did to save herself after you stupidly barreled in here last night. What were you thinking?"

"You didn't have anything last night. Is your head clear yet?"

Zack detached the explosive from the wall and unhooked it. "In our world, Kilgas, we follow orders, or people die. Which one do you want to be?"

"Zack, I'm sorry. I let emotions get in the way, but I'm good. Hannah is at the estate."

"I know. Is your head clear yet? This isn't going to be a cakewalk since you screwed us over with that stupid stunt last night. They know we're coming." Zack slid his knife into its sheath. He grabbed Kilgas' hand and helped him stand. "I need to know I can trust you to have my back. Hannah is going home alive this morning, Kilgas. Are you with me?"

"You're damn straight I am. Let's go get my daughter."

Zack examined the other chunk of explosives. The wiring left the inside of the underground room. "This must be on a timer or controlled remotely. I don't think they were going to drug you, Kilgas. I think they were going to blow you to bits and bury you under a hundred tons of earth." Zack disconnected the wires, removed the chunk and the detonator. "By the way, I found Angie. She's safe."

"You came for me last and leave that here. I don't want to be around when it explodes."

"You're lucky I came for you at all, and if you do as I say, you won't be."

Zack raced back up the stairs with Kilgas behind him. Zack stuck his head out just in time to see Dre return. The three men crouched outside the shed.

"I'm unarmed, Stack," Kilgas said.

"Right there," Zack pointed to the two men he incapacitated. "Body armor, a weapon, and ammo. Get it."

"The other two are clear," Dre said. "Though they are wired with some serious explosive. We don't want to be around when it blows."

Zack pointed to the lights at the far east end of the property. "Hannah is there."

"We're outnumbered maybe by a thirty or forty to one margin," Kilgas said. "I saw a lot of firepower before they threw me into that pit."

Zack checked his weapon. "Make it sixty to one. Dre isn't coming with us."

67

Zack put his hand on Dre's shoulder and squeezed. "This is where you're going home."

"Bullshit, I'm with you."

"No, partner. You're not. You're making sure Angie makes it back safely. You're going home to Alysha. Get Barnes and Kael out of here. This place will be swarming soon. The Colson's called in a favor, and if we get caught, we all get fried. That's why you, Barnes, and Kael are getting Angie far from here now. Most importantly, you're taking care of Julie and Cate for me. I need you there, Dre. They all need you there."

"No, Zack."

"Dre, it can't be any other way."

"Zack, goddamn it! That's not how we work!"

"It is today. I can do this; you can't. Get out of here. I'll make it back. I got this guy watching my back." Zack motioned to Kilgas.

"Make up your minds, boys." Kilgas kept his eye on the scope of the rifle in search of the enemy.

"Zack, don't do this."

"Dre, tell Lauren I'm sorry. Tell her I didn't miss Michelle with her. And tell Stefani she was the one."

Dre started to talk, but Zack cut him off.

"Brother, get your ass home to Alysha. That's what you're fighting for." Zack grabbed Dre's hand and squeezed it. "This is as far as you go."

"Zack," Dre started, but Zack stopped him.

"You saved my ass enough times. Now I'm saving yours. Get to the vehicle. Protect the girl. If I'm not back a half-hour after sunrise, leave."

"You'll never make it, Zack. Hell, we'll never make it. It's too far on foot in that amount of time."

Zack pointed to the path and a parked Jeep. "Courtesy of Lewis Colson. Keys are in it. Pick up Barnes, Kael, and the girl. Get to our vehicle and give me until thirty minutes past sunrise. We'll be there."

"Zack, no! Jules and Stef will never forgive me, neither will Alysha! We finish this together."

Kilgas suddenly spoke. "Boys, either kiss goodbye or let's get going."

Zack looked at Dre one last time. "Get out of here." Zack removed the grenade and two clips for the Bushmaster from Dre's equipment. "You need to trust me. The Feds already have my number. They're not getting yours."

"Zack," Dre shook his head.

"Dre, it was the greatest honor of my life to serve alongside you. I love you, man. Now get out of here."

Dre drooped his head. "Make it back. We're having words when you do." Dre wrapped his arm around Zack quickly, let go, got to his feet, and ran through the brush to the Jeep as the hues of orange and pink slowly overtook the black sky to the east. The vehicle started; Dre turned it around and sped down the path west. With Dre gone, Zack and Kilgas crouched low in the bush and waited.

"Now what, Stack? It would have been nice to have another trained man with us," Kilgas said.

"This isn't Dre's fight, and after we save your daughter, you're going to owe me. No one else dies tonight, Kilgas."

"No one else?"

Zack stuck the clips of ammo in his belt. "You and I know our fate. An agreement, remember? We sneak in, find Hannah, sneak out."

"And Sophie? She can't get away."

"Let me worry about her. You concentrate on Hannah. Let's move out. Keep alert."

68

There was nothing to like. Zack and Kilgas approached the estate but saw no one. The few lights were enough to show them the way. Zack crouched behind a large, round shrub near the patio on the opposite side of the pool and watched. Kilgas reached Zack and knelt beside him.

"What do you see?"

"Nothing," Zack said. "Your stupidity sucked us right into this trap."

"You knew this was a trap the moment you stepped foot on this property. I'm not the stupid one."

"And have to explain to Erin why she has to hire someone new to follow me? Not a chance."

Kilgas chuckled but went back to serious. "There's no way they know we're here," Kilgas said.

Zack pointed to the corner of the house. "Under the eaves on the patio. Look."

It was clear as the gun in Zack's hands. A camera. Kilgas frowned as he looked from end to end and saw video surveillance as far as he could see. "Ok. So what do we do?"

"We wait." Zack looked at his watch.

"For what?"

"For a favor." *I'm sure I'll regret asking for this.* Zack pointed to the rear of the house. "Open window second floor. I'll scale there and enter. You get in the lower level by those slider doors."

"Why are you going upstairs?"

"Because there's likely to be more bad guys downstairs."

Kilgas shook his head. "Total dick move. What are we waiting for?"

Zack remained silent as he kept tabs on time. Then, two minutes of long silence later, Zack looked at Kilgas. "Move fast when I tell you. Ready?"

"What?"

Just as quickly as Kilgas ended his sentence, the lights of the estate shut off. Power outage. Zack smiled and dashed to the rear of the house. Kilgas raced towards the patio doors, and the two lost sight of one another.

* * * *

Four men didn't typically occupy the control room. But this wasn't an ordinary situation. The previous night's visitor raised the stakes, and the boss ordered the entire regiment to operate and observe. The boss and his brother hoped they could get through at least Saturday's service before the planned hasty exit.

The four men watched different monitors from different cameras located all over the property and suspected they had more visitors. The east-end cameras showed black until one of the Colson Jeeps appeared, unexpectedly and unannounced, outside the gate and picked up three people. Garrett Colson expected this and had the trap set. For the next night. Not this one. Still, the four men watched nervously.

Then everything went black.

The leader of the four tech men snapped to attention. He moved his computer mouse and realized they had a problem. "Everyone, wake up!" Nothing worked. "Shit, we have a problem!"

The other three men snapped to attention. "What's going on?"

"The power is out. Dale, get to the generators now. Kevin, go wake Garrett. Syd, you stay with me and arm yourself. We have visitors."

One of the men stumbled in the dark, grabbed a flashlight from a drawer, opened the door, and a foot kicked him back inside. A man stepped inside, shut the door, and held a rifle in his hands pointed at the men. "Gentlemen, you do have a problem. The question is, are you going to be a part of the solution, or will you compound the problem?"

* * * *

Kilgas peeked around the corner. The power outage worked favorably, and Kilgas crept through the house. He spotted two guards posted outside a door down the hall. The two men spoke; one nodded and ran down the hall and disappeared. Kilgas took this as a bad sign. But the guard outside the door told him someone was inside, and Kilgas believed it to be his daughter.

Kilgas took a deep breath and remembered what Stack told him. No killing unless necessary. Well, to Kilgas, that was subjective. So he turned the corner quietly and approached the guard. The guard looked, saw the shadow, and ordered Kilgas to announce himself.

Kilgas did.

A single shot from the Bushmaster hit the man in the head, killed him instantly. The muzzle did its job. Kilgas kicked the man out of the way, entered the room, and saw a girl laid on the bed against the wall, asleep. Kilgas looked around the room carefully, expectant of trouble, but saw nothing beyond the girl.

He crept to the bed, knelt, and quickly put his hand over the girl's mouth. He flipped her to her back. "Hannah, don't scream," Kilgas said. "It's me, your father. I've come to take you home."

The girl cautiously moved her hair from her face and looked at the shadowy figure's face only inches from her. She didn't scream. The girl knew she had a chance if this man didn't kill her.

Kilgas's eyes opened wide. "It's you! Where's Hannah? And if you scream, I'll slit your throat faster than you can imagine. Where is she?"

Sophie Flowers offered her hands in surrender. "I won't scream," she said softly. "Please don't hurt me."

"I should kill you now. Where is Hannah?"

"She's with Garrett. He forced her to spend the night with him. All pledges do the night before their Enlightenment. It's down the hall, around the corner to the left. Is Mr. Stack with you?"

"Get dressed and be quiet."

Kilgas heard a low grumble. He heard thumps and crashes in the distance, and the black quickly changed. The generators flipped, and several lights illuminated the estate. A small lamp brightened the corner of Sophie's room, and Kilgas saw the red marks and bruising on the side of her face. She had been beaten.

"Hurry."

Kilgas readied by the door. He heard a commotion outside but then it was silent. He looked back and saw the girl who helped kidnap his daughter slide on a pair of grey sweatpants and a hooded sweatshirt. Running shoes without socks completed her rushed assembly.

"I'm sorry," Sophie said quickly. "I did what I did because,"

"Shut up. I don't want to hear it. Take me to Hannah."

Sophie lowered her head and walked to Kilgas, who peeked through the small opening in the doorway. Nothing. He opened it, grabbed Sophie, and pulled her along. The hallway remained dark. Kilgas crept until the end, ready for anything. Another hallway veered to Kilgas's left but ahead was the front door at the end of a great hall. Ceilings thirty feet high, a wide area filled with a fountain, furniture, large plants, giant windows, and more arched ceilings with a broad set of stairs along the wall to the second floor on the opposite side of the hallway to the left.

Kilgas looked through the night vision scope just as the lights brightened the room. The light burned his eyeball, and he looked away in pain. Then, as he blinked and forced himself to focus, Kilgas saw his predicament.

Surrounded.

Twenty men appeared, all carrying long rifles, all pointed at Kilgas. And in the center of the men, the front door immediately behind him stood the man Kilgas wanted to kill most. Garrett Colson. The man who defiled Kilgas's only daughter.

And then Kilgas saw Hannah Leary. Her long unkempt blonde hair flowed wild and free, fresh from waking, and her big blue eyes looked at the man in front of her. Kilgas took off the helmet and dropped it to the floor. Hannah stared at him. Perhaps a look of recognition from the many high school pictures of Kilgas back at her mother's house. Or maybe a look of dread for Hannah knew the man in front of her was about to die.

"Put it down, hero," Garrett demanded.

"Let her go, Colson. You don't need Hannah any longer," Kilgas said quickly.

"Her name is Suday," Garrett said. "I said drop the weapon."

"Her name is Hannah Leary!" Kilgas yelled. "Hannah, I'm taking you back to your mother. Let her go, Colson. Take your money and leave. But she stays with me."

"Who are you?"

"My name is Marcus Leary. I'm Hannah's father, and I'm here to take her home."

69

Kilgas hadn't used his real name in years. It felt liberating but scary as he stared at his daughter for the first time. She looked confused.

"Let the police know the people who threatened us have arrived," Garrett told one of his men who stepped out the front door cell phone in hand. Garrett stared at Kilgas. "She doesn't want to go with you, do you, Suday?"

"Your name is Hannah Leary, not Suday," Kilgas said. "This monster has been keeping you drugged to convince you he's a prophet when all he wants from you is sex, Hannah. He's a disgusting piece of garbage, and he's been lying to you since day one. We found your friend Angie. She's safe, Hannah, just like you are now." Kilgas inched closer. The odds stacked heavily against him. Kilgas didn't see Stack, and that upset him. He felt abandoned.

"What? What is he talking about? Is that true?" Hannah asked.

"Yes, what I said is the truth, Hannah. You don't want to be with that slimeball."

"Put it down, hero," Garrett barked. "You can't win here. Another fifty men are converging on this area right now. Where is Stack?"

"My father disappeared," Hannah said. "He left my mother before I was born."

"I did, and I'm sorry, Hannah. I made a mistake, but I am your father, and I'm here now. You are not Suday, and that man is a lie. I loved your mother, Sherry. I got her pregnant with you; I freaked out and left. I'm sorry, but I'm here now, Hannah. And your mother wants you home back in Annapolis."

"How touching," Garrett laughed. "Hannah is now Suday, hero, and she doesn't want to be with you," Garrett laughed.

Kilgas stared at Hannah. "Yes, she does. She wants her family, not this lie. His brother was going to kill Angie, your friend, Hannah. And he'll kill you if you leave here with him. Hannah, he doesn't care about you. Garrett, let her go. I'll forget about everything. Just let my daughter go."

"Kill him. NO! Wait," Garrett barked at his men before any could fire. "I'll do it myself." Garrett pointed the handgun at Kilgas. One bullet fired. Kilgas hit the floor.

* * * *

Hannah screamed. She tried to race to the man who claimed to be her father, but Garrett held her arm tight and yanked her back. "Stop!" Garrett looked at Kilgas, but Kilgas didn't move. Sophie stepped back, now alone, her hands over her mouth in shock. Garrett looked at her.

"Summer, I was going to throw you out of my private plane at thirty thousand feet to see if you could fly. But I think you've outlived your usefulness. Goodbye." Garrett raised the handgun at her when two metal canisters rattled on the floor from the balcony above.

Garrett looked at the flares from the ends of the canisters. They burned, grey smoke rose, and one exploded—the flashbang burst. The loud noise reverberated off the limestone columns and thick walls. The bright light temporarily blinded the men. The other canister blew, and red smoke poured out to fill the air.

Another two canisters hit the floor from above. Sophie crouched on the floor, her hands over her ears as the second flashbang exploded and more smoke poured out. A high-pitched beep shrieked from the smoke alarms. Hannah escaped the clutches of Garrett and ran to her father. She crouched on the floor.

The twenty men surrounding Garrett collected their wits and raised their rifles at the balcony above. They saw a dark object fly overhead. It hit the four-feet wide and twelve-feet tall wooden doors, bounced behind the men, and exploded.

Shrapnel tore through the men and blew them apart. Then, the culprit appeared at the top of the stairs with his rifle aimed and ready. The guards scrambled, some for their weapons, some for their lives, some were already dead. Garrett missed getting any shrapnel from the grenade but held his ears as the ringing slowly subsided. And he watched the man he wanted to kill mow down his guards one at a time. No hesitation. As soon as one of his guards grabbed a weapon or aimed to fire, a bullet from Zack Stack's rifle ended the threat.

Stack reached the bottom of the stairs and scanned the area, but no one offered resistance. Finally, Zack pointed the gun at Garrett. "Mr. Colson, you took the wrong girls."

* * * *

Zack watched as Hannah Leary stayed beside Kilgas but kept his rifle trained on anything that moved, mainly Garrett Colson. Sophie slowly stood as Kilgas finally moved. Kilgas held his chest but got to his knees. Kilgas unzipped a vest, and it hit the floor.

"What took you so long?" Kilgas rubbed his chest as he got to his feet.

Zack eyed the surroundings. "I was pacing myself." Kilgas gave him a pissed-off look. "Sometimes a bargaining chip is necessary for survival." Zack patted a bag on his hip. "That's twice now I saved your ass."

"For Pete's Sake!" Kilgas said.

"Who the hell is this Pete, and why does everyone care about his sake?" Zack shook his head while focused on Garrett. "Kilgas, grab your daughter and head out the back. There's transportation in the garage for us."

"You think you're getting out of here?" Garrett laughed. "You won't get anywhere. You did come here earlier than I expected; quite a daring move for you, Stack. But after I knew, I called the police, and my men surrounded this place. Friends in high places, Stack; I have some. You don't." Garrett laughed.

Zack walked over to Garrett and kicked Garrett's jaw. Garrett hit the floor face first. "Wanna bet?"

Kilgas looked at Garrett, dissatisfied that he didn't do that himself. Kilgas picked up a discarded rifle from a dead man in the hallway and turned to Sophie.

Zack watched the front door. "Down the hall to the right at the end is the garage. Get going."

"No, it's not done yet," Kilgas said. He looked at Stack and saw blood drip from Zack's left hand from under his shirt.

Zack turned around. "It is. We have to go. There's more than just the police on the way."

"No, she sold me out. She brought Hannah here. She has to pay."

Zack walked towards Sophie slowly, who suddenly looked scared for her life as Kilgas raised the rifle. "Mark, don't do it!" Zack yelled.

"They would have killed me! I had to do what I did," Sophie said. "I knew Zack would save us both!" She pleaded with her hands high. "Don't shoot me, please!"

"How many girls suffered because of you? HUH? MY DAUGHTER! Because of YOU!"

Kilgas put his finger on the trigger.

"Kilgas, don't do it! Put it down," Zack yelled again.

Kilgas spun and fired. Multiple bullets hit Zack, knocked him through the air backward, over a chair, and onto the floor.

"I'm sorry, Stack. I like you. But she's not walking out of here. She doesn't deserve it."

Kilgas looked at the motionless Zack and saw blood. The thought he just killed Stack registered. A wave of dizziness swept through him, an after effect of the drugs. He shook his head and looked at Sophie, who turned and ran down the hallway in a panic.

Kilgas, as everything appeared in slow motion, raised his gun, his daughter screamed no and reached for the gun, the front door burst open, Kilgas looked at the door as men raced in, their gun's pointed, and the gunfire erupted.

Bullets flew. Parts of the walls and floors splintered and sparked as bullets ricocheted and tore up the great room. Kilgas returned fire, pushed Hannah to the floor, grabbed her when the attackers paused to find cover, and ducked around the corner.

Zack Stack, blood at his side, didn't move.

70

Garrett Colson scrambled towards the front door as his army of protectors destroyed the inside of the house to help him escape. The noise deafened as bullets tore up the foyer and open areas inside the door. Garrett covered his head and felt two hands on his shoulders. One of his men dragged him towards the door. Garrett got to his feet at the door and saw the car. The shooting stopped.

Garrett stepped outside; he could hear faint sirens in the distance. "Get me out of here."

He took another step, and the grenade exploded. The blast knocked Garrett off his feet, and he felt the wounds and watched his men drop to the ground. The silence ended as another wave of guards rushed the building to protect their leader.

Gunfire erupted. Men raced in all directions; some fell to their deaths, smoke, and fire partially blocked the view, but Garrett managed to get to his car. Another grenade exploded, and Garrett watched his faithful servants fly through the air, torn apart by the blast. Garrett righted himself in the backseat of the car and looked at his once glorious estate. A fire burned on the edge of the front door and slowly engulfed the entranceway. Two men fell to the ground, bursts of blood from their backsides, and another two danced in the air like puppets as bullets ripped them apart. Garrett saw Zack Stack step through the doorway. His rifle fired round after round, and Garrett's loyal protectors failed; most dropped wounded or dead. As the car sped out of the driveway, Garrett watched a few of his men run for their lives. Just like Garrett, the strongest of them all did.

"GO! GO! GO!" Garrett ordered the driver.

The car tires squealed, and the car sped around the circular driveway, headed for the main road. Garrett peeked back, saw Zack Stack kneel, point his rifle, and the muzzle flashed. The window shattered. Garrett felt a bullet rip through him, and searing pain tore at his flesh. He fell back into the seat as the car straightened and took several more bullets. The driver screamed as one hit his arm, but the vehicle kept straight and accelerated.

The car hit the street and headed away. "Blow it!" Garrett screamed. "Destroy everything. NOW!"

* * * *

Zack heard the sirens as he watched the Colson car disappear. He listened to the thump-thumping of a distant helicopter. The grip of nighttime defeated by the ever-rising sun and the early morning heavy mist beat back by its warmth. Morning arrived. Zack stumbled through the growing fire into the house, staggered from the blows to his chest, looked to see the source of the screaming beep of the fire alarm, shot it to quiet it, and headed down the hallway. Then he saw her on the floor; her hands clutched to her stomach.

Zack saw the fear in Sophie's eyes and the wound in her stomach.

"Sophie," he knelt beside her. He looked at his watch.

"Hi, Zack," she said. The attempt to put on a brave face.

"Hey, you. Let's say we go have a drink, huh?"

She looked at him and put her bloody hand on his. "Zack, I'm sorry."

Zack took a breath. "Apologize later, ok? We have to get out of here now."

"Zack," Sophie tried but stopped and smiled.

"Come on," Zack lifted her, but she screamed in pain.

"It hurts, Zack. I'm going to die, I know it."

"No, you're not, Sophie. I've seen worse. No one else dies today," Zack said. Zack ripped off his camo shirt, wrapped it around her wounds, and tightened it with hopes to at least slow the bleeding. He scooped Sophie into his arms, and she put her bloody hands around his neck. "Hang on to me. We're going home."

Zack entered the garage as a massive explosion blew pieces of the roof off the second floor. Zack and Sophie hit the floor. The house shook and rumbled. Parts of the ceiling crashed on the floor near them. Zack fought off his pain, ignored the blood from his own body, and lifted Sophie again. At the end of the vast, eight double-door stalled garage parked several motorcycles and off-road vehicles. One motorcycle was missing. Kilgas and Hannah escaped.

313

Several small explosions ripped through the house. An air compressor tank at the end of the garage exploded. Zack and Sophie hit the floor again as debris and smoke blew over them. Windows of vehicles shattered, and fire scorched the far end of the garage.

"Is he blowing up his own house?"

"Just the evidence. I'm blowing up the evidence of us being here. That's why we have to go." Zack rushed to the motorcycle he wanted. The only BMW motorcycle in the lineup. A 1250 from the Adventure series. Zack put a helmet on Sophie and set her on the seat in front of him. "Sophie," he said softly, "hold on to me. Hold on tight. You're going to make it."

Sophie rested her head on his shoulder and wrapped her legs around his waist. Not the best way to ride but the only way to make sure she didn't fall off. Zack fired up the bike, revved the engine, and tore out of the garage.

In the early morning light, a helicopter approached and saw the motorcycle exit the garage amidst the smoke and fire from the house. Zack rode to the trail leading to the outside path surrounding the property. Zack twisted the throttle, and as the motorcycle sped off, the C4 Zack planted exploded. Part of the house exploded and shot a plume of smoke and debris high into the air. The helicopter quickly diverted its path to avoid a collision, and part of the house disintegrated. Well-placed detonations leveled the grand estate room by room. Flames consumed the property. The entranceway crumbled, the doors and windows shattered, and the ceilings fell. The thunder of the explosions reverberated the ground.

The blast wave rushed towards the motorcycle; the sound pounded at Zack's eardrums, but he throttled the handle, and the bike's speed pulled through the percussion. The billowing smoke wall blinded the helicopter, and the police descending on the estate halted immediately.

Zack didn't slow. There was no time. He raced the bike over the massive parcel of land, sheltered on both sides by trees and shrubs. They passed the outhouses, and Zack hoped he did enough to prevent their explosion. He needed that evidence uncovered.

But Zack knew justice wasn't served. The cowardice and evilness of the operation, hidden by the grandeur and faux holiness of the megachurch and its accepting religion, infuriated Zack. He felt the fire rage inside him hotter than the fire which consumed the estate. But Zack kept focused on his goal: to save Sophie.

Zack handled the bike expertly, and the fiery estate disappeared in the side-view mirrors. Sophie kept her grip on Zack as they raced away. Finally, they reached the gate at the far west end of the property, steered through it, and sped down the road. No one there like Zack hoped. "Hang on, Sophie. We're almost there."

* * * *

The motorcycle raced over the roads as they wound into the hills. Zack found where the minivan should have been, but it wasn't there. The Jeep remained. Zack looked at his watch to see he had arrived twenty minutes late. Zack heard a helicopter in the distance. Zack stopped the bike, ripped the rest of his shirt off, stuck it in the gas tank of the Jeep, and lit it. Matches in a pocket saved Zack and Dre more than once before. He got back on the bike and started it.

"Sophie," Zack said. "Hold on." Her head moved, and her eyes barely opened.

"I hurt, Zack."

Zack had seen enough death and dying. But this one felt different. This one, he *believed* he could save. She deserved that. She coughed and sputtered. "You're not done. Not until I say you are."

Zack revved the engine and raced off. Zack realized he may not have been right. One more person may die that day. But not on that mountain. Not near that estate. He owed Sophie that.

71

Sunday morning arrived in Fells Point, Maryland, the second week of June. Lauren Mayfield entered the office and fought off a shiver. She quickly went to the thermostat to change the temperature and saw Zack's door closed.

Lauren opened his office door and flicked on the light. She turned to the couch and saw Zack, on his back, one arm splayed to the side and a blanket over only his legs. His body lay bare save his boxer shorts, a bandage under his arm where a bullet from Kilgas passed through the small patch of skin above his armpit and another application around his bicep. She saw the severe bruising on his chest and cringed. But he didn't move. Thawed ice packs, an empty glass, and a half-empty bottle of bourbon rested on the floor. Lauren recognized the bottle and amount inside. One glass knocked Zack out. For that, she was thankful.

Lauren nudged him. "Wake up, Awesome Sauce."

Zack's eyes slowly opened but closed. "Go away."

"Mr. Stack, I'm not going away."

"Can I fire you?"

Lauren grabbed his arm. "No." She tried to pull him off the couch.

Zack groaned in pain and resisted. His chest hurt, but the vest saved his life. The discoloration and pain would last a long time. Zack wondered how long his heart stopped before somehow it started again. He thanked God, if God were responsible, for making sure the screwdriver jabbed into Zack's arm by the techs didn't break a bone or do any severe damage. Still hurt and bled a lot but could have been worse. "Why not? I'm still the boss, aren't I?"

"You may be the boss. But I'm the boss of what goes on in this office. So come on, Awesome Sauce. I gave you a few days."

Zack pulled Lauren to him, and she fell beside him on the couch. Zack put his arm around her and held her close to him. "It's Sunday. A day of rest. Even says so in the Bible."

Lauren rolled to her other side and faced him. "Now you're using religion to justify your actions?"

"Why can't I? It works for"

"Sir, stop," Lauren told him. "We'll find another way to help you then." She grabbed his good arm and pulled him off the couch. "Can you shower? Your wounds probably shouldn't get wet."

"They're only minor wounds. I'll be fine. I'll be in the shower. I know you won't bother me there."

"How do you know?"

Zack walked past her into the bathroom. He disrobed, turned on the shower, and stepped under the stream. "Why are you here?"

"Because you need me." Lauren sat on the counter and watched Zack lean under the showerhead.

Zack looked at her. "I'm sure I can manage being alone today."

Lauren stepped close to the shower. "Sweetie, not today you can't."

Zack stood in the shower; the water beat on him from every direction the shower allowed. Zack leaned against the wall with his head against his forearm. "If I see that sonofabitch again, I'm beating his ass."

Lauren couldn't resist and grinned as wide as she could. "Sir, I told you so. Didn't I?"

* * * *

Lauren walked into Zack's office at nine that morning. Zack turned the page on a birding magazine. Lauren stood beside him and looked at the picture of the pretty yellow bird with a thick conical bill. "What's that bird?"

"Evening Grosbeak," Zack said.

"It's beautiful. Can you take me to see one?"

"Sure. Call in sick next week, and we'll go to Canada to find them. I'll vouch for you," Zack said nonchalantly.

Lauren saw the bottle of Pepsi and an empty plate on his desk. At least she got him to eat. Lauren leaned over, put her arm around him, and made Zack look at her. "Hey," she said softly. "It will be ok. No one blames you."

"I blame myself."

"Those girls are alive because of you."

They stared at each other, and Lauren made sure she fixated on Zack's eyes.

"Come here, Awesome Sauce. Someone needs a hug." She sat on his lap and hugged him until they heard a buzz. "Sounds like someone is at the front door."

"I'll get it."

"No, stay there. I'll be right back." Zack watched Lauren walk away. He heard her talk, then the locks clicked. Moments later, Lauren walked back into the office.

"Sir, there are two gentlemen from the FBI here to see you."

Zack's shoulders slumped. "Terrific. Send them in."

Lauren disappeared and in walked Ty Campbell and Derek Larson. Campbell frowned at Zack. "Good morning, Mr. Stack. You remember Agent Larson, don't you?"

"Unfortunately. Where's your partner? What was his name?"

"Carter Nolen," Derek Larson said. "He's taking some time off."

Zack nodded. "Well, you two are here for a reason. So let's hear it."

Larson stepped forward. "Mr. Stack, do you know who Garrett and Lewis Colson are?"

"Nope. Never heard of them."

"We spent the last three days at their estate in Northern Virginia."

"Why? Did they have a party for FBI agents?"

"The place was blown to bits and burned to a crisp. We found over three dozen dead bodies inside the place. Most were shot, some blown to bits. You didn't hear anything about it?"

"I've been enjoying a quiet weekend. No television, internet, newspaper, nothing," Zack said.

Larson stepped forward. "We have reason to think you were there and part of the incident."

"You have reason to think that, huh?" Zack scratched his head. "Well, you're reasoning is wrong. I wasn't there."

"Where were you?"

"I went to the coast after I heard there was a report of a Magnificent Frigatebird seen. Spent the weekend chasing reports of it." The two men stared at Zack. "It's a bird. Up here, that would be a rare sighting."

"I don't believe you," Larson said.

"Of course you don't," Zack said.

Lauren walked behind Zack. "You should believe him. He was with me. We left work Wednesday and went to the coast as he said. Primehook National Wildlife Refuge. We spent the weekend in a little motel, came back yesterday afternoon, and haven't left here since."

"Can you verify that?"

"I'll give you the receipts of where we ate and stayed if you'd like, and I probably can get you a video of me checking into the motel," Lauren said. "If you knew Mr. Stack, you'd know he was already at the beach looking for that bird." She chuckled. "I never knew it was such an obsession with him. If you want, I'll even give you the name of the bartender who tried to overserve me." Lauren grinned. "I guess he thought Mr. Stack needed help with having his way with me." Lauren winked. "He didn't, not that's any of your business."

"You were in Primehook and here since Wednesday night?"

"I apologize, gentlemen, if I didn't annunciate clearly. I'll be more direct. Yes, but I don't think what Mr. Stack and I do in our private time is any of your business." She put her hand on Zack's shoulder. "Or do you want the details of how we made love?"

Larson shook his head. "Proof you were at the Colson's will surface. When it does, I'll be there."

"I don't even know what you're talking about or who the Colson's are." Zack smiled. "Sorry."

"What about my partner being framed for murder?"

"What murder?" Zack asked. "Listen, Larson, I know you don't like me and want a way to lock me up again, but you're barking up the wrong tree. I have no idea what

319

you are talking about, and you're wasting our Sunday." Zack put his hand on Lauren's hand on his shoulder. "We plan to do some unholy things this day of the Lord, so if you'll hurry up with this ridiculousness."

Larson turned and walked to the door. "I'm going home, Campbell." He left. Ty Campbell adjusted his position in the seat and smiled at Zack.

"You ruined his day."

"If you would have tried to take me to prison, I would have ruined a lot worse."

"I told him it was a wasted trip. But since I'm here, I might as well fill you in. We got an anonymous call Thursday at four in the morning. It came from a burner phone letting us know that some people were trying to escape the Colson estate. Said they were on a coach bus heading south, and if not stopped, everyone aboard would die via a rapture, meaning poison. We found the bus about an hour later. When the Virginia State Troopers stopped the bus, there was a shoot-out that left four people dead. Thirty-three people of some group called the Enlightenment started talking and gave us some weird stories. Not long after that, a call came from the estate saying there were four men with rifles attacking the place."

Zack looked surprised. *The first call came from Sophie.*

"When the local police arrived, they saw explosions take out part of the house. A helicopter arrived and saw a motorcycle speed out of the garage. Another explosion sent smoke and debris in the air; the helicopter lost sight of the bike. We arrived and found a whole bunch of dead body parts at the estate, but the Colson brothers weren't there."

Zack leaned forward. "Sounds like somebody had some fun."

"Oddly enough, the two girls you were searching for showed up alive at home. Both said they were captive there, although one needs some serious de-programming. The other thanked a man she didn't know. Said he was white and that he beat the crap out of one of the Colson brothers. She told us the man stopped her from being raped again and shot Lewis Colson in the knee after he smashed his face."

"So these Colson boys. It sounds like they were running a cult for sex with young girls. I fail to see why you're here."

"I came here to make sure you didn't kill Larson. He wants you locked up, so be careful. I told you people in high places don't like people peeking through their windows."

"They should either close their blinds or quit committing crimes then," Zack replied. Zack opened a desk drawer and pulled out a small paper bag. He put them on the desk. "You may need these."

"What are they?"

"The hard drives from the computers inside the Colson estate, I'm guessing," Zack said. "They detail every sordid little crime those two committed and how. You're going to solve a lot of missing girl cases in the next day or so. If I were you, I'd give them to Michelle Borman. I hear she's doing a great job."

Campbell looked at the bag, opened the top, and saw four hard drives. He took the bag. "I'll give them to her immediately." Ty Campbell looked at Zack. "How did you get these?"

"They came in the mail yesterday," Lauren said. "No return address. We don't know who sent them. But we're guessing if they wind up in the wrong hands, nothing will come of it. People in high places, remember?"

Agent Campbell liked what he heard. "Garrett Colson survived. We're not sure about his brother. My boss got a call from his boss. Somewhere along the line, the President got a call from Colson. Your name came up."

"Not sure how they got my name. Where are they?"

"Don't know. They own a private jet that left the states Thursday morning. People higher than me already swooped in and took over. If the truth gets out, it will look bad for the President."

"So despite the crimes that took place there, the kidnappings, the brainwashing, the drugs, the stealing, the rape, the murders, everything, will all get washed under the rug just so the President doesn't have to admit his spiritual advisor is a criminal?"

"You know how it works, Stack."

"Or does it go deeper than that? Is this one of those Lolita things?"

"You know how it works, Stack. And you know where you stand. Is there any chance that you'll be connected to any of this?"

"There's always a chance. This is America. Evidence is planted every damn day. I'm betting against it, though."

Campbell looked at Lauren and nodded. "We found one of the Colson jeeps about five miles west of the property in the hills burned. No evidence anywhere other than tire tracks that disappeared. Looked like a vehicle and a motorcycle. I'm sure someone will try to match the tracks to a tire, but that will lead nowhere."

Especially since we already put new tires on the minivan before we returned it, and the motorcycle has been destroyed. "That's too bad."

"Stack, what happened?"

"I have no idea, Agent Campbell," Zack said. "I was with Lauren."

"Are we going to find any trace of you on one of those hard drives?"

Zack smiled. *Like I'm that dumb.* "I can't imagine why I would be."

Ty stood. "All right. I better get back to work."

"Ty, if someone comes to me and says I need to take the fall for any of this, there will be bloodshed."

"I'll keep my eyes and ears open." Campbell walked to the door.

"Ty, that goes for the people in my life. I will fight back if there's a next time."

Ty Campbell waited for more, for a change in expression, for anything. There was nothing. "I understand. Listen, Stack; my suggestion is to keep quiet. Disappear. Maybe you and Lauren," Campbell stopped as if he doubted the bond between the two, "should go away for a month or so."

"I am not budging on my position."

"Because you're at the bottom and you know too much, you may have to." Ty nodded.

"Agent Campbell, do I need to reiterate my stance?"

"Stack, I like you. Be careful. Keep in touch."

Lauren watched Campbell leave, and she returned to Zack's lap.

"Thank you, Lauren. I now officially owe you."

"I know, sir. The month away part sounds good. You're still a relationship disaster in the making, but when do we leave?"

72

Zack entered the tavern and checked his watch. Two minutes early, which he hoped would put his host in a positive mood. He spotted her instantly. She sat alone at a table in the corner of the tavern, her back to the door but surrounded by tables filled with men Zack knew were there for one reason: to keep people away from her.

Addison Jones.

Being invited to McFaul's Ironhorse Tavern surprised Zack, but not enough to miss the meeting. He didn't dare. Zack scanned the restaurant and slowly approached the table. A man at each of the four tables around Addison Jones looked at Zack and looked away. They knew, and Zack knew they knew.

Addison Jones owned control.

Zack walked to the table, and the chair beside her slid away from the table. Zack took this as an order to sit immediately beside her. Zack suspected Addison would not raise her voice, and this talk was for his ears only.

Zack sat beside her, and two drinks placed instantly in front of them. Addison Jones casually looked away from the menu.

"Did you ride your ridiculous motorcycle?"

"I don't have one," Zack said. "The bad guys destroyed both."

"So you drove your car?"

Zack hesitated. "I don't have a car."

"What about the Jag our mutual friend bought for you?"

"It's not in my possession currently," Zack said. "Is one of these drinks for me?"

Addison lifted one off the table. "This is against my better judgment and my policy, but since I'm off duty." She winked. "One is. I decided you weren't drinking beer in my presence. I determined a Woodford Mint Julep would suffice."

"It will," Zack said. He grabbed the glass, lifted it, and tapped her glass. "To us, whatever the hell us is."

Addison Jones smiled. "To us." She sipped her drink. "How did you get here?"

"One of those ride services."

"Good. Let me start by saying I'm sorry about Sophie Flowers. I know you tried." Zack paused before he sipped his drink again.

"It wasn't your fault, Zack," she said softly. "At least now her parents know."

"Thanks, but that doesn't make me feel better."

"I suspect it won't from what I know about you." Out of character, she put her hand on his hand. "It will get better in time. I promise."

"No, it doesn't." Zack saw Addy's determination. "How?"

"In time, as I said. I talked to your new secretary, Lauren. She seems nice. I think she likes you."

"You going to send her to Europe, too?"

Addy pretended to consider it. "I may have to. She suggested you may have a hero complex."

"Hero complex. Seriously? Never has a guy been more misunderstood. I was trained to help those who can't help themselves. No different than an ICU nurse or doctor. I simply use different means. I may fire her."

Addy leaned back and sipped her drink. "Keep your emotions in check, Mr. Stack. They only get in the way and impair your judgment." She kept her eyes on him as she sipped her drink. "There is heat coming your way. And unfortunately for you, Mr. Stack, you won't be able to shoot your way out of this one."

"You never know. People respond amazingly accordingly with a properly placed .40 caliber projectile."

Addy motioned her hand. A waiter appeared on cue. "I'll have the Cassidy's Crab cakes, and he'll have the Sesame Crusted Tuna." The waiter nodded and disappeared. "Both look good to me, so this way, I can try both."

"That's very thoughtful of you," Zack said. "I would have gone for the fish and chips."

"Pity. What is your plan now?"

Zack reached in his pocket slowly and smiled. "Please don't have your men shoot me."

"I don't plan to. At least not until after dinner."

Zack pulled a zip drive from his pocket, placed it on the table, and slid it on the table to her. "This."

"What is it?"

"Leverage," Zack said. "It's everything I have on NPA. You wanted it; you got it."

Addison Jones looked at it. "And what do you want me to do?"

"I don't have to spell it out. You've already planned what to do." Zack sipped the drink. *Not bad.* He saw Addison's blue eyes stare at him. "Or I can spell it out. Once what is on this drive hits the airwaves, the people pissed at me because I upset their apple cart will be far too busy saving their asses to bother with me. I know an excellent reporter in the DC beltline that would love to take down some power-crazed jackoffs."

Addison Jones knew his direction. "Annette Caldwell. Did you tamper with this information in any way?"

"No. Didn't have to. Whoever kept track of all of this did a great job of incrimination. Any tampering would have been silly."

Addison put the device in her pocket. "How do you feel?"

"Like I've been shot in the chest by three bullets from a large gun at close range."

"But you survived."

"I put extra plates in my vest. Where is Kilgas?"

"Why?"

"I would like a word with him," Zack said. "I promise you I'll leave him alive. You didn't deny knowing him. Does he work for you, too?"

"Mr. Stack, remember me telling you about your vivid imagination."

"Jesus H. Christ on a popsicle stick. Why do you insist on this song and dance?"

Addy smiled and squeezed his hand. "Because I enjoy toying with you. You're fun." She sipped her drink. "This really is a good drink. So tell me, what is your plan now?"

"To keep my employees and friends safe."

"Job wise?"

"I have a case to close and some answers to get."

"About Stefani Oakley?" She waited until Zack looked at her. "I have something I want to show you that might help you with your predicament about your precious Stefani. But, that too will come in time."

"What aren't you telling me?" Zack asked quickly.

"Be patient, Mr. Stack. In time."

Zack chuckled. "Wow. This sure feels like you're using me."

Addy leaned closer with a huge grin. "I am using you, Mr. Stack. Now, I'll admit, a part of me does like you."

"Which part?"

She ignored him. "But this is not that type of relationship. So bottom line, Mr. Stack, is this: I get what I want from you. End of story." Addy smiled. "Judging by your reaction, you're not objecting."

"I don't see a problem with having a powerful yet secretive woman using me. To date, it hasn't upset me. But, when it does, well then, Addy, we'll have a different conversation. What about Stefani?"

She lightly scoffed with a grin. "Enough talk about the periphery, Zack. Let's enjoy our dinner."

"Stefani is not periphery."

Addison shook her head. "If she isn't, then what is Julie?" She finished her drink. "Let's have another."

73

Zack entered his office shortly after ten that night. He expected to be alone, and the sofa-bed called his name. Zack locked the doors, turned off the lights, left his clothes on the floor on his way to the soon-to-be-bed, fell onto it, and felt a leg underneath him.

The person on the other side moved, rolled over, and turned on the light. Zack saw Lauren.

"What are you doing here?"

"Waiting for you. How was your night?"

"What are you doing here?"

"I already said waiting for you. My job is to take care of you. Now let me do my job."

"I've had enough to drink to know you in the same bed with me dressed in your sleeping attire is not a wise idea."

"Let me be the judge of that. I'm a big girl, and you left alone leads to bad things. Besides, I have something for you that might cheer you up."

"If you get naked, I'm not fighting what happens next."

Lauren smiled. "I'm sure you won't. Let's go to your garage."

* * * *

Zack stood in the doorway of the garage speechless, his mouth open and his eyes wide. "What? How? Did you? I don't; what is this?"

Lauren grinned. "It's your baby, sir. The motorcycle you gave up. The bike you had since you left the military."

Zack looked at her. "Why?"

"Because," she said. "Oh, I did have the valves bored or whatever you said. The mechanic said it's carbon-free and will, and I quote, purr like a kitten but race like a cheetah. I told him I'm sure you'll understand." Lauren slid her hand into his. "Because sir. That's the only reason I needed," she said softly.

Zack stared at her, again speechless, a tear formed which he quickly wiped away.

"Are you going to stand here looking like a kid at his first Christmas, or are you going to take me for a ride?"

"Now?"

She giggled. "You're right. We should wait until morning since you've been drinking. We should go back upstairs and get you to bed."

Zack looked at Lauren and smiled. "I'm going to my place and call Jules. I'll stay there tonight."

"Definitely a wise choice, sir. Please stay there. I know you'll be safe there. At least I'll sleep knowing that."

"I doubt I'll sleep tonight." Zack kissed Lauren's cheek. "Thank you, Lauren. I'll see you tomorrow. Goodnight."

* * * *

Zack lay on his bed and watched an old movie. He doubted he'd sleep. The ring of his cell phone startled him, but he quickly answered with hopes it was Jules returning his call. "Stack here."

A brief hesitation before Zack heard a breath. "Uh, Stack, I think I owe you an apology. I wasn't myself. I don't know what happened after Sophie blamed everything on me. I lost it, man. I'm sorry for shooting you."

"If you're planning on visiting, I wouldn't. Lauren vowed to kill you, and I doubt she'll alter her vow."

"I'm sure. Look, I can't thank you enough. I'd be dead, and Hannah would be gone if it weren't for you."

"Well, my shortened life span due to the blunt force trauma on my heart can't thank you enough, either."

"I'm sorry, Stack. I like you, and before that happened, I thought you and I could have a friendship. I thought maybe I could work for you and make things right instead of, well, you know."

Zack remained silent.

"What happened to Sophie?"

"She's dead."

Kilgas paused. "I'm sorry."

"Where are you?" Zack ignored the apology.

"A private jet left a small Virginia airport the other morning with two injured passengers. I thought they might need my services."

"Where are they?"

"Right now, the Bahamas. Both are in a hospital." Kilgas exhaled. "Look, Stack, Erin warned me you don't trust easily, and I know I blew it when I flipped and shot you. Perhaps I'll get there with you someday. I know these words are hollow to you but trust me, I'm not going to kill you. As you said, if the time comes that someone pays me to do it, I'll come to you first. I owe you that."

"I suppose there is comfort in that."

"I don't want to step out of line, but knowing what you've been through the last couple of years and the shit we did, and what you and your unit did all over, I mean, that wears on a person, Stack. Any person. You might want to think about talking to someone about it."

Zack said nothing.

"I got close to you during the time we worked together, and I want to tell you I'm sorry for everything I did."

"I agree with you, Kilgas. Your words do seem hollow."

"I supposed they do. But, look, I'm sorry, and I'd appreciate it if you don't tell Erin I almost killed you. I doubt she'll be as calm as you are right now. And since I'm trying to live straight and hoping to get my daughter back in my life, me dying would be bad for business."

"Were the shots to my vest intentional?"

Kilgas was silent.

"Wow. And people call me an asshole. You dick. You could have killed me!"

"I said I lost it, and I'm sorry. It won't happen again, and I owe you big time. Keep that in mind. If you ever need something, let me know. I'll do whatever I can for you."

Zack said nothing.

"Just know if you need an ear, you know from someone who knows what you're dealing with, let me know."

"Kilgas, the Colson's have White House connections. I like knowing you're working for Erin. Perhaps you should hire out for that one. That's more your style anyway."

"Perhaps I'm evolving."

"It took me a year to figure out who Erin hired to follow me; I don't want to go through that again."

Kilgas couldn't show Zack his smile. "Thanks, Zack. I mean that."

"If you walked into my office tomorrow, I think I'd shoot you before Lauren could. However, you're kind of like a callous now. At first, you're irritating and hard to live with, so I keep scraping you off, but after a while, it's almost like protection. Still gross and ugly to look at, but at least I'm not getting a blister, know what I mean?"

"Wow, Stack. That was pure fricking poetry. You should publish that."

"If you ever point a gun at me again, you better make sure I'm dead. Because you will be."

Kilgas was silent.

"Watch your back and take care of your family, Marcus. Maybe guys like us can earn a second chance. Don't blow it."

"Thanks, Stack. And I'm sorry. And I kept six guys there to watch over you. My treat."

"When I talk to Erin, I'll forget about the four bullets that nearly killed me."

Kilgas exhaled over the phone. "I get it. I owe you. I think I'll take a walk around a hospital this morning. It's a beautiful day in the Bahamas. See you soon, Stack." The line disconnected.

Zack closed his eyes in vain. There would be no sleep this night.

74

Zack stood inside Lauren's new apartment the following evening and watched her organize things the way she wanted. Seeing her happy gave him some semblance of hope. *Maybe, just maybe, I can dig myself out of this mess.* She finished hanging a picture on the wall, which to Zack was a collection of random and squiggly lines in different colors that made no sense to him.

To Lauren, it was a piece of fine art that cost her five hundred dollars. She smiled and walked over to him. "What do you think?"

"I guess the colors match."

Lauren laughed. "It's art. It looks good on that wall. It's perfect, isn't it?"

"If you say so." Zack grabbed his leather jacket. It was warm enough not to need a coat when he rode, but out of habit and love for that jacket, the last thing Michelle got for him, he wore it. Plus, it kept the bugs off his clothes when he rode.

"Where are you going? I thought we could just order a pizza and have it delivered. You need to relax, Mr. Stack. Doctor's orders."

"And I'm sure that's sound advice. But,"

"There's always a but with you, isn't there?" Lauren straightened the collar of the jacket.

"I should talk to Mikayla. You wanted me to talk to people. I'll start with her since I know she's not happy with me."

"She's not. That is a long list. If you're going to start on that, I won't see you until Labor Day." She smiled and stepped close to him. "You're not the only one who can be a smartass, Mr. Stack."

"I see that. You're settling into your position nicely."

"Will I see you tonight?" Lauren moved closer. "You shouldn't be alone."

"I should get back to my place and clean before Jules comes home tomorrow."

Lauren frowned. "So you're going to try to make it work with her."

Zack's shoulders slumped. "What am I supposed to do? How can I not try?"

Lauren nodded her head, stepped forward, and put her arms around his neck. "Do what you think is best. You know I'll be here for you when things fall apart."

"You're so encouraging. Do you know something I don't?"

"I'm a woman. It's called intuition." She kissed him. "At least call me tonight when you get back to your place, so I know you're safe. Ok?"

"Ok."

"Promise me."

"I promise I'll call you later tonight."

Zack left the apartment and got on his motorcycle. With the helmet on, he dialed Mikayla's phone. She answered right away.

"What do you want? You should be resting after those bullets to your chest," Mikayla answered quickly.

"I know, but I wanted to meet with you. I thought we could talk. Yes, I said talk."

"Zack, I'm not getting drunk and having sex with you."

"I wasn't planning on getting drunk." No reply. "Is sex all you think I'm good for? I want to talk to you, ok? So we're on solid ground. That's what you said you needed from me, and frankly, I need that from you."

"Stack, this is not a good time. Let's meet tomorrow."

Zack heard something in her voice. "Are you on a date? It's ok, you can tell me."

"No, Stack. But I'm busy, ok? I'll call you in the morning."

"Mikayla, are you not telling me something?"

"Stack, I saw your chest. You need to rest. Call me tomorrow. Goodnight." She disconnected.

Mikayla was right. His chest did ache, and each breath hurt. But something was in her voice: apprehension, nervousness, anxiousness. Zack thought about the conversation. And then, he revved the bike, let go of the clutch, and the motorcycle squealed away.

* * * *

Mikayla Dorsey didn't like lying to Zack. But she did what she needed to do. Once Michelle left and Zack went to prison, Mikayla worked with Dre, but Zack was who she needed to impress. So Zack had the final say in the agency. Dre was cool with that and requested that in the first place. But to Mikayla, it meant she would never be equal.

She knew Zack protected her. Their relationship was odd, but Mikayla knew they shared a special relationship, as dysfunctional as it may have seemed. Mikayla needed to prove herself. She needed the training wheels to come off. She could do this job, and Mikayla needed Zack to realize it.

To that end, this case would solve that dilemma.

Mikayla sat in her car, knew if she told Zack the truth, he would have yelled at her, found her, and made her leave. Only that wasn't her plan.

Mikayla planned to solve this case by finding out why Zack didn't want her to investigate the mysterious death of Evan Rossum. But, somehow, she ended up here, parked down the street from a house that attracted nightly visits from different men regularly. The visitors stayed one-to-two hours, sometimes as many as four visitors in one night, five nights a week. And some nights, the equally mysterious Dan Banks would arrive, the man Mikayla and Zack met in a hot tub with a woman who was not his wife.

Zack proved it was a BDSM house; at least there was a room in the basement where the owner, Andrea Whitehead, tied up paying customers and performed whatever she performed. Mikayla wanted to know Dan Banks' involvement because the possibility he cheated on his wife, Susan Banks, the former wife of Evan Rossum, was evident. The weird triangle didn't surprise Mikayla. While part of the BPD, she investigated several murders involving love affairs, multiple lovers, one jilted, and murder seemed the only way to fix things.

It never did.

Her camera at the ready, she filled a memory card with pictures of men entering and leaving the house, and when she could, Mikayla got their license plates. Thorough, but to what end, Mikayla wasn't sure. She may have been wasting her time. But Mikayla persisted because this night was to prove she could do the job to Zack. If Mikayla was a partner in name, it was time to be treated like a partner on the job.

A black four-door Chevy Impala turned the corner and crept past. Mikayla kept her head low to keep unseen. The car parked across the street from the house she watched, and Mikayla readied her camera.

As soon as the man exited the car, Mikayla understood why Zack wanted her away from this case. She froze at the recognition but quickly regrouped.

Mikayla pressed the button, and the camera snapped frame after frame as the man crossed the street, his eyes alert for any other person around, walked to the front door, and pressed the doorbell. The door opened, and Mikayla got a shot of Andrea Whitehead kissing the man's cheek, the man entered the house, and the door closed.

"Oh my God," Mikayla whispered. Panic shot through her. Mikayla wanted to speed away, but another car appeared behind her, drove past, and parked behind the black Impala. No one got out of the vehicle. Mikayla disassembled the camera lenses and quickly stuffed them in the camera bag. Lastly, she popped the memory card out of the camera and slid it into her pants pocket. Then, her phone vibrated. Zack called again. She clutched it in her hand when the passenger door opened.

A man got in beside her, pointed a gun at Mikayla but didn't shut the door. "Hotel reviewer, huh? You've reviewed your last hotel. Where's your partner?"

"On his way," Mikayla said. "He'll be here any second. Get out of my car."

"I'm putting an end to this. You've snooped around too much." The man shut the door. "Drive and do exactly as I say. I won't hesitate to put a bullet in you."

"What do you have to do with Andrea Whitehead?" Mikayla asked. "What's going on in that house?"

"None of your concern, and you and your private eye friend are about to learn a lesson in why you shouldn't stick your noses in other people's businesses. Now drive. Take a left. No one is going to miss you or your boss. I promise you that." The man shoved the Glock into Mikayla's ribcage. "I said drive."

75

Mikayla followed instructions and drove north of town with her phone resting in the door pocket out of sight from her passenger. She tried to get the man she knew as Dan Banks to talk, but he didn't. Instead, he barked at her to shut up and continued to issue instructions. Mikayla knew what the end game was here. Disposal.

He had her pull off the road into a dark, empty area surrounded by forest. The parking area served as a launch point for hikers during the day, but the place was closed at night. Dan Banks didn't care about that. "Park here," he ordered her, the gun at the ready.

Mikayla put the car in park.

"Give me your gun," Banks demanded.

Mikayla removed her Sig pistol from her hip holster and handed it to him. "You don't have to do this," she said. "Whatever it is you're involved in, I'm sure we can help."

"I said shut up, and you don't understand. We don't want help. We want anonymity. The clients we have don't like snoops or people who talk, and you're both," Banks said. "Now, we're going to have a little accident."

"What?"

"You're committing suicide," Banks said. "You're about to decide life isn't worth it; there's no need to continue, so you're going to blow your brains out."

Mikayla wedged against the driver's side door. "No, please, you don't have to do this. I'll back off."

"I know you will because you'll be dead. And your PI boyfriend will either be back in prison or dead."

"Yeah, well, killing me won't save you. He'll know. Plus, women committing suicide typically don't shoot themselves. It's too violent. If you shoot me, you'll have to walk back to town. That walk will take forever, and people will see you walking.

There's only one way here, and that's on Fells Road. I mean, Lake Roland isn't a good place to dump a body."

Banks smiled. "Shut up and put the gun to your head."

"No, I won't do that, please," Mikayla begged as the man forced the gun into her right hand. She fought with the man. Mikayla resisted the weapon, but he overpowered her. He cupped his hand around hers, forced Mikayla's hand onto the handle of the gun, and tried to get her finger in place as Mikayla pressed against the door. Her left hand reached for the door handle.

Mikayla fought and kicked, scratched his face, then reached back again as the gun touched her temple. The door opened, and she fell backward. The gun went off but missed. Mikayla fell out of the car, kicked the man away, struggled to her feet, and ran. The man aimed and fired. Mikayla felt the bullet enter her back. She hit the ground.

The man exited the car, walked to Mikayla, and watched her breathing stop. Banks dropped the gun by her side, turned, and left. He drove off in Mikayla's car.

* * * *

Zack saw Mikayla's car pass him on the road headed to town. Stopping the car wasn't Zack's objective. He skidded the bike, ran to Mikayla, and knelt beside her. Zack saw the blood, checked the wound, and felt his emotions surge.

"No, Mikayla," Zack yelled at her.

Mikayla's eyes opened; she weakly coughed and touched Zack's face. "You're late." She coughed again.

"Yeah, well, so I'm late," Zack said, and he put his arms under her. "We're getting you out of here."

"No, Zack, don't."

Zack shook his head as he processed. "Guess what, you stubborn mule. I'm not re-naming our agency, The Mik-Dre-Zack Detective Agency if you don't do as I say, and I'm ordering you to live. There's no negotiation on that. So hold on tight."

"Zack, I'm glad I used you for sex." She smiled.

And then her eyes closed.

* * * *

Altered Vows

Andre Kitchell ran into the hospital at midnight, and he searched. He didn't care about manners or protocol; he jumped ahead of a couple at the desk. "Where is Mikayla Dorsey? I need to know now!"

"Sir, I'll be with you in a minute," said the receptionist.

"No, I don't have a minute. She's been shot. WHERE IS SHE?"

The couple in front of Dre, at first upset about his intrusion, suddenly backed away sympathetically. The receptionist took a deep breath. "Surgery 4," she said. "Down the hall, take a right at the third set of doors. There will be a waiting room. I think the man who brought her here is waiting."

Dre sprinted down the hall, found the doors, burst through them, and raced to the room. He stopped and saw Zack seated, knees on his elbows, face hidden by his hands, bloodstains on his clothes. Dylan Kael sat beside him. A doctor in surgery scrubs exited a room down the hall and walked somberly to the waiting room. He saw Zack and Kael. The doctor said something to Kael and Zack. Zack's shoulders convulsed, and he lowered his head. Kael said something to Zack, put his hand on Zack's back, patted it twice, followed the doctor through the doors, and disappeared.

Dre's mouth dropped open as he watched his best friend cry. He slowly walked to Zack. "Zack, what happened?"

Zack, eyes bloodshot and teary, looked at his partner. "Mikayla."

"What?"

Zack shook his head. He closed his eyes tight, and more liquid dripped from the corner of his eyes.

"Zack, what happened to Mikayla?"

"She's dead."

THE END

Andrew Gruse

Altered Vows

Acknowledgements

Getting this book out was more difficult due to several things, none of which matter to the reader. What matters is that book six is finally out and begins to answer/resolve several of the questions left at the end of Bad Blood.

A special thank you to Masa Radanic for the incredible cover design. I had no idea of what I wanted but after a few back-and-forth's, she did it. Masa, you went above and beyond, and I thank you yet again.

A huge thank you goes to my wife, Heidi. She may not understand my need to revise and edit, but she understands my passion and dreams. Fortunately, she supports me in this endeavor and believes that it will pay off.

As always, my two sons deserve a thank you simply for being two of the most incredible sons a dad could have. Not surprisingly, that is due to their mother. Although, I can take credit for some things. (And yes, sarcasm is a gift a parent can take credit for. LOL)

This may sound repetitious, but I cannot thank you, the reader, enough. Without you reading books or e-books, this would be a sad, sad world. Imagine a world without books. Or a country banning books or burning books. I mean, why? How could anyone be so close-minded or hateful that they would feel the need to ban books?

So thank you for reading.

And more importantly, a huge thank you for telling others about reading my books.

I talk about reviews all the time and the need for them. Some sites won't even acknowledge a book without a certain number of reviews, and of course, recommends to the author places where the author can pay for reviews.

Which, as you know, is a practice of which I am not a fan.

So, I am relying solely on you, the reader.

Again, thank you.

Typically, I write about one of my brothers, but I covered all four in the first four books. Sadly, both of my parents have passed at incredibly young ages since publishing my first novel, Stacked Case. Unfortunately, it doesn't get easier with time.

But they are always in my thoughts.

The next edition in the Zack Stack series is coming sooner than this one did. Still untitled but mostly finished, I won't tell you much other than the story will bring Zack back to the beginning.

Also, please follow me via my author page, Andrew Gruse, on FB or whatever it is called now, and I am not opposed to you sharing my page or posts I make about my latest novel. Is asking you to help me promote my books shameless? I don't think so. A guy needs every break he can get in this business.

Thank you again. Thank you for reading.

Andrew Gruse